RESUSCITATION

D.M. Annechino

RESUSCITATION

Text copyright ©2011 D.M. Annechino
All rights reserved.

Printed in the United States of America.

Published by Thomas & Mercer
P.O. Box 400818
Las Vegas, NV 89140

ISBN-13: 9781612180717
ISBN-10: 161218071X

This one's for you, Mom.
In loving memory of Josephine DiMarco-Montinarelli.

PROLOGUE

When Genevieve Foster awoke, she felt completely disoriented, like someone regaining consciousness after major surgery and a heavy dose of anesthesia. She lay on the bed, having no idea where she was or how she got there. When she tried to brush the hair out of her eyes, she found that her wrists were bound to a brass headboard with nylon straps. She lifted her throbbing head and could see that her ankles were also bound to the bed. She lay there spread-eagle. Next to the bed, she noticed the silhouette of an IV bag hanging from a metal pole. The line from the IV was inserted into the vein at the bend of her left elbow. Except for a thin sheet covering her from neck to toe, she was completely naked.

This can't *be happening.*

The only light in the room spilled in from passing cars, their headlights flashing across the floor-to-ceiling windows just long enough for Genevieve to get a glimpse of her surroundings. The room looked big, perhaps a loft, or maybe a small warehouse. By the volume of cars passing by, she guessed that she was in a populated area. Lying still, listening closely, she could hear what she believed was a refrigerator humming in the background. And somewhere on the other side of the room, she heard the steady rhythm of a clock.

Tick-tock. Tick-tock.

She felt as if the clock warned her of impending danger.

She closed her eyes and tried to piece together the hazy fragments of images floating around in her head. She looked to her left, then right, searching for something that might trigger her memory. But she saw no one and felt completely alone, isolated from the world. Strangely, she thought about the Tom Hanks movie, *Castaway*. Although she was not stranded on a deserted island like he had been, this dark, eerie prison seemed as lifeless.

Who would rescue *her*?

Breathing deeply, sucking in short, quivering gulps of air, she evoked every ounce of willpower to stay awake. Falling asleep was the last thing she wanted. She guessed that the IV was more than saline because as terrified as she was, she seemed way too composed for the situation. Shouldn't she be screaming her throat raw? Her body shivered uncontrollably, reminding her of a chilly November morning when her brother had double-dog-dared her to take a quick dip in the sixty-degree Pacific Ocean. Never one to back down from a challenge, a tomboy in every respect, Genevieve accepted the dare and not only went into the water, she swam to the end of Crystal Pier and back. Twice. So chilled was she that she couldn't stop shaking for more than an hour. Right now, at this exact moment, she would gladly trade her situation for a long swim in icy water.

Lying quietly, trying to suppress her utter feeling of helplessness, she vaguely recalled a sandy beach, watching the sun set, a handsome face. But none of those things fit together. There were far too many voids in her memory. About to surrender to the effects of the potent drug flowing through the IV, she heard the familiar sound of a key unlocking a deadbolt. Her head snapped toward the door, eyes suddenly alert and probing. A rectangular block of light flooded the hardwood floors, but only for a moment.

Darkness fell again.

Then, Genevieve Foster heard the most terrifying sound of all: heavy footsteps moving toward her.

CHAPTER ONE

He sat at the bar sipping his second glass of Johnny Walker Blue, searching for the courage he needed to do the unthinkable. *Unthinkable?* Wasn't there a word in the English language that would more accurately describe what he was about to do? He let the smooth Scotch reward his taste buds before taking a long, silky swallow. At two hundred dollars a bottle, it was worth every penny. Thinking about the events over the last several weeks, the life-changing letter he'd received from GAFF, the Global A-Fib Foundation, he couldn't believe what he was about to do. But what choice did he have? They had driven him to this crossroad. Here he sat, sipping Scotch at Tony's Bar & Grill as if it were happy hour on a Friday afternoon, when in reality, his intentions were far from lighthearted banter with his colleagues. Although he had worked with hundreds of volunteers, Julian's research findings were still limited. He had explored every possible solution, but no other option could solve his problem. His only hope to complete the research was to work on live subjects with no limitations. The decision had not come easily. After all, he was a healer, an esteemed cardiologist, not a murderer. But drastic situations often call for drastic remedies.

When he received the certified letter, at first he thought that the board of directors at GAFF were satisfied with the data from his research and had approved the ten-million-dollar grant. The first two paragraphs brought him to his knees.

"*Our committee painstakingly reviewed your research data and the statistics associated with the controlled study to develop new surgical treatments for atrial fibrillation. Although groundbreaking in some respects, we found the data insufficient to approve your grant. To be specific, the test results you submitted that support modifications to the current catheter ablation and Maze III procedures are incomplete, and we do not agree with your findings that the use of amiodarone in doses less than 200 milligrams can be effective. In light of your impressive efforts, however, we are pleased to offer you a six-month extension to complete and resubmit additional findings, at which time we will reevaluate.*

"*Enclosed please find a comprehensive summary of the data we require to reconsider your application.*"

Two years of long workdays, sleepless nights, neglecting his family, and setback after setback, and all he had to show for his efforts was a two-page letter that undermined his hard work.

After carefully reading the comments detailing the additional data they required, Julian concluded that he would need eight subjects to fulfill the GAFF request. At first, he had thought about using his own patients. After all, he archived every detail of their medical histories and could hand-select each of them based on specific parameters. But what would happen if his patients went missing, and the police investigated and connected the dots? He would be the common denominator. No, he did not have the luxury to select perfect specimens. Having no other choice, he had to rely on instincts and random selection in his search for ideal subjects. However, through the strategic use of medication and careful surgical procedures, he could produce just about any symptom or condition he needed to compile the data he sought.

Julian didn't feel comfortable sitting in this bar. He was out of his element. But he thought of it as a means to an end. The popular hot spot in the Gaslamp District of downtown San Diego pulsed with a rowdy crowd and made it easier for him to remain inconspicuous—just a face in the crowd.

He remembered when the Gaslamp District was little more than vacant, boarded-up buildings and a collection of drunks littering the streets. Now completely revitalized with renovated hotels, jazz clubs, trendy boutiques, and sidewalk cafes—not to mention PETCO Park, the new ballpark for the San Diego Padres—the area buzzed with activity.

Just forty-two years old, Julian hoped he hadn't lost his charm. In years past, women gravitated to him like steel to a magnet. Back in college, his smile and vivid blue eyes never failed to yield an eager companion. But that was twenty years ago, and no man can preserve his youthful appearance forever. Besides, he no longer had the physique of an athlete.

He made eye contact with a blonde woman sitting a few barstools away and presented his best smile, hoping that she'd respond. Married for over a decade, he didn't have the slightest idea how to meet women in a bar. Seemingly shy, the blonde looked away, took a long sip of a martini, and continued talking to another woman. When their eyes met again, he held up his glass and gestured toward her, offering a cordial salute. Then for the next few minutes, he glanced at her every few seconds and caught her looking his way, presumably wanting to continue with their innocent flirting.

He waited patiently, hoping she would approach him. Lost in his thoughts, he felt someone gently clutch his shoulder, and when he turned to look, he was happy to see the blonde standing next to him, noticeably nervous.

"I was hoping you'd come over," he said, delighted that she was young, relatively slim, and appeared to be healthy. He wanted to say, "*Do you mind if I listen to your heart with my stethoscope to be sure everything's okay?*"

"Oh, really?" the blonde said, with both hands parked on her hips.

"Didn't you get my signal?" he said.

"Well, I'm standing here, so I guess I got something."

He offered a handshake. "My name is Julian."

She firmly grasped his hand and pumped his arm. "Genevieve."

"Pretty name." Acting totally poised while his gut churned uncontrollably, he motioned for the bartender. "Can I buy you a drink?"

She shook her head. "I'm already past my limit."

"And what happens when you exceed it?"

"I'll never tell."

He sipped his drink. "Should I feel guilty that you abandoned your friend to talk to me?"

"She's a big girl. She can take care of herself."

"So, how often do you dump your girlfriends and pick up strange men?"

She set her small clutch purse on the bar and laughed. "Counting tonight?"

He nodded.

"This is my first."

This, he doubted. "Why me?"

"You look…interesting."

"And I should be flattered?"

"You damned well better be." She pointed to the crowd. "In case you haven't noticed, there are lots of possibilities here."

"You're feisty, Genevieve. I like that in a woman."

"What else do you like in a woman?"

"I think we both know the answer to that question." He ordered another Scotch and dropped a fifty-dollar bill on the bar. He could barely keep his hands from shaking. "Sure you wouldn't like another?"

"No thanks."

The bartender poured his drink and Julian took a sip. "So what's your gig, Genevieve? Are you a fashion model or a promising actor?"

"First year of law school."

"Impressive." He smiled like a bashful schoolboy. "I don't impress easily."

"It's not that big a deal. Attorneys are a dime a dozen these days."

"Where are you headed with your legal career?"

"Haven't figured that out yet. I'm kinda leaning toward corporate law." She curled her long hair around her fingers. "I know. It's boring."

"Hey, if it moves you, go for it." His confidence was building and he felt more relaxed.

"How about you, Julian? What's your deal?"

He hadn't prepared for such a question and had to think fast. "I dabble in real estate."

"Dabble?"

"I buy. I sell. I make a bundle. I lose a bundle."

"Sounds risky."

"Only when you lose more than you win."

They sat quietly for a few minutes, their eyes doing most of the talking.

He'd been told by many of the single doctors he worked with that younger women these days were easy. Time to find out. "Are you a betting woman, Genevieve?"

"If going to Barona Casino and playing the slots is betting, then I guess I am."

"How would you like to make a small wager—just for kicks and giggles?"

"What kind of wager?" Her eyes were markedly suspicious.

"Twenty bucks says you'll be sipping a glass of wine at my place by eleven thirty tonight."

"You already lost, Julian. Where's my twenty bucks?"

"I'm not following you."

She grinned. "I don't drink wine."

"Okay, you've got me there. Let me rephrase. I'll wager one portrait of Andrew Jackson that you'll be sitting in my apartment by eleven thirty."

"You're pretty damned sure of yourself, Buster."

Actually, he wasn't, and regretted this approach. But he couldn't back down now. "Sure enough to wager twenty dollars."

"Are you *trying* to make me walk out that door?"

"We both know you're not going to do that."

"Oh, really? Why's that?"

"'Cause we're having too much fun."

"My *God*. You're unbelievable." She snatched her purse off the bar. "Maybe your cocky bullshit charms other women, but…" She shook her head and turned to walk away.

This was his last shot. "Look me in the eyes, Genevieve, and tell me you really want to leave."

"Are you *always* this arrogant?"

"It's not arrogance. It's honesty. Why do we have to play some childish game of cat and mouse? If you weren't attracted to me, you wouldn't have approached me. And if I wasn't interested, the conversation would have been over in a New York minute. You like me and I like you. So why don't we take it to the next level?"

"Next *level*? I don't even kiss on a first date and you want to make a wager about getting me in *bed*?"

"That's not what I said."

"But it's what you meant. I've been around long enough to read between the lines. Do I look like some cheap tramp?"

"No, Genevieve. You look like a woman who never lets her guard down."

She couldn't suppress her smile. "So, it's that obvious, huh?"

He lifted a shoulder. "I see what I see."

"It's tough out here," she motioned toward the crowd. "Lots of assholes."

Right now, he felt like an asshole. "If I offended you, I'm sorry. Alcohol doesn't bring out my charming side. How about giving me another chance?"

It appeared that she was considering his request. But then, she offered her hand. "It's been...*interesting*, Julian. Maybe we'll bump into each other again some time when alcohol hasn't dampened your charm. And if there *is* a next time, you might want to consider toning it down a bit."

"So you're leaving?"

"You can bet your last pair of knickers on it."

"Do I at least get an innocent kiss goodbye?"

"I don't think there's anything innocent about you. You really don't let up, do you?"

"Not with a woman like you."

"Okay, will you settle for a peck on the cheek?"

"Not what I was hoping for, but sure."

She leaned toward him and pressed her lips against his cheek. She was just about to pull away when Julian grasped her shoulders. Their eyes met, faces only inches apart. He moved toward her and kissed her softly on the mouth. "My apartment is only a few blocks away."

Unable to believe how effortless it had been to pick up Genevieve, or more accurately, how easily she had picked him up, Julian led her to his rental car. They got into a pearl-white Cadillac CTS and headed for the loft apartment he had rented only a few weeks ago. Four blocks away from Tony's Bar & Grill, it took only minutes to arrive. Julian hadn't kissed another woman in over ten years. As much as he wished the kiss hadn't fazed him, he was terribly excited and hated himself for feeling this way.

Genevieve pawed through her oversized purse. "Mind if I text my friend, Katie? I feel a little guilty that I left her at the bar."

"And what are you going to tell her?"

"Not to wait for me."

Julian couldn't be more pleased. He pushed the remote and the security gate lifted so he could park the Cadillac in the dimly lit underground garage. His was the only car.

"This is a little spooky, Julian," Genevieve said, her fingers dancing on the cell phone keypad.

"Sorry. The garage does look like a dungeon. I've completely renovated the building. But I haven't had time to deal with the garage yet. It seems less important than the rest of the place. My loft spans the entire second floor, and I don't mind saying that it's remarkable. The architects who rent the lower level are rarely here, so I pretty much have the place to myself. It's hard to find that kind of privacy in downtown San Diego."

They stepped into the elevator and the moment the door closed, Julian's arms were around her and he kissed her long and hard. This had not been his intention, not part of the plan. His actions were purely of a primal nature. He almost forgot why he'd brought her to his loft.

It's the alcohol, Julian. Stay on task.

She backed away slightly, nearly out of breath.

Julian recognized that he was heading down a dangerous path. What was he thinking? If he wasn't careful, he could easily get distracted. He couldn't afford to jeopardize his research in any way. But kissing this lovely, young woman so passionately brought back images of Rebecca and Marianne, visions of the dark shed behind their house, and of the game they had forced him to play so many years ago, a game that helped mold his sexuality.

"You don't waste any time, do you?"

"I'm a very impatient man."

"Can we slow down just a bit?"

The reality of it all was unfolding in a way he hadn't imagined. He never thought he'd get sidetracked. But images of sexual grandeur tugged at his conscience. He had to remain focused on his only goal: recognition for his breakthrough research. He could not afford to lose sight of his primary objective.

Her knees nearly buckled at a vision of Julian making love to her. She'd been with her share of men, some inhibited and insecure, others like charging bulls. But she felt certain Julian was a different breed, and guessed that soon she'd be in his bed. She felt inexplicably attracted to him. Out-of-control attracted to him. So much so, that she'd abandoned all reason. As much as she wanted to ravish him, that little voice in the back of her head waved a red flag.

She had not been truthful with him. He wasn't the first man she'd picked up in a bar. Far from it. But unlike with other men where she was merely looking for a wild evening with no strings attached, with Julian she wanted more. Genevieve could not fathom why—she hardly knew him—but of this fact she was sure. She imagined meeting him for coffee, sharing a romantic dinner, taking long walks on the beach—all the corny things she'd seen in a hundred chick-flicks. She could also see him clearing off the dining room table, tearing off her clothes, throwing her down, and taking her. But if she gave him what he wanted tonight, there might not be flowers, or candy, or courting. It puzzled her that at such an early juncture she fantasized about a storybook outcome. Something about Julian set her heart ablaze.

For a moment, she thought about coming up with a believable excuse of why she had to leave. When the elevator door opened, long before she had a chance to step out, Julian's arms surrounded her again, but this time he kissed her gently. It wasn't like his last kiss. It was more of a first-date kiss, with an all-consuming intensity.

"Welcome to my humble abode."

The spacious loft was anything but humble. It looked like something you might see on the cover of *House & Garden* magazine. From the Brazilian cherry floors to the granite countertops and gourmet kitchen to the Ethan Allen furnishings, it looked like a hip loft you might find in SoHo, New York.

"*Humble* isn't quite the adjective I would choose to describe this place," Genevieve said.

"Charming, isn't it? How about a little snifter of Bailey's or Grand Marnier? Just to take the edge off."

She certainly needed to take the edge off. She remembered what he'd admitted about alcohol and his behavior. "Are you having one?"

"I'm already past *my* limit."

"In that case I'll have just a whisper of Bailey's, please. On ice."

Julian pointed to the Victorian sofa. "Make yourself comfy while I get the drinks."

He went into the kitchen to the wet bar where he kept a generous assortment of wines and liquor. Julian kept his back to her and spoke over his shoulder while doctoring her drink. "Would you like a snack—crackers and cheese, bruschetta with some crusty bread, Godiva chocolate?"

"Mmm. How could anyone turn down Godiva?"

He put a few ice cubes in her snifter, added some Bailey's, and stirred her drink to be sure the potent drug dissolved. He sat next to her on the sofa, handed her the drink, and set the box of truffles on the cocktail table. He gestured toward her with a glass of sparkling water.

"To you, Genevieve. May all your dreams come true."

Julian stood over Genevieve, alarmed that she was still sound asleep. She hadn't so much as uttered a sound. Had he miscalculated the amount of sedative he'd given her when he had spiked her drink? As he was about to check her vital signs, she moaned, turned her head, and opened her eyes.

"Welcome back," Julian said. He smiled warmly, then turned away from her and adjusted the flow on the IV bag. When finished, he sat on the edge of the bed. Genevieve turned her head away from Julian and he noticed her gaze at the video camera mounted on a tripod.

Her voice barely audible, she whispered, "Why are you doing...this?"

"I don't have a choice, Genevieve."

"You...*do* have a choice. You can cut these damned straps... give me my clothes...and let me go."

"I'm afraid we're beyond the point of no return."

"I don't understand what you mean."

"The wheels of fate are already in motion."

This was now a game of riddles. "What did you do to me... while I was unconscious?"

"I undressed you and covered you with a sheet."

"You raped me, didn't you? Videotaped yourself...fucking me."

"I'm not a rapist."

"Then why am I naked?"

"It's complicated."

"You're a fucking liar!"

"If I *had* raped you, you'd know it. Wouldn't you sense that your body was violated?"

"I can't even see straight. How would I know if you—?"

"Your anger is only going to make it more difficult."

Genevieve began to sob. "*Please*...don't hurt me. *Please* let me go."

He stood up and walked to the corner of the room. Several minutes later, Julian returned to her bedside wheeling an LCD screen mounted on a steel pole with tripod legs and squeaky wheels.

"Is that a...heart monitor?" she asked.

He sat on the corner of the bed and gently stroked her arm. "Have you ever heard the quote, 'The needs of the many outweigh the needs of the few'?"

She shook her head.

"Spock said that in one of the *Star Trek* movies. But he plagiarized. Aristotle, in a much more complex and philosophical way, said basically the same thing thousands of years ago."

"What does Spock's quote have to do with anything?"

"Unfortunately, Genevieve, you represent the few."

CHAPTER TWO

Sami Rizzo raised her wine glass and motioned toward Alberto Diaz. "To you, my dear."

He returned the gesture and gently clicked his glass of non-alcoholic beer against Sami's glass of Merlot. "I can't believe we've been a couple for two years."

She reached across the table and laid her hand on top of his. "Any regrets?"

"Only that I should have fessed up a long time ago. We should be celebrating our fourth year together."

"It's all about timing. And yours was perfect. Any sooner and I wouldn't have been ready for more than friendship."

"I do wish I could toast you with a glass of wine," he said.

"I'm afraid that you and alcohol will never be friends again."

"Booze and I never *were* friends."

Considering what he was about to tell her, Al wished he had a stiff drink in front of him. Since Sami's brush with death at the hands of Simon, the serial killer who held her hostage in his Room of Redemption with the intention of crucifying her like he'd done to four other women, Al and she had agreed never to speak of Simon again.

But in spite of their efforts to manage the residual shock-waves, Sami still suffered from violent nightmares. Although the frequency of these graphic and terrifying dreams had decreased considerably—thanks to a solid year of intense therapy—not a week passed without Sami bolting upright in the middle of the night, dripping cold sweat, and shaking uncontrollably. She had shared these episodes with Al many times. The memory of the breathlessness she felt as she hung on that cross, and how it made her heart pound out of her chest. Al wondered how many times she had felt the cold steel piercing her wrists. How often were her dreams so real that she was sure someone was driving spikes into her feet? After over one hundred sessions of therapy, she still had a long way to go.

For several days now, Al felt that he should break their pact and ask Sami if she'd heard the news. It was all over the newspapers and on every TV station, but she hadn't mentioned anything about it. It *was* possible that her crazy schedule shielded her from current events. She *was* taking four difficult classes at San Diego University, tending to her daughter, and spending some time with her mother, who of late had not been feeling well. But this was a news item that would most certainly interest Sami.

"Have you been watching the news lately?" Al asked.

"And when would I find time to do that? I barely have time to pee. No one knows that more than my terribly neglected lover."

He didn't need to be reminded. They hadn't had sex in…what was it now, a month, six weeks? And as much as Al loved Sami, adored her, this platonic aspect of their relationship was starting to take its toll. Angelina was sound asleep, rarely known to awaken in the middle of the night, and considering that today they celebrated their second anniversary, he hoped the evening would end with some quality lovemaking.

"Simon refused an appeal," Al blurted. "Some nonsense about wanting to appeal to a higher power."

Sami fixed her stare on Al but didn't say a word.

"It usually takes years to execute a murderer, but once Simon refused an appeal, Judge Carter, a woman with bigger balls than a gorilla, had no problem pushing the law to its limits. No mercy from her."

"Death by lethal injection?" Sami asked.

Al nodded.

She processed his announcement for a few minutes. "That's too damned merciful. I wanted the bastard to rot in jail for the rest of his perverted life."

"It might take awhile before they do him in."

"One can only hope."

"Sorry I broke our agreement, but—"

"I'm glad you told me."

Sami excused herself, went into the kitchen, returned with two steaming hot dinner plates, and set them on the table.

"Looks wonderful," he said. He tasted a forkful of the sea bass and made a yummy sound. "You kept your promise."

"What promise is that?"

"In two short years you've gone from frozen pizzas and Chinese takeout to wonderful home-cooked meals. I can't imagine how you manage things with such a crazy schedule."

"Love can make a woman do a lot of things she didn't think she could do."

"You're going to make me blush."

"You're blushing because I love my daughter?" Sami could barely suppress her laugh.

He laughed. "I'm glad your workload hasn't diluted your sense of humor."

"Hey, if I lost my sense of humor, you'd be in a heap of shit."

They ate dinner, sipped their drinks, and engaged in small talk. Sami served dessert—New York–style cheesecake with fresh strawberries.

"Do you miss detective work?" he asked.

The question caught her off guard. "I get my fix through you."

"Is a fix enough? What I mean is, now that you've been away from homicide for a couple of years, do you still feel as strongly about becoming a social worker?"

"My view of social work has been somewhat tainted. There's quite a difference between my idealistic image and the real world. Two of my professors have been more than blunt about some of the challenges social workers face. And to be honest, I'm not totally positive I can deal with the political BS."

"Just to be the devil's advocate," he said, "don't you have to deal with politics no matter where you work?"

"True, but I paid my dues as a detective and learned how to work the system. With social work, it's uncharted water."

Al helped Sami clean the table and load the dishes in the dishwasher. When they finished, he pulled her toward him and gave her a firm hug. "This is a bit cliché, but you really light up my life."

"Don't ever apologize for saying something sweet."

He kissed her softly on the lips and handed her a beautifully wrapped present. "Happy anniversary, Sweetheart."

She looked at it for a moment and slowly peeled the paper away. Inside the velvet box she found a diamond-studded heart on a gold chain. "It's beautiful. Thank you so much." She looked at the floor and shook her head. "Um, I didn't get you—"

"Let's go to bed and make love all night long."

"That's a wonderful idea."

Genevieve watched Julian adjust the IV, increasing its flow. She tried desperately to fight, but with her arms and legs securely bound to the bed, there was little she could do. Moments after her fruitless struggle, she felt dizzy and nauseous. Her body and mind seemed suspended in a barely conscious twilight state. Julian carefully placed the heart monitor electrodes, ironically, at places that might be a lover's point of caress, four on her bare chest, one on each wrist, one on each shoulder, and one on each ankle. He turned on the heart monitor, and Genevieve, eyes fighting to stay open, could see the rhythm of her heart displayed across the LCD screen. She wasn't sure what a normal rhythm looked like, but she could barely see that her pulse rate was ninety-seven beats a minute.

Dressed in green hospital scrubs, Julian turned on the video camera and stood at the edge of the bed beside a small table crowded with various surgical instruments. He treasured these brilliantly crafted tools. To some, they were merely cold steel. But to a surgeon, they had sacred meaning. He examined each one, making certain he had everything he needed. He checked Genevieve to be sure that the anesthesia rendered her completely unconscious. Once that was confirmed, he selected a scalpel and stood frozen for a moment over her naked body, poised to make the critical first incision.

He realized that he faced certain limitations. If he were in a hospital surgery room, he'd be working with other surgeons, an anesthesiologist, several nurses, and a surgical technician. But he stood alone. And his loft, of course, was not a sterile environment. On the other hand, infection was not an issue he needed to be concerned about because none of his subjects would survive the experiments.

From this moment forward, everything Julian held sacred about his life, career, his relationship with family and friends, and his conception of the Hippocratic Oath would forever change. Once he found the courage to press the scalpel against her sternum, he could never go back.

He forced himself to focus on the most important goal of the research: global recognition. He longed to be validated as a pioneer among surgeons.

Looking at her exquisitely proportioned body, its total vulnerability, the soft curves from shoulder to breasts to hips, her perfectly manicured Brazilian wax, he retracted the scalpel. As much as it violated every ounce of reason remaining in his conflicted mind, he wanted her. Oh, how he wanted her. If he took her, he had only his conscience to deal with.

He hadn't noticed the resemblance until now, but Genevieve reminded him of a girl he had dated in college. Well, it could hardly be called "dating." She had been a senior and he a sophomore. Eva something or other. A foreign student from Iceland. He could never pronounce her last name. In fact, no one could pronounce it. It was as long as a city block.

Until he had met Eva, a wild-eyed party girl with natural platinum hair and the shapeliest ass he had ever seen, Julian never realized that he could derive so much pleasure from bondage. Before Eva, he'd had a dim view of anything kinky, particularly bondage, and felt that anyone who found twisted sex enjoyable should be locked in a padded cell.

One day, Eva changed all of that when he went to her apartment and found her lying in bed with both wrists tied to the brass headboard, securely held by satin strips of fabric. To this day, he had no idea how she had bound herself without assistance. He never asked. She never told.

"Fuck me," she had said. "Fuck me hard."

Her invitation, so simple yet so direct, sent his desire to levels he'd never thought possible. Even now, those words were like a magical symphony playing in his head. He could never remember feeling so aroused. It was as if he overdosed on some exotic aphrodisiac. Excited beyond anything he had ever experienced, Julian ravaged her and savored every exquisite minute of it. And Eva, moaning like a wounded cat, must have loved it as well. So pleasurable was the experience, the mere thought that he could take her any way he wanted, that he had complete control over her, that he could be totally selfish and pleasure only himself if he chose, evoked a fear that he might never truly enjoy traditional sex again.

But there was more to the story. The whole time he penetrated her, with each thrust, he spoke these words in his mind: "This-is-for-you-Rebecca. This-is-for-you-Marianne." It was like a silent triumph, as if he were getting even.

Forcing his thoughts to the present, Julian somehow found the strength to overcome temptation. He pressed the scalpel against Genevieve's breastbone and made the incision. Then, he reached for the circular saw as he had so many times in his career while performing legitimate surgery. Halfway through her sternum, he had to set down the saw. Overwhelmed with nausea, he tried to make it to the bathroom but threw up all over the floor. He hadn't expected such a reaction. It was as if he were a surgical intern witnessing his first open heart procedure. How many chests had he cut open? More than he could remember. How many hearts had he held in his hand? But this was different. Concerned that she could bleed to death, he found the strength to rush back to the bed.

This is more difficult than I thought.

He finished cutting through her sternum, carefully placed the rib spreaders into her chest, and cranked her ribcage open. Julian then cut her femoral vein high on her thigh, and inserted a catheter into the vessel. Then, he gently inched it forward to her heart. When he positioned it properly, he injected a mixture of epinephrine and potassium chloride into the IV and introduced a high-frequency electrical impulse through the catheter. After several minutes, her heart went into a sporadic arrhythmia, and shortly afterwards, she converted to full atrial fibrillation.

Now the tricky part. Locating the exact area of the heart producing the faulty electrical impulse induced by the drugs and catheter would not be easy. Under normal circumstances, two, sometimes three surgeons would perform corrective surgery related to A-Fib. But Julian had to make do with only two hands. Not having to be overly concerned with the long-term consequences of the procedures, Julian could afford to boldly experiment without medical limitations. His primary objective was to keep her alive as long as possible. He removed the catheter and in its place inserted a different catheter to perform a radio frequency ablation. He checked to be sure the automated external defibrillator was close at hand.

"Forgive me, Genevieve, but the needs of the many outweigh the needs of the few."

This was now his credo.

CHAPTER THREE

When the phone rang at 3:45 a.m., Sami, roused from a deep sleep, blindly reached for the receiver, almost knocking the clock radio off the nightstand.

"Hello," she whispered, her voice raspy.

"Sami? This is Captain Davidson. Sorry to call in the wee hours, but I have to speak to Al."

She hadn't spoken to Captain Davidson for several months, but this was not the time for chitchat. Al, snoring like a hibernating grizzly bear, was obviously sound asleep. She gently grasped his shoulder and shook him.

Al moaned but didn't say a word. He did, however, continue to snore.

She shook him again, harder this time. "Wake up, Al."

"What the hell's going on?"

She handed Al the phone, then rolled on her side. "It's the captain."

It took him a few moments to get oriented. He combed his fingers through his hair, feeling certain that the captain wasn't calling to invite him to an early-morning breakfast.

"What's up at this ungodly hour?" Al said.

"Get dressed and shuffle your ass to Mission Bay Park," the captain ordered.

"It's a little early for a picnic."

"Cut the cute shit and hightail it over to the parking lot east of the Tourist Information Center. Know where it is?"

Now Al was wide awake. "What's going on?"

"Homicide is going on."

The next thing Al heard was a dial tone. Trying hard not to disturb Sami, he got dressed as quickly as he could in the dark. But halfway through the process, she turned on the nightstand light.

"What is it?"

"Sketchy information." Even if he knew all the gory details, he'd never share them with her. Over the last two years he'd become a master at telling Sami everything about his homicide investigations without telling her anything. It was like boot camp for a politician.

"Is there a body?" Sami asked.

"Not sure. I gotta get going. Try to go back to sleep."

"Fat chance of that." She kicked off the covers, stood up, and stretched for the ceiling. Her daily stretching exercises really helped with her lower back problems. She stood in front of Al as he hurriedly buttoned his shirt. "Last night was amazing."

"Would you expect anything less from a hot-blooded Latino like me?"

She smiled. "If I'm not here when you get home, call me on my cell. I'm taking Angelina to my mother's later this morning."

"Weren't you there just yesterday?"

"I'm worried about her. She can barely catch her breath just walking down the street. And her memory? I'm surprised she even recognizes me when I walk in the door."

Al strapped on his shoulder holster and eased into his leather jacket. "Has she seen her doctor?"

"He's got her on some new medication, but I'm not sure it's helping much. I worry about her living alone. If something happened in the middle of the—"

"Maybe she should stay with us for a while."

Al's suggestion caught her completely off guard. "And you'd be okay with that?"

"As long as we put a lock on our bedroom door, I'm fine."

She cradled his face with both hands and kissed him softly. "You're a real gem."

Just before he headed out the door, she grabbed his shoulder. "No need to protect me from the bogeyman anymore, Al. I'm a big girl, so don't feel like you have to filter everything you tell me. I can handle it."

"Nothing to tell. Yet."

"Well, when there is, don't be afraid to share."

Now at his family home, thoughts of Genevieve flooded Julian's mind. Some exciting. Others haunting. She had been his first, a maiden voyage to a world unknown. No matter how he had tried to predict his reaction, or visualize what to expect, nothing could have prepared him for the overwhelming surge of mixed emotions he was now feeling. On one hand, he felt like a pioneer, a man who might soon make medical history. On the other, he felt like a monster, a hypocrite, a murderer of innocent people.

He faced the ultimate paradox. As a skilled cardiothoracic surgeon, he had saved many lives and lost only a few. But he could not let himself think of Genevieve as an ordinary patient. Although unwillingly, she was now a fundamental first step in his research. The data he had collected before all desperate attempts to resuscitate her failed, made it painfully obvious that the answers he sought could only come from live subjects.

He had to indisputably prove to the Global A-Fib Foundation that the success rate to eradicate atrial fibrillation by modifying both catheter ablation and the Maze III procedures could be as high as 95 percent. He had feared from the onset of this project that controlled test studies and working with cadavers would never yield the data he needed to complete his research. Genevieve now confirmed his theory.

In a dreamlike state, Julian walked in the kitchen, shaky and uneasy. He stood behind his wife, who was standing at the counter cutting an apple. He kissed Nicole on the neck, more obligatory than purposeful. She turned and looked at him.

"Lord," Nicole said, "you're as white as a ghost. Are you feeling ill?"

"Just a touch of the flu."

"And you're *kissing* me? Stay the hell away from the girls. The last thing I need is a couple of sickly kids."

"Sorry," he said. Lately, it seemed that "sorry" was the most overused word in his vocabulary. At least with Nicole.

"I have to ask you something," Nicole said. "This is a touchy subject, I know, but how would you feel about turning over the A-Fib project to one of your colleagues?"

"Are you *kidding* me?"

"I really want you to consider it."

"Do you have any idea how humiliated I'd be in front of the entire medical community?"

"What's more important, your precious ego or your family?"

Julian wanted his motivation to be humanitarian; he wished that a desire to save the world drove him. But in truth, helping to eradicate A-Fib worldwide was merely a fringe benefit. No, as much as it prickled his conscience, this research project was totally about him: the fame, the recognition, seeing his photo on the cover of the *American Journal of Medicine*, and maybe even earning a prestigious nomination for the Nobel Prize in Medicine. Oh, how he hungered for the admiration and prestige.

"You want me to flush two years of busting my ass down the toilet? Working twelve-hour days. Not taking any vacations—not even a three-day weekend in Big Bear. How would I feel about giving up? Are you shitting me? I'm almost there and you want me to abandon ship?"

"So the rejection letter from the Global A-Fib Foundation hasn't discouraged you?"

"Of course it did. It knocked the feathers right out of me. But it also gave me hope and made me realize that I'm this close." He held up his hand and gestured with his thumb and index finger.

"Hey, Julian, it's your career. Do whatever you think is right. To hell with me and to hell with the girls. But if you're looking for support from me? I've got two words for you. And they ain't Merry Christmas."

At 4:35 a.m., Al pulled into the parking lot near the Tourist Information Center at Mission Bay Park. The area buzzed with activity. Red beacons flashing, yellow tape everywhere, cameras lighting up the landscape, detectives milling about, and the forensic staff huddled around what Al assumed would be a dead body. He even spotted a news van sitting in the corner of the parking lot with its satellite dish reaching for the stars. How did they hear about this homicide so quickly? he wondered. The morning air still hung on to its late-spring bite. The reflection of the full moon danced on the bay.

Al slid out of his car and headed for Captain Davidson, easy to single out among the dozen or so worker bees. Who else would be dressed in a suit with a cigarette in one hand and a cup of coffee in the other this early in the morning? Seeing the captain on the scene surprised Al. Davidson usually worked the privileged nine-to-five gig. So, seeing him milling about at a crime scene before sunrise suggested that this was no ordinary homicide. Then again, Al had never really seen anything ordinary about a murder.

As always, Davidson sucked on his cigarette with the passion of a man drawing his last breath. "Sorry to interrupt your beauty rest, Detective Diaz."

"Wouldn't miss it for the world." Al watched three forensic experts examining the remains. He caught a whiff of Davidson's cigarette and urgently wanted a puff. "Have they identified the body?"

The captain shook his head. "This is a creepy one. The victim is not only fully clothed, she looks like she's going to the opera. I've never seen a victim so perfectly groomed."

"What do you make of it?"

"I haven't the slightest clue."

"Was she assaulted?"

"Betsy's working on that as we speak."

"Cause of death?"

"Her sternum was split in half, and it looks as though her ribs were pulled apart with one of those rib spreaders surgeons use during open heart surgery."

Al felt chilled and zipped up his jacket. "Who found the body?"

"A couple teenagers." The captain pointed to a smoldering fire pit near the edge of the water. "A bunch of kids were doing an all-nighter. Bonfire. Beer. Pot. Two of the boys had to take a leak and found the body lying next to the restrooms."

Al understood that it was part of his job to examine the body. He'd seen dozens of corpses. Shot. Stabbed. Bludgeoned. Dis-

membered. But since Sami's ordeal two years ago at the hands
of Simon, he had begun to find it difficult to examine murder
victims, which for a homicide detective was as absurd as a scuba
diver being afraid of water.

"I want you to take the lead on this," the captain said.

Al's gut reaction was to say, "No fucking way!" But to argue
would be futile. "And who am I partnering with?"

"I was thinking Ramirez. But I want everyone working this
investigation."

"Does my vote count?"

"This is not a democracy."

"Can I at least plead my case?"

The captain folded his arms across his chest. "I'm listening."

"Ramirez sucks. Ever since his promotion to lieutenant, his
ass has been stuck to the chair in his cushy office. He's not a frontline cop anymore."

"Your concerns are noted."

Al hated to be dismissed like a child.

The captain dropped his cigarette on the grass and crushed it
with his size 13 shoe. "How's Sami doing these days?"

"She's holding her own."

"Haven't seen her in a long time. She used to stop by the precinct once in a while. Doesn't she love us anymore?"

"Don't take it personally, Captain. We live together and I have
to make an appointment just to have dinner with her."

The captain searched his pockets for another cigarette. "How
are things working out for you two?"

"We're not without our little tiffs, but things are good so far."
This was only half true. Of late, he wasn't really sure how he felt
about their relationship. Strange as it sounded, he loved her but
wasn't sure if he wanted to be with her.

"What you've got is the brass ring. Don't fuck it up."

"I'm trying my best not to, Captain."

Al walked toward the body, feeling more uncomfortable than usual. The corpse, partially covered from neck to ankles with a white sheet, lay face up on the freshly cut grass. With flashlight in hand, he lowered himself to his knees next to the body and studied the murdered woman's remains. Her blonde hair looked like she'd just left a beauty salon. Not a strand was out of place. For such a young woman—she appeared to be in her thirties—the dark circles and the puffy bags under her eyes seemed strange. He was so focused on her, he jumped when he felt someone squeeze his shoulder. Betsy, the crime scene investigator, stood over him and smiled. "A little jumpy there, hey, Diaz?"

"I'm always on edge when I'm kneeling next to a corpse." He stood with a slight moan. "These old bones ain't what they used to be."

"Ah," Betsy said. "But you still have that pretty face."

"That's what a forty-year-old man really wants to hear." Still craving the relaxing effects of nicotine since he'd quit smoking a couple years ago, he would gladly pay a hundred dollars for one—fifty just for one long drag. "What have you got so far?"

"This is a strange one," Betsy said. "The body was fully clothed when we arrived on the scene. And when I say 'fully,' I mean dressed to the nines—including very expensive high heels."

"How expensive?"

"Well, she was wearing a Carolina Herrera cocktail dress—that probably doesn't mean anything to you, but get this. The friggin' sales tag is still on the dress. I found it attached to a button on the underside of the hemline. It was purchased at Saks Fifth Avenue, and guess how much?"

"I haven't a clue."

"Five bucks shy of *three thousand dollars.*"

It took a minute for him to digest this. "What do you make of it?"

"Unless her parents are loaded or she just won the Lotto, I can't imagine that she bought it."

"So, you think that our guy cranked her fucking chest open, did unspeakable things to the poor thing, and then dressed her in a three-thousand-dollar dress?"

"Seems that way. But that's just part of the mystery. No price tag on the shoes but they're Jimmy Choos, and I'll bet they cost close to a thousand."

"I don't get it. He kills her and then spends four Gs on clothes?"

"It sure is puzzling," Betsy said.

"Sounds like he suffered from serious regrets after he killed her."

"Either that, or there's some hidden message he's trying to convey."

"Any prints on the price tag?"

"It's clean as a whistle."

"Anything else?"

"I don't think he raped her, but can't verify it until we do a complete exam and analysis in the lab." She shook her head. "Can't imagine why he killed her the way he did. It's a new one on me."

Al knelt again and slowly uncovered her chest. "Un-fuckin'-believable." He remembered the last serial killer and how he had removed his victims' hearts as trophies. "He stapled her chest?"

"Neatly and with precision."

"Any other bruises or wounds?"

"That's the weird thing. The rest of her body—at least here on-sight—looks unharmed. But I can't really answer that until we get her on a slab."

"Call me as soon as you have a full report."

"Will do, Detective." A moment of awkward silence. "Tell Sami I said hi. And that I really miss her."

CHAPTER FOUR

Sami and Angelina had arrived at Josephine's home before noon, just in time for lunch. Angelina loved her grandmother's macaroni and cheese, and Grandma Rizzo had promised to make some. Concerned that her mother's health of late had seriously deteriorated, Sami felt guilty asking her mom to cook. But Sami knew her mother well. Josephine was a tough old woman and it would take more than a weak heart and fading memory to ground her. Besides, Josephine's cardiologist told Sami that keeping her mom busy with tasks that were not too strenuous would be a good thing. And she could think of nothing that pleased her mom more than cooking—particularly for Angelina.

They sat at the kitchen table, Josephine barely eating a forkful of the macaroni and cheese. Angelina cleaned her dish and was licking the bowl.

"Honey," Sami said. "How many times have I told you that young ladies don't lick their bowls?"

"But Mommy," the six-year-old pleaded, "I'm still a little girl. Can't *little* girls lick their bowls?"

Josephine gave Sami the "look." "Leave the girl be. She doesn't need restaurant manners at my house. If she wants to lick the bowl, let her."

"But Mom—"

"Don't 'but Mom' me, Samantha Marie Rizzo. Remember what *you* used to do with ice cream bowls when you were Angelina's age? You used to lick them clean and put 'em back in the cupboard."

"I most certainly did not."

Josephine placed her left hand over her heart and raised her right hand to the heavens. "God is my witness."

No reason to argue. Sami guessed that this was just another example of her mom's senility. Josephine could remember things that happened thirty years ago, but couldn't recall what she ate for breakfast yesterday. The doctor had warned Sami that her short-term memory would fade fast. And over the last few months, her mom's condition had noticeably worsened. "Are you still feeling chest pains and shortness of breath, Mom?"

"It comes and goes."

"Are you taking your medications every day?"

"When I remember."

"That's why I bought you that seven-day pill container. Remember how we talked about you filling it every Sunday and taking the blue pill in the morning and the white and pink pills with dinner?"

Josephine waved her arm as if to dismiss the reminder. "I wrote it down on a piece of paper but don't remember where I put it."

"I'll write it down again and put it on the refrigerator."

Suddenly, the color drained from Josephine's face and she clutched her chest.

Sami sprang up and her legs pushed the chair backwards, knocking it over. "What is it, Mom?"

"The macaroni and cheese didn't agree with me. I should know better than to eat rich foods."

"But you only ate a couple of forkfuls."

"My stomach isn't what it used to be."

Sami could see Josephine struggling to breathe, clearly in distress. Her forehead was dripping perspiration. Sami frantically searched through her purse for her cell phone. "I'm calling nine-one-one."

Now Josephine was leaning forward, her upper body almost resting on the table. "I'm okay. It will pass. It's just a stomach thing."

Sami ignored her and called 9-1-1.

Al was on his way to the precinct when Sami called. He stuck the magnetic light on top of the roof, turned it on, engaged his siren, made a U-turn, and headed for Saint Michael's Hospital.

In less than ten minutes, he squealed his tires as he pulled into the emergency department driveway and parked next to the painted-yellow curb where the sign said "Ambulances Only." He flipped down the visor with the "Official Police Business" placard and the San Diego Police Department logo. He dashed through the front doors and approached the main check-in desk. After a brief conversation, the nurse directed Al to a small waiting room just outside the emergency department.

He spotted Sami sitting in the corner of the dim room with her head down and her hands neatly folded on her lap. The last time he'd seen her look so forlorn was at the funeral of her ex-husband, Tommy DiSalvo. Angelina was nowhere in sight. He slowly walked toward her, purposely clearing his throat several times, so he wouldn't startle her. He sat beside her and draped his arm around her shoulders.

"How is she?"

She looked up at him with puffy red eyes. "She had a heart attack. They're doing an angiogram right now to see if there are any blockages. They haven't yet determined if her heart was damaged."

Al kissed Sami on the cheek. "She's a tough cookie. She'll be fine." He didn't feel as though he convinced her. "Where's Angelina?"

"Emily is watching her."

"Where?"

"At the house."

"Want me to go pick her up and bring her here?"

"Not the best place for a hyperactive six-year-old. Besides, Angelina loves Emily." Emily was Sami's only cousin on the Rizzo side of the family. Sami grasped Al's hand. "Can you stay with me?"

He stared at his scuffed shoes and shook his head. "I hate to do this, Sami, but—"

"I understand." She kissed him on the cheek. "Not too long ago I was a cop, too. Does it have to do with Davidson's call early this morning?"

"We found the body of a young woman at Mission Bay Park. The parents have identified the body and I have to interview them. Not looking forward to it." Al checked his cell phone. "If you hear anything—and I mean anything—call me."

Sami craved a cup of coffee, even the rotgut they served at the hospital cafeteria. But she didn't dare leave the waiting room for fear she'd miss the doctor. She tried to concentrate on a two-month-old article about Paris Hilton in *People* magazine, but the words did not register in her brain.

She looked around the room, at the dilapidated cloth chairs, the worn carpeting, the crooked picture of a surfer riding a huge wave, the coffee table littered with outdated magazines. She caught a whiff of the antiseptic smell so prevalent in all hospitals. Alone with her thoughts, she remembered the last time she sat in this same waiting room while her father lay in intensive care fighting for his life. Somewhere in this hospital, her mother might be doing the same thing. At this very moment, her mother could be lying in a bed with tubes up her nose, IVs in her arms, and a breathing tube down her throat. She'd been waiting for more than two hours and not one person had even popped their head in the room to offer an update. To sit alone in this smelly room seemed like cruel and inhumane treatment.

Sami's daughter, Angelina, had already lost her father, and the only family left was Grandma Rizzo and Cousin Emily. Once Sami's biggest critic, Josephine had become her strongest supporter after her daughter's brush with death at the hands of Simon. For so many years, Josephine had made Sami's life a living hell with her meddlesome, manipulating ways. But somehow, the old crotchety woman had been reborn. This was not to say that Josephine didn't often take a cheap shot at her daughter. But the frequency and intensity had diminished considerably, leading Sami to believe that even senility had its benefits.

Sami didn't pray very often. But at this particular moment, she found herself pleading with God to save her mother.

She lifted her head and noticed a young doctor standing in the doorway, wearing the customary white lab coat and stethoscope draped around his neck. He smiled warmly and approached Sami.

"Ms. Rizzo?" He extended his right arm and firmly grasped her hand.

She stood and the doctor affectionately sandwiched her hand between his.

Odd, Sami thought, that he would be so cordial. Most of the doctors she'd met over the years had been like icebergs. She was certain they had never met, yet he seemed vaguely familiar.

"I'm Doctor Templeton, chief of cardiothoracic surgery."

Templeton? Was this *the* Templeton, the Chamber of Commerce Man-of-the-Year Templeton she'd read about only a few days ago? The chairman of a committee that advised the president himself on matters of health? He seemed much too young for such a prestigious title. She tried to read his eyes but they offered no clues for her to foresee what he was about to tell her.

"Why don't you have a seat, Ms. Rizzo."

Al arrived at the precinct and parked his car in the underground garage. Guilt-ridden that he'd left Sami alone at the hospital, he felt as though he had betrayed her. She'd been fragile since her near-death experience, but he felt sure she'd bounce back. Except for her father's passing, there had never been a time when she needed his support so desperately. He saw the neediness in her eyes when he'd left her. Al tried to negotiate a delicate balance between his personal life and his career. But police work demanded his undivided attention. And once in a while, he had to choose between Sami's well-being and his duties as a homicide detective. Frankly, he wasn't completely certain he wanted the responsibility that went along with a committed relationship.

Al wrestled with his feelings for Sami constantly. When they were together, he felt completely content and certain this was where he should be. But when they were apart, he savored every precious moment of his freedom. After living alone for his entire adult life, doing whatever he wanted to do whenever he wanted to do it, letting the laundry pile up to the ceiling, eating pizza and takeout seven nights a week, scratching his balls, watching sports until his eyes bugged out, he was now faced with some sense of structure in his life, and having to consider someone else's welfare. He did not feel that Sami and he were at the same point in their relationship. Clearly, Sami wanted more. But scared to death to make a commitment, he felt himself pulling away, and wasn't so sure he was capable of giving more. This was not about love. He couldn't imagine loving her more. But love came at a hefty price. He had sacrificed his independence. Perhaps he'd even forfeited his identity. Was it any wonder he'd never been married?

And of course, the other huge issue was Angelina. He'd never wanted kids—never wanted the responsibility. But the six-year-old was part of the package. Although Sami never once put any pressure on him, or even hinted that he should assume the role of a parent, how could he live with Sami, under the same roof, lie beside her every night, and not accept the unwritten obligation?

Feeling a wave of panic, he glanced at his watch and rushed into the building. In less than thirty minutes, he would meet with Genevieve Foster's parents, and he'd be asking tough questions and offering few answers. Al had not yet seen the full autopsy report, so he headed for Captain Davidson's office for a quick briefing.

Doctor Templeton sat beside Sami and coughed into his hand. "Ms. Rizzo—"

"Please call me Sami."

"Okay, then, Sami, the very good news is that your mom's heart shows no signs of major muscle damage. In fact, the test results are very positive. However..."

At this particular moment, she hated the word *however*.

He hesitated for a moment and fixed his eyes on hers. "Four major arteries are over eighty percent blocked, and the only effective treatment is bypass surgery."

It took a moment for Sami to process this announcement. "And you feel this is a safe procedure, all things considered?"

"Well, there are ways to manage this condition with special diet and medications, but to be honest, I really don't see that as a reasonable option. Open heart surgery these days has become routine. And the ten-year survival rate is over eighty-five percent."

As Sami tried to grasp his words, she wondered why the chief of cardiothoracic surgery would be sitting next to her, delivering the news. Why was she receiving such special treatment? Surely, a man who advises the president must have more pressing issues to deal with.

"Can I speak to the doctor who will actually perform the surgery?"

"You *are* talking to him, Sami." He rubbed his palms on the front of his lab coat. "My role as chief of cardiothoracic surgery is split between administrative duties and research. In fact, I'm working on an intense controlled study right now. But to be honest, I'm more of a hands-on surgeon. So, I try to perform about four or five surgical procedures every month—both for my sanity and to keep my skills honed."

"I don't know what to say, Doctor. I feel privileged that a surgeon of your caliber is willing to operate on my mother."

"Well, Sami, I must make a little confession." His lips curled to a smile. "I'm a big fan of yours. Of course, half the county genuflects whenever they hear your name. You're the Super Cop who arrested that insane serial killer two years ago. I can't even imagine what a harrowing experience that must have been—being locked up in his cage, waiting to be crucified."

"Actually, Doctor Templeton, I deserve little credit. Had it not been for my partner, I wouldn't be sitting here talking to you."

"You can minimize your heroic escape if you want to, but you've got lots of fans out there."

Feeling somewhat flattered, yet unworthy of his praise, she wanted to confess to him that if she was all he claimed her to be, she wouldn't have bailed out of the police force. Since doing so, she had struggled with a profound feeling of guilt. Guilt because she had promised her father she'd become a detective. And guilt because her desire to be a social worker was fading fast. Perhaps the whole social-worker idea was merely a convenient excuse. Maybe Samantha Marie Rizzo was not the gallant figure she appeared to be. Maybe she was a coward. At this particular moment, however, she couldn't trouble herself with deep self-evaluation. She had to focus her attention on her mother.

"So, Doctor, when will you perform the surgery?"

"Barring any unforeseen medical issues, and as long as your mother signs the consent form, my team and I can operate in forty-eight hours."

Sami thought about this for a moment. "When can I see her?"

"I can take you to see her right now."

CHAPTER FIVE

Al walked into Captain Davidson's office and sat down without an invitation to do so. As usual, Captain Davidson sat erect behind his messy desk, puffing on a cigarette. Oh, how Al wanted to fill his lungs with the comforting smoke.

"So," Al said, "what were the results of the autopsy?"

Davidson slapped his hands on the metal desk. "There *is* no fucking autopsy."

"It's not done yet?"

"It's not going to be done," Davidson said.

"What gives?"

"Does the last name Foster mean anything to you? Does it ring any bells?"

Considering that the name was common, he wasn't sure where the captain was going. "Nothing jumps out at me, Captain."

"The victim is *Judge* Foster's daughter. The Supreme Court Judge for the State of California. Not exactly a lightweight."

"What does his stature have to do with an autopsy?"

"Judge Foster will not give his consent." The captain sucked on his cigarette. "If he wasn't such a high-profile person, we could turn the thumbscrews and convince him to approve it. But we have to handle him with kid gloves. And that's a direct order from Police Chief Larson."

"Fuck Larson," Al almost yelled. "Without an autopsy, we're pissing in the wind. Besides, who more than a judge knows first-hand the importance of an autopsy?"

"*I* know that, and *you* know that. But we don't make the rules."

"So when I meet with Judge Foster, what the hell am I supposed to do, kiss his hairy ass?"

"And his balls."

"So I should wave a magic wand and make the judge change his mind?"

"Look, Al, what I want you to do is to be firm yet diplomatic, which isn't exactly your strong suit. You're leading this investigation because of your experience in apprehending that fucking nutcase who was crucifying young women. Sami and you did a stand-up job. I need you on board." Davidson's voice softened. "Get his approval, but don't kick the shit out of him. If Larson gets a call from the judge—"

"Okay, okay. I get it. Does Larson want me to give him a blow job, too?" Before the captain could respond, Al bolted out of the office, slamming the door harder than he'd wanted to. He wished he could pass this interview with Judge Foster off to Ramirez. But this was a task he needed to handle himself.

Sami tiptoed to the side of the bed and gently grasped her mother's hand. Josephine lay on her back, her eyes barely open. "Hi, Mom," Sami said, her voice little more than a shaky whisper. She inventoried the numerous tubes and IVs attached to her mother. Under her nose, a small plastic hose provided oxygen. Wires hung from beneath her hospital gown and snaked over to a heart monitor. The room smelled like Pine-Sol.

Josephine adjusted her body and moaned. "Who's watching Angelina?" The question didn't surprise Sami. Even lying in intensive care, fighting for her life, Grandma Rizzo put her only granddaughter first.

"Emily's with her, Mom."

Josephine forced a smile. "Then she's in good hands."

"Are you in pain?"

"Of course I'm in pain. I just had a heart attack."

"Let me find a nurse and get you some pain medication."

"No need. I don't think there's much more they can do."

Sami wanted to press it, but feared it was futile. "Has Doctor Templeton been in to see you?"

She nodded.

"Then he's told you about the bypass surgery?"

Josephine's face tightened. "He told me."

"He's one of the best surgeons in the country."

"Makes no difference. I'm not going to let them cut me open."

Sami stepped back as if her mother had shoved her. "What the hell are you talking about? You've *got* to have the surgery."

"I don't have to do nothing but pay taxes and die."

"Well, if you don't have the surgery, you *will* die."

"So be it. If it's my time, it's my time. It's all in the Lord's plan."

Sami had to enlist every ounce of energy to suppress her anger. "Open heart surgery has become routine. It's like getting your appendix removed."

"Then let them take my appendix out. I'm not going to let them cut me open like a dead fish."

"Mom, you're only sixty-seven years old. With this surgery, you can live another twenty years or longer. Don't you want to be around to watch Angelina grow up?"

Josephine squeezed her eyes shut but could not stop the tears from streaming down her face. "I'm scared, Sami. Really scared." She reached for the box of tissues on the table next to the bed.

"When they cut you open, you're never the same again. Remember our neighbor Helen? As soon as they cut her open, everything went wrong."

"Helen had stage-four stomach cancer, and her prognosis was terrible. They gave her a ten percent chance of survival."

"I love you, Sami, and I love Angelina. But I'm not signing the release form."

Still seething from his talk with Captain Davidson, Al took a couple deep breaths before he walked into the interrogation room where Genevieve Foster's parents waited. The Fosters stood and each graciously shook his hand.

"I'm Joseph Foster and this is my wife, Katherine. And you are?"

Al thought it odd that Foster did not introduce himself as Judge Foster. Most judges demanded that everyone address them formally. "I'm Detective Diaz. But please call me Al."

Judge Foster, a tall, lean man with a full head of mostly silver hair, looked to be a generation older than his strikingly attractive wife. Only a few inches shorter than her husband, Katherine carried a few extra pounds but hid them well. Her eyes, swollen and bloodshot, were the color of dark chocolate. And her hair, flowing to her shoulders, was jet-black.

"First, let me offer my deep condolences for your loss," Al said softly. "I can't begin to imagine how difficult this is for you. So I will try to make this as brief as possible. Please understand that some of my questions may be of a sensitive nature, but as you know, Judge, they're necessary." He removed a digital tape recorder from his pocket and set it on the desk. "Do you mind if I record this interview?"

"I'd be upset if you didn't," Judge Foster said. "What is your capacity regarding this investigation, Detective?"

"I'm lead."

"Good. I don't want to waste my time talking to subordinates. Turn on that little recorder and let's get down to business."

"Thank you for cooperating," Al said.

"So, Detective, what can you tell us thus far?" the judge asked.

And Al thought *he* was conducting this interview. "Not much at this point. But I'm hoping that you and your wife might be able to fill in a few blanks that will point us in the right direction."

"What can we do to help you?" Katherine said.

"When was the last time you saw your daughter?"

"She recently moved into her own apartment in downtown San Diego, and hinted that she felt a bit lonely," Judge Foster said. "She was twenty-three years old and had never been on her own—not even when she was in college. We invited her home for dinner the Saturday evening she went missing. My daughter is…I mean *was*…not the domestic type. In spite of my wife's coaching, Genevieve didn't have much of a command in the kitchen. We figured that she'd enjoy a home-cooked meal."

"She wasn't by any chance wearing an expensive cocktail dress, was she?"

"Can't remember the last time I saw her in a dress," Katherine said. "If my memory serves me correctly, she was wearing her favorite worn-out jeans and a green sweater."

"What time did she leave your home?"

"Her best friend, Katie, picked her up around nine p.m.," Judge Foster said.

"Do you have Katie's last name?"

"Mitchell. Katie Mitchell."

Al noted her name on his yellow pad. "Did they say where they were going?"

The judge looked at his wife as if to pass the baton.

"Detective," Katherine said, "Genevieve was a wonderful daughter." She paused for a moment and combed her fingers through her hair. "But no matter how hard we tried, neither my husband nor I could influence her lifestyle. She loved the bar scene, the nightlife, drinking way too much and…" Her eyes began to tear. The judge slipped his arm around her shoulders and pulled her toward him.

Al sat quietly and let her regain her composure.

"My daughter was not discreet," the judge admitted. "From one week to the next, there was no telling what questionable person would be her latest flame. Some of the men she dated, well, let me just say that they were from the wrong side of town. But what can you expect when you're looking for a quality person in a bar?"

"Where did she like to go?"

"Mostly the Gaslamp District," the judge said. "She'd try to convince us that the crowd there was upscale, that it was where the in-crowd gathered. Whatever that means."

"Did you ever meet any of her boyfriends?" Al asked.

"The ones who could put two sentences together without stuttering. For obvious reasons, she was very selective about who we got to meet."

"Did she have a recent boyfriend, or a steady relationship?"

"She hasn't brought anyone home for months."

Al made more notes on his pad. "Do you have a recent photo of her?"

Katherine searched through her purse, opened her wallet, and handed Al a photograph. "This…is her…graduation photo." Again, the tears seeped out of her eyes.

"This investigation is our top priority, and I promise you, we will hit the streets hard and check out every bar and pub in a ten-block radius of the Gaslamp District. And I personally will speak with Genevieve's friend, Katie. With your permission, I would also like to examine Genevieve's apartment." He paused for a moment, sensing that this was the perfect time to go in for the kill. "I have to be honest with both of you. Unless we stumble upon some extraordinary evidence, or someone comes forward with some crucial information, we have very little to go on right now."

Al, of course, knew that he was downplaying the evidence. But how else could he convince the judge to approve a full autopsy?

The judge sat forward and locked his stare on Al. "So what you're telling me is this maniac that brutalized my daughter might never be brought to justice? He's free to kill someone else's daughter?"

"I'm only trying to point out that all we have to go on right now is a handful of circumstantial evidence."

"What do you need from us, Detective?" the judge asked. "What can we do to ensure that you apprehend this monster?"

This was the opening he had been hoping for. "Judge Foster, you have many years of experience on the bench, and you've tried countless cases where forensic evidence helped us lock up hundreds of criminals. Even when there is a weapon and fingerprints, or even eye witnesses, there is still the possibility of error. But forensic evidence leaves no room for subjectivity because it's scientific, and juries believe science."

Now that Al had offered his most compelling argument, he remained silent and his eyes ping-ponged between the judge and Katherine Foster.

"So what are you saying, Detective?" the judge asked. "Is there a question or request hidden somewhere in your narrative?"

"If there is any hope of finding the monster who killed your daughter, then we must perform a thorough autopsy."

The judge stood up and wagged his finger at Al. "You need not lecture me on the merits of autopsies. But it's much different when it's a stranger. I want to preserve what little dignity my daughter has left. She's not a laboratory animal or a cadaver, Detective. She's our *daughter!*"

"I respect your position, Judge. And please understand that it is not my place to browbeat you or try to convince you to approve something you're uncomfortable with. But I must tell you that a preliminary exam of your daughter strongly suggests that the perpetrator may have left a roadmap to his doorstep. He was careless, and the only way to benefit from his mistakes is through an autopsy. I can see how grief-stricken your wife and you are, Judge. My heart goes out to you. All I'm trying to do is to see justice served and to ensure that no other parents have to share your pain. I want to see this lunatic behind bars for the rest of his miserable life."

Judge Foster glanced at his wife, his lips tight and his eyes glassy. Katherine nodded her head ever so slightly. "Okay, Detective," the judge said. "This totally goes against our will, but you have my permission to perform an autopsy. But be warned. If it doesn't further the investigation and lead you to her murderer, prepare yourself for professional suicide."

CHAPTER SIX

Lingering longer than he had anticipated, Julian could still envision every detail of his experiments on Genevieve. Although the data he'd obtained moved him closer to his ultimate goal, he still felt haunted by the deep moral issues. He had gone through a period of self-recrimination, weighing carefully the delicate balance between righteousness and arrogance, clinging to the quote that now represented his conscience: "The needs of the many outweigh the needs of the few."

After her death, however, these comforting words had lost their potency for Julian, so he found himself digging deeper into his psyche for further moral justification of his actions. Every fallen soldier back to the Revolutionary War died for the needs of the many. Had they not, America might still be under British rule. Every soldier in Iraq and Afghanistan risked their lives for the sake of all Americans. And during the Vietnam War, most of the 50,000 fallen troops were drafted into the armed forces and had no choice but to die for the many. Wasn't it the same with Genevieve? Was she not "drafted" for the needs of the many?

He'd struggled with the notion of completely disposing of her body. That would have been his safest option, dramatically hampering the efforts of the police. No body. No evidence. It would start out as a missing person's report. But after an extensive investigation, the authorities would file the case under Unsolved Homicides. By leaving her body at Mission Bay Park, Julian had placed himself at great risk. But he was not a barbaric murderer; he was a medical professional. How could he live with himself if he'd chopped Genevieve up in little pieces and dropped her remains in the ocean? It lacked dignity and proper respect. After all, in a sense she was a martyr.

When the idea to dress Genevieve in designer clothes first struck Julian, he immediately dismissed it as insane. But he was so burdened with guilt, the more he thought about it the more it appealed to him. He could have wrapped her in a burlap bag and it wouldn't have made any difference. She'd still be dead, her chest nearly cut in half, her heart sliced open. As pointless and illogical as it was, in a twisted kind of way, it was his way of honoring her, and it simply made Julian feel better.

He wished he had found a more fitting location to leave her body. Surely, he could come up with a more suitable place than a park. For subject number two, he would rethink his options and search for a more appropriate setting.

Julian sat on his sofa, rested his head, and drifted back to his childhood.

His parents, affluent and successful, provided everything his obsessed curiosity desired throughout his childhood and teenage years. Everything but love. He always felt a void in his life, an emptiness he could never fill. No one in his family—not mother, father, or siblings—would openly show affection. Why didn't his parents understand that they had a responsibility to provide more than just food, clothing, and shelter?

On his birthday and special occasions like Christmas, they would shower him with expensive gifts, spoil him rotten, but the greatest affection he could expect was a peck on the cheek or a firm pat on the shoulder. Didn't they realize that he would gladly trade all of his belongings just to hear his mother say "I love you"?

Although he was a straight-A student, neither of his parents so much as acknowledged his performance in school. They quickly scanned his report card, scribbled their signature, and tossed it on the kitchen counter. He had been an exemplary Boy Scout, earning nearly every award from a square-knot patch to a medal of merit. He was first in his class throughout elementary school and won a national award for "Science Project of the Year." Why wasn't he able to get their attention and earn their respect? What did he have to do before his parents would acknowledge his accomplishments?

Consequently, he turned to other areas of his life to find what he thought was true affection and recognition. So vulnerable and naïve was twelve-year-old Julian that his two older cousins, Marianne and Rebecca, barely past puberty, took full advantage of his hunger for love. They introduced him to a secret little game they called "Ticklish."

After school, nearly every day, long before their parents got home from work, his two cousins would lead him to a small shed in the backyard of his home. There, in the shadowy wood structure filled with garden tools and trash cans, he watched the girls pull down their panties. Taking turns, each cousin guided Julian's hand under their Nazareth Academy pleated skirts and gave him specific instructions how to "tickle" them.

"Right there," Rebecca would say, sounding almost out of breath.

"A little to the left," Marianne would order. "Yes, yes, right there! Harder! Faster!"

At times he thought his whole hand would go numb.

Although it aroused him—after all, he was well on his way to puberty—he didn't really like this game of Ticklish, and could never quite figure out why they moaned instead of laughed. For the first couple of weeks he thought he was hurting them. But they had convinced him that this is how you show your love. This is what cousins do. Afterwards, they would always offer to touch him "down there," but even at such a young age he felt too embarrassed.

"We let you touch us," Rebecca would point out. "Why can't we touch you?"

"We'll make you feel real good," Marianne would add.

They cautioned him that if he ever told anyone about their secret game, they would no longer be his cousins.

When Julian had told his best friend about the secret game of Ticklish, George, two years Julian's senior, nearly soiled himself laughing so hard.

"Are you messing with me?" George had asked. "They're letting you touch their *pussies*? Did you screw them?"

Julian stood silent.

He finally understood that the game of Ticklish was no game at all, and he swore that one day he'd get even. After two years of this abuse, he pretty much kept to himself and spent hours in his room reading books about the human anatomy, life after death, and biographies about famous physicians, never understanding that the "game" was far from over.

The memories plagued Julian but he had to dismiss them. At any moment, Julian's wife and two children would return from a Friday evening shopping spree, and once again he would be forced to suppress his internal struggles and play the role of loving husband and father. His life was a mixture of responsibilities and details, his weeks burdened with endless meetings, intense research, national teleconferences, and emergency surgeries. But in the scheme of things, he now felt as though he was living a double life. On one hand, he was a gifted cardiologist and revered research leader. But on the other hand, he was something beyond definition.

The media, no doubt, would label his work the deeds of a madman. The police would hunt him down as a deranged serial killer. But in truth, he was a pioneer, a man willing to risk it all—his family, career, and life itself—for the recognition he deserved. Success eclipsed everything.

In the morning, the gods would bless him with a free weekend to continue with his research. His wife would drive to Los Angeles with the children and not return until Sunday evening, giving him enough time to search for his next subject.

After his meeting with the Fosters, Al's head was spinning out of control. He wasn't sure if he had roughed up the judge, but felt certain if he had, Chief Larson would take a big bite out of his ass. At this point, Al didn't really care. He had a job to get done, and if it required that he abandoned political correctness, too bad. In fact, now that he thought about it, he actually hated PC. It seemed to Al that society had become so super sensitive about everything from religion to ethnicity, you had to walk on eggshells every time you opened your mouth for fear you would offend someone.

Years ago, if you lived on the streets you were a bum. Plain and simple. Then, some do-gooder decided that bums should be called homeless people. Most recently, the politically correct term was "financially disadvantaged." He shook his head and laughed out loud. If he had learned anything at all since joining homicide, it was that a detective without balls might as well work at Walmart as a greeter. So if he had to bend a few noses out of place to get results, he was willing to take some heat for his blatant disregard of PC.

Al headed for the evidence room, popularly called the "Cage," appropriately named because that's exactly what it was. Along the way, he passed several colleagues who looked as if they wanted to stop and talk about everything from *American Idol* to fishing. Wanting to avoid any mingling, he acknowledged them with a simple nod and kept walking, careful not to make eye contact, which was generally an invitation to chitchat. This wouldn't be the first time they accused him of being a self-centered asshole.

Al thought he had escaped, then saw Ramirez approaching. He wanted to ignore him, but even though he'd contributed almost nothing to the investigation, he was still Al's partner, even if in title only. Since becoming a lieutenant, Ramirez didn't like to get his hands dirty.

"How'd it go with Judge Foster?" Ramirez asked.

"If you were there, you'd know." Normally, Al wasn't this curt, but Ramirez's lack of work ethic really pissed him off.

"I was busy with other things."

Al didn't want to go there, but couldn't help himself. "Like what? Getting a fucking pedicure, or getting a little afternoon shag from the hottie in Permits?"

"You're stepping way over a line here, Al."

"Fuck you. And fuck your line."

Al didn't wait for him to respond. He did a one-eighty and spotted the Cage a few steps away.

"Hi, Charlie," Al said as he leaned on the counter. Portly and nearly bald, Charlie Brown, as one might imagine, had been harassed most of his life for having the same name as the dubious character in the comic section of every newspaper in the country. Charlie even looked like his namesake and shared the same small tuft of hair just above his forehead. Al wondered if his parents had even the slightest inkling how they'd cursed their only son. Charlie had more insecurities than a turkey two days before Thanksgiving. Whenever he spoke to Charlie, a selection of one-liners hung in the back of Al's throat. The possibilities to mock him were endless. But to piss off Charlie, the guy in charge of every piece of evidence ever associated with a crime, would be a hugely consequential mistake.

"How they hangin', Detective?"

"I need a little help, Charlie. I'm investigating the Foster homicide and need to sign out a small price tag that we found at the scene. It's about this big." Al referenced the approximate size with his fingers. "It's from Saks Fifth Avenue."

"Is this the gal we found at Mission Bay Park dressed like a prom queen?"

"I wouldn't say 'prom queen.' More like someone on the cover of *Vogue.*"

Charlie did an about-face and looked over his shoulder at Al as he headed down one of the aisles. "Be back in a flash."

Al felt that the price tag could yield something significant. After all, it did contain the store name, price, and UPC code. Besides, how many three-thousand-dollar dresses did they sell every day? Surely the salesperson would remember the perp. He likely paid for the dress with a credit card and this could prove to be a significant piece of information.

Charlie returned with a small sandwich bag, price tag inside. He set it on the counter and wrote something on a clipboard. "Sign right here, Detective, and it's yours for twenty-four hours."

Al just couldn't help it. "Thanks, Charlie. Tell Lucy and Linus I said hi."

"Bite me!"

Because of the exigency of the situation and the importance of determining Genevieve Foster's cause of death, Maggie Fox, Medical Examiner, began the autopsy almost immediately after receiving Judge Foster's written consent. Al made it a point whenever he could to observe the autopsies of homicide victims so he could view the body firsthand and ask questions that might give him a lead. He had intended to drive to Fashion Valley Mall and speak to the manager of women's apparel at Saks, but the autopsy loomed more important. Besides, no matter how thorough or skilled the medical examiner, four eyes were always better than two—even considering his limited medical knowledge. In this particular instance, his presence might prove to be more critical. Doctor Fox had been part of the forensics team for only six months, and he wasn't yet convinced that she possessed the same skills as her more experienced colleagues. She just didn't *look* like a medical examiner. To Al, a medical examiner should look like Mr. Magoo. Doctor Fox was anything but Mr. Magoo.

Al walked into Exam Room 3, and as in the past, he felt uneasy. He wasn't sure if it was the indescribable odor, what he was about to observe, or a little of both. From the outside looking in, one might believe that a seasoned homicide detective could witness an autopsy with casual indifference. But even though Al would never outwardly show his emotions, inside, his stomach felt like it was trying to digest itself.

Lying on a stainless-steel table, the curves and contours of Genevieve Foster's body clung to the blood-stained white sheet. Her right foot stuck out from under the sheet and he could see the yellow ID tag on the victim's big toe. Doctor Fox stood next to the body, latex gloves covering her hands, white lab coat neatly buttoned, an assortment of surgical instruments positioned on the table adjacent to the remains of the victim.

"Detective Diaz," Doctor Fox said, more cheerful than what seemed appropriate for the situation. "It's nice to see you again. Sorry we're not meeting under different circumstances." Her honey-brown eyes locked on Al's, lingering for just a bit.

"Not my favorite part of the job, Doctor Fox."

"Mine either. It's one thing to dissect an eighty-year-old man with heart problems and quite another when it's a young woman with her whole life ahead of her. Makes you wonder if God is really paying attention."

"Well, he wasn't paying attention in this case."

The medical examiner grasped one corner of the sheet. "Shall we begin?"

Al nodded.

She handed him a mask and latex gloves and removed the sheet with one swift motion, almost like a matador waving his red cape at a bull. He surveyed the woman's body, noticing extensive bruises in the center of her stapled-shut chest, and burn-like marks on her upper left and lower right torso. He also noticed an incision on her upper thigh. But the rest of her body showed no signs of trauma. He didn't even see a mosquito bite.

Before making any incisions, Doctor Fox poked and prodded the victim's chest, carefully evaluating the bruises and running her fingers up and down and side to side on the woman's ribcage. "I can't imagine why, but it looks like our man performed open heart surgery on this poor gal."

She looked more closely, her focus on the burn marks. "It appears that the killer repeatedly tried to resuscitate her with a defibrillator and with CPR." Her eyes drifted to her lower body. "That's interesting."

"What is it?"

"There's a small incision on her thigh. Right above the femoral artery and vein."

"Any suspicions why?"

"That's generally the area where a cardiologist would insert a catheter to perform an angiogram."

Al shook his head. "What the hell did this nutcase do to her?"

She examined both arms, wrist to triceps. Ran her hands down the victim's torso and checked every rib, her breasts, her nipples. Then, Doctor Fox gently spread her knees apart and poked and prodded her genital area. "No evidence of trauma. I don't think she was raped or assaulted in any way."

"So he performed some kind of mock surgery and tried to revive her?"

"Seems that way."

The superficial exam went on for twenty minutes. The doctor recorded her observations on a digital tape recorder while Al scribbled on his notepad. After putting on a protective face shield, Doctor Fox used a surgical staple remover that resembled special needle-nose pliers, and one by one removed the stainless-steel staples.

As if she were working on a live patient, Doctor Fox's gentle precision stuck Al as peculiar. Was it respect for Genevieve Foster, or the tentative actions of an inexperienced ME?

When finished, Doctor Fox carefully inserted a Finochietto rib spreader into the victim's chest and cranked it open, exposing the heart and other internal organs. Her fingers began to probe, squeeze, and examine.

The medical examiner pointed to Genevieve Foster's heart. "See that area on the right lower part of her heart? That's the right ventricle. Notice that it's bluish and the rest of the heart is mostly red? That bluish area is a myocardial contusion. In other words, her heart is actually bruised."

"And what would cause such injuries?"

"A couple of possibilities. Injuries such as this generally suggest that the victim fell twenty or thirty feet and landed square on her chest. However, there is no evidence of head trauma, so although it's possible, it's unlikely. Second, she could have been in a head-on collision, but in most cases, we find facial injuries from the impact of the air bag. As you can see, her face is perfectly normal."

"So, Doctor Fox—"

"If we're going to be working together closely, Detective Diaz, why don't we dispense with the formalities and address each other by our first names? You okay with that?"

"Sure. Call me Al." He wasn't positive, but it sure seemed like the medical examiner was flirting with him. He had noticed her wedding ring just before she put on the latex gloves, but based on Al's years as a detective looking into people's backgrounds, marriage didn't guarantee fidelity.

"And please call me Maggie rather than Doctor Fox."

"Deal," Al said. "So tell me, Maggie, what caused the victim's death?"

"I still have to examine her lungs, throat, skull, and stomach, and run a series of blood tests before I can determine the cause of death. However, whatever killed her was directly related to her heart."

"When do you think you'll be finished with the autopsy?"

"Give me a couple hours. By then, I should have it wrapped up and I'll also get a complete blood workup and toxicity report."

Al scribbled on a piece of paper and handed it to Maggie. "Call me on my cell as soon as you know something."

She smiled. "Will do, Al."

Al turned and just before he took a step, Maggie grabbed his arm. "Maybe you and I can grab a cup of coffee sometime soon."

He just smiled.

CHAPTER SEVEN

"Hi, Sweetie," Al said. "I'm on my way to check out a lead. Traffic is at a standstill so I thought I'd touch base. Did the doctor convince your mother to have the surgery?"

"Not yet," Sami said. "I'm meeting him at the hospital in an hour."

"How is your mom?"

"Ornery as ever, which I suppose is a good thing."

"Want me to come home and stay with Angelina?"

"Thanks for the offer, but Emily's on her way over as we speak."

"Gotta love that Emily," Al said. "We should adopt her."

"I'm not so sure you can legally adopt a twenty-two-year-old cousin."

He exited Freeway 5 and headed for Friar's Road. "I'll keep my fingers crossed that Doctor Templeton is a convincing litigator."

"That's all we can hope for."

"Okay, Sami, I gotta run."

"We need to talk about something when you get home. Think you'll find time for dinner?"

"Not sure, but I'll do my best. I have a witness to interview a little later, but I don't think it should take me too long." Al turned into the Fashion Valley Mall and headed for the parking ramp. "Am I in hot water again?"

"Could be."

"You really know how to hurt a guy, Samantha Marie."

"And you love every minute of it."

"Sure I do. I love hangin' by my fingernails, waiting to find out if I'm going to spend the next two weeks sleeping on the sofa."

"I was thinking more of the garage, Honey."

"Terrific."

"Drive carefully."

"Good luck with the doctor."

"I'm going to need more than luck."

"I'll speak to you later," Al said. He tossed the cell phone on the passenger seat.

After parking his car next to the red curb, Al weaved his way through the crowded mall and found a directory that indicated where Saks Fifth Avenue was located. He'd never been in this store let alone purchased something there. And if three-thousand-dollar cocktail dresses and thousand-dollar shoes represented their mainstream prices, then he seriously doubted he would *ever* be a patron. This was not a store that catered to the middle class.

The busyness of retail stores and restaurants in San Diego never ceased to amaze Al. No matter what time of day, most places were packed with customers. If there truly were a recession, apparently no one told San Diegans.

He walked in the front door and immediately recognized that he was not in JCPenney. The sales people were impeccably dressed and the store was beautifully decorated. From the rich wood-covered walls to the stunning light fixtures to the marble floors, the place smelled of money. Every customer looked like they'd just left the beauty salon and had that air of snobbery so prevalent in people with deep pockets. At this particular moment, he really appreciated Sami.

He found a salesperson and told her he needed to speak to the manager of women's apparel. He waited by designer handbags while the salesperson paged the manager to the sales floor. Curious, Al looked at the price tag on a Prada handbag: four hundred and fifty dollars. What could be so special about a hunk of leather that it would cost so much? He owned two pair of Docker knockoffs he'd bought on sale for nineteen bucks apiece, he never paid more than thirty dollars for a pair of jeans, and even the one suit he reserved for weddings and funerals cost a hundred and twenty-five dollars. Then again, Al had never been particularly fashion conscious.

After a short wait, Al spotted a tall, slender woman walking toward him with purpose in her step. Her hair, a few shades darker than auburn, barely touched her shoulders. She wore a perfectly tailored, navy-blue pantsuit with a stark-white blouse.

"Are you Detective Diaz?" she asked.

Al extended his hand and nodded.

"Katherine Levy." Her grip put a man's to shame. "Let's go to my office, shall we?"

He followed her past racks of dresses, skirts, business suits, and lingerie. She led him to a small office next to the dressing rooms, and when Al walked inside, the first thing he noticed was the stark difference between the pristine store and Katherine's shabby office. It looked more like the kind of office you might find in the back of a convenience store.

"Please have a seat, Detective."

"Thanks for taking the time to talk to me," Al said. "I just want to assure you that this conversation is strictly confidential."

"What exactly can I do for you?" Levy asked.

"I'm working on a murder investigation—"

"Is it that girl they found at Mission Bay Park?"

It wasn't a secret. Everyone who could read had heard about Genevieve Foster's murder. The story dominated both newspapers and television. "It is."

"What a shame. Is it true they found her dressed in designer clothes?"

"Her outfit was purchased here, Ms. Levy." Al pulled the sales tag, still in a plastic bag, out of his shirt pocket and handed it to her. "Is there any way to identify who bought that cocktail dress?"

"It really makes my skin crawl to think that the murderer might have been right here in this store." She grabbed the plastic bag and examined the sales tag. "Well, I can tell by looking at the UPC code that it's a Herrera designer dress. One of our more expensive items. Unlike general merchandise that uses a generic UPC code, designer items have a unique number specific to that particular item." She set down the tag, planted her elbows on the desk, and rested her chin on folded hands.

"So, what does that mean?"

"Well, I can scan the code in our database, and we should have the buyer's name and address on record."

Al wanted to jump up and down and yell, "Yippee!" But from past experiences, he had learned that many promising leads led nowhere.

"You do have a warrant, correct?"

"It's in process as we speak. I can have one in your hands in an hour."

"I'm afraid that places me in a rather difficult situation. Saks Fifth Avenue is very rigid on customer confidentiality. I could lose my job if I gave you this information without proper authorization."

"And another young woman could lose her life while you and I debate company policies and procedures, Ms. Levy. I can appreciate your situation. Truly. And I'll be happy to get you a warrant, but time is absolutely critical. How would you feel if Genevieve Foster's murderer abducted another woman while I was chasing down a warrant? I give you my word that I'll—"

"I'll be right back, Detective."

After several minutes, Katherine Levy returned to the office and shut the door behind her. Instead of sitting at her desk, she plopped down next to Al and crossed her legs. "Unfortunately, the gentleman who purchased the cocktail dress paid cash."

"So what does that mean?"

"The name on the sales receipt is 'John Smith,' and the address he gave us is a post office box."

"John Smith? That doesn't give me a cozy feeling."

"Then this should ruin your day," Levy said. "The address he gave us is PO Box 1234, Vancouver, Canada. No zip code."

No need to check out the name or address, Al thought. Obviously, both were bogus. Then again, he couldn't take anything for granted. "Can I speak to the salesperson who sold him the dress?"

"I figured you might want to speak to her, but her shift doesn't start for another two hours. So, I called her and asked if she could come in immediately."

"And?"

Levy glanced at her watch. "She'll be here in twenty minutes."

"Terrific. Mind if I hang around until she shows up?"

"Not at all. In fact, our lounge is on the second floor. Grab a coffee or muffin—whatever you like—and I'll come get you when she arrives."

"I really appreciate your cooperation."

"No problem."

✡ ✡ ✡

"Do you want to come with me when I speak to your mom?" Doctor Templeton asked. "Or would you prefer that I go solo?"

"I think you might have more impact one-on-one," Sami said.

"Make yourself comfortable in the visitor's lounge while I speak to your mom."

She was no stranger to this lounge. "Thank you, Doctor. I can't tell you how much I appreciate what you're doing."

"It's part of what I do, Ms. Rizzo. You'd be surprised at the number of people who have to be pressured into consenting to surgery."

"If you don't mind me asking, have you been successful in convincing reluctant patients?"

"At the risk of sounding pompous, I have a pretty impressive track record. I can only think of two holdouts that stood firm and refused." The doctor's lips tightened. "Their outcomes were not pleasant. They both died within weeks of being discharged."

"Do you have a special dialogue that you use to persuade them?'

"Yes, I do." Doctor Templeton adjusted the stethoscope hanging around his neck. "I simply tell them in no uncertain terms that by not signing the consent form, they just signed their death certificate. It's harsh, and might even violate my Hippocratic Oath, but if it saves even one life, I'm willing to push the envelope."

Sami thought about that for a moment, rather stunned at Doctor Templeton's candor. "And if my mother refuses, what is her prognosis?"

"It's not good, Ms. Rizzo." The doctor shook his head. "I give her six months."

"Well then, you have my permission to hit my mother with a two-by-four if necessary. Whatever works."

"So you don't mind if I rough her up a bit?"

"I'm more concerned about her roughing you up."

"I love a challenge." Doctor Templeton looked at his watch. "I'll be back in less than thirty minutes with a signed consent form."

"That sounds like a promise."

"It is."

As she watched him walk away, she found herself surprised by his casual, easy-going demeanor. Her experiences with doctors in the past, particularly while her father lay in a hospital bed dying of cancer, had been unsavory to say the least. Most of the doctors she'd encountered had been arrogant and cold. Dr. Templeton was anything but self-centered. She hoped that he remained this cooperative and pleasant.

"Detective Diaz," Katherine Levy, Saks manager, said. "This is Robin Westcott, one of our sales associates."

"It was kind of you to come in early," Al said.

"I just hope I can be of assistance to you."

Katherine's cell phone rang. "I have to take this call. I'll be right outside my office if you need me."

"No problem," Al said. He reached in his pocket and removed a photo of the designer dress and showed it to Robin. "Do you recall selling that dress?"

Robin pinched her chin between thumb and index finger. "I distinctly remember the dress—and the guy who bought it."

"What did he look like?" Al asked.

"He wore a Chargers baseball cap but took it off a couple of times and ran his fingers through his hair. He had a full head of pitch-black hair."

"Any distinguishing features?"

"His eyes were sky-blue. Just beautiful. And to be honest, Detective, he was a real looker. I'm talking Hugh Jackman,

George Clooney good-looking. He was tall—over six feet. And he had an average build."

"How old would you say he was?"

"I'd say fortyish."

"Could you pick him out of a lineup?"

"Oh, yeah."

"Do you think you could sit down with a sketch artist and help us with a composite drawing?"

Robin's face tightened. "If I saw him again I'm pretty sure I'd recognize him, but his face just isn't clear in my mind. I'm afraid if I tried to help you with a drawing, I'd be wasting your time."

"Tell me about your conversation with him."

"The one thing that stuck out in my mind is that he was really nervous. Looked like he just drank a pot of high-test coffee. Strange thing was, he hadn't a clue what size to buy. That seemed odd to me. I mean how do you *not* know the dress size of someone you'd buy a three-thousand-dollar dress for? I didn't want to jeopardize the sale, so I guessed the size based on his description of her."

"How did he land on that particular dress?"

"Well, the first thing he said when I approached him on the sales floor was, 'I'm looking for a stunning cocktail dress. And money is no object.' When a commissioned salesperson hears a customer say that, which isn't very often, what they really hear is, 'cha-ching.' Not that we would ever take advantage of a customer, but hey, a gal's gotta make a living, and when a guy opens up his wallet…what can I say?"

"Anything else you can tell me about the way he looked or acted?"

She shook her head. "Nothing unusual rings a bell."

"Did he have any scars, a tattoo, a limp—anything at all that might distinguish him?"

She contemplated his question for a moment, then shook her head. "Nothing that strikes me."

Al reached in his pocket and handed Robin a business card. "If anything pops into your head, anything at all, please call me right away."

Al left Saks and headed downtown.

When he walked into the precinct, Al all but ignored his fellow detectives, and headed straight for the break room. After his conversation with Robin Westcott, he needed a pick-me-up before he could find the strength to interview another witness. At this time of day, it seemed unlikely, but he hoped that he'd find a freshly brewed pot of coffee. When he entered the break room, he spotted the red light on the base of the coffee maker glowing like a laser pen. As he approached the coffee maker with high hopes, he could see the almost empty pot. He flipped up the lid on the cardboard donut box and found the remains of a cinnamon twist that pretty much looked like it had been attacked by a hungry rat. Slightly annoyed, he headed for the interrogation room.

Genevieve Foster's best friend, Katie Mitchell, curly red hair resting on her shoulders, freckles highlighting her cheeks, and prominent lips painted with pink lipstick, sat nervously on the metal chair, twisting a tissue as if it were wringing wet. Her hazel eyes looked like they were covered with a clear glaze.

Al extended his hand. "Ms. Mitchell, I'm Detective Diaz." Her hands felt cold and clammy. "Thanks so much for coming. Can I get you some water or a soda?"

"No thank you."

Al pulled out the chair, turned it 180 degrees, and straddled the seat. Normally, two detectives would conduct an interview, but evidently, Ramirez had better things to do than track down a serial killer. He set a digital tape recorder on the desk and pushed the "Record" button.

"Do we have to record this conversation?" Katie Mitchell asked.

"Is there something you're going to say that you don't want recorded?"

The question seemed to stun her. "Well, um, I just don't want to get myself in trouble."

"Did you do something that *might* get you in trouble?"

"No. No. Of course not."

"Then there's nothing to be concerned about."

She fingered her curly hair. "Can we get this over with, please?"

"That ball is in *your* court, Ms. Mitchell."

"I'm sorry if I seem a little...a little nervous. I still can't get past what happened to Genevieve."

"I totally understand. And believe me, I will try to make this as painless as possible." He pulled a notepad and pen out of his shirt pocket and flipped open the notepad. "What was your relationship with Ms. Foster?"

"She was my best friend in the whole world. We went to the same elementary school and high school together and lived only a few blocks away from each other."

"How often did you see her?"

"Not much during the workweek, although we texted each other regularly. Neither of us had boyfriends—at least not recently—so on the weekends we'd do some bar-hopping."

"Did you go to the same bars every weekend?"

"Not usually. But Tony's was our favorite."

"Tony's Bar and Grill in the Gaslamp District?"

She nodded.

"Why was it your favorite?"

"Can I be really, really honest?"

"I wouldn't have it any other way."

"You're going to think I'm some superficial dingbat, but Tony's has the hottest guys."

"And by 'hot' I assume you mean attractive, right?"

"Totally to die for." Katie Mitchell covered her mouth and gasped, looking like she'd just seen a ghost. "Oh, my God. I didn't mean that. I was just—"

"No need to apologize, Ms. Mitchell. It was merely a slip of the tongue."

Al gave her a moment to regain her composure. "Are you okay?"

"As okay as I'm going to be."

"Were you with Ms. Foster the night she disappeared?"

"Yes. I picked her up at her parents' home and we went to Tony's for drinks."

"Tell me everything you remember about the evening."

"Well, Gen and I were sitting at the bar, sipping a couple of martinis, and talking about things that girls talk about. A few barstools away, this gorgeous guy—and I mean drop-dead gorgeous—keeps smiling at Gen and making eye contact. They were definitely checking each other out. Before I even realized what was happening, Gen leaves me and walks over to the guy. I was a little pissed, but it wasn't unusual for us to go our separate ways if one of us…"

"Met a hot guy?"

"Exactly. So anyway, they talk for a bit and without even saying a word to me, I see Gen and this guy heading for the exit. A couple of minutes later I get a text message from her."

"And what did it say?"

"'I think I'm in love. Call me tomorrow.'"

"And that was the last time you heard from her?"

All teary-eyed, Katie Mitchell nodded.

"Other than saying that the man Ms. Foster left with was 'drop-dead gorgeous,' can you tell me what he looked like. Any striking characteristics?"

"Like most bars, the lights are pretty dim. That's so average-looking girls like me rank a couple of notches higher than we are. Dim lights can do wonders for those of us not blessed with high cheekbones and a cute little turned-up nose. I do remember that he was a tall guy—over six-foot—and his hair was jet-black."

"What was he wearing?"

"I remember his navy-blue Chargers cap."

"If you sat down with a sketch artist, could you give us enough detail of his face for us to do a composite drawing?"

"I doubt it, Detective. I only remember what I told you."

"Do you think you could pick him out of a lineup?"

"Not sure. But I'd love to give it a whirl."

"Anything else you can tell me?"

"Only that I want you to find this asshole and cut his dick off."

"Nothing would please me more."

Late for dinner with Sami and company, Al left a voice mail for her so she wouldn't get worried. He walked into a crowded Starbucks, craned his neck, and spotted Maggie sitting at a table for two, waving her arm.

"We meet again," Maggie said. "Get yourself a drink. On me." She handed Al a ten-dollar bill. He ordered a double espresso and sat opposite Maggie, dropping her change in the middle of the table.

"The autopsy results are going to knock your socks off," Maggie said.

When Maggie had called Al and suggested they meet for coffee to discuss the results of the autopsy, at first his radar kicked into high gear. He recognized a come-on when he heard one. But Maggie convinced him that getting away from the "coal mines" would be good for both of them. He had to admit that he was running on reserve power and ready to shut down. So relaxing and drinking a stiff espresso wasn't the worst idea.

After their prior meeting, and Maggie's subtle yet obvious attempt to flirt, he wasn't totally comfortable with this rendezvous. He'd be lying if he didn't admit that he found her attractive. And he'd also be lying if he denied the fact that his love life with Sami wasn't exactly the fabric from which steamy romance novels were written. Although his intentions were honorable, he felt vulnerable right now.

"Go ahead and knock them off."

"First of all, the blood tests proved very interesting. The lab found traces of sevoflurane, and higher doses of epinephrine and potassium chloride in her blood, but not enough to kill her."

"Epinephrine is what they use for anaphylactic shock, no?"

"Among other uses," Maggie said, "it's the drug used in an EPI pen."

"For people who go into shock from a severe allergic reaction, bee sting—"

"Exactly."

"And the potassium chloride?"

"It's the third drug used for lethal injection. And the correct dosage, based on subject's weight, can permanently stop a heart."

"And what about the sevoflurane?"

"It's a general anesthesia administered in gas form to keep the patient unconscious."

"What do you make of it, Maggie?"

"It's very peculiar. When I examined her heart, it looked like it had been kicked around like a soccer ball. For a twenty-something girl, her heart was pretty much worn out. And she suffered from a moderate case of ventricular hypertrophy, which causes the walls of the heart to thicken. Hypertrophic cardiomyopathy is caused by untreated hypertension, but to be honest, it's generally an age-related disease. I seriously doubt that this young woman had a blood pressure problem."

"Anything else unusual in her blood?"

"As a matter of fact, yes. We found high levels of a drug called amiodarone."

"Ami-what?" Al asked.

"Amiodarone. It's a drug used in the treatment of two conditions: atrial fibrillation, commonly known as A-Fib. And ventricular fibrillation, referred to as—"

"Let me guess. V-Fib?"

"Very good, Detective. You just might have a future in forensics."

"No thanks." Al tried to process all this information but felt like his brain was close to a complete meltdown. "So why the hell would the killer inject so many drugs into her?"

"I haven't the foggiest, Detective. But what I do know is that each of these drugs has a direct connection to heart rhythm and function. And the effect of these drugs varies dramatically. It seems to me that our guy was using the victim for some kind of perverse experiments or maybe even playing torture games."

"So, whatever horrific experiments he conducted on the Foster girl ultimately stopped her heart and killed her? That would make cause of death cardiac arrest, right?"

"Here's where it gets spooky." Maggie finished her latte. "Genevieve Foster died of a massive stroke. In technical terms, COD was a thrombotic stroke in the middle cerebral artery. This is the granddaddy of all strokes. At best, it leaves the patient in a complete vegetative state, but rarely do they live for more than a few days."

"And what the hell would cause such a stroke?"

"A huge blood clot."

This was way too much for Al to absorb. He gulped the double espresso as if he were downing a shot of tequila, and the hot liquid burned a trail to his stomach. "So, I'm guessing whatever wild experiments he performed on this young girl ultimately formed a blood clot in her brain?"

"Here's my read," Maggie said. "Epinephrine and potassium chloride dangerously affect heart rhythms and any pooling of blood in the heart can cause blood clots. I can't tell you why he did what he did, but ultimately, the victim's blood flow and heart rhythm were dramatically compromised—enough so that blood pooled in her left ventricle, formed clots, and they found their way to her brain."

"Based on your autopsy and all the issues we've discussed, do you believe our killer is medically trained or even a doctor?"

"I can't imagine anyone without medical training performing these kinds of complicated procedures."

He felt uncomfortable asking this question but had to. "Did she suffer?"

"If she was properly anesthetized, which seems logical considering that her blood contained trace amounts of sevoflurane, not to mention the epinephrine and potassium chloride, I'd bet she was in the Twilight Zone."

"And your written report?"

"It's in your mailbox back at the precinct."

He felt an obligation to chat with Maggie, but his head pounded unmercifully and he wanted to at least salvage part of the evening with Sami. Before he had a chance to gather his thoughts, Maggie confirmed his suspicions.

"So, Al, when you're not hunting down the bad guys, what do you do for fun?"

"I try not to have too much fun because it distracts me."

"Sounds utterly boring."

"It serves a purpose."

"Life's too short not to have a little fun, don't you think?"

"I think fun is overrated."

Maggie unzipped and removed her leather jacket and draped it around the back of her chair. She sat upright, as if she was conscious of her posture. Her low-cut blouse gave Al an eyeful. "What does a gal have to do to get a rise out of you?"

Rise? Al wasn't sure if her double entendre was intentional or an innocent miscue. *Time to play dumb.* "I'm not sure I understand the question."

"Let me take out the blocks, Al." She leaned forward, giving him full view of her generous cleavage. "I'd like to have dinner with you sometime soon and get to know you on a more personal level."

"You heard that I'm involved, right?"

"Everyone knows about you and the former Detective Rizzo. Hope you two weren't trying to keep it a secret."

"Our lives are an open book. In fact, just last week we were running naked through Balboa Park."

"So, you *do* have a sense of humor."

Time to set her straight. "Look, Maggie, I'm really flattered. Honestly, but—"

"Is this the big letdown?"

"If I weren't in a committed relationship, I would love to have dinner with you and learn more about you on a personal level. But I'm a one-woman guy."

"I'm disappointed, but I respect that."

Al looked at his watch. "I really have to run. Thanks for getting the autopsy report done so quickly."

"Good luck. I hope you find this nutcase before he strikes again."

"That's my plan."

"Sorry I missed dinner," Al said. He hung his jacket on the coat tree by the front door, feeling guilty about meeting Maggie. But why should he? He had been a perfect gentleman. Then again, if she didn't give up the chase and pursued him again, he wasn't absolutely sure he would be so noble. "Are there any leftovers?"

Sami took a long swig of her Corona and pointed toward the kitchen. "Didn't have time to cook, but there's some pizza in the fridge."

Terrific. Just what I need after a twelve-hour day. He walked over and kissed her on the cheek, remembering how they used to kiss. "So, what's the deal with your mother?"

"I can't even guess what Doctor Templeton said to her, but she's having the surgery on Monday."

"Did he give you any details of their conversation?"

"Not really. But I did talk to my mother afterwards and all she said was that she didn't want Angelina to grow up without a grandmother."

"That's terrific news!"

"It shocked the shit out of me." Sami didn't look as happy as Al thought she should be. "After you gobble down your dinner, can we talk?"

"Let's talk first," he said.

Sami patted the sofa. "Sit next to me."

He plopped down and draped his arm around Sami. "What gives?"

"I'm really uncomfortable with my mother being alone."

"You made that point quite clear."

"Well, now that she's had a heart attack, I'm even more concerned."

"Totally understandable."

"Were you serious when you said you're okay with her living with us for a while after her surgery, or was it one of those impulsive things you wished you hadn't said?"

"I was dead serious. We've got two spare bedrooms. She can stay as long as she likes."

Sami let out a heavy breath.

"There's only one problem," Al said. "With my schedule and your schedule, she's still going to be living here alone."

"That's part B of the equation." Sami swigged her beer. "Cousin Emily agreed to stay with Mom while we're doing our thing. But I don't want her schlepping back and forth from East County every day. Forgetting about traffic delays, it would take her almost an hour one way. So, we talked, and with your blessing, she's willing to move in for as long as my mother needs her."

"But I thought she was looking for a nursing job."

"Well, she just got her nursing degree and I guess it was grueling. So, she wants to take a few months off just to veg-out before she searches for a job."

"And she thinks tending to your mother is vegging-out?"

"Don't be a smartass."

"Sorry. It's in my nature." Al stroked Sami's back. "But seriously, does she have any idea what she's getting herself into?"

"I told her it wouldn't be a day at the beach, but Emily loves my mother, and really wants to do this. Besides, Angelina is crazy about Emily, so it would be good for her, too."

"If you're okay with it, Sami, I'm okay with it." Deep in his gut, he feared what little sex they had right now would almost completely end when Josephine and Emily moved in. The moment his thoughts faded, he felt horribly guilty and selfish. Was he really this self-centered?

CHAPTER EIGHT

Julian could barely contain his excitement as he stood on the front porch and waved goodbye to his wife and two daughters. Watching them drive away, he felt a surge of exhilaration. He could not continue his research with his wife and kids in town. How would he explain his long hours away from home? He could only get so much mileage out of medical emergencies. Besides, he could not afford any distractions while he conducted his research. To be successful, his experiments required his undivided attention.

His wife reversed the Range Rover out of the driveway, waved back at him, and headed north for Los Angeles. She wouldn't return until late Sunday. This gave Julian plenty of time to search for his next subject. He didn't feel comfortable with his wife driving at night, but a two-million-dollar real estate deal had derailed her plan to leave early in the morning. Julian made plenty of money, enough so Nicole didn't have to work. But she loved selling real estate. And loved the five-figure commissions even more.

He dashed up the stairs, two steps at a time, unbuttoning his shirt as he made his way toward the master bath. He felt like Superman running down the street, tearing off his civilian clothes. A quick shower and shave, and he'd be out the door. Before stepping into the shower, he stood in front of the full-length mirror and appraised his reflection. There was a time when his body was nearly perfect, as if made of clay and molded by a gifted sculptor.

Before starting the A-Fib research project, he followed a strict diet and visited the gym five times a week. But he found little time to continue with a workout regimen. Although he felt as handsome as ever, his body was no longer lean and muscular. In fact, looking at his flabby midsection, he felt disgusted with himself. But his priorities offered no apologies for his less-than-perfect physique.

Tonight, he would face a new challenge. His next subject needed to be a young male, someone who would be attracted to him. This would be the easiest way to find his next subject. Using his charm would be less risky than trying to abduct some unwilling man. But how would he go about meeting a gay man? Being straight, he had no idea how to give off the right vibe or say the right thing. He hadn't a clue how to *act* gay. Surely, there was a difference in their behaviors and body language. Julian wasn't yet sure how he would meet his next subject. The anticipation of venturing into uncharted waters overwhelmed him with excitement and trepidation.

He stepped into the shower, turned on the water, closed his eyes, and gently stroked himself. "What to do," he whispered. He slowly turned in circles, gradually increasing the rhythm, trying to clear his mind of all arbitrary thoughts. Then at the exact moment he reached paradise, an event from the past flashed before him, and a vivid image unfolded in his mind.

Julian hadn't seen his cousins Rebecca and Marianne in months. And that's the way he had wanted it. The more he thought about what they'd done to him, the deeper his anger. They had made it clear that if he stopped playing the game of "Ticklish" with them, he'd regret it. But he'd ignored their warning and done everything possible to avoid them—even to the point of finding excuses not to attend family get-togethers. As a naïve teenager, still trying to figure out the ways of the world, he felt haunted by two burning questions: First, how could his cousins—his own flesh and blood—commit such an unspeakable act? And second, were all women this evil?

On one particular day, right after school, Julian had just walked in the front door of his home, and was stunned to see a living room crowded with family members—including Rebecca and Marianne. Just seeing them made his temples pulse. As he stood in the foyer taking a head count, he noticed that everyone in the room was staring at him. They gawked at him as if he had stolen money from their church. His mother's eyes were red and puffy. Julian feared that a family member had died.

"What's going on?" Julian asked.

His father stood and walked toward him. "I'm disgusted with you, Julian. *Totally* disgusted."

Julian made eye contact with Rebecca and could see her lips curled ever-so-slightly to a smile.

"What did I do, Dad?"

"Tell us about the incident in the shed," his mother ordered.

Julian fixed his stare on Marianne and saw the same smile he'd seen on Rebecca. His palms felt moist and he found it hard to swallow.

"I don't know what you're talking about," Julian said.

"If you lie, Julian," his father warned, "you're only going to make it tougher on yourself."

Julian had no idea what was happening. Why would Rebecca and Marianne tell his parents about their little game? Why would they confess? Shouldn't *they* be the ones getting grilled? Wouldn't *their* little asses be in trouble?

"Well, um, I don't know what you want me to say."

"Get on your knees and say you're sorry, you little shit," his father said. "You're lucky that Rebecca isn't going to file criminal charges."

"*What*?" At first, Julian didn't get it. "*Criminal* charges?" Then, like a tsunami crashing over him, he realized that his cousins had kept their promise.

"It's a good thing Marianne heard Rebecca's scream before you had a chance to…" His mother couldn't finish her sentence.

Julian's Uncle Sam, Rebecca's father, stood and wagged his fist at Julian. "If you *ever* go near my daughter again, I'm going to forget that you're my nephew."

For a fleeting moment, Julian thought about pleading his case, telling the real story. But who would believe him? His cousins had woven a web from which he could not break free. He wanted to scream and stamp his feet and proclaim his innocence. Swear on the Holy Book. Anything to exonerate himself. He wanted everyone to know that Rebecca and Marianne were the criminals. But Julian knew it was a losing battle.

"Apologize to Rebecca," his father ordered.

Julian stood silently, unable to utter a sound. His gut welled with anger. At this particular point in time, he felt as if he could actually kill his cousins. Painfully and with great angst, Julian whispered, "I'm sorry." They were, perhaps, the most insincere words he would ever speak.

"For the next three months," his father said, "your ass is grounded. You go to school. You come home. You do your homework. No TV. No music. No going outside. No nothing. When you're home, you stay in your room. I want you to feel what it's like to be locked up like the animal you are."

From this day forward, Julian's entire family would think of him as dirt beneath their feet. Even his parents. Prior to this momentous day, he had to deal with a mother and father incapable of showing love or affection. But now things would be worse. He would be an outcast and reach a new depth of insignificance. It was a stigma from which he could never escape. If there had ever been a chance for Julian to break through the barrier his parents had built around their hearts, it was now hopeless. After all, his family had tried, convicted, and sentenced him as an attempted rapist. It wasn't like shoplifting or smoking pot. He now regretted not taking advantage of his cousins in that little shed. He wanted one more afternoon with them, one more chance to teach them a lesson, but he knew that would never happen. All eyes were on him now; he was an insect sitting under a microscope. Somehow, he'd find a way to get even.

"I'll be up to bed in a few minutes, Sami," Al said. "I just have to make one more phone call."

"Talk about burning the candle at both ends," she said. "How long can you keep up this pace?"

"Until I collapse."

"I won't lecture you, 'cause I've tried that before."

"I'll just be a minute or two."

This was not a telephone call Al wanted to make. But part of his responsibility as a detective was to deliver the results of autopsy reports to the family of a homicide victim. It was difficult enough dealing with the average family, but faced with calling a Supreme Court judge in the state of California, and especially considering the strange cause of death, he wished he could delegate the task to someone else. But who? Ramirez?

He picked up the cell phone and dialed the judge's home number.

One ring. Two rings. Three rings. Voice mail.

"Judge Foster, this is Detective Diaz—"

"Detective? Sorry about the voice mail, but for obvious reasons, I always screen my calls."

"No problem, Judge. I totally understand. Sorry to call so late."

"Do you have the results of the autopsy report?"

Obviously, the judge was a get-down-to-business man. "I do. I'd like to set up an appointment with Mrs. Foster and you—"

"Appointment? No need for that, Detective. Just give me all the details over the telephone."

"With all due respect, Judge, normal protocol requires that we meet face to face. I'm sure you can understand the sensitivity of the situation. I can come to your home whenever it's convenient."

"It's *never* going to be convenient, Detective Diaz. My daughter was brutally murdered. As you might imagine, our lives have been turned upside down. I do appreciate your gesture for this personal service, but please indulge me. You can send me a complete copy of the medical examiner's report, but for the moment, I just want to find out how Genevieve died."

He thought about debating the issue further, but Judge Foster seemed rigid on his position. Rigid enough to get him off the hook.

"Your daughter's cause of death was a massive stroke." As soon as the words rolled off his tongue, Al wished he could retract them. They seemed so cold and without diplomacy. But was there really a tactful way to deliver this information?

Silence.

"Judge Foster?"

"I heard you, Detective. I'm just trying to understand how a healthy twenty-three-year-old woman died of a stroke."

"It's complicated. In fact, even the medical examiner is puzzled. Blood tests confirmed your daughter had several very potent prescription drugs in her system. Why, we don't know. Two of these drugs have an effect on heart function and it's possible that an erratic heartbeat formed a blood clot that traveled to her brain."

"That is medically possible?"

"One of the drugs in your daughter's blood can cause what they call fibrillation, where the heart flutters instead of pumping blood normally. This fluttering causes the blood to pool and form clots that can travel anywhere in your body."

"What would motivate anyone to give her these drugs?"

"That's the question we need to answer."

"Tell me, Detective." The judge hesitated for a few moments. "Was she…sexually assaulted?"

Al didn't think his answer would give the judge much comfort, but this was the only piece of information that let Al breathe easy. "No, Judge. We found no evidence that Genevieve was sexually harmed in any way."

"Thank you, Detective."

Al didn't want to push it, but the judge seemed like he was in a cooperative mood. "You can help us tremendously by answering a few questions."

"Like what?"

"First off, was Genevieve taking any prescription medication?

"None. She didn't even take vitamins."

"Did she have any allergies that would require she keep an EPI pen handy?"

"Absolutely not. Other than a few sniffles in the fall during hay fever season, to the best of my knowledge, she wasn't allergic to anything."

"One last question, Judge. Did your daughter have any medical condition that required a doctor's care?"

"She was healthy since the day she was born."

"Thank you, Judge. That's it for now. I'll be sure to get you a complete copy of the autopsy report."

"I have one more question, Detective Diaz. Unfortunately, I'm aware of what goes on during these gruesome autopsies. That's why I was so dead set against it. What I want to know is this. Can we have an open casket at her wake, or will we never see her beautiful face again?"

Al knew exactly what he was asking: *Did the ME fillet my daughter like a dead fish and crack her skull open like a coconut? Will she be presentable lying in that casket, or will she be a collection of body parts?*

"When you see her, Judge, there will be no evidence that she ever even had a mosquito bite."

"That's what I wanted to hear." The phone went silent again. "You deal with this sort of thing every day. And as a judge, I've seen my fair share of violent criminals and acts of brutality that make me question the civility of mankind. But no matter what you're exposed to each and every day, nothing, I mean nothing can prepare you for a loss like this." The judge's voice was a little unsteady. "But how do you deal with not knowing? How do you sleep at night wondering what that monster did to our daughter? What she felt the last few minutes of her life. How do you go on when you try to imagine how much she suffered?"

Al searched his mind, but could not find one comforting word. All he could say was, "I'm really sorry, Judge Foster. I promise you that I won't rest until I find Genevieve's murderer."

✡ ✡ ✡

Sami lay on her side, facing Al. It was one of those moments she loved when their eyes and body language did most of the talking. He seemed a bit restless and distant tonight, but she hoped she could improve his mood. "This might be the last time you get to jump my bones without having to stifle yourself, Cowboy. Wanna make whoopee?"

"Sounds inviting, but I'm completely out of gas."

"Well, maybe I can fill up your tank," Sami said playfully. She kissed him softly on the lips. "When have you *ever* refused a roll in the hay?"

"Will you give me a rain check?"

Something didn't feel right. He never refused an opportunity for sex. Okay, so their sex life had tapered off. With his schedule and her hurried life, they found it nearly impossible to carve out any time for themselves. But wouldn't that make her invitation even more appealing?

Al kissed Sami on the cheek. "I'm sorry, Sami. It was just one of those days."

She felt a knot in the back of her throat. "Are we okay?"

He nodded. "Of course we are."

She wasn't convinced. Sami's romance with Al had taken a turn she never expected. Early in their relationship, the passion between them was so intense that she felt certain it would fade quickly. Yes, the frequency of their lovemaking had diminished; their hurried lives often distracted them. But she thought that the fire still burned hot. Was she wrong? Had he really turned down sex? She'd never expected to fall in love with him. He'd always seemed like a rogue, a heartbreaker. But since their love affair began, Al had shed his protective armor and exposed a kind and sensitive man. A man worthy of her love. Perhaps they had reached a crossroads, and Al and she were headed in different directions.

Before Sami could complete her thoughts, the telephone rang.

"Let the answering machine pick up," Al said.

She reached for the telephone before the second ring. "It could be the hospital calling about my mom."

"Hello. Yes. Yes. And your name is?" Sami covered the mouthpiece. "It's Ricardo Menendez?"

"Who?" He grabbed the phone.

As Al silently listened, Sami watched the color drain from his face. His hand began to shake and he nearly dropped the telephone. "What hospital?" Al asked. "Give me your cell phone number." Al reached past Sami and grabbed a pen and pad sitting on the nightstand. He scribbled hastily. "Thank you, Ricardo. I'll be there as quickly as I can."

Al dropped the cordless telephone on the bed. "That was my sister's boyfriend calling from Rio." He couldn't find his voice. "Aleta was in a head-on collision. She's in an intensive care unit in Rio." Al's eyes filled with tears. "She's in a coma and they don't think she's going to make it."

Sami sprang out of bed and put her arms around Al. "I'm so, so sorry." There were no words that would comfort him.

"I have to get there as soon as I can."

"Let me fire up the computer and search for tickets," she offered.

"Make a pot of coffee," Al said. "I think it's going to be a long night."

Julian's destination this evening required that he dress down. He slipped on a pair of stylishly worn-out blue jeans and a pink polo shirt. He completed the ensemble with black Converse sneakers and he clasped a thick gold chain around his neck. He'd never been to Henry's Hideaway before—why would he patronize a gay bar? But tonight he had a purpose and felt certain the crowd would fulfill his expectations. Located in the heart of Hillcrest, an area of San Diego famous for its trendy eateries, chic boutiques, and being a hot spot for the gay community, Henry's was the hottest new pub and bistro in the area.

Ordinarily, Julian wore his hair neatly parted on the side with just a touch of styling gel. But in an effort to blend in with the crowd, tonight he decided to grease it up with Bed Head and let it run wild. He was certain that none of his friends or work colleagues would ever patronize a place like Henry's, so he felt secure his covert operation would go unnoticed by anyone significant. Not wanting to deal with explaining to his wife why he required a rental car, Julian had parked it in the far corner of a Food Mart only a few blocks away from Henry's.

Julian stood in front of the full-length mirror and appraised his appearance one last time before he left the house. "Perfect," he whispered. Satisfied that he looked the part, he headed for Henry's, confident that tonight he would steal someone's heart.

Sami had no idea how to comfort Al, except to keep her distance and make herself available if he needed to talk. She also kept topping off his coffee. Since receiving the phone call from Ricardo, Al had been on the Internet searching for the quickest flight to Rio, but hadn't uttered a sound. Aleta was Al's only living relative. And even though he hadn't seen his sister in years, they talked on the telephone every couple months and stayed in touch with brief e-mails. He'd been saying for ages that he wanted to visit her, but every time he seriously thought about it, either he was knee-deep in a murder investigation or Aleta was globetrotting with her wealthy boyfriend.

"Shit," Al muttered. He slammed the lid on the laptop computer and stood up, pushing the chair so forcefully it fell backwards. "Except for a red-eye late tonight, not a single fucking flight out of here until Monday."

"Then book the red-eye," Sami suggested.

"It's twenty-two hundred dollars. I've got five-hundred to my name and not enough available credit on my Visa."

"Then use *my* credit card."

"I *hate* to borrow money from you. This is *your* house and *your* furniture. All I pay for is food and utilities."

"If you want to argue gender roles in this relationship or debate financial responsibilities, this is neither the time nor place." Under the circumstances, this was not the way she wanted to speak to him. But sometimes he just pushed her buttons. "Cut the macho bullshit, Al. Get your ass on that damn computer right now, while there's still a ticket available."

His stern face relaxed and the corners of his mouth turned up ever so slightly. He walked over to Sami and gave her a bear hug. "I'm a little wired, Sami. Sorry."

"You have every right to be. Now book the damn flight and get packed."

Julian eased out of the rental car and handed the valet parking attendant a ten-dollar bill. A big burly man with a shaved head sat near the entrance checking IDs. Julian tried to walk past the man, but he pressed the palm of his enormous hand against Julian's chest.

"ID please," the man said with a deep, throaty voice.

"You're kidding me, right?"

"I don't kid, Bro. I have no sense of humor."

"I'm forty-two years old."

"Well you look pretty fucking good for your age. Where's your ID?"

Julian opened his wallet and handed the man the phony driver's license he'd bought in Tijuana.

The man checked the license, looked at Julian, and checked the license again.

"You having a bad-hair day, Bro?"

"Just trying to look stylish."

"I don't think it's working, Bro."

"I thought you said you didn't have a sense of humor."

"I don't."

The man yielded and let Julian through the door to Henry's Hideaway. Julian hadn't been proofed in years and felt more complimented than insulted that the bouncer asked for ID. But he didn't appreciate the man's wise-ass attitude. He'd been worried about his appearance of late, noticing crow's-feet and slight puffiness under his eyes. Not to mention that his once six-pack abs had surrendered to a muffin-top. He hated the aging process and wished he could stay young forever.

Julian walked toward the bar, weaving his way through a sea of people, mostly men. Music blared in the background and the tiny dance floor couldn't hold another soul. He surveyed the long bar and couldn't find a place to sit or even order a drink. He squeezed between two men sitting on bar stools and tried to flag the bartender. The place buzzed with energy. The booming techno-music and its irritating repetitive beat gave way to a ballad, and the rockers, acting like someone had just tossed a live grenade among them, immediately evacuated the dance floor, replaced by a more subdued group. With heightened curiosity and an ample share of fascination, Julian watched men dancing with men and women dancing with women.

After several unsuccessful attempts, Julian finally got the bartender's attention.

"Sorry you had to wait, sir. This place is nuts tonight. What'll it be?"

"How about an extra-dry Belvedere martini, up—with two olives."

"Yes, sir. Coming right up."

Sandwiched between two young men at the bar, Julian could barely sip his drink. He made his way through the crowd and eased toward the dance floor. Now only a few feet away, he could clearly see the interactions between dancers, the firm embraces, hands exploring intimate areas, kissing that should take place only in a private room.

There was nothing inhibited about this crowd.

Julian felt a hand squeeze his shoulder. He turned to see a young man with sun-bleached blond hair and a dark tan. He looked like he could be the centerfold for *Surfer* magazine. Couldn't have been more than twenty-five.

"Would you like to dance?" the blond asked, his voice gentle and polite.

"The dance floor's a little too crowded for me."

"This place is always hopping—especially on weekends." The blond pointed to Julian's shirt. "Love the pink polo."

"Actually," Julian said, "it's faded. When I bought it, it was shocking pink. Don't believe those Tide commercials."

"You're funny," the blond said.

He extended his hand. "I'm Julian."

"Connor Stevens." Despite his firm grip, the young man's hands were as soft as lambskin.

"Are you a regular?" Connor asked.

"First time."

"So what do you think?"

"It's quite a lively place but not my cup of tea."

"And what *is* your cup of tea?"

"I prefer a little less noise and a little more intimacy. Guess I'm getting crotchety in my old age."

Connor laughed. "Yeah, right. Old age. What are ya, thirty-two, maybe thirty-three?"

"Only in my dreams."

"Well, whatever you're doing to stay young-looking, keep it up 'cause it's really working." An awkward silence ensued. "Want to go someplace a little quieter and have a drink?"

Julian looked intensely into Connor's sky-blue eyes and smiled. "Are you trying to pick me up?"

"Actually, I was hoping to park my slippers under your cabana."

"So you think I'm easy, huh?"

"I'm getting that vibe," Connor said.

"Would you believe me if I told you I've never been with a man?"

"Would you believe me if I said I was Santa Claus?"

"Look, Connor. You're a very handsome young man and I'd be lying if I didn't say that I'm attracted to you. But I'm here because I'm curious. That's all. I've been married and divorced twice, and for years I've been in denial. This is all new to me and I'm a little intimidated by the whole game. I need someone who's going to be patient and understanding and let me move at my own pace. I'm going through a really confusing sexual crisis right now. So if you're looking to score tonight, then you're wasting my time and yours."

Julian was fascinated by his ability to lie with a straight face and deliver a totally believable story without the slightest hesitation.

"Wow, Julian. I can't tell you how refreshing it is to hear someone bare their soul. To be honest, everyone in this place is full of shit. There's no sincerity. The whole gay scene is a hoax. I've been looking to be with someone legitimate for a long time. Someone who isn't afraid to be vulnerable. You've really blown me away, and I'm deeply sorry if I insulted you."

"Tell you what," Julian said. "Now that we've played true confessions, why don't we go back to my place, have a drink, and learn more about each other—strictly as friends. My loft is about ten minutes away."

"I'd love that, Julian."

As the two men headed for the exit, Julian realized that he was completely out of touch with the dating scene. He couldn't believe how easy it had been to meet someone willing to leave with a complete stranger. Was that what the single life was like today? Was there no discretion or good judgment? How could Connor be sure that Julian wasn't an axe murderer? Wasn't the young man concerned about his welfare? Just because Julian crafted an outrageous story of his sexual crisis, the young man seemed ready to hop in bed.

As they walked toward the rental car, Connor grabbed Julian's hand and held it as if they were lovers walking on a sandy beach.

What is this world coming to?

CHAPTER NINE

"Have a safe flight," Sami said. She helped Al remove his luggage from the trunk.

"Thanks for dropping me off," Al said.

"Call me as soon as you get there, okay?"

"Will do."

Silence.

"Think positive thoughts, Al. She's going to be okay. I feel it in my bones."

Al looked deep into Sami's eyes. "Tell your mom I'm sorry I can't—"

"She'll understand."

Al put his arms around Sami and held her close. He wished she could come with him, but understood that it just wasn't meant to be. About to walk away, he remembered.

"Shit!"

"What's wrong?"

"I forgot to mail Selena's birthday card and gift. I already signed and addressed the card. Would you mind dropping them in the mail tomorrow? They're in the bedroom closet."

"Be happy to. Another gift card from Walmart?"

He nodded. "Yeah, I know. A little impersonal. But since a Walmart opened a mile away from the orphanage, it sure has made shopping easier. Better a gift card than something she hates. Besides, I spoke to one of the gals in the office and she said that the staff love to take the kids shopping."

Selena was one of five orphans Al sponsored at Casa de los Niños in Tijuana. Having endured a poverty-stricken childhood himself, losing his hardworking parents when he was still a teenager, Al swore that one day he would do his part to help other deprived Mexican children. He wished he could do more, even sponsor more children, but his budget was stretched to the max. Although his Spanish was a bit rusty, he made quarterly visits to the Tijuana orphanage and loved seeing "his" kids and spending time with them.

"I'll get it in the mail first thing in the morning," Sami offered.

"Let's move it along, folks," the security guard said as he motioned with his flashlight.

He kissed Sami on the lips. "Let me know how your mom's surgery goes."

"I promise to call."

Julian and Connor sat on the leather sofa, sipping glasses of Cabernet.

"This wine is really going to my head," Connor said. "I suddenly feel terribly dizzy."

"Have you had anything to eat?"

"Not since lunch."

"Maybe that's why. Let me get some cheese and crackers."

"Actually, I feel a bit nauseous. May I use your bathroom?"

"Of course." Julian pointed. "It's just to the left of the kitchen."

The drug was working quicker than Julian had thought. He felt concerned that Connor might pass out in the bathroom. He didn't want him to fall and injure himself. That was not part of the plan. He listened, but couldn't hear a sound coming from the bathroom, so he walked over and gently knocked on the door.

"You okay, Connor?"

No answer.

He knocked harder this time.

Nothing.

Julian slowly pushed on the door but it only opened halfway. He squeezed through the opening and saw Connor lying unconscious on the floor, his body snug against the door. Julian checked his pulse and looked at the second hand on his watch. Sixty-six beats a minute. Perfect. He checked Connor's head for any sign of an injury, but it didn't appear that he'd hit his head when he passed out.

Julian firmly grasped Connor's forearms and dragged him out of the bathroom, toward the bed on the far side of the loft. He felt a bit concerned lifting the dead weight, especially with the height of the bed. The last thing he wanted was to pull a muscle in his back. He guessed that Connor, tall and lean, weighed around a hundred sixty pounds.

Julian gripped Connor under his armpits and lifted his torso onto the bed. Then he grabbed his legs and swung them up as well. He figured that Connor would remain unconscious for two to three hours, so Julian secured his wrists and ankles to the bedposts with thick nylon straps. Then, he went back to the sofa and started making notes to himself about the instruments he needed, and the drugs and the dosages. As he sat quietly, Julian tried to emotionally prepare himself for the impending experiments. Unlike with Genevieve, who was completely unconscious from beginning to end, Connor Stevens would not be as fortunate. The next series of tests required that the subject be sedated but awake.

He wasn't sure what the pain threshold was before a subject would pass out. But soon he'd find out.

The captain turned on the PA system and announced that for the next fifteen or twenty minutes, the ride would be a little bumpy.

"Great," Al whispered. There were few things he dreaded more than turbulence at 37,000 feet. Second to that, he abhorred being wedged between two overweight people in a center seat. But when you book a flight hours before it takes off, you should feel lucky that you even got a seat.

Halfway to Charlotte, where he'd catch his connecting flight to Rio, he couldn't relax or clear his mind of troubling thoughts. When the flight attendants stopped right next to him with their little serving cart, and asked if he'd like something to drink, for a fleeting moment he wanted to scream "yes." This moment represented a true test of his sobriety, seven miles from the ground and fifteen hundred miles away from Sami.

But he did not fail. Not yet. He worried more about his nine-hour flight from Charlotte to Rio. On that flight, he would have more time to think. More time to be tempted. More time to justify having just one drink. How many "just one drinks" had he had over the years? He couldn't even begin to count.

Sami, of course, weighed heavily on Al's desire to remain sober. He had promised her that he would never touch another drop of alcohol no matter what the circumstance. But he never thought he'd be faced with a situation like this. If he made it to Rio without having a drink, it would be a miracle.

Al tried to sleep, but all he could think about was his sister lying in intensive care in a coma. In their younger years, Alberto and Aleta were very close. With both of their parents long gone before either reached adulthood, they clung to each other for support and companionship. For a period of time, they even shared an apartment.

But when Aleta took a Caribbean cruise and met Ricardo, an older Brazilian gentleman with charm, money, and a breathtaking mansion in Rio de Janeiro, everything changed. Aleta, quite to Al's dismay, had always been a gold digger, a woman searching for a sugar daddy. She had found this with Ricardo, but in the process had compromised her relationship with Al.

Al could never understand why his sister didn't visit him frequently. She had the means to do so. Although he never blatantly asked the obvious question, he'd hinted numerous times that he wanted to see his sister more often.

If Aleta didn't make it, if she never regained consciousness again, Al would not be able to speak the words he needed to speak. Words that lived quietly in a dark corner of his subconscious. He would be forced to relive the loss of his parents all over again. There were so many things he should have said to them, but he waited too long. Al's mother and father both died never knowing how much he loved them and appreciated all their sacrifices when he was growing up. He had been a selfish, rebellious little shit. It wasn't until they were both gone that he realized how much they had done for him.

Al—tired, troubled, and regretful—leaned back in the cramped seat, his knees rubbing against the seat in front of him, closed his eyes, and tried to fall asleep.

Just at the point in time when Julian began to doze off on the leather sofa, he heard Connor moaning. Julian shook his head, and slowly walked toward the bed.

"Well," Julian said, "glad you returned from your little nap."

Not yet realizing that his wrists and ankles were bound to the bed, Connor tried to sit up. "What the fuck is going on?"

"At this moment, not much."

"Are you out of your *fucking* mind?" Connor screamed. "Cut me loose, you fucking asshole!"

"There, there," Julian said. "No need to be uncivilized. It would be much easier for you if you just relaxed."

"You're a sick, twisted *fuck!*"

Julian ignored his rant and walked past the kitchen and into a small storage room. He wheeled out the heart monitor and positioned it beside the bed. Still dazed and foggy from the effects of the sedative, Connor squirmed like a man covered with spiders. As Julian shaved his chest, Connor opened his mouth, but nothing came out. When Julian finished connecting the ten electrodes to Connor's chest, wrists, ankles, and shoulders, he stepped back and surveyed what he'd done as if he were appraising a beautiful painting.

"Perfect," Julian said. He turned on the heart monitor and studied the screen carefully. Connor's pulse rate was over ninety beats a minute. The elevated reading seemed perfectly normal under the circumstances, so Julian did not feel alarmed. But he also noticed signs of an irregular heartbeat. At this point, the abnormal sinus rhythm did not pose a problem. In fact, most people under severe stress experience mild arrhythmias. This could turn out to be an unexpected bonus. If Connor suffered from a benign case of atrial fibrillation, it might reveal critical data Julian did not anticipate.

Julian went into the closet and opened his leather satchel. He pawed through a myriad of medical paraphernalia and sample bottles of various heart medications: Coumadin, Toprol XL, Bystolic, Cardizem, Lipitor. About to give up, he found the last plastic bottle: amiodarone.

Julian opened the bottle and removed four 200 mg tablets. This amount, called a loading dose, would hopefully stabilize Connor's heart and return it to normal sinus rhythm. Julian filled a twelve-ounce glass with water and sat on the side of the bed. "You need to take these pills, Connor."

"Do I look fucking stupid to you?"

"My, oh my, we certainly have a foul mouth, don't we though?"

"Cut me loose, you asshole, and I'll show you foul."

Julian stood up and pointed to the heart monitor. "See this wavy line at the bottom of the heart cycle? Without getting into technical definitions, it represents an irregular heartbeat, which could lead to what we call A-Fib. If that happens, your heart rate could reach two hundred plus beats a minute. If the blood pools in your left ventricle, it could result in a blood clot to your brain, or cause a pulmonary embolism. Either way, you'd be dead in less than five minutes."

Connor processed the information. "Why do you know so much about hearts? Are you a doctor?"

"You could say that." Julian grabbed a pair of scissors sitting on the nightstand and cut the nylon strap securing Connor's left wrist. He placed the pills in Connor's free hand. "You need to take these pills and you need to take them *now*."

Connor wasn't sure what to think. In this particular situation, his options were few. Never in his wildest dreams had he expected Julian to be a nutcase. He'd met lots of men in local bars and nightspots. And once in a while he'd picked up a guy who was a little kinky. But this was more than kinky. Whatever Julian— if that was even his real name—had planned for him, Connor feared that it wasn't going to be pleasant. Maybe Julian was into bondage and just wanted rough, submissive sex, which was fine with him. But why the heart monitor?

Now that Connor's brain was nearly wide-awake, a wave of panic crashed over him. He was in a predicament he never imagined possible. He could either cooperate with Julian and hopefully survive this ordeal, or he could continue to yell expletives and provoke him further. It seemed like a lose-lose situation.

"So," Julian said, "are you going to take the pills or risk a stroke?"

"Tell me what I'm taking."

"It's called amiodarone, and it's used for various types of irregular heartbeats."

"I don't get it," Connor said. "You've got me strapped to this bed like an animal, and it's pretty obvious you've got some sick, twisted agenda. Yet you're concerned about my health? How can I be sure that this amio—whatever it's called—is what you say it is?"

Julian walked over to the cocktail table and returned with his laptop computer. Once booted and connected to the Internet, he Googled "amiodarone." He clicked on the link to Wikipedia and set the laptop on the edge of the mattress so Connor could see the screen. "If I wanted to kill you with lethal drugs, I'd be sticking them in your veins," Julian said.

Connor read the first few sentences and concluded that the drug was a legitimate treatment for an irregular heartbeat. "If I take these pills and it stabilizes my heart, then what?"

"You and I will conduct a little experiment."

"Emily?" Sami said into the phone.

"Please tell me your mom's okay."

"She's stable. At least for the moment."

"Thank God."

"I'm really sorry to call so late, Emily." Sami told her cousin about Al's sister and his hasty departure to Rio.

"That's terrible. Anything I can do?"

"I just needed to hear a friendly voice. That's all."

"Hey, that's what cousins are for."

Sami regretted making the call. "Get some rest, Cuz. We'll talk in the morning. Okay?"

"I've got a better idea. Why don't I drive over and spend the night?"

"That's sweet of you, Honey, but I'm okay. Really. Just feeling some overwhelming emotions. Between my mom's surgery and Al—"

"Hey, it'll be like a sleepover. We can make popcorn, throw down a few brews, and watch old movies."

"You're sweet, Honey, but—"

"I'll be there in less than an hour."

Julian wanted to take a little nap himself, while the amiodarone worked its magic and stabilized Connor's irregular heartbeat, but his mind was filled with unsettling thoughts. He rested his head against the soft leather sofa and closed his eyes. He drifted back to a day he wished he could forget.

As if God had a vendetta against him, his mother was diagnosed with chronic atrial fibrillation on his eighteenth birthday. After five surgical procedures, the doctors concluded that her condition was irreversible and that another attack would ultimately be fatal. As much as Julian prayed for her to be healed, his plea fell on deaf ears. On the day she died, he stood outside her hospital room and watched in horror as the doctors frantically tried to revive her with CPR and an external defibrillator, no one realizing that the young man had a front-row seat to watch the event. After repeated attempts, the doctors pronounced her dead. While all this happened, Julian's father sat in the hospital cafeteria.

He witnessed his mother's death all alone.

He watched a nurse pull a white sheet over his mother's face, and before the doctors and nurses filed out of the room, Julian ran down the hall, went into an unlocked closet, and cried his eyes out. After several minutes, he found his way back to his mother's room. The room was still and quiet. A small fluorescent lamp on the wall behind his mother's bed lighted the room. It cast eerie shadows across the floor. He stood by his mother, staring at the white sheet, feeling as if his body were frozen. Carefully, and as if the process were some sort of devout ceremony, Julian pulled the sheet far enough so he could see his mother's face. Beautiful as ever, even in death, he kissed her on the cheek.

"Goodbye, Mom. I know you can't hear me but I have to tell you something anyway. Something that's been tearing me apart for years. I never tried to…hurt Cousin Rebecca. It was actually the other way around. Dad and you have been so distant. And I know it's because of what you thought I did. But I swear to you, I'm the victim. I just wanted you to know that."

About to cover her face again and leave the room, a strange feeling overwhelmed Julian. He couldn't understand why the doctors and nurses with all of their medical knowledge could not save his mother. Then, as if some mysterious force controlled his actions, he removed the sheet, and began administering CPR, using the same technique he had witnessed earlier.

Over and over, he pressed on his mother's chest, trying desperately to revive her. He heard cracking sounds, probably ribs snapping. But he continued thumping on her chest. Every so often he'd stop and put his ear near her nose for any sign of breathing and pressed his fingers to the side of her neck, searching for a pulse. He continued with the chest compressions until his arms were so fatigued he could hardly move them.

"Please wake up, Mom. Please."

Just as he was about to give up and pull the sheet up over her face, his mother's eyes opened, and she seemed to look right into his eyes. Before he could even begin to react, two nurses rushed into the room, each one grabbing an arm.

"You shouldn't be in here, young man."

"She's alive. My mother is *alive!*"

"Please, son," one of the nurses said. "You must leave this room immediately."

"But she's alive! Her eyes are open. She looked right at me."

"I'm sorry, son, but she's *not* alive. Her open eyes are merely a reflex."

The nurses tried to lead Julian out of the room, but he wasn't going anywhere. Noticing the commotion as he walked by the room, a security guard came in to find out what was going on. Once briefed, he secured Julian and literally dragged him out of the room.

Over the next few months, everyone tried to convince him that he had not resuscitated his mother. But he knew better. He *had* revived her, and no one could convince him otherwise. He now felt that he had a special gift. And to waste these extraordinary skills would be tragic. So, once wanting to be a college-level chemistry teacher, Julian accepted the event as a divine message, and felt absolutely certain that one day he'd be a gifted cardiologist specializing in A-Fib research.

When Sami heard a knock at the front door, she glanced at the clock above the TV. Wow, she thought. Almost two in the morning. Always overcautious and a little paranoid since her ordeal with Simon, she looked through the door scope and felt relieved when she saw Emily.

"Hey, you," Sami said. "I feel like a seven-year-old kid who just saw a scary movie."

Emily walked in and Sami closed and locked the front door. They both sat on the sofa in front of the TV.

"You're dealing with a lot of shit, Cuz," Emily said. "You've always been the Rock of Gibraltar for everyone. It's time you get to lean on someone else for a change."

"But you know how damn independent I am. I hate to rely on anyone."

"Get over it, Cuz. It's called being human."

"You're wise beyond your years, Emily."

"And I owe a bunch of it to you."

Up until four years ago when Emily went to college in San Francisco for her nursing degree, Sami spent a lot of time with her. Sami was more of a surrogate mom than cousin. Recently graduated, Emily now lived in a small studio apartment in East San Diego. "You've got your choice. Corona Lite. Dos Equis Amber. Or we can uncork a bottle of Cabernet and really get shit-faced."

"We can also get shit-faced on the beer," Emily said. "A Dos Equis sounds great."

Sami popped the caps on a couple of beers and handed one to Emily. "Here's to my favorite cousin." They clicked bottles.

"You mean *only* cousin, don't you?"

They talked for over an hour about nothing in particular. They were three beers into the conversation, both feeling the effects of the alcohol.

"How's everything going with school?" Emily asked.

"Good question. To be honest, I'm seriously thinking about dropping out." Sami couldn't believe what she'd just said.

"But you've got nearly two years invested."

"More like two years *wasted*."

"For as long as I can remember you've dreamt about being a social worker. And now that you're almost there you want to flush it down the toilet? I don't get it."

"I guess investigating homicides was more in my blood than I thought. Maybe I still feel guilty about bailing out. I'm still a little haunted by my stupidity trying to apprehend a serial killer with no backup. Maybe I can't deal with breaking a promise to my father just before he died. The fucking walls are closing in and I haven't a clue what to do."

"Does Al have any idea how you feel?"

"We've talked, and I've explained the great divide between my idealistic view of social work and the reality. But I never even hinted that I was thinking about dropping out."

For several minutes, neither uttered a word.

"Have you discussed this with your therapist?" Emily asked.

"Extensively."

"And what does she say?"

"She always hits the ball back in my court."

"If you're really that unhappy, Sami, maybe you should follow your gut."

"But what the hell would I do, watch soap operas and eat chocolate bonbons?"

"Have you considered going back to police work?" Emily asked.

"It has been on my mind."

"Then why are you hesitating?"

"Do you have any idea what I'd have to go through to get reinstated? I don't think they'd welcome me with open arms."

"Don't be so humble. You were one hell of a detective."

"Yes, I was. But the operative word is *was*."

"Isn't Al investigating the murder of that girl they found near Mission Bay?"

"He is. Or at least he was. Who knows how long he's going to be in Rio?"

"Exactly. This would be the perfect time for you to lobby for your old job."

"It's just not that simple, Emily. It's not like asking to be rehired at some discount clothing store. This is a civil service job with lots of red tape and truckloads of bullshit."

"Well, I'm not going to nag. But I really think you should go for it."

"I'll give it some thought."

Emily swigged the last of the warm beer. "You still okay with me moving in to take care of Aunt Josephine while she recovers?"

Sami, a little teary-eyed, slipped her arm around Emily and gave her a firm hug. "You're a sweetheart, Cuz, and I truly appreciate the gesture. But I really can't ask you to do that."

"Is it Al?"

"Of course not. He's all for it. But you had your heart set on taking the summer off before searching for a nursing job. How do you possibly expect to unwind if you're caring for a cranky old lady who just had major surgery? Trust me. You have no idea what you're getting yourself into."

"You're really stubborn, Cuz. This is something I *want* to do. Honestly. Who would be a better caretaker than your favorite cousin, who just happens to be a nurse?"

"Let me think about it, Emily."

"Well, don't think too long. My offer expires at sunrise."

Julian awoke from his disturbing nap and felt as though he had just revisited his mother's death. It wasn't the first time and he suspected it wouldn't be the last. To this day, he felt haunted by the whole incident, certain that he had indeed revived his mother. But the incident, as traumatic as it was, proved beneficial. Had he not experienced such a life-changing event, he might be in front of a classroom right now, pointing to a chart of the elements, instead of standing on the threshold of a medical discovery that could fulfill his desire for fame and recognition, and change the lives of one hundred million people worldwide suffering from atrial fibrillation.

He could hear Connor mumbling something under his breath. He made his way to the bed. "Did you say something, Connor?"

"I was praying."

"For salvation?"

"No. Praying that your balls fall off the next time you take a piss. You're a pathetic pile of dog shit."

"Those are some pretty harsh words, Connor." Julian sat on the side of the bed and gently brushed Connor's hair out of his eyes.

Connor turned his head in a defiant manner, trying to avoid Julian's touch. "Don't you *dare* put your hands on me!"

"Please try to understand that I'm doing this because I have no choice."

"That's total bullshit and you know it."

"What would you say if I told you that you had the power to save thousands of lives every year, to literally change the world?"

"I'd say you've been watching way too many science fiction movies."

"It's true, Connor. You will be instrumental in the treatment and cure of a debilitating medical condition."

"And how exactly can I do that?"

"Through some of the experiments we're going to conduct."

"What kind of experiments?"

"I can't give you specific details but you'll find out soon enough."

"And if I'm not interested in being a lab rat?"

"Sorry. You don't have that option."

Connor squeezed his eyes shut and tears leaked out of the corners. "You're going to fucking kill me, aren't you?"

"The needs of the many," Julian said, sounding like an echo in his own ears—did he even believe it? Did he have a choice?—"outweigh the needs of the few."

CHAPTER TEN

Slightly hung over from her evening with Emily, her mind whirling with conflicting thoughts, Sami lay in bed waiting for the Excedrin to kick in. She checked the clock radio and wondered why she hadn't heard from Al yet. He, needless to say, had his hands full, but she had hoped to hear something by now.

Just as she was about to roll over and hopefully get a little more sleep, her cell phone played "No Ordinary Love," Al's exclusive ring.

"You must be a mind reader," Sami said, sitting upright and swinging her legs to the side of the bed. "Please tell me you have good news about Aleta."

"It's not good." His voice sounded weak and raspy. "She's been in a coma since the accident and she suffered a massive concussion. Her brain is severely swollen. She's on a respirator and the only good news is that she has strong brain activity."

"What are the doctors saying?"

"Only that they've done everything they could. Now it's just a wait-and-see situation." Al breathed heavily into the phone. "How you holding up? How's your mom?"

"I'm pretty much a basket case but my mom is doing okay. Her surgery is scheduled for nine tomorrow morning."

"Send her my love."

It wasn't the ideal time, but Sami had to ask. "Can I run something by you, Al?"

"As long as it's not too heavy. Don't think I could handle much more."

Sami gathered her thoughts. "Emily slept over last night and we got to talking about mom's surgery and recovery. Remember when we talked about her moving in temporarily while my mom recovers? You still okay with that arrangement?"

"Absolutely. It would be good for your mom, good for Emily, fantastic for Angelina, not to mention that it would keep us out of the looney bin."

"Thanks for being so supportive."

"Hey, we're a partnership. Remember?"

"Please call me if anything changes with your sister."

"And call me after your mom has her surgery."

"I will."

She could hear him breathing into the cell phone. "You still there?"

"I don't think I can deal with this without unraveling. It all seems so surreal. I look at my sister lying in that hospital bed, tubes coming out of everywhere, and I can't believe it's her. I can't believe this is happening. What am I going to do if she…doesn't make it? How will I function? Aleta is my only living relative. If she dies…"

"I wish I had the answer for you. But all I can tell you is that you have to be strong for *her*. You have to keep the faith for *her*. Otherwise you're going to self-destruct."

"Love you," Al said.

"Love you more."

✲ ✲ ✲

Julian tried to focus his attention on Connor and the impending experiments, but found himself too distracted for surgical procedures that required his undivided attention and a rock-steady hand. No matter how hard he tried, he could not free himself from disturbing visions of Genevieve or the events soon to take place with Connor. The internal struggles were beyond anything he could deal with on his own. There had to be a way for him to cleanse his mind and concentrate on the task at hand. There was too much at stake.

Julian walked over to the bed, gave Connor another mild sedative, and walked out the door.

Saint Thomas Aquinas Catholic Church was only a fifteen-minute drive from Julian's loft. Born and raised Catholic, he, like so many other young people, drifted away from God and his faith when he was a teenager. But through his life experiences, he had learned that he could always find solace in the quiet solitude of church. Faith or not, it was spiritually therapeutic, like salve for the soul.

When Julian walked into the church on this cloudy Saturday afternoon, he expected it to be nearly empty. But surprisingly, he noticed a dozen or so people scattered about. Some knelt in pews desperately praying for God to heal a loved one, others sat quietly, lost in their own misery, and a few stood in line just outside the confession booth.

Confession?

Julian hadn't been to confession in decades. He always thought it was a silly ritual designed for the truly naïve. How could a priest—a flesh and blood human—forgive your sins by telling you to say ten Hail Marys and ten Our Fathers and blessing you with the sign of the cross? The arrogance of this so-called sacrament bothered Julian even as a child.

As he sat there, trying to sort out his troubling thoughts, something occurred to him. He'd been taught that a priest is bound to secrecy regarding sins revealed to him in sacramental confession. He cannot divulge them directly or indirectly by giving information based on what he learns through confession.

Silly ritual or not, perhaps this was the sanctuary Julian needed to purge his guilt without the risk of consequence. In the shelter of confession, Julian could tell all, without editing or whitewashing the details. And the priest would go to his grave with Julian's confession. Maybe confession was just what he needed to deal with his troubled conscience. He didn't care about divine forgiveness; he just needed a sympathetic ear.

Next in line for the confessional, Julian anxiously waited. As much as this exercise violated everything that he believed to be true about religion, God, and the hereafter, Julian felt it was the only possible way for him to continue with his research without distraction.

He glanced at the woman standing behind him. Bent forward, her wrinkled hands clutching rosary beads, a kerchief covering her head, she paid little attention to him.

Guessing that the old woman had a difficult time standing, he asked her if she wanted to go ahead of him.

"Thank you, Honey, but no." She held up the rosary. "I'd like to finish praying before I go in."

The door opened on the confession booth and a young man stepped out and headed for the front door. Julian took a couple of steps toward the booth but stopped.

Who am I kidding? I can't do this.

Now facing the reality of kneeling before a priest and pouring out his heart, Julian realized it was foolish and self-destructive. Just because the priest had made a vow of secrecy, how could

Julian be certain he wouldn't contact the police? How many altar boys had been victimized by priests who had taken the vow of chastity? Confession was not the answer. This was a problem he had to resolve all alone. More determined than ever to complete his research regardless of the emotional shockwaves, Julian left the church like a man fleeing a burning building.

Monday morning came quicker than Sami had thought. Her therapist had made a special concession for her and scheduled an early-morning appointment, so she could get to the hospital an hour before her mom's surgery. Sami hadn't wanted this appointment with Doctor Janowitz. In fact, she tried everything to postpone this session. But Doctor J, as Sami affectionately referred to her, convinced her that it would be beneficial for them to talk before her mother's surgery.

Before getting ready for a day that would be a true test of her sanity, Sami looked in on Angelina, and then Emily. Both were sleeping soundly. Emily was such a blessing. Sami turned on the TV and listened to the local news channel. From the bathroom she couldn't see the screen but could hear the audio clearly. Just as she was about to brush her teeth, she heard a familiar voice. She ran into the living room and turned up the volume. Police Chief Larson stood on the front steps of City Hall addressing the media. At this early hour, whatever he was about to say must be significant.

"At approximately four a.m. this morning," Chief Larson said, *"some early-morning joggers discovered the body of a young man at the Mount Hope Cemetery in La Mesa. We have not yet identified the body, but we're working around the clock to determine who it is."*

The reporters fired a barrage of questions at the police chief. Most of the questions he could not or would not answer. Then a reporter asked, *"Is there any connection between this murder and the murder of Genevieve Foster?"*

"There are similarities, but I'm unable to give you any details at this time."

Sami grabbed the remote and turned off the television, her hand shaking uncontrollably. A million thoughts flashed through her mind—all of them revolving around the possibility of another serial killer stalking the streets of San Diego. Maybe another Simon. At this particular point in time, Sami had to focus her attention on her mother's surgery. But forcing these disturbing thoughts out of her mind could prove to be a challenge for which she was not prepared.

Sami pulled into the parking lot on La Jolla Village Drive, and as she'd done dozens of times before, she sat in the car for a few minutes mentally psyching herself up for a mind-draining conversation with Doctor Janowitz. Of course, it was difficult for Sami to call their get-togethers a conversation. They were more like Sami pouring out her heart and Doctor Janowitz asking the same question: *"And how do you feel about that, Sami?"* So many times she wanted to say, *"I don't know* how *the fuck I feel, Doctor, that's why I'm lying on this cold leather sofa."*

The fiftyish PhD had been divorced twice, was as thin as a pencil, and had perfect teeth. Her office walls were covered with accreditations and wall plaques from umpteen universities, and had she chosen law as a career, she would have been a ferocious litigator. The veteran therapist had heard it all over the last twenty-five years—every argument, every excuse, every pretext. And Sami felt certain that no one ever got the best of her.

Instead of riding the elevator to suite 605, Sami walked up the six flights of stairs, struggling all the way, proof positive that her body was trying to tell her something. The frequency of her power walks had dwindled to once or twice a week. And the pace had slowed from heart pounding to little more than a Sunday afternoon stroll. Like anyone falling short of a healthy exercise routine, she kept her little bag of excuses close by. *"It's too hot." "It's too cold." "My back is ready to go out." "I have to study for a test." "Still got that blister on my foot."* She could bullshit her classmates with the best of them. And Al? No contest. Even her mother, who redefined the word *suspicious*, bought her excuses now and then. But she couldn't lie to herself. She just wasn't motivated right now. So what if she carried a few extra pounds? Would anyone really care?

Of course they would, stupid. You care. Who are you trying to kid? And Al most certainly cares. Maybe that's why he had refused sex. Not a good time for this psycho-babble.

As usual, when Sami walked into Doctor J's office, she found the doctor sitting at her desk, reading glasses resting on the tip of her nose, engrossed in paperwork. Today, the impeccably dressed therapist wore a forest-green business suit, a white silk blouse, and a pearl necklace. Sami had been coming to Doctor J for almost a year and could never remember seeing the same outfit twice. She could only imagine the size of her closets.

Considering Doctor J's stature and reputation with high-profile patients, many of whom were wealthy, her office wasn't at all impressive. It was functional and adequate, but modestly furnished and frugally decorated. If dollars and cents measured a therapist's success, however, at a rate of three hundred fifty dollars for a fifty-minute session, one could say that Doctor J was indeed successful. Sami, of course, didn't pay these exorbitant rates. How could a college student with a dwindling savings account and negligible income dole out this kind of money? After she'd resigned, the San Diego Police Department offered to pay a generous portion of her therapy expenses. Sami never confirmed it, but felt certain that this generous perk came directly from Mayor Sullivan.

"Good morning, Doctor J," Sami said. "Lovely suit." Familiar with the routine, Sami fell heavily onto the worn leather sofa.

"Give me just a minute, Sami." Doctor J shuffled some papers and made some notes. After a few minutes, she glanced at the clock, wrote something on the yellow pad, and dropped her reading glasses on her desk. "Now you've got my undivided attention. What's the latest in your life?"

"If just one more crisis rears its ugly head, I think my brain's going to shut down."

"Well, I'm aware of your mom's surgery this morning and Al's situation with his sister in Rio, but talk to me. What's going on?"

"The nightmares have returned."

"Simon?"

Sami nodded. "I was okay for a while, but as soon as Al left for Rio..."

"Same as in the past?"

"Worse. More vivid."

"Tell me about them."

"As I've mentioned, in the past I could never see Simon's face clearly, and when he nailed me to the cross, I didn't feel any pain in my dream. Well, now I see his face clearly and swear I can feel those spikes going into my wrists."

Doctor J made notes. "Are you still taking Valium every night?"

"I miss a night every now and then, but—"

"You have to take this medication *every* night, Sami." Doctor J stood, walked over to the chair adjacent to Sami, and sat down.

"You've made it clear how much you hate to medicate yourself, but the benefits outweigh the side effects." Doctor J paused for a moment. "Does Simon say anything to you in these nightmares?"

"Not a word. But he has this hideous grin on his face. The sinister look of a madman."

"Tell me about the pain. Does it wake you?"

"Bolts me upright as if a rush of electricity was surging through my body. I'm cold and clammy. My hands shake uncontrollably, and my heart is pounding. Feels like I'm going to have a coronary."

"Classic anxiety attack. We've discussed them before." Doctor J lightly tapped her index finger against her temple as if she were deep in thought. "When you suffer from an attack like this do you immediately start the breathing exercises we discussed?"

"I do."

"And do they help calm you down?"

"Most of the time."

"When you go to sleep at night, what's usually on your mind?"

"Everything. The minute my head hits the pillow, my brain is bombarded with thoughts—all coming at me like a machine gun."

"What dominates your thoughts?"

"That all depends on what issue is on top of the heap on that particular evening."

"What have you thought about most recently?"

"My mom's surgery. Al's sister. What I'm going to do with the rest of my life. If I made the right decision resigning from the police department. Al's unusual behavior. Should I go on?"

"Talk to me about Al. What's changed?"

"Nothing I can put my finger on. It's just that he doesn't seem invested in our relationship like he used to be. We're disconnected."

"Has he done anything to make you feel this way?"

"Well, among other things, he refused sex the other day. Considering his past appetite and the fact that we rarely make love anymore, I'd say that's significant."

"You mentioned the last time we met that Al was leading the investigation in the Foster homicide, correct?"

Sami nodded. "Until he left for Rio, he was."

"When did his behavior change?"

"Within the last few weeks."

"Maybe he's been preoccupied with this case."

"But his behavior changed before he was assigned to investigate the Foster homicide."

"And what was he working on prior to this case?"

Sami thought for a minute. "He was investigating the Jenkins homicides, the teenager that butchered his whole family— mother, father, and four-year-old sister."

"I'm sure that each homicide investigation comes with its share of riled emotions and stress. But I would guess that some affect you more than others, no?"

"Absolutely."

"Maybe Al is merely absorbed with his job. It's not uncommon for even the healthiest relationship to experience setbacks from career pressure."

"Never thought of it that way. But if you live on planet Earth, when do you *not* have stress?"

"Everyone has their limit, Sami. Stress is cumulative. Ever heard the saying, 'the straw that broke the camel's back'?"

"I see your point."

Dr. J fiddled with her pearls. "Any word on Aleta's condition?"

"It's not looking real good."

"How long do you think Al is going to stay in Rio?"

"I wish I knew."

"Under the current situation, there is no accurate way to measure the solvency of your relationship with Al. Both of you are way too distracted. When things settle down—and I promise they will—sit down with him face-to-face and tell him how you feel. A little candid communication goes a long way."

Sami sat quietly and processed Doctor J's advice. Today, for some reason, the doctor seemed much more expressive than in past sessions. Sami hadn't heard the words she dreaded most: "Tell me how you feel about that." Why was she so gregarious today?

"So," Dr. J said, "you're still wrestling with your resignation from the homicide division?"

"Every day."

"What happened to your passion for becoming a social worker?"

"Reality happened. I think maybe I was living in a utopian world."

"You've invested nearly two years in school. Are you ready to abort your plan and forfeit all your hard work?"

"That's the compelling question, Doctor J."

"What would you do if you dropped out of school?"

"Pray that the department would reinstate me."

"*Really*? Is that even possible?"

"Not sure."

Doctor J stood, leaned her backside against her desk, and folded her arms. "Until today, you've been firm on your conviction that you were simply not cut out to be a cop and that the reason you pursued a law enforcement career was because of a promise you made to your father, correct?"

"That's right."

"What has changed? How can you suddenly reverse your position? What happened?"

"People change their minds every day, don't they?"

"Yes, but you survived a near-death experience, an event that altered your entire paradigm. Are you really prepared to deal with violence and murder every day of your life?"

"When you put it that way, I'm not so sure." Tears began to well up in her eyes. "I'm not sure how I feel about anything anymore."

"We all go through that, Sami. It's not uncommon to feel like your life is a runaway train. It's part of the human condition." Doctor J sat next to Sami and draped her arm around her shoulders. "Maybe we should stop for today. You've got a big day ahead and I—"

"I'm okay, Doctor. Really. Just a temporary meltdown."

"Are you sure you want to go on?"

Sami glanced at her watch. "We've got another twenty minutes before you throw me out of here and I want to get every penny's worth."

"I'm not going to walk on eggshells," Doctor J said.

"Take your best shot, Doctor."

Doctor J planted her elbows on the armrests and rested her chin on her folded hands. "When you told me what you think about when you go to bed, you mentioned everything, but didn't say a word about Simon. Don't you think about him?"

"If I do think about him, I'm not consciously aware of it."

"But even though you don't believe he's on your mind when you go to sleep, you still have vivid nightmares about him?"

"I do."

Doctor J made more notes on the yellow pad. She stared at something across the office. "Simon is scheduled to be put to death by lethal injection very soon, correct?"

"Yes."

"Tell me how you feel about that."

Ah, there it was. Finally. The question Sami hated most. She almost felt relieved. "I don't want to see the son-of-a-bitch put out of his misery. I want him to live in a cage like the animal he is for the next forty years. I want some big hulk of a man to make him his bitch. I want the fucker to suffer."

"You don't think he should be put to death?"

"Death is too merciful."

"In all the time we've spent together, I can never remember you expressing yourself with such anger and raw hatred."

"My animosity toward this bastard grows every day."

"You do realize that you're letting him control your life, right?"

"What the hell are you talking about? He doesn't control anything. Not even *his* life."

"Oh, really? Have you ever considered that all these uncertainties in your life circle right back to your ordeal with Simon? Did it ever occur to you that you don't yet have closure on this situation and that you're never going to have closure until you confront Simon face-to-face and tell him how you feel?"

"Face-to-face? How do you propose I do that? He sits in a jail cell in Northern California, a few days away from an appointment with his Creator."

"People visit inmates every day. Even death row inmates."

"Not true, Doctor. It takes an act of Congress to get approval to visit a death row inmate—even for a detective."

"Even for the *arresting* detective that put him behind bars? Find a believable reason why you need to talk to him."

"Are you suggesting I lie?"

"Of course not. But I am suggesting you get creative."

"Okay, let's pretend I *could* get approval to visit him. I should just hop on a plane, fly up north, and meet Simon for coffee?"

"No, Sami. You should fly up north and free yourself from this crushing grip he has on your life."

When Julian arrived at the hospital, he headed directly for the lab. Once inside, he found his staff huddled around the coffee machine like a bunch of Monday morning football fans analyzing Sunday's Chargers game. Why wasn't anyone working and conducting their assigned research experiments? Nothing made Julian angrier than walking in on his staff and finding them wasting away precious time. Particularly because he had told each member of his team how critical the timeline was for them to produce the research results GAFF requested.

Julian stomped toward the group finding it difficult to suppress his anger. "Did I not get an invitation to the coffee klatch?"

"Sorry, Boss," Judy Forester said. "Have you read the newspaper or watched the news?"

He hated to be called "Boss." But in such a confined environment, he tolerated it because he believed that creating a casual atmosphere reduced stress and increased productivity. "What's going on?"

Forester pointed to the headlines. "That woman who was murdered and dumped at Mission Bay Park? Well, there's a second victim. It seems that whoever killed them performed surgical experiments that are similar to some of the procedures in our A-Fib research. In fact, the first victim died of an A-Fib–induced stroke. But they haven't yet determined cause of death for the second victim. Isn't that bizarre?"

"Remarkable." He swallowed hard. "Any suspects?"

"No," Burns said.

"Only God knows what he did to the guy," Forester added.

In that one defining moment, Julian realized the critical flaw in his plan. Why hadn't this consequential oversight occurred to him? If the research was ultimately successful and he received recognition for perfecting new procedures to treat A-Fib, wouldn't the police eventually make the connection and want to question him or his staff? Wouldn't an alert cop want to interrogate the foremost authority on A-Fib? Wouldn't they conclude that the actions of the killer were too similar to the research to be a coincidence? His thoughts were a flurry of panic and disbelief. He wondered how many other mistakes he'd made along the way, how many clues he'd left for the police. Maybe because he wasn't a hardened killer, he didn't know how to be cunning and devious. The only thing he knew for sure at this particular moment was that he had to create a diversion, something to take the spotlight off of his research. But how?

"I'd like to see you in my office, Judy," Julian said. "The rest of you, please get to work."

Julian sat at his desk and Judy Forester sat opposite him.

"Sorry about that, Boss. I guess I should have kicked some butt and got everyone back to work."

"Two things," Julian said. "First, don't *ever*, under any circumstances, call me 'Boss' again."

"I apologize, Doctor."

"Second." Julian looked at his watch. "It's seven forty-five. I want all your personal belongings packed in a box and I want you out of here no later than eight-thirty."

The color drained from Forester's face. "Are you serious?"

"Does it sound like I'm kidding?"

"But why? Just because the staff took a few minutes to talk about the article in the paper?"

"I pay you to be the team leader and to make sure I get eight solid hours out of every staff member. You, more than anyone, know how critical our timeline is, yet you let the staff lollygag around. I've warned you before that you're too easy on them. And you gave me your word you'd make some changes. I need a leader who can make this lab run like a well-tuned machine. Obviously, that's not you."

"Please, Doctor, you know that Nate and I just bought a house. Geez, we haven't even made the first mortgage payment yet. If you let me go, I'm screwed. Please, please give me another chance. I've been with you since the research began. I helped you select the team. I promise—"

"I really don't want to hear your sob story, Judy. You made your bed. Now sleep in it." Julian looked at his watch again. "If you're not out of the building in thirty minutes, I'm calling security."

Until he could find a suitable replacement for Judy Forester, Julian left David Burns temporarily in charge. Time was of the essence, and finding a competent candidate with the proper research background to head one of the most sophisticated studies in the world would not be easy. But with unemployment approaching double digits, it was an employer's market and he felt comfortable he'd have someone on board soon. Julian believed that heading a research team for such a high-profile project was a man's job. Julian knew this going in. His opinion was based on personal experience, not sexism. The only reason he had hired Forester in the first place was because the human resources manager, Cathy Ferguson, an overweight, overbearing feminist, had flexed her executive muscles and insisted that he *consider* a woman. Julian, of course, understood that her suggestion was a mandate. Politics or not, he wouldn't make the same mistake twice.

Julian left the lab and walked over to the Chest Pain Center. He never quite understood why they didn't name this area Cardiac Care. After all, not all heart-related problems produced pain. He'd gotten a call earlier about an A-Fib patient he'd been treating for five years. He had undergone three catheter ablations, and two different Maze procedures, yet chronic attacks of A-Fib still plagued the seventy-five-year-old man. Scheduled to perform bypass surgery a little later this morning, Julian wanted to check in on Mr. Reznik to evaluate his condition.

He walked into the Chest Pain Center and waved to the nurses. Noticing Mr. Reznik lying in a bed, Julian walked into room 4 and grabbed the patient's chart. He glanced at the heart monitor and saw the erratic image confirming that the patient suffered from a severe A-Fib episode. His heart rate approached two hundred beats a minute.

"Good morning, Mr. Reznik."

"What the hell is good about it?"

"Come on, now. You know we're going to take good care of you."

"Been lying here for over two hours and the drugs still haven't converted my heart to normal. How long before you have to use those dang-blasted electric paddles? They scare the crap right out of me."

"The drugs should do the trick. No need to worry about that at this time."

"I'm getting really tired of spending more time in the hospital than at home." The elderly man scratched his bald head. "Am I going to make it this time, or should we call a rabbi?"

"I think you've got quite a few years left, Mr. Reznik."

"Sure doesn't feel that way."

"How long have you been in A-Fib?"

"It all started early this morning—about five-thirty. I drank a glass of prune juice and as soon as I took the last swallow, I felt this flutter, and my heart started pounding out of my chest. I'll tell you, Doctor, it feels like a hummingbird is trapped in my left lung."

"Do you drink prune juice every morning?"

"If I didn't, my stool would be like concrete."

"Was the prune juice ice-cold?"

He thought for a minute. "Shit. I usually let it sit on the counter for a while before I drink it."

"You remember what I told you about drinking ice-cold liquids, right?" Julian had warned Mr. Reznik years ago that no one diagnosed with A-Fib should drink ice-cold liquids because in some patients it can trigger an attack.

"I guess I forgot."

"Write yourself a note that says 'No Cold Liquids' and tape it to the front of the refrigerator."

"I did this to myself?"

"Just try to be more mindful in the future."

"I guess I can't drink a cold beer now and then, right, Doctor?"

"Drink red wine. It's better for you." Julian flipped through Mr. Reznik's chart. "Are you still taking your medications every day?"

"I ran out of the amiodarone but still have a few of the Coumadin left."

"When did you run out of the amiodarone?"

"About a week ago."

"Why didn't you renew the prescription?"

"I just can't afford them anymore. Since Helen died and her Social Security checks stopped..." Mr. Reznik bit his lower lip and his eyes filled with tears. "I miss her so much."

Julian couldn't imagine what it was like to be old, sickly, and alone. He waited for him to regain his composure. "Doesn't Medicare pay part of your prescription costs?"

"Never signed up for Part D."

"Why?"

"Can't afford the premiums."

Julian wanted to lecture Mr. Reznik and once again make him understand the importance of taking his medication. He even thought about trying to scare him into it, but he figured that the lonely man might not be opposed to joining Helen more quickly than nature intended. Maybe he purposely ignored Julian's medical advice.

"Here's what we're going to do, Mr. Reznik. The pharmaceutical reps that call on me regularly give me a truckload of samples. You have follow-up appointments scheduled with me every three months, and if I remember correctly, you're booked through the end of the year. When you come in for your checkups, I'll be sure my assistant gives you a ninety-day supply of both medications. Just promise me that you'll take them every day and that you'll stay away from ice-cold liquids."

Mr. Reznik wiped the tears off his face. "You're a good man, Doctor. Wish my son was half as good."

Sami stood outside her mother's hospital room while the nurse prepped Josephine for open heart surgery. No matter how hard she tried, Sami could not stop thinking about her session with Doctor J. More than two years had passed since Sami had escaped from Simon's Room of Redemption and helped put him behind bars. She thought she'd gotten past the fear and the nightmares and the haunting memories of what might have happened if Al hadn't come to her rescue. But she now realized that her journey to closure was far from over. The mere thought of meeting Simon face-to-face jabbed at her nerves like a hot poker.

Although Sami tried to deny the bitter truth, in her heart she felt strongly that the near-death experience had changed her forever. A piece of her had died in that Room of Redemption. Simon hadn't carried out his plan to crucify her, but he won the battle by killing part of her spirit. Doctor J had been right. No matter how hard she tried to deny it, Simon controlled her. Barring another appeal, Simon was scheduled to be executed by lethal injection in less than a week. At this particular point in time, her mind flooded with thoughts of her mother and Al and Aleta and Angelina and Emily. There was no room in her brain to think about Simon, yet somehow he hovered over her like a buzzard ready to dive. One more troubling thought and she would surely end up in a padded cell.

She glanced down the hall and spotted Doctor Templeton briskly walking toward her, limping slightly. She brushed her sweaty palms across the front of her jeans and tried to force a smile.

"Good morning, Ms. Rizzo," Doctor Templeton said. "We should be able to begin surgery in about an hour." He squeezed her arm. "How are you holding up?"

"Nervous as hell, Doctor."

"Not to worry. Your mom is in good hands. I have the best surgical staff in Southern California. There are no guarantees, of course, but if the surgery is successful, she's going to feel much better. I promise."

"I don't know how to thank you, Doctor. I still can't believe you convinced my mother to have the surgery."

"You can thank me after the surgery."

He leaned against the wall and Sami noticed him grimace. "Not to stick my nose where it doesn't belong," she said, "but I noticed you limping."

"Foolish me. I reached in my trunk to remove a case of spring water and tweaked my lower back." He reached behind and gently massaged the muscles. "Don't be alarmed. My back doesn't affect my hands."

For the first time since meeting Doctor Templeton, she saw him as a man rather than a doctor—a strikingly good-looking man.

Captain Derrance Davidson sat across from Police Chief Larson reasonably sure what was coming.

"I just got off the phone with Mayor Sullivan, and she's not a happy camper this morning," Chief Larson said. "In fact, she took a big bite out of my fat ass. We need to pull out all the stops on this one." Larson stood up and walked to the window, turning his back on Davidson. "How the fuck could such a beautiful city produce two serial killers in less than three years?"

"We haven't yet determined if the two homicides are connected, Sir."

"What world are you living in, Captain?"

"I just think that before we get our undies all twisted in a knot, we should wait for the autopsy to be completed."

Larson tossed a manila folder across his desk. "Read this."

Davidson opened the folder and read the preliminary autopsy report. "Mother of Mercy."

"The second victim died of cardiac arrest," Larson said. "Same stapled chest. Same burn marks on his ribcage."

Davidson shook his head. "This one was dressed in an *Armani* suit?"

"Our guy has good taste in clothing." Larson let out a heavy breath. "But the perp wasn't kind enough to leave us a price tag this time."

"He's been careless to this point. Maybe he's tightening his act."

"I hope not," Larson said. "Ramirez still partnering with Diaz on this investigation?"

"Diaz is off the case."

Larson parked his hands on his hips. "This better be good, Captain."

Davidson explained the situation. "I found out yesterday morning."

"He's the best we've got," Larson said. "What's your contingency plan?"

"I've assigned Osbourn and D'Angelo." He hesitated. "Ramirez wasn't working out."

Larson's face tightened. "D'Angelo's two months away from retirement and Osbourn is still wet behind the ears."

"With all the budget cuts, Chief, we're running the show really lean."

"I want to be in the loop on every fucking development—no matter how insignificant. Is that clear, Captain?"

"Absolutely, Sir."

"And tell Osbourn and D'Angelo to get their asses in gear and find this fucking douche bag."

CHAPTER ELEVEN

Slouched forward, half asleep, Sami was startled when Doctor Templeton walked in the visitor's waiting room and called her name. Completely disoriented and not remembering where she was, she stood up quickly and felt a wave of dizziness. She steadied herself by grasping the arm of the chair. If she didn't know better, she'd think she was drunk.

"Sorry, Doctor, I must have dozed off." She searched his eyes for a hint of what he might say, but they offered no clues.

"The bypass went even better than I anticipated. Your mom came through the surgery aces."

"Thank you, Doctor. I...I can't thank you enough." Sami squeezed her eyes shut and tears ran down her face. Her mind flooded with memories of the extremes in her relationship with her mom. There were good times and bad, conflict and harmony, trepidations and words of support. Their relationship had been the proverbial roller-coaster ride—most of the time racing along dangerous curves. She had no delusions about their compatibility. But she hoped that however many years her mom had left, they could form an allegiance and build a strong, loving mother-daughter connection.

Doctor Templeton draped his arm around her shoulders and gave her a side hug. "Those are happy tears, right?"

Sami nodded. "When can I see her?"

"She's going to be in recovery for a while. When she wakes up, they'll move her to the ICU. She's likely going to be unconscious for an hour or so, and even when she comes out of it, expect her to be groggy for another twenty-four hours." Doctor Templeton hesitated for a moment, his lips tensed to a thin line. "The next couple weeks are going to be tough. Your mother is going to experience both physical and psychological challenges. I'll prescribe some pain pills and a sedative to relax her. Just don't be alarmed if her behavior is out of sorts. It's perfectly normal. I'll have someone come and get you as soon as she comes out of the anesthesia."

As inappropriate as it would be, Sami almost laughed at the doctor's comment about her mother's behavior being out of sorts. What Doctor Templeton hadn't yet discovered was that her mother's behavior was *always* out of sorts.

"I keep saying 'thank you' because I don't know what else to say, but thank you again."

He offered his hand. "It's been my pleasure, Ms. Rizzo. Hope we meet again under less stressful circumstances."

"Aleta," Al whispered, his mouth almost touching her ear. "It's Alberto." Only his sister and Sami's mother called him by his given name. "Please open your eyes."

Although Aleta remained unconscious, the doctor cautioned Al to be careful what he said in front of her, warning him that people in a coma can generally hear very well. They can't necessarily react to what they hear, but every word is comprehensible.

As Al stood over his sister, shocked by her black and blue eyes, severely bruised forehead, and swollen nose, what struck him most were the plastic tubes invading her body. She looked like a subject in some sick experiment. He stepped out in the hall, out of earshot, where the doctor waited for him.

"Be straight with me, Doctor. What are her chances?" Al asked.

The young Brazilian doctor spoke perfect English but with a thick Portuguese accent. "It is not looking so good," Doctor Souza said. "The longer she remains in a coma, the more concerned I become. But try not to despair. Although her brain is swollen from the impact of the collision, her brain activity is still strong, and the MRI did not reveal extensive brain damage."

"Then why is she in a coma?" Al asked.

"It's the swelling of her brain, Mr. Diaz, causing intracranial pressure. We are administering medications that I hope will reduce the swelling, but until they do, she will likely remain comatose."

"Not to insult you, Doctor, but are there other hospitals better equipped to deal with her condition?"

"I assure you, Mr. Diaz, we are doing everything possible to treat your sister with the most medically advanced techniques."

The doctor left and Al bolted out the door a few steps behind him, and headed for the exit. He didn't want to leave his sister's side, even for a moment, but he needed some fresh air, some time to absorb everything the doctor said. When he stepped outside, the brisk autumn air gave him a chill. When he'd left San Diego, the temperature flirted with eighty degrees.

Al leaned against the cold concrete wall and inhaled the refreshing air. He was ready to scoot back to his sister's room when his cell phone rang.

"Hi, Sami," Al said. "Good news?"

"Mom went through the surgery with flying colors."

"Fantastic."

"What's the latest with Aleta?"

"Nothing's changed. She looks terrible—like someone beat her with a lead pipe. It's really tough to see her this way."

"Stay there as long as you like. But just be sure to touch base and keep me posted."

"I promise."

"Captain Davidson must be having a coronary," she said.

"He wasn't overjoyed when I left. And he's already called me twice."

"So he told you?"

"Told me what?"

"There's been another homicide. According to the news, it looks like the same MO."

"Fuck," Al said. "Now the captain's really going to give me shit."

"You need to be with your sister. No matter what. Besides, everything's been cleared through HR."

"*I* realize that. And *you* realize that. But the captain is a whole 'nother story."

"Family first, Love."

Sami could hear Al breathing heavily into the cell phone. Burdening him with more to think about was the last thing she wanted, but she felt so conflicted and confused, she just couldn't help herself.

"I realize your plate's full right now, and I hate to give you even more shit to deal with, but I really have to run something by you before my head explodes."

"Sounds serious."

Sami wasn't quite sure how to deliver this announcement in a gentle fashion, so she got right to the point. "You're going to think I'm some unstable dingbat, but I've been thinking about approaching Captain Davidson and Chief Larson to see if it's possible for me to get reinstated."

"*Reinstated*?"

"Considering what's going on right now, my timing might be perfect."

"But how about school and social work?

"I'm bored to death with school, and the whole social-worker gig just isn't what I expected. To make it in that world, you have to get your master's degree, and I understood that going in. But now that I've got two years invested in school, there's no way I can sit in a classroom for another couple years."

"But Sami, after your ordeal with Simon, I thought you'd had it with detective work."

"So did I. But times change. Circumstances change. I guess detective work is more in my blood than I thought."

"Well, Sami, you just knocked the piss right out of me. But, if you've really thought this through carefully, and this is what you want, hey, you have my total support."

"Thank you. How do you think the captain and chief will respond?"

"To be honest, with the current hiring freeze and restricted budget, I think you're facing an uphill battle."

"Wouldn't be the first time I tangled asses with the two of them."

"And it likely won't be the last." Al paused. "I hate to cut you short, but I've got to get back to my sister's room. Tell your mom she's in my thoughts. And give her a kiss for me."

"I will. If anything changes with Aleta, call me right away— no matter what time."

"Good luck with Davidson and Larson."

"I'm going to need more than luck."

The medical experiments Julian had conducted on Connor did not yield sufficient evidence to support his research conclusions. In fact, they hadn't produced one piece of evidence to uphold his theories about new surgical treatments for the cure or control of atrial fibrillation. At first, when Julian discovered that Connor suffered from an arrhythmia, he couldn't believe it. Considering that only about three percent of the population suffers from A-Fib, and the majority are over sixty years old, what were the chances that he would randomly meet someone with this condition—particularly a man so young? Julian had made some incorrect medical judgments that cut his experiments short. Now faced with a profound feeling of guilt—*oh, how Connor had suffered*—he had to remove all distractions and moral arguments and look at the big picture.

The needs of the many outweigh the needs of the few.

He had thought long and hard about how he could cut the connection between his laboratory experiments and the research he performed on live subjects, how to sidetrack the police. The solution was so obvious; he couldn't believe he'd overlooked it. It was a simple strategy: divert attention away from surgical procedures on hearts by performing mock procedures on other organs.

Such a simple concept, yet utterly brilliant.

Now Julian could focus all of his attention on the only issue that mattered. If he could support his theories through controlled studies and develop a new surgical procedure that far surpassed catheter ablation and the three Maze procedures, Julian would likely see his photo on the cover of every medical publication in the world. Not to mention that he would gain the respect of the entire medical community, the recognition he urgently longed for. And if he was painstakingly careful with the data, no one would ever know that he'd gathered it from live subjects.

Having conducted his research on two subjects, a renewed urgency rose in him, an uncontrollable desire to continue with his experiments. He had to get past Genevieve and Connor and press on. But he did not have the luxury to come and go as he pleased. His family had now become his most formidable road-block.

He could only conduct his research on live subjects when his family was out of the picture. After all, he couldn't just vanish for several days without a credible explanation. As a cardiologist, his work often required that he travel and attend conferences. But how often could he use this excuse without his wife getting suspicious? Once or twice a month, Nicole drove the kids to Los Angeles to spend a weekend with her parents, but they had just returned from a visit, so Julian didn't expect them to make another trip soon. For him to complete his research and meet the six-month deadline GAFF had given him, he had to find a way around this logistical problem. Even if it required drastic measures.

CHAPTER TWELVE

Feeling as if she were returning from a short vacation, Sami walked into the precinct and the only face she recognized belonged to veteran homicide investigator Chuck D'Angelo. The precinct hummed with activity, detectives as well as support staff buzzing around. Out of pure courtesy, she thought about approaching D'Angelo, even though she couldn't stand the guy, but he looked busy talking to a young man she had never seen before. Likely a newbie, she guessed. Maybe her replacement?

Sami made her way over to what used to be her desk. Whoever sat there was nowhere in sight. She had never seen the desk so neat and orderly, unlike when she had occupied this space. She was overwhelmingly tempted to sit in the chair just to see how it felt, but Captain Davidson just happened to pop his head out of his office, yelling for D'Angelo, and he fixed his gaze on her.

Davidson marched over to Sami and extended his hand. "Well, well, well. Look what the cat dragged in."

She grasped his hand and pumped his arm. "You're looking well, Captain."

"That's good, 'cause I feel like shit. Blood pressure's through the roof." He motioned to D'Angelo.

"I'm a bit early," she said, "so I'll wait until you're free."

The captain displayed a rare smile. "Shouldn't take more than five minutes for me to nibble on his ass."

"Nice to see that some things never change," Sami said with a big grin.

"And some never will. Make yourself comfortable."

D'Angelo didn't say a word, but waved and smiled at her as he followed the captain, looking like a kid on his way to the principal's office. Oh, how she remembered those closed-door thrashings. Not able to resist it any longer, she plopped down on her old chair. Whoever sat here, she thought, must be a tall one. Her toes barely touched the floor.

Preoccupied with her old desk and the familiar surroundings, she hadn't noticed the man standing to her side.

"Sami Rizzo?" the young man said.

"In the flesh. And you are?"

"Detective Osbourn. Call me Richard."

"Pleased to meet you, Richard."

He folded his arms and leaned against the desk. "I've heard a lot about you, Ms. Rizzo."

"My mother is Ms. Rizzo. I'm Sami. And a word of caution: Don't believe what you hear. People around here have a tendency to exaggerate."

"Even when they say good things?"

"Particularly when they do."

"Detective Diaz thinks you're the best detective this precinct has ever seen."

"Does he, now?" Obviously, Detective Osbourn wasn't aware of their relationship. "That's only because I'm sleeping with him."

Osbourn laughed. "He also told me you have a great sense of humor."

"Anyone sleeping with Al has to have a sense of humor."

Osbourn still didn't get it.

"How long have you been in homicide, Richard?"

141

"Nearly two years."

"So you started shortly after I left?"

"Actually, I replaced you—in a manner of speaking."

"I see," Sami said, easing out of the chair. He seemed way too young to be a homicide detective. He looked like he'd just graduated from high school. "So, this is *your* desk?"

Osbourn nodded. "You're more than welcome to sit there. I'm on my way out anyway."

"Thank you, Richard." Sami extended her arm. "Can you keep a secret?"

"Sure."

"I really am sleeping with Al."

Sami took a few minutes to gather her thoughts, then headed for the captain's office. Except that his desk looked even more cluttered than Sami remembered, not much had changed in his office. She did notice that the stench from cigarettes seemed even more overpowering, and the mountain of cigarette butts piled in his ashtray was worthy of a call to the people at Guinness.

"I see you haven't quit smoking, Captain."

"You sound like my wife."

"I'll take that as a compliment."

"Have you seen her recently?"

The door squeaked open and in walked Police Chief Larson. "Nice to see you, Sami." He nodded to the captain.

"Likewise, Chief," Sami said.

Larson sat next to her. "What's the good word?"

"I'm not going to beat around the bush and share pleasantries or small talk," she said. "I've given the situation careful thought and I want to be reinstated as a homicide investigator."

The room was as quiet as a mortuary. "After two-plus years out of this place, you want me to snap my fingers and rehire you?" Larson said.

"I understand that there's red tape and protocol, but—"

"*Protocol*? I need approval from the City Council to buy a fucking roll of toilet paper these days."

"Then let's talk to the City Council," she suggested.

"Our budget is for shit," Captain Davidson said. "We can't hire anybody right now. Not even a part-time janitor."

"So you're telling me that even faced with the second serial killer in little more than two years, you boys aren't going to pull out all the stops to get this guy? How's Mayor Sullivan feel about that?"

Davidson and Larson locked eyeballs.

She leaned toward Larson. "Look, Chief, who else in this place has experience dealing with serial killers?"

"No one," Larson shot back. "You had fucking dinner with the son of a bitch, and didn't even call for backup. That little stunt could have put you in the morgue. The last thing I need is some reckless loner going off half-cocked."

He blindsided her with that comment. But she deserved it. "You don't have to remind me, Chief. Do you have any idea how many times I lie awake at night and wish I could go back and relive that day? Considering that I almost died and made my daughter an orphan, do you honestly think I would ever do such a foolish thing again?"

"I sure hope not," Larson said.

Captain Davidson stood up and parked his hands on his hips. "Any idea when Al might be back?"

Sami shook her head. "His sister is still in a coma and there's no way of telling if or when she'll snap out of it. I can tell you this, though, he'll stay with his sister as long as necessary."

The three of them sat quietly, staring at one another. Chief Larson stood up. "Let me run it by the mayor. Give me a day or so. But to be honest, it's more than a long shot." He shook her hand. "If by the grace of God we do get a thumbs up, how soon are you available?"

She thought about that for a minute. The hospital would discharge her mom in a few days and Emily had already started moving her things. And of course, she had to deal with dropping out of college. "Is immediately soon enough?"

CHAPTER THIRTEEN

"Sorry it's such late notice, Nicole," Julian said. "But Doctor Hastings got the flu at the last minute, so I have to go in his place." Lately, Julian was finding it painfully easy to lie to his wife, but he had his priorities. He could tell by the look in her eyes that she was not pleased.

"Who the hell is Doctor Hastings?"

"He started at the hospital only a couple of months ago. He relocated from Chicago General. Real sharp guy."

"Why you? Can't somebody else go to LA?"

"Only Ted Hastings and I are qualified to lecture on this new procedure." He put his arms around her and hugged her for a minute, rubbing her back and kissing her cheek.

"It's not fair," Nicole whispered.

"Do you like your new Range Rover and living two blocks from the ocean?"

"Is that a rhetorical question?"

"I'm merely trying to point out that there is a price to be paid for our upscale lifestyle. It's not a nine-to-five job, Nicole. Sometimes it requires that I go out of town. It's only two nights. I'll be home by noon on Wednesday."

"I'd rather see you take the train than drive," Nicole suggested.

"And I'd rather fly, but the hospital's budget is really tight. I'm okay with driving. It's only two hours."

"Two hours if the freeway's moving. It's crazy anywhere near LA."

"I'll be fine."

"This really pisses me off, Julian."

Julian feared that the discussion might escalate. Wouldn't be the first time, he thought. But before Nicole could sharpen her fangs, their daughters, Isabel and Lorena, rescued him. They came in from outside, sweaty cheeks and out of breath. Each grasped one of his legs and held tight.

"We were playing hopscotch, Daddy," Isabel said. Only five years old, she was already reading books for children twice her age. "And guess who won?"

"I'll bet it was your sister." He winked at Lorena. Unlike Isabel, Lorena, three years older, was not blessed with her sister's intellect or her physical agility.

"I won, Daddy!" Lorena yelled.

The moment Lorena looked the other way, Isabel cupped her hands around her mouth and spoke as softly as she could. "I *let* her win, Daddy."

Julian was not surprised that the younger of his two daughters could be so kind and generous at such a young age. During a recent parent-teacher meeting, Ms. Taylor had called Isabel a "gentle soul."

Julian squatted down and hugged his girls. There was nothing in the universe he cherished more than Isabel and Lorena. The highlight of his day was sitting on their beds and reading them a bedtime story. Shortly after Lorena's birth, it was obvious that she was a special needs child. The doctors never gave Julian a firm diagnosis. All they could say was that for some reason, she would be slow to learn and never be particularly agile. She didn't take her first step until she was eighteen months old, and couldn't put a complete sentence together until she was four. Nicole, devastated by Lorena's handicap, feeling totally responsible, wanted no part of another baby. But Julian pleaded and begged until finally Nicole gave in. It was tough for Julian to admit, but had he not wanted children so desperately, he might never have gotten married.

"Who wants to go get ice cream?" Julian asked. At their age, the girls didn't realize that the "ice cream" was actually fat-free frozen yogurt.

"I do! I do!" they both yelled.

Nicole gave him the "look," and Julian knew from past experiences what was coming.

"Our conversation is far from over," Nicole said.

At times like this, he wished he was a single parent.

Doctor Templeton discharged Josephine a day sooner than Sami expected. "She's coming along very well," he had told Sami.

Aware that Simon would meet his fate with a lethal injection in less than a week, Sami had no choice but to confront her longstanding issues with him despite a profound feeling of guilt for having to leave her mother just a few days after her surgery. And she had to do it quickly. There was no time for deliberation. In spite of her ability to deny the truth, on some issues, she now realized that no amount of therapy or counseling could ever give her complete closure. She had to look him in the eyes and ask the questions that haunted her every night.

The decision had not come easy.

Doctor Janowitz had made it clear that Sami would never put the ordeal to rest until she confronted Simon face-to-face. And Sami, too, now felt certain that in order to live a productive life, she had to find peace once and for all. The idea of actually meeting him, however, seemed beyond anything Sami could imagine. Where would she find the courage and strength to carry out such a daunting feat? How might she react when she was just inches away from him, looking into those steel-blue eyes, and her mind flashed back to her life-changing experience?

She'd spent the last two years struggling to make sense of her life, trying desperately to get it back on track, to feel like a whole woman again. Yes, she and Al were now lovers, and for the most part their relationship was stable. Or was it? His behavior of late puzzled her. But she could not think about this right now. Her focus was Simon. It was a matter of survival. Deep in the pit of her gut, Sami feared that even though Simon lived in a cage awaiting his execution, ironically and pitifully, he had won. She was the one imprisoned. She had learned, painfully, through two years of misery, that death was not always the worst punishment. Sometimes living life with a head full of baggage was the ultimate hell. Her only solace, the thread of hope she clung to, was believing in Doctor J and believing in herself.

Sami felt totally confident leaving her mother with Emily. In fact, Emily was better suited to care for her mother than anyone. Yet if something were to happen while Sami was away, she'd never be able to forgive herself. Doctor Templeton had told Sami that no one could predict if a bypass patient would ever suffer from another heart attack. But he assured her that her mother's prognosis was favorable. And as long as she was willing to modify her lifestyle, she could live to a ripe old age.

It hadn't been easy for Sami to get the warden's approval to visit Simon one-on-one, particularly because she was no longer a detective. But having connections not only with the police department, but also with the corrections community, Sami, through the lieutenant governor in Sacramento, convinced the warden that she, more than anyone in the world, was entitled to visit Simon before the State of California put him to death.

Of one thing Sami felt certain: After confronting Simon, if she could not take control of her life, then dead or alive, he would forever have her in his grip.

Wearing a Chargers baseball cap, Julian met the man at an out-of-the-way coffee shop in a quiet strip mall in La Mesa. Feeling a little conspicuous, he panned the area, looking for a familiar face. Comfortable that no one observed or cared about his activities, Julian pulled out a wad of money and peeled off a hundred-dollar bill. "Here's a little something for you." He handed the man the money and a folded piece of paper. "The phone number and specific instructions are written on this paper. Make sure you call at seven p.m. sharp."

The man pointed to the note. "And that's all I have to do is make the call, say that I'm Doctor Hastings, and follow these instructions?"

Julian nodded. "That's it." He leaned toward the man. "Any questions?"

The man thought for a minute. "None."

As Julian turned, ready to walk away, the man grabbed his arm. "If ever you need me again, Bud, I'm always available to make an easy buck."

The California Courts had imprisoned Simon Kwosokowski in Pelican Bay State Prison, a two-hundred-seventy-five-acre Supermax facility located in Crescent City, three hundred seventy miles north of San Francisco. It was home to some of California's most dangerous inmates. Opened in 1989, half of the prison—an X-shaped cluster of buildings set apart by electrified fencing—

was a Security Housing Unit, one of the first maximum security facilities in the country. Inmates confined to this area were held in isolation twenty-three hours a day and spent the remaining hour in a heavily guarded exercise area. Home to infamous gang members, rapists, and mass murderers, Pelican Bay State Prison housed the worst of the worst.

Fortunately for Sami, when she'd made reservations, she was able to coordinate a flight from San Francisco directly to Crescent City via a regional jet. When she arrived at Jack McNamara Field, a tiny airport by any definition, she could smell the ocean. The salty air seemed like the only characteristic this area shared with San Diego. She saw two small buildings, which she guessed represented the sum total of the airport.

A young man with a dark tan and thick accent whisked Sami and three other passengers to the main building in a golf cart. The building was slightly bigger than a two-car garage. The sky looked ominous, as if at any moment the clouds would open up and release sheets of rain. She saw one broken-down taxicab in front of the building and the driver was sitting in the front seat sound asleep.

Not wanting to stay overnight—she'd been careful when making reservations to be certain she could return to San Diego the same day—she carried no luggage, just an oversize handbag. She was uncertain whether or not to tip the polite young man, but saw one of the other passengers hand him some money, so she pawed through her bag, found her wallet, and handed the guy five bucks.

She gently knocked on the taxicab's window and startled the sleeping driver. After a brief conversation, he agreed to drive her to the prison.

With proper ID, a lengthy explanation, notarized authorization documents from the lieutenant governor, and a series of endless phone calls made by the corrections officer stationed at the main gate, Sami managed to get through security. Getting into this gigantic fortress seemed a lot easier than getting out, Sami thought. In her second golf-cart ride of the day, the corrections officer shuttled Sami toward the warden's office. She passed one concrete structure after another, one electric fence after another. The place looked completely abandoned, as if the corrections officer and she were the only two living beings in this complex of buildings. She knew, though, that behind these concrete walls, there lived quite another world.

Just when she thought the concrete structures would never end, she spotted a building that looked completely out of character and guessed that this was, among other things, the warden's office.

The corrections officer had hardly spoken a word to Sami, and his silence continued as he led her into the building and onto the elevator. The warden's office sat by itself at the end of the hall. The corrections officer knocked gently on the heavy-gauge steel door and waited for an invitation to come in. Once inside, he quickly retreated and left her standing just inside the doorway.

Standing up and making his way toward Sami, the warden, portly and bald, offered his hand. "Sebastian Marshall." He vigorously pumped her arm. "So you're the famous Sami Rizzo."

"I think famous is a stretch, Warden," Sami said.

"I'm sure a lot of people would beg to differ with you, particularly in San Diego." He moved toward his desk. "Please have a seat."

He wedged his wide hips into the leather chair. "May I ask you a rather personal question?"

"I can't guarantee I'll be able to answer, but sure, go ahead."

"I can totally understand why you would be compelled to witness Simon Kwosokowski's execution, but why in the name of God would you want to visit him?"

"Because dead people can't answer questions."

"What questions?"

She wiped her clammy palms on the front of her slacks. "Let's just say that Simon and I have some unfinished business."

"I hope you clearly understand what you're getting yourself into. Simon is a shrewd fellow and he can really get into your head and mess with your brain."

She didn't need the warden's warning. She'd already played a little game of chess with him. "I appreciate your concern."

"You do realize that you've been given a special privilege here, right? The only people authorized to visit a death row inmate are immediate family, priests, attorneys, and select law enforcement people."

"I'm aware of that, Warden. And thank you for cooperating."

"Don't thank me. I lobbied against it when Lieutenant Governor Bertolino contacted me, but he's not the kind of guy who takes no for an answer."

Sami had met Bertolino at a conference in Sacramento a few years ago. For some reason, he took an immediate shine to her. To this day she wasn't sure why. But she guessed either it was an Italian thing or he just liked woman with full hips and a generous ass. Whatever the case, she was happy she'd met him.

"One last question, Ms. Rizzo, and then you can shuffle off. Do you really think that getting into Simon's head is going to benefit you in some way?"

"I guess I'm about to find out."

CHAPTER FOURTEEN

Al, drained of energy, cranky, concerned, and utterly frustrated, succumbed to the overpowering urge and bought a pack of Marlboros at the local convenient store two blocks from the hospital. It had been a struggle, but under the circumstances, he could come up with a dozen reasons why he needed a cigarette. Al had always found it easy to justify his addictions. A short distance away from the hospital grounds, he paced back and forth, puffing on his fourth consecutive cigarette. He'd almost forgotten how soothing the raw smoke could be. He wondered how long before a bottle of Jack Daniels called his name.

He hadn't heard from Sami and wondered how her mother was doing, and if Sami had, in fact, talked to Captain Davidson about being reinstated as a homicide investigator. Always supportive, Al hadn't shared his true feelings with her, but the last thing in the world he wanted was to see her wearing a gold badge. He had never worked with a detective as competent and smart as Sami. Her sixth sense and keen ability to sniff out clues from the most obscure pieces of evidence always amazed Al. But that was then.

Since her life-threatening ordeal, and her foolhardy plan to apprehend Simon completely on her own, without backup and without a logical plan, Al had lost faith in Sami's judgment. And his biggest fear was that someday, circumstances might compel her to make a similar mistake.

Then there was also the issue of her mother. Suppose she didn't fully recover from the open heart surgery? What if she needed special care? Sure, Emily was a godsend, but by the end of the summer, she'd be employed and for the most part unavailable. And of course, Al couldn't dismiss the possibility that Josephine could have another heart attack and die. How would that affect Sami's judgment? Lots of questions, but few answers.

One burning question stuck in Al's mind: Now that Sami and he were lovers, how could they possibly work together? Even if the captain assigned them to different precincts, it would be impossible to keep their distance. So how could they deal with the stress of detective work and maintain a productive personal relationship?

Al still wrestled with his feelings for Sami. Well, not really his feelings—he felt in his heart that he loved her—but relationships were not like Hollywood movies. Was there really a "happily ever after"? Relationships were about compromise and sacrifice, two things with which Al had little experience. He had never lived with a woman, nor had he been exposed to a child. He had no idea what it might be like. Maybe his love affair with her was a screenplay for a romantic tragedy.

Al's cell phone interrupted his thoughts. "Alberto Diaz."

"Mr. Diaz, this is Doctor Souza."

Hearing the doctor's voice, Al could feel his pulse racing. "What's going on, Doctor?"

"Please come to your sister's room as soon as possible."

The corrections officer led Sami to a small room. "I'll be right outside if you need me."

Somehow, this didn't comfort her.

In this room, she saw a single chair placed in front of a panel of thick Plexiglas. Next to the Plexiglas, mounted on the wall, was a telephone. She sat on the chair, a knot growing at the base of her skull, her hands trembling.

What the fuck am I doing here?

At this particular moment, she wanted to be anywhere on the planet but here. Except for her ordeal awaiting crucifixion, she could never remember feeling so utterly terrified. But what was she worried about? He couldn't touch her or physically harm her in any way. Of course, that wasn't what she feared. The warden was right: Simon was a master at getting into your head. And once in there, he wreaked havoc with your mind.

She closed her eyes and flashed back to her ordeal. She could clearly see Simon's Room of Redemption. The furniture. The bed. The concrete walls. She could smell the musty air and hear the dead silence. She could see Angelina sitting in front of the TV, not understanding what was going on. Sami remembered her long conversations with Simon, her attempts to outwit him. She had failed. He had gotten the best of her and at any moment—*God, my heart is pounding*—he'd walk through that door.

In a state of sheer panic, she stood up, now believing that she had made a huge mistake.

What was I thinking?

She could no longer deny the truth. Samantha Marie Rizzo was a coward. She was not the Super Cop the newspapers had labeled her to be. She was a weak, incompetent fool.

The door on the other side of the Plexiglas opened. Now feeling trapped, with no place to hide, Sami sat down and felt her pulse pounding in her temples.

This is it, girl. You're screwed.

Two corrections officers—one on each side—escorted Simon into the room. His ankles were shackled and his wrists hand-cuffed and secured to a thick link chain around his waist. He wore a standard issue orange jumpsuit. The long thick hair Sami remembered now looked like a crew cut.

Simon shuffled toward the chair and sat down. One of the corrections officers un-cuffed Simon's right hand. He fixed his stare on Sami and smiled the warm smile of a blood relative who hadn't seen her in years. For a few moments, neither moved. They sat quietly, eyes locked in place. Almost as if cued, they both picked up the telephones.

"Welcome to my humble home," he said.

She didn't say a word.

"I'm really surprised to see you here."

"And why is that?"

"Maybe because I frighten you."

"I think I'm fairly safe."

"Are you? Are you really safe? Tell me I don't haunt your dreams." Simon tilted his head to the side and Sami sensed that he was about to pounce. "I dream about you a lot."

She could actually feel her skin crawling.

"I think about what could have been," he said.

She had no idea what to say.

The staring game continued.

"You've come a few days early. The festivities don't begin until Friday at noon. No dress rehearsals and no rain checks."

She didn't want to exchange barbs with him. "Are you enjoy-ing your brief stay here?"

"It's like the Ritz. Twenty-three hours of solitary confinement, three gourmet meals a day, a warm shower, an hour of R and R, and the good ole boys have only tried to rape me twice."

"Seriously?"

"Want to see the scars?"

"But you're in solitary."

"Not when I'm taking a shower."

She felt no pity for him. "Prison life was never meant to be like a holiday, but—"

"Please, spare me the philosophical sermon. I'm a big boy and I can take care of myself."

"Obviously not."

"The three guys gumming their food might disagree." He cranked his neck from side to side as if trying to get out a kink. "So, Sami, tell me why you resigned from the police department."

"That's none of your business."

"But you were supposed to be a female Dirty Harry. Why did you quit?"

She leaned forward, her face a few inches away from the Plexiglas. "You know you're going to burn in hell, right?"

He ignored her comment. "You quit because of me, didn't you?"

"Don't flatter yourself. They were personal reasons."

"C'mon, Sami, let's be honest here. I haunt your dreams, don't I? You think about me every day and every night."

"You are nothing more than a faint memory."

"Oh, really? I have a theory that might interest you. I don't think you're a smart cop at all. In fact, I think you're pretty damn stupid. Having dinner with a man you hardly knew. In his *home*? Honestly, Sami. Just how desperate were you? What were you thinking?"

"I *wasn't* thinking. But I'm out here and you're in there."

"You know what surprises me more than anything?" he said. "All I had to do was smile and wink and you were ready to spread your legs. You're a bigger tramp than the four whores I crucified."

She could feel her face ablaze. He was doing what he did best.

"And you know what the real irony is? As much as you wanted to have sex with me, I found you totally unattractive and repulsive."

"Fuck you, Simon."

"My dear Sami, is that the best you can do? Does the truth really hurt that much? Why did you come here?"

She couldn't answer that question. She remembered that during the many hours she'd spent in Simon's Room of Redemption, he was a champion at keeping her on the defensive. But now he seemed even more intense.

"You know what I regret most?" he said. "That I only had one opportunity with Angelina." He licked his lips. "She was the sweetest flower I ever tasted."

Now Sami wanted to kill him, her rage nearly uncontrollable. "You *miserable* son of a bitch! And you're supposed to be a man of *God*?" She stood and pounded her fist on the Plexiglas.

In less than ten seconds, the two corrections officers standing ten feet behind Simon charged toward him. Each grasped one arm and stood him up. Sami had a few more things to say but Simon had dropped the telephone. He fixed his stare on her and smiled.

The officers led him to the door.

Al jogged back to his sister's hospital room. Out of breath and frenzied, his thoughts were dark and unsettling. He wanted to remain optimistic, but he thought the worst. Al walked into his sister's room and saw two physicians, one nurse, and Ricardo, Aleta's boyfriend. He took one look at Ricardo and had every reason to be alarmed.

"Mr. Diaz," Doctor Souza said, "your sister has taken a turn for the worse."

Al didn't utter a sound.

"The latest EEG," Souza continued, "indicates abnormal brain activity."

"What the hell does that mean in layman's terms?"

"If the EEG goes flat, which indicates no brain activity at all, we can only sustain her with the use of life support. Now I must be clear. It is entirely possible that her current state is only temporary. That is not uncommon with head trauma. I just don't want to give you any false expectations."

"What's the bottom line?"

"If her EEG remains abnormal, she could remain in a vegetative state."

"For a week? For a month?" Al asked. "How long?"

"Indefinitely."

"And if this happens?"

"Then as her only living relative, you will be faced with the decision of whether or not she should remain on life support."

CHAPTER FIFTEEN

Still furious that Julian had to give a lecture in Los Angeles, Nicole sat quietly in her living room sipping her third glass of crisp La Crema Chardonnay. Not normally a drinker, tonight she wished to numb her brain. Isabel and Lorena occupied themselves playing the Wii in the family room.

When the telephone rang, she guessed it was Julian. Before picking up the cordless, Nicole glanced at the Caller ID and it indicated "Private Number." Thinking it was likely a telemarketer, she let the answering machine pick up, but listened carefully.

"This is Ted Hastings calling for Julian—"

Nicole snatched the telephone. "Hello."

"Sorry to bother you, but I'd like to speak with Julian, please."

"Is this *Doctor* Ted Hastings?"

"Why yes, it is."

"I'm Nicole, Julian's wife. We haven't met but my husband's mentioned your name."

"Nice to talk to you, Nicole."

"I'm a little confused. Why would you be calling for Julian when he's giving a lecture for *you* in LA?"

"Excuse me?"

"Don't you have the flu?"

"Um, well, I really don't know what you're talking about."

"Weren't you supposed to be giving a lecture in LA?"

"Sorry, but I'm not following you."

The blood rushed to her face. "Maybe I'm confused." She had to enlist every ounce of willpower not to bounce the cordless off the far wall. "Julian will be back tomorrow. I'll tell him to call you. Unless you'd like his cell phone number."

"Nothing urgent. I just wanted to speak to him about the upcoming golf tournament."

"Have a good night, Doctor Hastings."

"You as well, Nicole."

"Where can Julian reach you?"

"He has my number."

And I have his.

Julian walked into Cutty's Bar & Grill, located in North Park, an eclectic neighborhood in San Diego, and as he'd done before, he made himself comfortable at the bar. He didn't expect that any of his colleagues patronized this place, unless, of course, they were living a double life like him. So, for the most part, he felt reasonably comfortable. Gazing at the crowd, he could see that men outnumbered women two-to-one. His goal tonight was to search for another young woman, so the selection was limited.

What troubled him most was that by researching only one subject at a time, he hadn't figured out how he could possibly gather the data he needed in only six months. And when he added his limited availability to the equation because of his fulltime job and obligation to his wife and daughters, these responsibilities carved out a big chunk of time. There had to be a way for him to study multiple subjects. But how?

Julian swiveled on the barstool to get a better look at the crowd. No one of particular interest caught his eye. Then, a tall redhead walked in the front door, swinging her hips like a model walking a runway. Her curly hair grazed her shoulders and bounced in harmony with her stride. Her lips, full and glossy, pouted ever so slightly. She waved and smiled at someone as she headed for the bar. His expectations crashed when he watched her embrace a man and kiss him on the lips. Of one thing he was certain: the guy wasn't her brother or best friend.

Julian's first thought was to forget about the redhead and search for someone else. But then he wondered if he could benefit from the situation. Was there a way for the redhead *and* her boyfriend to become his next subjects? He had no plan. He couldn't imagine that they would voluntarily go back to his loft. But his instincts told him to take the next step to see how things unfolded. What could it hurt?

With each of his subjects, Julian faced the same major obstacle. How could he know for sure that a potential subject's heart was healthy? The only factors he could rely on were their approximate age and physical appearance—both based on his visual evaluation. If potential subjects were young and slender, he had to presume that they were relatively healthy. But even if they weren't ideal subjects, no matter what their health situation, every heart in every chest offered potential for data.

As much as he hated to admit it, good-looking women got his attention. The risk with this mindset was that he tempted fate by selecting women to whom he felt attracted. With Genevieve, he almost compromised his research by letting his lustful desires overpower him. Was it possible to satisfy both his research and his appetite for raw sex?

As inconspicuously as possible, he watched the redhead's boyfriend downing bottles of beer as if he were chugging shot glasses of tequila. Soon, the guy would likely be stumbling drunk.

Irrational. Disoriented. Defenseless. Julian guessed that eventually he'd have to empty his bladder.

Could be risky, he thought, but maybe there was a way for him to study two subjects at the same time. Maybe Lady Luck had dealt him a straight flush.

He waited as patiently as he could, nursing the last mouthful of his cocktail, a scenario playing out in his mind.

"Another drink, sir?" the bartender said, interrupting Julian's deep thoughts.

Normally, he'd enjoy a second drink. But in a low-end pub like this, the best Scotch they offered was Dewar's White Label, and Julian's palate had grown accustomed to the silkiness of Johnny Walker Blue. Besides, he had drunk just enough to relax. The last thing he wanted was to compromise his alertness. "No thanks. I'm good."

Glancing to his left every so often, keeping an eye on "Beer-Man," Julian saw him ease off a barstool and hightail it in the direction of the men's room. Not wanting to squander even a minute, yet having no idea how to proceed, he sucked in a heavy breath and headed toward the redhead.

"Anyone sitting here?" Julian asked her, smiling as innocently as he could.

"Yes, as a matter of fact, someone *is* sitting there—my fiancé."

He found her tone particularly annoying. But she was as sexy as they come. "He'd have to be out of his mind to leave a looker like you alone."

"A '*looker*'?" she said. "You're shitting me, right? That expression went out with high-fives. What century are you living in?"

Julian forced a laugh. *She's a feisty one.* "If I had a woman like you, I'd never leave her side."

"Not even if you had to piss?"

"I guess that's the only exception."

"Then I suppose you'll forgive my fiancé for emptying his bladder."

"Can I buy you a drink?" Julian asked.

"Obviously, you can't take a hint, can you?" the words flowed off her tongue with bold contempt.

He didn't like the way things were going. He almost turned and walked away.

"I'm not trying to offend you, and I'm not proposing. I was just asking you to have a drink with me. Totally innocent."

"And when my fiancé finishes business in the bathroom, are *you* going to explain why I'm having a drink with a stranger?"

Before he could respond, the fiancé returned, a little stagger in his walk. He eyeballed Julian, then put his arm around the red-head. He looked like a guy who could be leader of a biker gang. "This guy a friend of yours, Sugar?"

"He's trying to be."

"Is that right, Bud?"

"No harm done. Just being cordial."

"How about being cordial someplace else. Or would you rather I tear your fucking tonsils out?"

Julian raised his hands, palms out, as if he were about to push a heavy object. "No need to get all hostile on me. I get the message."

More humiliated than he'd ever believed possible, infuriated at Beer-Man's threat, Julian worked his way to the front door for some cool evening air. Once outside, he paced up and down University Avenue angry with himself and angry with Redhead and Beer-Man. He had wasted valuable time and would have to go someplace else looking for a subject.

As he stood there, feeling a fever rise, it felt almost as if the couple had flipped a switch in him, that suddenly the whole A-Fib research project didn't matter. He could never recall feeling so much anger. The more he paced, the greater his rage. Having a woman reject him was uncharted water for him. He never knew what it felt like to crash and burn. Overwhelmed with a strong primitive impulse, a desire for revenge, he could not find the strength to just walk away.

What am I doing? *Get in the car, drive to another bar, and search for someone else! Forget about this couple. Let. It. Go. The only thing that matters is the research.*

Julian found his way to his rental car parked at the curb only a hundred feet away from Cutty's. When he got inside, he slammed the door harder than he intended to. What to do, he thought. Maybe there *was* a way for him to salvage the evening. He grabbed the leather satchel from the back seat, turned on the reading light, and pawed through an assortment of medical items. When he found what he was looking for, he grabbed the remote garage door opener clipped to the visor, got out of the car, crossed the busy road, and parked himself in front of a closed boutique, making certain he had a clear view of Cutty's entrance.

I think I'm losing my grip.

About to abort his idea altogether, Julian spotted Beer-Man and Redhead walking out the front door of the bar. What were the chances, he thought. Maybe it's an omen. The man, teetering slightly from left to right, appeared to be intoxicated.

Walking a safe distance behind the couple, Julian followed them. He hoped that they'd parked their car on a side street with less traffic and fewer inquisitive onlookers. At the next intersection, the couple turned left into a dark alley.

Julian picked up the pace a bit and closed the gap, mindful to remain in the shadows of the buildings he passed. What he was about to do violated everything he believed about right and wrong. To stay focused, he had to whisper his credo.

The needs of the many outweigh the needs of the few.

He watched the couple approach a black GMC Envoy. Beer-Man, apparently sober enough to remember the basics of chivalry, unlocked the passenger door for his fiancée. The moment before Redhead entered the car, Julian, unnoticed by either of them, snuck up behind Redhead, firmly grabbed her around the torso with one arm, and with the other, he pressed his Berretta .380 automatic handgun against Redhead's temple. Neither she nor Beer-Man realized that the pistol was empty. But Julian seriously doubted they would call his bluff.

"Remember me, Sweetheart?" Julian said, his face pressed against her curly red hair.

"What the *fuck*!" Beer-Man yelled.

"You're driving, shithead. Get in." Julian ordered. "Try anything heroic and your girlfriend's brains are going to decorate the inside of your shiny new SUV."

"Please, man," Beer-Man pleaded, "don't hurt her."

"That's entirely up to you. Now get in the fucking car and drive."

Julian forced Redhead into the back seat and sat next to her. Still holding the gun against her temple, he barked directions to Beer-Man. During the short ride to his loft, he kept a close eye on Beer-Man, talking to him constantly, making sure he didn't speed or drive erratically. Neither Redhead nor Beer-Man said a word.

With his body pressed firmly against her, his arm wrapped around her waist, and his face nestled in her curly red hair, Julian caught a whiff of Redhead's coconut shampoo. He adjusted his hand and could feel it brush against her breast. Her denim mini-skirt left little to his imagination. The last thing Julian needed was a distraction. But his thoughts moved toward tantalizing possibilities.

Julian felt as though he were dreaming, unable to fathom what was going on. Some force had taken hold of him and he was incapable of breaking free. The more he thought about what he'd just done, the more excited he became. But his excitement quickly turned to paranoia. Suppose someone had seen this abduction? What if they'd called the police? His entire life, all the hard work, all the hours of sweat and blood, could be gone in a blink of an eye. And what about his family? How would they feel when his photo was plastered all over the front page of the newspaper? He could see the headlines now:

"Esteemed Cardiologist Arrested for Kidnapping."

How would his family survive the humiliation? At this juncture, the situation was beyond the point of no return. His only option was to move forward and turn this madness into something productive. After all, he had hoped to find a way to experiment on two subjects simultaneously. So, he had to clear his mind of these troubling thoughts and focus on his objective.

Still pressing the gun against Redhead's temple, he released his grip on her long enough to reach in his jacket pocket and push the garage door remote. The steel gate swung open and Julian told Beer-Man where to park.

Having only a one-bedroom loft, Julian sat Redhead on a wooden chair next to the bed, and pointed the gun at Beer-Man. He motioned with the .380. "Lie on the bed, face down." He swung the gun toward Redhead. "And don't you even think about moving."

Beer-Man did as he was told, and Redhead sat frozen.

Julian opened the drawer on the cart holding the surgical instruments and grabbed a handful of nylon straps.

"Get over here," he yelled at Redhead.

Once there, Julian tapped his gun on Beer-Man's shoulder. "Roll over."

He handed four nylon straps to Redhead. "I want you to secure this asshole's wrists and ankles to the bed. And make them tight."

When Redhead was finished, Julian checked to be sure the straps were secure.

"Back on the chair," he ordered.

Once Redhead sat down, Julian bound her ankles to the legs of the chair and secured her hands behind her back.

From the moment they'd set foot in the loft apartment, the cocky-confidant woman who'd insulted Julian with her wiseass attitude was reduced to a sobbing little girl who'd just lost her Barbie doll. "Why are you doing this? Please let us go."

Julian found no logical reason to explain. Not yet.

"Are you some kind of fucking pervert, or what?" Beer-Man shouted, the fight in him still very much alive.

Ignoring him completely, Julian went into the storage closet and returned pushing a heart monitor. He wheeled it next to the cart with an assortment of surgical instruments and related items. He picked up an instrument looking like fancy pliers and held them up as if examining them.

"What the fuck is all that shit?" Beer-Man shouted.

"What was that you were saying about tearing out my tonsils?"

CHAPTER SIXTEEN

"Did you enjoy staying with Emily?" Sami asked Angelina.

"Yes, Mommy. Emily played with me. Lots."

"How can I thank you, Emily? I owe you big time."

"Well, if you run into any rich doctors looking for a trophy wife, we can call it even."

If Doctor Templeton hadn't been married, Sami thought, she would have loved playing cupid. "I'll keep my eyes peeled."

As Sami and Emily chatted about nothing in particular, each sipping a cold Corona, Angelina sat cross-legged in front of the TV watching *Sponge Bob*. Shuffling her feet across the hardwood floors, Josephine appeared through the archway.

"Are you okay, Mom?" Sami asked, launching off the sofa and dashing to her side.

"Every time I cough, it feels like the incision on my chest is going to split wide open."

"Are you holding the pillow tight against your chest?" Emily asked.

Josephine waved her hand as if dismissing Emily's question. "Pillow, schmillow. My body doesn't always warn me when it wants to cough or sneeze."

"There's an extra pillow in the closet," Sami said. "I'll put it on your nightstand."

Josephine eased her body into the recliner. "I'm a little hungry. Any leftovers in the fridge?"

Sami looked at Emily.

"There's a little meatloaf and some mashed potatoes left over from dinner," Emily said.

"I'd rather have something Italian."

"Want me to order some takeout from DeMarco's?"

Josephine's eyes lit up. "Eggplant parm with a side of ziti. And tell them not to overcook the ziti. I hate mushy pasta."

The Rizzo family called DeMarco's for takeout regularly, so Sami had their number programmed in her cell phone. After she called in the takeout order, Emily volunteered to pick it up and walked out the door.

"Can I talk to you about something, Sami?" Josephine asked.

By the stern look on Josephine's face, Sami guessed that her mom wanted to talk about something important. "Sure, Mom, what is it?"

"Since my heart attack and the surgery and all the time I've had to lie around and do nothing but think, I've been talking to God a lot."

The announcement caught Sami off guard. Her mother hadn't mentioned God in years, and hadn't been to church since Sami's father died. Her only reference to God was blaming Him for Angelo Rizzo's untimely death.

Josephine continued. "I want to go to confession and start going to mass again on Sundays." She pointed to Sami and then Angelina. "And I want you two to come with me."

Sami lay wide awake, twisting her pillow in every possible direction to get comfortable, but she couldn't fall asleep. Flooded with so many consequential issues, she couldn't turn off her frenzied brain. Foremost in her mind—at least at this particular moment—was her mother's request that Angelina and Sami accompany her to church.

Her mom's announcement brought back bitter memories. There was a time when Sami attended church every Sunday without fail. And what she enjoyed most was the fellowship with other churchgoers. She felt as if she were part of something special. Something sacred. She had thought that the friendships she had built through the church community were lifelong. And she foolishly believed that her fellow Christians would stand by her side through thick and thin. But when she went through her awful divorce, a period in her life when she needed support and understanding more than ever, she learned firsthand the hypocrisy of those who proclaim to be godly people.

One woman in particular, Margaret, a woman with whom Sami had spent many holidays—Thanksgiving and Christmas in particular—went from dear friend, sister in Christ, to judge and jury. Because Sami went through a divorce, an event the Catholic Church and the Bible condemn, Margaret completely turned her back on Sami and dissolved their friendship. She had become part of Margaret's family, almost as if she were adopted. So when Margaret figuratively tossed her to the curb, Sami lost not only Margaret's friendship but also her relationship with Margaret's family. Sami felt such a deep sense of loss that she swore she'd never go to church again. But now, her mother's request forced Sami to reconsider.

Sami was still reeling from her earlier conversation with Al. She had never seen him like this. So desperate. So emotional. He had told her that Aleta's EEG was abnormal, and if it went flat, he would have to make the decision whether or not to keep her on life support. Sami so desperately wanted to be by Al's side, but she respected his wishes. She had considered telling him about her rendezvous with Simon, but what purpose would it serve? In time, she would.

She closed her eyes, feeling certain that it would be a long night.

"Please, please," Redhead begged, "Don't hurt my fiancé." She was still bound to the chair adjacent to the bed where Beer-Man lay, but Julian noticed that she'd stopped struggling to break free. Even her voice lacked spirit. Had he broken her will?

He stood next to Beer-Man, ignoring her plea, and focused his attention on the task at hand. He quickly inventoried the surgical tools lying on the cart and untangled the ten leads attached to the heart monitor.

"Enough is enough!" Beer-Man shouted. "Now let us go!"

Julian found a fresh razor and started shaving Beer-Man's chest.

Squirming like a worm on a fish hook, Beer-Man violently twisted his body but could not break free. "What the fuck are you doing?"

Julian pressed on Beer-Man's shoulder, trying to hold him steady. "This will be much easier for you if you relax."

Beer-Man's face changed from angry to terrified. "I'm sorry, man, I really am. I didn't mean what I said. I was a little shit-faced and thought you were hitting on my fiancée."

"I was."

"You rotten son of a *bitch*!"

"You haven't figured it out yet, have you? This is not a game and I'm not trying to get even." Julian's voice grew louder. "Now shut the fuck up before I really give you something to scream about."

Beer-man finally broke down, sniffling and sobbing with breathless bouts of tears.

"Mister," Redhead called out, her voice utterly desperate. "I'll do anything you ask. You can have me *any* way you want. Just let us go."

Finished shaving Beer-Man's chest, Julian set down the razor, moved toward Redhead, and knelt next to her. His mouth was inches from her ear. "Tell me," he whispered. "When you say I can have you any way I want you, what does that mean exactly?"

"Do I have to spell it out?"

"As a matter of fact, you do."

"If you let us go...I'll, um, have sex with you."

"You think that's what I want?"

"You're a man aren't you? Has there ever been a man in history who's turned down a sure thing?"

"I don't see how your offer benefits me. I can take you right now without your consent, so why should I make a deal?"

Julian noticed that Beer-Man was leaning toward them, stretching his neck as far as the restraints would allow, obviously trying to hear what they were talking about.

Redhead didn't answer right away. Julian guessed she would choose her words carefully.

"Even if you force me to have sex with you, there will still be limits on what you can do. Wouldn't it be better for you if I cooperated *completely*?"

"Maybe I don't like it that way. Maybe I *want* you to fight."

"However you want me, I'm yours."

"How can you be sure I'll honor my end of the bargain?"

"I can't. But what other options do I have?"

"Let me think about it."

"What the fuck are you two talking about?" Beer-Man shouted.

Julian walked back to the bed.

"Your fiancée is trying to make a deal."

"What kind of deal?"

"She wants to trade her body for your freedom."

Beer-Man fixed his stare on his fiancée, his eyes nearly bulging out of his head. "Don't you *dare* fuck this asshole! I'd rather die than have him touch you!"

Beer-Man glanced at the heart monitor and the assortment of surgical tools on the cart. "Go ahead, fuck-straw. Perform your sick experiments."

"As you wish." Julian started connecting the heart monitor leads to Beer-Man's chest, shoulders, wrists, and ankles. "Sick is not the appropriate word. Call it medical research."

Beer-Man sat forward as far as the nylon straps would allow. "Are you a *doctor*?"

Julian mounted the IV bag on the rolling stand and turned on the heart monitor. "A cardiologist."

"You're going to do something to our hearts, aren't you?" Redhead asked.

"Your hearts will be central to my experiments."

"What are you going to do?" Redhead asked.

"Even if I explained it you wouldn't understand."

"Try."

No need for him to get too technical. "I'm going to use certain drugs to induce a condition called atrial fibrillation, which is an arrhythmia. The drugs will cause your heart to go into a spasm. Then, I'll perform specific surgical experiments to determine how your heart responds."

Beer-Man looked as though someone just told him that his entire family had been murdered. "Are you *fucking* serious? You're going to operate on us like we're some kind of lab rats?"

"I'd hardly call you lab rats. I'd rather think of you as martyrs."

"We're going to die, aren't we?" Redhead asked, her voice barely a whisper.

"It's not my agenda, but that, I'm afraid, may be the unfortunate outcome."

Beer-Man pleaded again, his tone completely resigned. "Please, don't do this. We have money in the bank for our wedding. About thirteen thousand dollars. You can have it all. Every penny. And I swear on my dead mother's soul, we won't say a thing to anyone."

His comment enraged Julian. He had to teach Beer-Man a lesson. "You should *never, ever* swear *anything* on your dead mother's soul!"

Julian stood over Beer-Man with a syringe in his hand. "I have to warn you that this is going to be terribly unpleasant. It can't be helped. When I inject you with this drug, your muscles will be almost completely paralyzed. However, your nervous system will be very much awake."

Beer-Man was now sobbing like a hungry newborn baby, rolling from side to side, trying to break free. "You're a monster! A fucking monster!"

Julian tore off a piece of duct tape and carefully placed it over Beer-Man's mouth.

Redhead, barely able to speak, made one last attempt to save her fiancé. "Let him go. *Please!* What about our deal?"

"We haven't made a deal, remember?"

"I'll make it worth your while. I promise."

CHAPTER SEVENTEEN

Dressed in scrubs, a scalpel in his hand, Julian prepared himself mentally to proceed. He had placed duct tape over Redhead's mouth and turned the chair to face away from the bed. Why torment her by letting her observe her fiancé's surgery? He'd already tortured her enough on the living room floor. He never thought it possible that anyone could please him more than Eva. But the tall redhead had come close. Apparently, fear of death brought out the raw animal in her. He had learned that her name was Rachael; family and friends called her Rae. How foolish she had been to think he'd have his way with her and simply let Beer-Man and her walk out the door. What was it about forcing himself on women that made it so pleasurable?

He had considered using a condom, but only for an instant. He had learned with Eva that nothing was more pleasurable than skin against skin. Besides, what difference did it make if the police harvested a sample of his semen? He was a model citizen, had never even gotten a parking ticket in his life. From a DNA perspective, Julian didn't exist.

Not sure if Beer-Man's vocal cords would be capable of making any sound, Julian wadded up some toilet paper and stuffed it in Redhead's ears. If Beer-Man *was* capable of screaming, Julian couldn't imagine that the makeshift ear plugs would suppress the violent screams. But it was better than nothing. After all, he wasn't cold-blooded.

"Try to move your toes," Julian said to Beer-Man.

Nothing.

"Move your fingers."

Still nothing.

Julian glanced first at the IV bag to be sure the drip was adequate. Then he looked at the heart monitor. Except for a rapid heartbeat, which Julian expected, Beer-Man's EKG looked normal. He pressed the scalpel against Beer-Man's chest and looked into his wide-open eyes. Beer-Man stared at the ceiling, pupils fully dilated. No blinking and no eye movement at all. A steady stream of tears seeped out of his eyes.

He made a deep incision in Beer-Man's sternum, from the manubrim, just below his neck, to the xiphoid process, two inches above his stomach.

Julian heard a strange gurgling sound coming from Beer-Man's throat, an obvious reaction to the pain. The young man's head and face were dripping with sweat. Julian again checked the heart monitor: 150 beats a minute. Prepared for this possible reaction, he grabbed a syringe he had already prepared, and injected Beer-Man with a strong dose of propranolol.

Julian studied the monitor.

139. 122. 109.

In less than five minutes, Beer-Man's heart rate dropped to 87 beats a minute, a suitable level for Julian to continue.

He reached for the surgical saw. The level of pain he expected Beer-Man to endure when he cut through his sternum and then spread his ribs apart, would no doubt make the incision feel like a mere paper cut. Julian pulled down the plastic shield to protect his face from splattered blood, and began to cut. The deafening sounds coming from Beer-Man's throat drowned out the sound of the circular blade ripping through his chest.

"This is Police Chief Larson."

Sami had just stepped out of the shower, ready to dry her hair. Running a little late for her 9:00 a.m. class, she'd been thinking about blowing it off. She hadn't cut a class since starting school, and if ever there was a time when she needed a break, today topped the list. "Good morning, Chief Larson."

"I've spoken to Mayor Sullivan."

By the formal tone in his voice, she suspected that his announcement would not be positive.

"As much as we'd love to have you back in homicide, it's just not possible. At least for the time being. With the budget restraints and hiring freeze in place right now, we'd need special approval from the City Council *and* the mayor. And you worked here long enough to realize that the red tape involved with any major decision is like asking Congress to overturn a veto."

She thought about debating the issue one last time, but felt it would be futile. Besides, Larson wasn't the decision maker anyway. "I understand, Chief. And I really appreciate your efforts."

Moments after hanging up, Sami felt overwhelmed with disappointment. Aware that the possibility she'd be reinstated as a detective was a long shot, she hadn't set her expectations too high. But in spite of her cautious optimism, she had already mentally prepared herself to drop out of school; she saw herself in the thick of things again. Emotionally, she couldn't handle school much longer. In fact, Chief Larson's phone call made the thought of going to class this morning virtually unbearable. How had she gone from idealistic enthusiast to complete cynic in less than two years? She tried to tell herself that she was a victim of the system, that the system had tainted her. But she remembered something Captain Davidson had told her years ago: "There are no victims, only volunteers."

There were few things she wanted right now more than skipping her class. But ingrained in Sami's psyche was a profound sense of right and wrong. She was addicted to the principles her father had literally forced on her throughout her childhood and even into her adult life. In grammar school, she was a model student. She didn't so much as steal a pencil. And in high school, not once had any teacher sent her to detention.

She almost called the administrative offices of San Diego University to alert them that she'd be missing her classes today. But her father's voice whispering in her ear forced her to stay on the straight and narrow. She picked up the hair dryer instead of the telephone and did the right thing.

Julian walked in the front door and set his luggage on the floor. Before the door closed behind him, Nicole seemed to appear from nowhere.

"How was the conference?" Nicole asked, her voice edgy.

Julian saw something in Nicole's eyes. "Boring. Glad it's over."

"I'll bet you are."

"Did you wake up on the wrong side of the bed? No kiss. No hug. Nothing."

"Where the hell have you been?" Nicole shouted.

"Are you seriously asking me that question?"

"Ted Hastings called while you were gone. *Doctor* Ted Hastings."

Julian waited for the explosion. He didn't have to wait long.

"There *was* no conference, Julian, you lying sack of horseshit." Nicole's eyes glazed over. "Is it another woman?"

"Of course not." Julian's plan kicked into high gear. He carefully scripted his explanation. "Do you want the truth?"

"No. I want you to feed me a load of crap."

"I drove up to Big Bear."

"What the fuck for?"

"It was supposed to be a surprise. You love it up there, especially during ski season. So, I tried to buy a little cabin. I wanted it to be a birthday present." Wow, he thought. His ability to lie with a straight face almost scared him.

Nicole seemed to be processing the information. "And did you buy one?"

Julian shook his head. "It was a private sale and the guy wouldn't budge on the price. It was about a hundred K more than we could afford."

"Why don't I believe you?"

"Have I ever given you reason to distrust me?"

"Just because I haven't caught you lying doesn't mean you haven't."

"I'm telling you the truth."

"Okay then. I've got an idea. I'm a much better negotiator than you, so give me the guy's name and phone number and *I'll* work him over on price."

Julian recognized that Nicole was testing his story. "Don't bother. There are plenty of properties for sale—especially the way the economy is right now. We'll take a leisurely ride up there together for a weekend. It won't be a surprise, but—"

"You are so full of fucking shit." Nicole moved toward Julian, her chest touching his, her face inches from his. "What's the bitch's name?"

"Look, I'm sorry that I had to lie. But I really wanted to surprise you."

"Oh, you surprised me all right." Nicole stormed out of the room and two-stepped it up the stairs.

"Where the hell are you going?" Julian shouted.

"I'm taking the kids and driving up to see my parents. I need time to think."

Julian had to employ all his willpower not to grin like a crazy man. He loved a well executed plan. A little elaborate, perhaps, but it worked. With Nicole and the kids out of the way, he could continue with his research.

"It's bad, Sami. Really bad."

She tried to squint the clock radio into focus, but couldn't quite make out the time. The dark room suggested early morning. She had never heard Al's voice so desperate. She closed her eyes, hoping that the worst hadn't happened. "What's going on?"

"Aleta's latest brain scan shows very little brain activity—less than the last EEG. Technically, she's not brain-dead, but as close as you can get."

"But there's still hope?"

"Very little."

Sami wanted to cry, but if she did, she believed it would make things even more difficult for him. She choked back the tears. "I'm so, so sorry, Honey."

"If the EEG goes flat, as the only living relative I have to decide whether or not to pull the plug." He now sounded angry. "Can you fucking believe it? I have to decide whether or not my sister lives or *dies*."

"I can't even imagine what it must feel like." Sami wished she could comfort Al, but what could she possibly say to soothe his pain? "As soon as we hang up, I'll check airfares and see how quickly I can get a flight out."

"I appreciate it. Really. But you're a few weeks away from finals—"

"Fuck finals. You're more important."

She could hear him breathing into the phone.

"I'll be there as soon as I can."

"Please, Sami, it's thoughtful of you, and I love you for it, but there is nothing you can do for me. Your mom just had bypass surgery. She needs you more than I do."

She realized that he was right, but oh, how she wanted to argue. "Listen to me. Emily can take care of my mom better than I can, so—"

"No, Sami. Please."

She thought about standing her ground, but the last thing she wanted was to put him under more stress. "If anything—anything at all happens, if you need to speak to me, don't you dare hesitate to call. Understand?"

"Thank you, Samantha Marie."

After taking a long hot shower, Julian wrapped a terrycloth robe around his body, slicked back his wet hair, and headed for the wet bar in the family room. He poured himself a tall glass of Johnny Walker Blue and sat in his favorite recliner, enjoying a rare opportunity to savor the peaceful serenity of his home.

Under normal circumstances, watching his daughters drive away with Nicole for a trip to LA would nearly bring him to tears. But, with the prospect of finding another subject for his research, he had found himself curiously excited when Nicole backed the Range Rover out of the driveway, even though he had no idea when he'd see his family again. When he had waved goodbye to his daughters, he hadn't felt the same emptiness he'd felt in the past.

In spite of the perfectly tranquil setting and the numbing effect of the Scotch, turbulent emotions stirred in Julian. It had been so easy for him to lie to Nicole about the supposed conference in LA. And he further extended the lie by manufacturing a story about Big Bear. He felt no guilt about lying, and this was a first for him. Something strange was happening. It felt as if he was going through a bizarre metamorphosis. A real-life Dr. Jekyll and Mr. Hyde. Had he become so fanatical with his research project that it had taken hold of him? Altered his value system? Was his desire for fame and recognition so overpowering that he was willing to risk everything?

But it wasn't just his obsession with the research project that gripped him, nor his growing apathy toward his family. There was another issue that weighed heavily on his mind. Why the sudden uncontrollable fixation with sex? Somehow, he had managed to defeat the temptation to have his way with Genevieve. Whatever honorable values remained in his character at that time, he had been able to overcome his raw desires. But with Rachael, it had been quite another story. He had not been the same man who spared Genevieve. Not only did he take Rachael without regret or the slightest compassion, he had deceived her into believing that he would set her free.

He gulped the last of the Scotch and poured another. This time, nearly to the brim.

His first instinct was to blame his preoccupation with sex on his lackluster physical relationship with Nicole. He had tried unsuccessfully to ignore his frustrations for years. He loved her. At least he thought it was love. But a nymph she was not. With her, he would never fulfill his deepest, darkest sexual fantasies. She could never be Eva. Or Rachael. Conservative and inhibited, Nicole would never consider experimentation or anything even remotely unconventional. He almost dreaded those rare occasions when she was actually "in the mood." Every time they made love—if that's what you could call it—he felt as though he was performing as a circus animal, trained to obey her every whim. He had never imagined that he would force himself on a woman, never dreamed how delightful it could be. But oh, how much he had enjoyed ravishing Rachael. His one regret was that he had never had the opportunity to take his cousins so brutally. But he remembered them every time he penetrated a woman.

He still couldn't understand why he hadn't felt compassion for Beer-Man. It was as if he had been operating on a cadaver rather than a human. The experiments he'd performed were beyond excruciating; Julian knew this, yet he felt no empathy for Beer-Man's suffering. Granted, Beer-Man had humiliated him. But did that give him reason to treat him so sadistically?

At one point during the experiments, he had not given Beer-Man sufficient anesthesia to paralyze his muscles. Right in the middle of a major surgical procedure, Beer-Man's ribcage spread wide open, his heart completely exposed, Julian was ready to perform an ablation on the posterior of the left atrial wall with radio-frequency energy when Beer-Man's entire body began to spasm, and, remarkably, he screamed so loudly that the duct tape broke free from his mouth and Julian thought for sure a passerby would hear him. Fortunately, he had a syringe of anesthesia handy. But something strange happened. Instead of immediately injecting the potent drug into Beer-Man to render him unconscious and relieve his agony, Julian hesitated as if he had derived pleasure from Beer-Man's suffering. He remembered glancing at the pliers sitting on the surgical cart and feeling a wave of excitement. Had he lost all sense of reason and humanity?

He finished his second Scotch, the smooth alcohol doing what it did best. His thoughts shifted to another disturbing issue. For now, he would enjoy his sovereignty and continue with his surgical experiments. But in a few days, Nicole, Isabel, and Lorena would return, and again they would restrict his activities. How could he be husband and father and still complete his research? He had no answers, at least not yet, but he started to see that the situation called for a permanent solution.

CHAPTER EIGHTEEN

Emily had just prepared breakfast: chocolate-chip pancakes for Angelina, Eggbeaters and turkey sausage for Josephine, and a Spanish omelet for Sami. Emily sipped orange spice herbal tea.

"You're a gift from the gods, Emily," Sami said.

"You might change your mind when you taste the omelet."

"And what's with you, Cuz?" Sami said. "You on a diet?"

"Trying to lose a few pounds."

"You look fine to me," Josephine said. "I could understand it if you had hips like my Sami."

"Gee, thanks, Mom, I can always count on you for support."

"Would you rather have me lie?"

"Yes," Sami said. "As a matter of fact I would."

Emily, five-foot-eight, silky black hair to the middle of her back, chocolate brown eyes, and an absolutely perfectly proportioned figure, needed to be on a diet about as much as Sami needed to eat a pound of Godiva chocolates every day. Sami was about to taste the first bite of her omelet when her cell phone rang. She shuddered instinctually, thinking that it might be Al with bad news. But then she realized she had not heard his personalized ring. Relieved, she excused herself, walked into the living room, and opened the Motorola flip phone.

"This is Sami."

"Ms. Rizzo, this is Mayor Sullivan. Is this a convenient time for us to talk?"

When would it not *be convenient to speak with the mayor of San Diego?* "Absolutely, Mayor."

"Just so you know," the mayor said, "Captain Davidson and Police Chief Larson are conferencing on this call."

Sami wasn't sure what to think. That the three of them called could only mean that whatever they wished to discuss had to be important. No, more than important. Monumental. "What can I do for you, Mayor?"

"This is Chief Larson, Sami. Are you still interested in being reinstated as a homicide investigator?"

Her first thought was to pinch herself. Since Chief Larson had rejected her request, she'd completely wiped the possibility from her thoughts and decided to focus on school, regardless of her apprehensions about the life of a social worker. "To be honest, Chief, I kind of put it on the back burner."

"Well," the mayor said, "I'd like you to consider putting it on the *front* burner."

"Sami," Captain Davidson said, "we've just been informed that two more bodies were found at the Fanuel Street Park."

A long silence.

Chief Larson chimed in. "There are many similarities between these homicides and the two previous, but our killer has kicked it up a notch."

"What do you mean?" Sami asked.

"We'd rather discuss the details face to face," Captain Davidson said.

"Boy," Sami said, "I don't know what to say. But I'd like to at least bounce this off Al."

"Ms. Rizzo," the mayor interrupted, "we now know for certain that we've got another serial killer on our hands. You've got more experience dealing with one than anyone else in homicide. Detective Diaz is in Rio and no one has a clue when he'll return. In the meantime, we've got some lunatic walking and stalking the streets of San Diego. This is not what people expect in America's Finest City."

Sami wished she could talk to Al. "As much as I'd like to say yes, I need a little time."

"In all honesty, Ms. Rizzo," the mayor said, "we don't have the luxury of time."

Another long silence.

"Agree to be reinstated," the mayor said, "and I'll personally guarantee that all your benefits and seniority will be restored. We can't pussyfoot around. If we can't make a deal with you, we'll be forced to seek help elsewhere. We need your decision right now."

"If I accept your offer, I have two questions. First, how quickly do you expect me to start? Second, who will I partner with?"

"We want you yesterday," Chief Larson said. "We have to locate this maniac before there's a fifth victim."

"The entire homicide squad will be at your disposal," Mayor Sullivan said. "But be warned. If you're not making significant progress within the next week, the FBI will muscle in and take over."

Fraught with uncertainty, Sami now realized that her idealistic vision of once again carrying the title of Homicide Investigator suddenly seemed like the foolish ambition of a spoiled child.

"Just give me twenty-four hours," Sami said.

"Twelve hours, Ms. Rizzo," the mayor said. "That's the best I can do. Call me on my cell no later than ten tonight. Can you live with that?"

"I guess I have little choice."

Sami scribbled the number she gave her on an envelope.

"One more thing," the mayor added. "If you agree to be reinstated, I want you in Captain Davidson's office tomorrow morning at eight sharp for a comprehensive briefing."

After Sami hung up, she was astonished that both her mom and Emily said they supported her regardless of her decision—her mom reminded her that she'd broken a promise to her father. Sami sequestered herself in her bedroom and carefully weighed the pros and cons. Was she really prepared to be a homicide detective again?

For some reason, it was not the impending offer from the mayor or Al's sister on the brink of death that first came to her mind. It was Simon. Her visit to Pelican Bay State Prison did not go as planned. She thought that she could control the situation, keep Simon on the defensive, but he had proved otherwise. She had gone to see him with hopes that a face-to-face encounter would give her closure. But Simon, true to his nature, completely took control and forced her to literally bolt out the door before she had a chance to say what she needed to say.

She now clearly understood that the missing words from their dialogue were, "I forgive you, Simon." This was the declaration that would have freed her soul and given her closure. How could she find peace and harmony in her life with so much hatred in her heart? All her anger and rage didn't hurt Simon one bit. But it had been eating her up. She remembered a quote she'd heard a few years ago:

"Resentment is like drinking poison and waiting for the other person to die."

Sami had been feeding herself a steady dose of poison for nearly two years. She had to let it go.

After a few hours of teetering back and forth, her mind aswarm with morbid visions of what might happen if she once again wore the prestigious badge of a homicide investigator, she concluded that she was incapable of making the decision on her own and needed to speak with Al. Guilt-ridden to be burdening her lover with the trials of her life, she reluctantly made the call.

"Hello, Sweetheart," Al said, his voice flat and lifeless.

"Any change in Aleta's condition?"

"Negative."

"That's good news, right?"

"If you look at the glass as half-full, I guess it is."

She struggled to find the appropriate words. "I'm sure my timing is for shit, but can I ask for a little advice?"

"The most independent woman of the new millennium actually wants advice from *me*?" For the first time since he had gotten the call about his sister, his witty sense of humor peeked out from behind his dwindling hope.

"I'm really at my wits' end." She gave him a recap of her conversation with Mayor Sullivan and company. "I feel like I'm between a rock and hard spot."

"I'm not sure I can help you. You're a great cop. Top notch. But I can't feel…as you know…what's in your heart. Working as a homicide investigator is unlike any other career. You can't approach it with a lukewarm attitude. It's gotta be one thousand percent. Every day. Every minute." He paused for a moment. "There's only one question for you to consider: are you capable of giving it your all?"

She could never expect viable advice from Al if she didn't share every detail with him. It would be like expecting him to complete a five-hundred-piece puzzle with four hundred fifty pieces. "I flew up to Pelican Bay State Prison and visited Simon."

She hadn't expected that her announcement would slip off her tongue so effortlessly.

"Are you fucking *serious*?"

"Please don't be pissed at me, Al. No one knows more than you that I haven't been myself since the incident with Simon. I needed closure, and Doctor Janowitz felt that the only way to put this to rest once and for all was for me to confront Simon face-to-face."

"So you're telling me that you actually feel closure?"

"I blew it. I really blew it."

"Talk to me."

She told Al how Simon took control and derailed her plan to forgive him. There was a long silence before he spoke.

"In my opinion, I think it's time for you to slay the dragon. Doctor Janowitz was right. You have to face your fears head on. When you resigned, I had to enlist every ounce of willpower to keep my big mouth shut. You're a social worker about as much as I'm a rocket scientist. Whether you accept it or not, detective work is in your blood. It's what you were meant to do. I'd be lying if I didn't tell you that I have concerns. But I have to deal with them myself. Personally, I think you've been out of sorts more because you resigned than because of your ordeal with Simon. It's been over two years. You have suffered and our relationship has been strained. Brush yourself off, climb back up on that horse, and ride like there's no tomorrow. Cause there isn't. Not for you. And not for us as a couple.

"If you feel in your heart that you have to forgive Simon to put this to rest once and for all, then write him a damned letter telling him exactly how you feel. Forgive him, Sami. And forgive yourself for hating him."

His was the taut dialogue of a warrior. Sami felt his words like a face full of ice-cold water. "Thank you for being so honest."

"Now call the mayor, write the letter, and get on with your life."

CHAPTER NINETEEN

Anxious, overtired, yet surprisingly energized, Sami arrived at the main precinct at seven thirty. No longer having a valid parking permit, she had to park in a visitor's spot. She felt a rush of awkwardness when she walked into the precinct, as if she were the only foreigner among a roomful of locals. She quick-scanned the room, looking for a familiar face, but she saw no one she recognized.

On her way to the captain's office, she passed her old desk, now occupied by rookie detective Richard Osbourn. Al had talked about the kid a few times, saying that he had real potential. She noticed a photograph in an eight-by-ten frame sitting on the desk. Richard stood with his arm around an attractive blond, and two young girls sat in front of them. His family, no doubt.

She was about to knock on Captain Davidson's door, when a familiar voice—one she found most irritating—called her name. She turned and saw Chuck D'Angelo, veteran detective, vulgar chauvinist, hustling toward her, trying hard not to spill his coffee. More overweight than she remembered, but still a victim of his wardrobe, D'Angelo reached out and shook her hand, pumping her arm as if he were purging a well.

"Sami Rizzo," D'Angelo said. "How the hell are you?"

Of all the homicide investigators she had worked with over the years, D'Angelo was the last person she wanted to see.

"Hangin' tough. I hear you're turning in your key to the executive washroom."

"Thirty years of this bullshit is quite enough. I bought a small ranch up in Montana. Me and the wife are going to live the easy life."

I pity your wife. "Good for you, Chuck." Sami wondered how he could possibly afford a ranch in Montana on detective wages. Then again, he wasn't the cleanest cop.

"So, Sami, I guess the rumor is true."

"No, Chuck, I'm not pregnant."

D'Angelo let out a hearty guffaw. "Are you really coming back for another go at it?"

"Looks that way. Meeting with the captain in a few minutes."

D'Angelo shook his head. "We've got a real nut-job on our hands. A fucking psycho."

"That's what I've heard."

"Is it true that you're going to head the investigation?" His eyes narrowed and she wasn't surprised he was fishing.

"Haven't a clue what the captain has in mind."

"Well, if you're lead on this case and need a solid partner, I'm not the least bit interested. I'm on cruise control for the next two months and have no desire to track down a fucking wacko."

"I'll keep that in mind, Chuck." *From what I remember, you've been on cruise control for years.* "Anyone in the department you would recommend—assuming of course I—"

"This new kid, Osbourn, is sharp as a tack. He's gonna be a good one if he hangs in there. I hear that his wife ain't too happy with him working in homicide."

"Thanks for the info." She glanced at her watch. "I really have to get moving, Chuck. Nice to see you." It pained her to be so cordial.

He nodded. "By the way. Is Al still in Rio?"

"Looks like he's going to be there for a while."

"Tough break. His sister going to make it?"

"It's a day-to-day thing." She could see his expression completely change. So much so, that she expected devil horns to sprout on his head.

"Who's keeping your bed warm in Al's absence?"

She wanted to kick him square in the nuts. "An electric blanket and my favorite vibrator."

"Well, if you ever—"

"If you were the only man in the universe, Chuck, I'd be a lesbian. Have a lovely day." She turned her back and knocked on Davidson's door.

Julian had just finished breakfast and was heading out the door for two early-morning surgeries when his cell phone rang with a ringtone he really didn't want to hear. He thought about letting it go to voice mail, but eventually she'd track him down.

"Mornin', Nicole," Julian said, trying to be as amiable as possible. "It's good to hear your voice. How are you and the kids doing?"

"Kids are okay, but I'm not so good."

"It's my fault."

"No it's not. I'm such a spoiled bitch."

Yeah, you are. He let her comment slide by.

"I miss you," she said.

This is not what he wanted to hear. He *didn't* want her to miss him.

"I'm coming home, but the kids want to stay here with my parents for a while. You okay with that?"

No, he was anything but okay with Nicole coming home. Besides, he needed a few more days to search for subject number five. "Why don't you take a few days and veg-out. Take the kids to Disneyland—"

"Sounds like you don't *want* me to come home."

"Nicole, how can you say that? You've already made the trip up there. Why not enjoy the time with your parents? I've got a crazy week at the hospital."

"I'm getting a strange vibe from you."

His plan to have some time for himself was slowly crumbling. "Look, I really have to get to the hospital. I'll call you later this morning, right after my surgeries, and we can talk."

"Don't bother. I'll be there when you get home."

Feeling like a suspect ready to be interrogated by three angry detectives, Sami sat in front of Captain Davidson, Police Chief Larson, and a young woman she'd never met. The office still reeked of stale cigarette smoke, supporting her notion that the captain's addiction to nicotine had reached new heights.

"Well, Sami," Police Chief Larson said, "I can't tell you how pleased I am to have you back on board." He pointed to the young woman and then to Sami. "Have you two met?"

The two ladies shook their heads in harmony.

"Sami Rizzo, this is Medical Examiner, Doctor Maggie Fox."

Sami stood and grasped the medical examiner's hand, thinking that this woman was barely old enough to drink alcohol, let alone be an ME. "Nice to meet you, Doctor Fox."

"I've heard some great things about you," Maggie said.

"Hopefully, some of what you heard is true."

After a moment of lightheartedness, the mood in the room shifted to the serious matter at hand.

"The purpose of this meeting," Larson said, "is to bring you up to speed on the investigation. Thus far, there are four victims, all murdered with certain similarities. However, with each new victim, our guy gets more diabolical."

Police Chief Larson paused for a minute, his head lowered as if he were studying the pattern in the carpeting. "Doctor Fox, why don't you share the autopsy results with Detective Rizzo."

Detective Rizzo? Sami had to admit to herself that she loved the sound of her restored title.

"Victims one and two pretty much have the same wounds," Maggie said. "The perp split their sternums right down the middle with surgical precision and it appears that their ribs were spread open as if they had undergone open heart surgery. In fact, their incisions were stapled shut meticulously. Whoever committed this atrocity knew what they were doing." Maggie opened a manila folder and studied the autopsy reports. "The Foster girl died of a massive stroke, and Connor Stevens died of cardiac arrest. However, there's more."

Sami listened carefully.

"Our perp got a little more aggressive with victims three and four."

"In what way?" Sami asked.

"Well, unlike with the Foster girl and Connor Stevens, he wasn't satisfied with operating only on their hearts."

"What do you mean?" Sami asked.

"All of their major organs were dissected. Liver. Kidneys. Pancreas. And lungs."

"Any idea why?"

"I don't have the slightest clue," Maggie said.

Sami tried to process Maggie's words. "What else can you tell me?"

"Cause of death is still a mystery. Unlike the first two victims, our perp performed several different surgical procedures on their hearts."

"What kind of surgical procedures?" Sami asked.

"All I can tell you for sure, Detective, is that I discovered identical scar tissue on the left and right atria of both hearts."

"The upper chambers of the heart?" Sami asked.

"Exactly," Maggie said. "And it seemed that these were caused by some kind of heat source. Microwave. Laser. Or perhaps a high-energy ultrasound."

"It appears," Larson said, "that our perp likes to play doctor."

"Our best guess," Captain Davidson said, "is that this lunatic definitely has advanced medical training."

Sami sat stone-still for a minute, stunned at this theory, trying to absorb the concept that any human walking the planet could be so evil. But then again, there was Simon. "Tell me something, Maggie. Do you have any idea why our guy would perform this particular kind of surgery?"

"Good question. I had never seen bruised tissue like this before, so I did a little research and discovered that the area of the heart scarred by the procedure plays a role in regulating sinus rhythm."

"But what's the motive?" Sami asked.

"Therein lies the mystery," Maggie said.

"So maybe we need to consult a cardiothoracic surgeon to find out if there is any medical significance to the area of the heart in question."

"Already in the works, Sami," Larson said. "I happen to be good friends with Doctor Templeton, chief of cardiothoracic surgery at Saint Michael's Hospital. Perhaps you've heard of him."

"*Heard* of him?" Sami said. "He performed my mother's bypass surgery."

"Small world," Larson said. "He's meeting with Doctor Fox tomorrow morning to examine victims three and four. He's the best, so hopefully he'll be able to fill in the blanks."

"There's more," Maggie said. "Unlike with the first three victims, who were not sexually assaulted, I found traces of semen in the fourth victim's vagina, rectum, and mouth. And the killer wasn't gentle."

"Have you submitted samples to the FBI's DNA Index System?"

"No matches."

Sami felt her hopes nosedive. She noticed Maggie's expression change.

"Victim number three must have really pissed off our perp."

"Why?"

"Because the victim's tonsils were ripped out of his throat."

Sami had to take a few deep breaths before continuing. "Ripped?"

"Like with pliers," Maggie said. "Which is really strange because every other procedure was performed with surgical precision."

Sami gathered her thoughts for a minute. "Let me see if I'm clear on this. Victim one died of a massive stroke, and victim two of cardiac arrest, correct?"

Maggie nodded.

"Cause of death for victims three and four is unclear, but the procedures he performed on their hearts were more complicated?"

"That's right," Maggie said.

"And our guy performed additional surgical procedures on the major organs of victims three and four. And he literally ripped out victim number three's tonsils? Do I have these facts straight?"

"Absolutely."

Everyone in the room seemed absorbed in their private thoughts.

"Thank you, Doctor Fox," Police Chief Larson said, breaking the silence. "We'll take it from here."

Maggie gathered her things and headed for the door. "It was a pleasure meeting you, Detective Rizzo. If you need any further feedback, feel free to contact me." Maggie handed Sami a business card. "Call me day or night."

"Thanks."

The moment the door closed, Police Chief Larson stood and leaned against the file cabinet, arms folded across his chest, eyes on Sami. "See what you've gotten yourself into?"

Quite to her surprise, nothing she had heard in this meeting made her second-guess the decision to rejoin the police department. In fact, she couldn't wait to roll up her sleeves and dig in. Perhaps, she thought, even though Simon had gotten the best of her, the little trip to Pelican Bay State Prison hadn't been crazy after all. She felt a renewed enthusiasm.

"What else do we have?" Sami asked.

"We have a few solid leads." Davidson pointed to the folder in Sami's hand. "Al interviewed the victim's roommate, but she couldn't tell us much more than the perp was tall, dark, and handsome, and apparently he's a football fan 'cause he wore a Chargers cap."

"Terrific," Sami said. "That ought to narrow the field down to about a hundred thousand possible suspects."

"Well, Detective Rizzo," Larson said, "you've got a good place to start. On that note, we need to talk about who's riding shotgun for you. Any preferences?"

"Who are my choices?"

"You've got your pick of the lot," Larson assured her, reinforcing the mayor's promise to Sami. "Then again, there are a couple of new faces out there. So, if you need our help, the captain and I would be more than happy to offer some feedback."

"I've heard good things about this Osbourn kid," Sami said. She had placed more faith in what Al had told her about the young detective and pretty much dismissed D'Angelo's endorsement.

"He's a crackerjack all right," Davidson said. "But wouldn't you want someone with more experience?"

Yes, she thought. *There's nothing I would enjoy more than partnering with a veteran asshole like D'Angelo.* "Let me have a little chat with the kid and I'll get back to you."

An awkward silence ensued. The three of them exchanged glances but nobody uttered a sound. They seemed to be playing some kind of childhood game and the first one to talk loses.

"Can I speak freely?" Larson said.

"Of course, Chief."

"My nuts are really in a vice on this one. The mayor is calling me five times a day. The press is having a field day, and the members of City Council are camping on my doorstep. San Diego hadn't seen a serial killer in decades and suddenly we're dealing with the second one in a little over two years. As police chief, it's my responsibility to keep San Diegans safe. At this particular moment, few people think I'm doing my job. I hate to lay this bullshit on you, but you've got to track down this fucker before he kills again." Larson walked toward Sami, bent forward, and fixed his stare on her. "You've got carte blanche. Anything you want. Anything you need. The entire department is at your disposal. Just find this fucking prick."

CHAPTER TWENTY

Like a man waiting for the results of a biopsy, Julian paced the floors, impatiently anticipating Nicole's return from Los Angeles. Angry and frustrated at his wife for sabotaging his plan and returning home much sooner than he had hoped for, he could feel the blood throbbing in his temples. A woman with an acutely suspicious nature, Nicole would force a conversation about the cabin Julian supposedly tried to buy in Big Bear. Cunning in the fine art of spousal debate, she would likely pose pointed questions that Julian was not fully prepared to answer. Questions to trap him. Having been married for over ten years, he felt certain that her attack would be thorough and strategic. He tried to anticipate what she might ask, hoping to compose a carefully thought-out script, but he found it impossible to focus his thoughts. All he could think about was when he would have the opportunity to perform his research on another subject. And of course, thoughts of what he had done to Rachael hung in the back of his mind.

Nicole's premature return also interfered with Julian's task to dispose of Beer-Man's vehicle. It sat in the underground garage below his loft, and he still wasn't sure how to get rid of it. It was a loose end he needed to take care of immediately. Fortunately, it was tucked away in a dark corner, so he doubted anyone would notice it.

About to grab a cold beer from the refrigerator, he heard a tire squeal. He poked his fingers through the wooden blinds and looked out the window. His wife's silver Range Rover sat in the driveway.

In an effort to reduce the possibility for conflict, Julian dashed out the door and greeted Nicole with a firm hug, hoping his gesture might temper another clash. "Welcome back, Sweetheart. It's so good to see you."

"Can you grab my luggage, please." Her voice was cold as dry ice. She followed him into the living room.

"How was traffic?" Julian asked, hoping to keep the conversation benign.

"It was nuts getting out of LA, but once I hit the San Diego freeway, I got in the left lane and didn't once touch the brake pedal."

"Girls okay?"

"They're fine. They love staying with my parents."

"Want something cold to drink or a little snack?"

"No, I'm good." She plopped down on the leather sofa. "But I would like a couple of Advils. My head is pounding."

"Sure thing."

Nicole swallowed the medication and drank the entire glass of water.

"My parents are moving back to San Diego," Nicole said, her abrupt announcement blindsiding Julian. "In fact, they're working with a real estate agent right now, looking for a home in La Jolla."

He felt as if a bomb exploded inside his head. Her statement caught him completely off guard. When she had said, "We have to talk," he was sure she wanted to discuss the Big Bear incident. Never in his wildest dreams did he expect such a consequential bit of news. "But I thought your parents loved living in Santa Clarita."

"They do. But they love Isabel, Lorena, and me more. Even though I take the kids up there a couple times a month, it's just not enough for them."

Except for a SWAT team breaking down the front door with a battering ram and arresting him for murder, Julian didn't think anything could possibly be worse than Nicole's announcement. "How soon is this going to happen?"

"They already accepted an offer on their home. They just need to find a place here."

With that statement—a stake driven through his heart— Julian watched all of his dreams and expectations evaporate before his eyes. If this were to actually happen, unless he could find small windows of time for his research, having his family there all the time would clip his wings forever.

"You don't seem all that thrilled," Nicole said.

"You're misreading me. I'm happy for them. I'm just surprised."

"Look at it this way. We'll have access to the best babysitters on the planet anytime we want them. Think of the possibilities." Nicole smiled for the first time since returning home.

Oh, how Julian thought of the possibilities. None of them having to do with his family or Nicole's parents. He had reached a defining moment in his life. As each day passed, and he moved closer to the research grant, closer to fulfilling his dream, everything else in his life had become secondary—even his daughters. It was a bitter realization, one he'd been wrestling with for months, but he could no longer lie to himself. The grant meant everything. Recognition meant everything. And one thing was certain: No force in the world could stop him.

✳ ✳ ✳

For privacy, and to ensure that no one would hear their conversation, Detectives Sami Rizzo and Richard Osbourn grabbed a couple of coffees from Starbucks in Pacific Beach, drove to Crown Point Park, and walked on the boardwalk. As was typical this time of year, dark puffy clouds dominated the sky anywhere near the ocean. It was a phenomenon San Diegans call May Grey and June Gloom. But in spite of the unfriendly-looking skies, the air blowing in off the bay felt warm.

Unlike the weekends, when the area buzzed with activities—picnickers, joggers, Rollerbladers, kids doing tricks on their skateboards—today, like most weekdays, there was very little going on in the park.

Sami sipped her soy milk latte. "Never in my wildest dreams did I ever think I'd pay six bucks for a fancy cup of coffee."

Osbourn laughed. "Starbucks sure has made the whole concept of coffee chic."

She picked up the pace a bit. "Tell me a little about yourself, Richard."

"There's not too much to tell. Born and raised in Ocean Beach. Love to surf. Got my degree in criminal justice from SDSU. Married my high school sweetheart. Two lovely daughters. Wanted to be a cop since I was twelve."

"What brought you to homicide?"

"This may sound a little cliché, but I really want to make a difference. It seems naïve, but it's how I feel. I watched my drunken father regularly use my mother as a punching bag. Until one day, when I was a teenager and strong enough to stand toe-to-toe with the son of a bitch. I beat the shit out of him. He never touched my mother again. Since that day, I vowed never to hurt another human being unless in self-defense." Osbourn took a long gulp of his coffee. "I really want to lock up the bad guys."

"How does your wife feel about you working in homicide?"

"She hates that I'm a cop—tries to convince me to quit nearly every day. But take my word for it, as much as I love my wife, if it ever comes down to police work or her…I'm not sure what I'd do."

"Don't you think the constant controversy with your wife will distract you?"

Osbourn shook his head. "We all have distractions. Some can deal with them. Others can't."

Who knew more about distractions than she did? Her lover's sister lay in a coma. Her mom had just undergone open heart surgery. She'd just dropped out of school. She narrowly escaped an appointment with the Grim Reaper at the hands of a serial killer. And she now wore the gold badge she swore she'd never wear again. Yes, Sami thought, she had the market cornered on distractions.

"I have the option to partner with whomever I choose on the serial killer investigation. And I have to make that decision quickly."

"I suppose I haven't earned the department's respect yet, Sami. But I assure you, if you give me a shot, I'll work my butt off to nail this asshole."

"The pressure to apprehend this guy is going to be intense," she warned. "From the mayor on down, everybody's got this investigation on their radar."

"I spent four years in the Marines, two of which were in Iraq disarming IEDs. So I guess you can say that I'm somewhat familiar with pressure, Detective Rizzo."

His last statement pretty much closed the deal. "So that explains the military buzz cut."

"Guess I kind of got used to no-maintenance hair."

"Are you sure you want to place your marriage under this kind of strain?"

"Makes little difference whether I'm investigating a single murder or serial killer. Either way, my wife won't be a happy camper."

If Sami based her decision totally on logic, she'd be compelled to partner with a more experienced detective. But, as she had done so many times in the past, she relied more on her instincts than reason. "Let's head back to the car and get to the precinct. We've got lots of work to do, partner."

Sami stood in front of the whiteboard and paced back and forth. Detective Osbourn sat on a chair and planted his elbows on the metal table, next to the case folder. The murky twelve-by-twelve room, normally used to interrogate suspects and interview witnesses, smelled like a high school locker room.

"This is what we've learned thus far," she said. She turned her back and started writing on the whiteboard. "All four victims— two male and two female—had their chests cut open and their ribcages spread apart. Cause of death for victim one was a massive stroke, and for victim two, cardiac arrest. Victims three and four were identified a short while ago but we have very little information on them, and we're still waiting for COD." Sami opened the case folder and flipped through the pages. "Victim three was Robert Winters, and number four was Rachael Manning, both twenty-eight years old. They were engaged. Unlike victim one and two, our guy performed surgical experiments on their kidneys, liver, lungs, and pancreas. The perp sexually assaulted victim four, a female, and the ME found traces of semen in her vagina, rectum, and mouth. Their chests were stapled with surgical precision. And our guy performed some sort of experiments on their hearts that do not look like the work of a hack. Except for victim three, a white male found wrapped in a sheet, each victim was dressed in expensive, designer clothes. Our guy left the price tag on the outfit the Foster girl was wearing and it was from Saks Fifth Avenue. Al spoke to the salesperson that sold him the outfit, but she gave us only a few clues. Our perp is tall, attractive, and has black hair. And one witness said he wore a navy-blue Chargers cap."

Sami turned and faced Osbourn. "Am I missing anything?"

"Only that the first victim," Osbourn shuffled through the folder, "the Foster girl, met the perp at a restaurant called Tony's Bar and Grill, in the Gaslamp District, and Detective Diaz interviewed Foster's friend who was with her the night she disappeared."

"Good catch," Sami said. "What's the friend's name?"

Osbourn searched the folder. "Katie Mitchell."

"Knowing Al, I'm sure he did a thorough job interviewing her, but—"

"Want me to give her a call?" Osbourn offered.

Sami nodded. "That's all we've got right now. If she can't come to the precinct today, we'll go to her." She picked up the folder and looked through every piece of paper. "While we're at it, let's check out Tony's Bar and Grill and see if anyone remembers seeing Foster or our guy."

Instead of cooking, as he often did, Julian convinced Nicole to pick up some Chinese takeout from the Dragon Palace, their favorite Asian restaurant. He felt more nauseous than hungry, but had to get something into his stomach. Enjoying the brief period of solitude, he sat on the leather recliner and turned on the television, curious to see if the police department had released any new information. He flipped from channel to channel until he found the local news.

"This just in," the female newscaster said. "A KNET exclusive. An undisclosed source tells us that Mayor Sullivan personally contacted veteran homicide investigator Samantha Rizzo and convinced her to return to the police department and lead the ongoing investigation into the recent serial murders in San Diego.

"Detective Rizzo is best known for her harrowing experience apprehending Simon Kwosokowski, the serial killer who crucified four women a little more than two years ago. Unless the governor issues a stay of execution, which seems highly unlikely, Kwosokowski is scheduled to be put to death by lethal injection on Friday at noon."

Julian grabbed the remote and turned off the television. "Detective Rizzo," he whispered. Bad enough having to deal with Nicole and the kids, and now his in-laws, but having Sami Rizzo leading the investigation added a whole new dimension to the hunt. She had earned a reputation as one of San Diego's best cops.

This could get interesting.

CHAPTER TWENTY-ONE

Feeling somewhat deflated after her first full day back with Homicide, Sami grabbed a cold Corona, pinched in a wedge of lime, and sat on the sofa. Neither Katie Mitchell—the first victim's best friend—nor anyone working at Tony's Bar & Grill could offer a single shred of new evidence to help with the investigation. Sami knew going in that tracking down the serial killer would be a formidable challenge, but she hoped she'd have more to go on than the few bits and pieces of information.

Josephine walked into the living room and sat next to Sami.

"How you feeling, Mom?"

"So-so."

"What's bothering you?"

Josephine shook her head. "No matter how much I sleep, I'm still exhausted."

"Doctor Templeton told us that you'd feel this way for a few months." Sami took a long swig of her beer. "Where are Emily and Angelina?"

"They walked down to the Tot Lot."

"Why didn't you go with them?"

"Too tired."

"No matter how tired you feel, you have to walk at least to the corner and back every day. That's the only way you're going to get your strength back."

"I lose my breath after walking only half a block."

"Do you feel any chest pain?"

"No. Just out of breath."

"If you want to feel better, you have to force yourself to walk."

"Maybe tomorrow."

Josephine squeezed Sami's leg. "Have you thought about going to church with me on Sunday like I asked?"

With all that had been going on, Sami had forgotten about her mother's request. But she felt forced to lie. "Been thinking about it."

"And?"

Born and raised Catholic, Sami had wandered away from the church and religion shortly after she divorced. Hoping to avoid any serious discussions, when asked about her religious beliefs, she would kiddingly say that she was a recovering Catholic.

"Still thinking about it, Mom."

"Well, don't think too long. God is not all that patient."

Sami believed in God, or more accurately, a Supreme Being or Higher Power, but she had never been able to clearly define Him, or feel a strong connection. No matter how hard she tried, Sami just couldn't accept the fact that a righteous, all-powerful God could allow so much pain and suffering in the world. As a homicide investigator, exposed to evil deeds beyond imagination, her feelings were skewed. Unlike the average citizen, she'd seen more than her share of death—innocent children strangled and burned and tortured unmercifully, shootings, stabbings, victims beaten beyond recognition. How could a just God let so much evil exist?

"If you don't want to go to church, that's fine," Josephine said. "But at least drop me off and pick me up."

"Of course." Sami realized that her mother's sudden urge to reunite with God was driven by her recent surgery and the very real possibility that her life could be over in an instant. "I'm not so sure I'll join you though."

"You've been angry with God for a long time," Josephine said. "Ever since He took your father. It's time to make peace before it's too late."

Julian and Nicole had just finished the Chinese takeout and a bottle of Jordan Cabernet, and were settled into the cushy leather sofa. The critics of *Wine Spectator* magazine would turn up their noses at such an incompatible food and wine combo, but Jordan was Julian's favorite red, so he could easily drink it with popcorn.

"Tell me about this cabin in Big Bear," Nicole said.

Julian had feared she wouldn't let it rest. "Considering that we're never going to buy it, I'd rather not."

"Would you just stop being so difficult and *please* tell me about the fucking cabin?"

There were few things about Nicole that Julian hated more than her sharp tongue.

"It's about two hundred feet from the lake, has three bedrooms, two baths, and a fireplace. And it's a hundred thousand dollars more than we can afford."

"Why did you even look at it in the first place? Did you really think you'd have that much wiggle room in the price?"

Knowing Nicole, he had anticipated that his little white lie would turn into a grand inquisition. "Look, Nicole, I wanted to surprise you and it just didn't work out. It seems that the only thank you I get is you breaking my balls. Can we just drop it?"

"You can be such an asshole sometimes." She stood up, but Julian grabbed her arm. "Let go of me."

"I'm not finished yet," he almost shouted.

"Well, I am." She twisted her forearm and broke free of his grip. "I'm going to bed. Why don't you sleep in the spare bedroom tonight."

"Are you serious?"

"Fucking totally."

At that particular moment in time, as he watched his wife disappear up the stairway, it became glaringly apparent to him that sometimes he actually hated Nicole. Both high-strung, they had many shouting matches during their marriage, some standing toe to toe. But never had he felt as much animosity toward her as he did right now. She was his wife and the mother of his children. But something in this marriage had to change. Someone had to give in. And he'd be damned if it was him.

He had his choice of two upstairs bedrooms, but he didn't even want to hear her breathing tonight. He grabbed a set of sheets and a cotton blanket from the linen closet, haphazardly made up the sofa, kicked off his shoes, and eased into bed. He closed his eyes and couldn't wait for morning. Tomorrow wouldn't come soon enough.

CHAPTER TWENTY-TWO

Wearing Oakley sunglasses and a Chargers baseball cap, the visor resting low on his forehead, Julian sat at a small table in the quiet, out-of-the-way coffee shop. He watched customers zoom in and out until a man fitting the PI's description walked in the front door and cranked his head from side to side. The squatty man, at least fifty pounds overweight, full head of silver hair, fixed his stare on Julian's cap and walked over to the table.

"Mr. Spencer?" Julian asked.

The man nodded.

Julian gestured. "Please have a seat."

Spencer offered his clammy hand. When Julian grasped it, he regretted doing so. They barely shook and Julian quickly withdrew his hand.

"Before we get started," Julian said. "You're okay with me remaining completely anonymous, is that correct?"

"As long as your cash is legal tender, I don't give a hoot who you are." The man leaned in and lowered his voice. "I'm the King of Discretion."

Julian slid an envelope across the table. "Three thousand, right?"

Without checking the contents, Spencer slid the envelope in the inside pocket of his sport jacket. "If it takes more than a week, three hundred a day."

"And it's okay to call your cell phone?" Julian asked.

"That's the only way to reach me."

Spencer removed a notepad and pencil from his side pocket. "Subject's name?"

"Sami Rizzo."

Spencer cocked his head. "*Detective* Sami Rizzo?"

"Is that a problem?"

"I don't give a shit who it is. If the money's right, I'll tail the Pope. I only asked cause I'm curious."

"And you're absolutely okay with it?"

"No problem." He scribbled on his notepad. "What am I looking for?"

"I want to know where she goes. Who she's working with. When she takes a piss. And I want to know who she lives with. Their names. Relationship to her. Their daily routines."

Julian realized it was risky for him to expose himself to a private investigator. But as much as he didn't want to admit it, he feared Detective Rizzo, and if through the PI's efforts Julian was tipped off that she was getting close, he might find a way to sidetrack her.

Spencer continued making notes. "That's a tall order and it's not going to be easy. Her being a cop and all. It might take longer than a week."

"How much longer?"

Spencer lifted a shoulder. "Don't know."

They sat silently, fixed stares, as if trying to read each other's minds.

"I have to ask the obligatory question," Spencer said. "I push the envelope beyond legal limits more often than not, but I *do* have limits." His voice softened to a whisper. "There's nothing criminal going on here, right?"

"Look, Mr. Spencer. This is totally personal. Sami and I used to date. Need I say more?"

"How do I reach you?" Spencer asked.

"You don't. I reach you."

"But how do I get information to you?"

Julian handed Spencer a piece of paper. "Mail it to this PO box."

He examined the note and laughed. "John Smith, huh?" He folded the paper and stuffed it in his pocket. "And if I need to reach you immediately?"

"I'll call you twice a day."

Spencer thought about that for a minute. "Fair enough."

"There is one more thing," Julian said. "This is the first and last time we'll ever meet face to face."

In spite of all the police-related tasks Sami faced, not to mention the tremendous pressure she felt to apprehend the serial killer, Friday at 11:00 a.m., she set everything aside, outlined a list of things to do for Detective Osbourn, and discretely checked out of the precinct.

She sat in her car for several minutes, thinking about where she could find a quiet, remote setting. After careful thought, she decided that Presidio Park, a fifty-acre haven of lush greenery overlooking Mission Bay and the Pacific Ocean, would work perfectly.

When she exited Freeway 8 and pulled into the unpaved parking lot, Sami let out a sigh of relief when she saw only three cars. "Terrific." Considering the size of the park, she felt confident she'd find a secluded spot where she could be alone with her thoughts.

As she laced her Timberland hiking boots, she glanced at her watch: 11:30. In thirty minutes, Simon Kwosokowski had a long-overdue appointment with his God.

Sami found a trail leading up a steep hill, snaking through a dense patch of trees. Near the top of the hill, she discovered an open area covered with a bed of dried leaves, pinecones, and green moss. She picked a spot that looked most comfortable and sat on the dirt.

Again she glanced at her watch: 11:53.

She closed her eyes and wondered if Simon had read the letter she'd mailed him. She'd sent it FedEx overnight, and even called Warden Marshall and asked him to personally see to it that Simon got the letter. But even if he had gotten it, how could she be sure he read it? She didn't feel any different, except that the rage in her belly had calmed down a bit. Perhaps, she thought, at twelve noon, when lethal poison coursed through Simon's veins and life drained from his body, and he could never hurt Angelina or her again, maybe she'd feel the sense of relief she'd been longing for.

The sun, shaded by the thick of trees, could not warm the uncharacteristically chilly air. Usually, June brought with it warmer air from the deserts and cool ocean breezes. But today, Sami felt as if it were February. Her mind, a kaleidoscope of colorful thoughts, raced out of control. She pulled her knees to her chest and hugged her legs, trying to force herself to focus on Simon.

As she watched the minute hand on her Seiko moving closer to noon, she tried to piece together all the components of her harrowing experience with Simon, hoping to find some grain of comfort. His execution would of course end his physical existence. But how could she get his emotional presence lifted from her mind?

Just before noon, Simon Kwosokowski stands next to a padded table, facing an anxious group of onlookers ready to witness his execution. The warden stands to his side.

"Any last words?" the warden asks.

"I deeply regret not being able to fulfill my promise to the Almighty. I can only hope and pray that another true believer walks in my shoes and carries on with God's work."

A crowd of restless onlookers sits silently and observes. As death draws near, Simon smiles at them, hoping they understand that he doesn't feel even the slightest bit of remorse. Two prison guards strap Simon to a padded table—arms, legs, and torso. The technician places an IV drip in Simon's arm. He can see the three glass cylinders sitting adjacent to the table, each filled with a lethal drug that will end his life. He glances at the warden and sees the smug look of victory in his eyes. Simon can't see the witnesses on the other side of the one-way glass, but wonders if Sami Rizzo sits among the crowd. He has read her letter three times, each time feeling more perplexed. That she could forgive him was beyond anything he could imagine. For the first time since meeting Sami, he admires her. For he could never be so forgiving. And in a sense, she has defeated him.

At exactly twelve noon, Warden Marshall gives the technician a nod and he pushes a red button marked number one. Slowly, a plunger in one of the three glass cylinders compresses the first drug, and forces the sodium thiopental, a powerful anesthetic, into Simon's IV. Making his eyes heavy, and his body feeling like he just drank a bottle of bourbon, the strong sedative takes hold almost immediately. Moments before the drug renders him unconsciousness, he thinks of his mother.

After four minutes, the technician pushes button number two, and a heavy dose of pancuronium bromide is pushed into Simon's vein. The drug causes complete muscle paralysis. He is not only unconscious, he can't even breathe. Last, the technician administers a lethal dose of a barbiturate and potassium chloride solution that permanently stops his heart. The entire process is over in less than eight minutes.

I'm coming, Mother. In a few minutes, we will be reunited.

Foolish boy. In a few minutes, the Lord will pass judgment on you and sentence you to spend eternity in the fires of hell.

Simon Kwosokowski's last earthy thought grips his heart and crushes it. He now realizes that his beloved mother had betrayed him and led him down a path to eternal condemnation. What was once righteous was now a disgrace.

A doctor presses a stethoscope to his chest and gives the warden a quick nod. The doctor pronounces Simon Kwosokowski dead at 12:10 p.m.

Andrew McDonald, husband of Peggy McDonald, Simon's fourth victim, sits among the onlookers. Before he leaves the room, he looks at Simon for the first and last time. "Rot in hell, you son of a bitch."

Sitting on the leaves, Sami looked at her watch. It was now twelve fifteen. Unless the governor issued a stay of execution, Sami felt certain that Simon Kwosokowski no longer breathed earthly air. She had hoped to feel significant relief from his grip, but she felt no different than she did last week or last year for that matter. She had no lofty expectations that her experience with him would be erased completely from her mind, but she did think she'd feel some relief.

Disappointed that such a significant event had little effect on her, she brushed herself off and made her way to her car. Once inside she changed her shoes and sat quietly for a moment with her eyes closed. Like so many times when she'd made a significant decision, Sami felt the angst of buyer's remorse. She had little doubt that police work was her calling. But she didn't feel prepared to lead the serial killer investigation. Enthusiasm was not the problem. But a lack of confidence was. All eyes were on her. Most people, her supporters. But some, male chauvinists like D'Angelo, licked their chops waiting for her to fail. Many social and cultural issues regarding equality had evolved, but female cops still rode in the back of the bus.

Never in her wildest dreams did she believe that her return to police work would instantly place her in a pressure cooker. Sami shouldered tremendous stress right now—not only as a homicide investigator, but also in her personal life. Aleta was on her mind constantly, and she was deeply concerned for her mother's well-being. And of course, she missed having Al next to her at night when she crawled into bed.

She started her car, ready to head back to the precinct.

Time to be a cop again.

Just as she grasped the shift lever, her cell phone rang.

"Hi, Detective Rizzo. This is Maggie Fox. Doctor Templeton just left the lab. Is this a good time to talk?"

"Absolutely. Did he offer any insights about the surgical procedures?"

"Only that there is a technique called the Maze Procedure to treat an ailment called atrial fibrillation—A-Fib for short. And the incisions are in the same area of the heart where this procedure is usually performed."

"What exactly is A-Fib?"

"It's a particular type of arrhythmia. It's generally associated with a rapid heartbeat or a quivering of the upper chambers of the heart. It's a malfunction in the heart's electrical system. The Maze Procedure is about eighty percent effective in curing this condition."

"I don't get it," Sami said. "Did all of the victims have this A-Fib condition?"

"That's highly unlikely. We can get a court order to obtain the medical records to see if there is any history of A-Fib in any of the four victims. But I seriously doubt it."

"Why?"

"Because typically, this condition occurs in people fifty years and older. That's not carved in granite, but that's the norm."

"What did Doctor Templeton have to say about the procedures our perp performed on the victims' other organs?"

"No logical explanation."

"Is there anything logical about this guy?"

"Here's what really puzzles me," Maggie said. "It seems obvious to me that the killer performed CPR and also used a defibrillator to resuscitate each victim. So, whatever his motive, it appears that he tried to keep them alive as long as possible."

"But why?"

"That, Detective, is the million-dollar question."

CHAPTER TWENTY-THREE

Peter Spencer, Private Investigator, a man who specialized in shady surveillances and questionable background checks, sat in his twelve-by-twelve office, chewing on an unlit Dutch Masters cigar. He pulled the envelope out of his inside pocket, tore it open, and poured the stack of hundred-dollar bills on his desk. Oh, how he loved Ben Franklin.

There was a time when Peter J. Spencer III occupied a plush suite atop an executive office building and employed a staff of ten. That was before his wife filed for divorce and took nearly everything but his underwear. California, at least in theory, was supposed to be a community-property state, unless you hired the right attorney. And that's exactly what Helen had done. She had brought new meaning to the cliché, "Took him to the cleaners."

When his business collapsed, he decided that he could make more money catering to clients with a shady agenda. Why? Because he could pretty much set his fees ridiculously high. And most clients would pay anything to get what they wanted. What he found most curious was the fact that nearly all of his clients were wealthy. Not six-figure wealthy, *obscenely* wealthy. This peculiar fact lead Spencer to believe that the super-rich were all dubious characters.

He fired up his desktop computer and waited patiently for the system to boot up. PI work had really evolved over the last decade. He remembered the days when it would take weeks, if not months to gather background and family-related information. Back then, a PI really earned his money. The Internet had opened up a whole new world. In this day and age, no identity was safe, nor could a person manage their affairs privately. The world had become a melting pot of names, dates, places, and people, each and every one of them as transparent as Saran wrap—if you knew where to look. The information he had uncovered with just a few clicks of his mouse and a valid credit card could make the CIA jealous.

Staring at the computer screen, Spencer felt overwhelmed with curiosity. Why was his new client, "Mr. John Smith," so afraid to divulge his identity? Why did he want so much information on a homicide detective? Spencer had promised the mysterious client total discretion, but who would find out if the PI conducted his own little covert operation?

Spencer went into his favorites menu and clicked on www.anyfamilyhistory.com. He typed "Samantha Rizzo" in the first field, added the city and state, then waited for the Web site to perform its magic.

Sami pulled into the precinct parking lot and sat in her car for a few minutes. She expected that Captain Davidson and Police Chief Larson would bushwhack her the moment she walked in the door, demanding to know what progress she'd made in the investigation. Thus far, she had little to share with them. Soon the pressure would be unbearable.

All serial killers shared certain characteristics. Sami searched her brain, trying to remember everything she could about Simon, hoping that it might trigger something she'd overlooked. She remembered their dinner, the time she'd spent locked in his Room of Redemption, how he'd kidnapped Angelina, the long conversations they'd had trying to outwit each other, his deceptive charm.

She was just about to step out of the car when it hit her like a Louisville Slugger. In one clarifying moment, two years of confusion, countless sleepless nights, overwhelming fear, and an inability to end this dark chapter in her life came into full focus. She now understood why she couldn't let go. Why Simon had such a firm grip on her. Why she couldn't purge the haunting memory from her thoughts. Why forgiving him fell short. Simon hadn't abducted Angelina and Sami the way he had the other four women. Sami's reckless heroics, her ego-driven desire to solve this case completely on her own, with no backup and no viable plan, had placed Angelina and her in a life-threatening situation. It was not Simon who had placed her in harm's way. She had been the architect of her own near-demise.

For over two years, she'd misunderstood her emotions and it had quietly tortured her. Her guilt, hidden to the point that she lived in denial, never allowed her to take responsibility for her reckless actions. And the one factor that made the situation so utterly unbearable was the painful fact that Sami had not only placed herself in a dangerous situation, she had also jeopardized Angelina's life, the one person she loved and cherished more than anyone else. Sami now understood that her inability to confront this issue head-on served as a roadblock to her recovery.

It all made sense.

She had learned through a year of intense therapy that the first step toward healing an open wound was to first acknowledge that you actually have one, and step two was to take responsibility, something she hadn't done. For over two years, she had pointed an accusing finger at Simon, when she should have pointed it at her reflection in the mirror.

She stepped out of the car and felt light on her feet, as if a yoke had been removed from her shoulders and neck. She didn't expect that this sudden revelation in and of itself would close the chapter. She had lots of work to do. More sessions with Doctor J. But for the first time since her ordeal, she eagerly welcomed a modest sense of peace.

"I think it's time for us to kiss and make up. Don't you?" Nicole said.

Julian had just stepped out of the shower. He stood in the bathroom doorway, toweling off his body, his hair dripping on the travertine floor. Nicole lay on the bed, just awake from a short nap. This was the kind of workday Julian loved. Two early-morning surgeries and home by noon. It didn't happen often, but when it did, he took advantage of it.

Nicole sat up and let her robe fall off her shoulders, exposing a completely tanned, golden bronze body with not one bikini line. Julian studied her carefully, pleased that her personal trainer had earned his hefty fee.

"Come over here," Nicole ordered.

A bit skeptical, Julian sauntered toward the bed, bath towel wrapped around his waist and legs. At first, he assumed that for whatever reason, Nicole was uncharacteristically horny today, but even so, he had no hope for more than another hundred-yard dash. He did, however, see an unusually playful look in Nicole's eyes.

When she sat on the side of the bed, he noticed that her Brazilian bikini wax was gone and she was now cleanly-shaved. How many times had he tried unsuccessfully to convince her to completely shave? Why now? Was she extending a rare invitation to make love without the hang-ups and inhibitions, or was it business as usual with a little twist?

Nicole slid her hand inside the towel and gently stroked him. His body responded immediately. Still uncertain of her intentions, Julian stood frozen.

"I've been such a bitch lately," she admitted. "It's as if I've had my period for six months. I think it's time I make it up to you."

He had no expectations. Based on past experiences, how could he? She had trained him well, and he'd been down this path before. He guessed that she would lie on her back like a corpse, let him have his way with her, and like a well-practiced routine, the encounter would be over with no fanfare and no surprises. He believed hookers called it a "straight lay."

"Would you like to try something different?" she offered.

This heightened his curiosity.

"What did you have in mind?" he asked, an air of reservation in his voice.

"How do you want me?"

A loaded question, he thought. If he told her the truth, surely she'd think her husband was a depraved pervert. "What are my options?"

Nicole smiled a mischievous smile he had never seen before. She stroked him with more resolve. "I'm feeling a bit naughty today. In fact, I'm feeling wicked. You can fuck me any way your little heart desires."

Her comment caught him totally off guard. Rachael, formerly referred to as Redhead, had said something similar to him, and he had given her everything. He didn't want to question Nicole's supposed willingness to accommodate him in any way he desired, but he guessed there would be limits to her naughtiness. "Are you serious?"

"There's only one way to find out."

"I want to tie your wrists to the bed and take you from behind." An image of his cousins, Rebecca and Marianne, flashed through his mind. He waited for a harsh response.

"Sounds interesting. One question though. When you say 'behind,' are you talking—"

"Yes." He didn't let her finish.

"Will it hurt?"

He shrugged. "Never done it."

There was a long silence.

"Go get two of your neckties."

Totally aware that Nicole had never done this before, Julian's rhythm was slow and gentle at first and he proceeded cautiously. But as his excitement heightened, as memories of his cousins' abuse illuminated in his mind, his actions were more forceful.

"That *hurts*," Nicole almost yelled.

He ignored her and continued thrusting without restraint or concern for her comfort.

"*Stop!*" she yelled. "You're fucking hurting me."

Without awareness or forethought, totally involuntary, Julian grasped Nicole's shoulders and lost all control. Now his actions were borderline violent. His excitement grew to a wildly familiar level. He could see the shadowy shed and hear his cousins moaning.

This is for you, Marianne.

This is for you, Rebecca.

Crying uncontrollably now, helplessly trying to stop Julian, Nicole frantically struggled to free her wrists from the headboard. "Please, Julian." Her voice was barely audible.

Suddenly, the moment Julian climaxed, reality returned. Nicole collapsed on the bed and began to cry hysterically.

He had no idea what to say.

Sami walked into the precinct and headed straight for Detective Osbourn's desk. He had a telephone pressed to his ear and rocked back and forth in the chair. When he spotted Sami, he acknowledged her with a quick wave. He held the telephone away from his ear, but standing a few feet away she could still hear whoever was on the other end of the line speaking loudly.

Osbourn covered the mouthpiece. "Judge Foster," he whispered. "And he ain't happy."

Sami gestured for him to give her the phone.

"Judge Foster, Detective Rizzo just walked in. Please hang on." He handed the phone to Sami and mouthed, *Good luck.*

"This is Detective Rizzo, Judge."

"Why did I have to read in the newspaper that you are now heading the serial killer investigation? What happened to Detective Diaz?"

"He got called away to a family emergency."

"What could possibly be more important than finding my daughter's killer?"

"I can understand your concern, Judge, but I am perfectly capable of taking over."

"Have you found him yet? Is the son of a bitch behind bars?"

"Not yet, I'm afraid."

"You'd better be afraid, Detective. Afraid for your job. Detective Diaz convinced me to give my consent for a thorough autopsy, and even though it went against my better judgment, I agreed." He huffed. "I let them fillet my daughter like a laboratory animal and what did it yield? Did it get you even one millimeter closer to apprehending this maniac?"

"We're piecing lots of things together right now, and I really believe we'll arrest this guy soon." If only she could believe her own words.

"Don't patronize me, Detective. I've been in this business way too long. Do you have any suspects at all?"

"Not at this time."

"So, thus far, four young people have been brutally murdered, and you don't even have a *lead*?"

"I truly understand your frustrations, Judge Foster, however—"

"*Frustrations*, Detective? Let me make *my* frustrations perfectly clear. If this monster isn't behind bars in the next week, I strongly suggest you update your résumé. Is that clear enough?"

Sami heard a click.

Osbourn rested his elbows on his desk and steepled his fingers. "So, Detective Rizzo, how was *your* day?" He grinned like a crazed chimpanzee.

"Oh, I've had better. But then again, I've had worse." She leaned against his desk and folded her arms. "I don't suppose you made any headway today."

He shook his head. "All we've got is Katie Mitchell's description of this guy. The autopsies yielded nothing we can sink our teeth into, except that the perp is probably some renegade doctor. Where do we go from here?"

"We pray, Detective Osbourn. We pray."

CHAPTER TWENTY-FOUR

Using the most reliable and sophisticated Web sites available, and utilizing his extensive resources, in less than two days of intense research, Peter Spencer learned just about everything there was to know about Sami Rizzo and her entire family. What he couldn't find in public records, he found through a network of "back-door" cronies. He knew more about her than about his own brother. Unlike the average citizen living a quiet life away from the public limelight, Detective Rizzo's visibility in the media made it much easier for him to access even the most obscure facts.

He knew when Sami had made her confirmation, where she made it, and who sponsored her. He knew the amount of life insurance she received when her ex-husband was murdered, and where she deposited the check. He knew the exact hour her father, Angelo Rizzo, died; how long he'd been a cop; and whom he'd partnered with for eleven years. He knew Angelina's birth date and that Detective Diaz currently occupied her bed. He learned that her mother, Josephine Rizzo, just underwent open heart surgery, and he knew where she had the operation. He found out that her cousin, Emily Rizzo, just received her nursing degree from the Bay Area College of Nursing and maintained a 3.8 grade point average. He even discovered that Sami had been in therapy with Doctor Theresa Janowitz for more than a year. He uncovered details about Samantha Marie Rizzo that her mother didn't even know.

Peter J. Spencer III could write Sami Rizzo's biography.

Now that he had this information, the next step was surveillance, the part of PI work he hated most. Although the Internet yielded significant personal data on everyone from a garbage collector to the president, PI work still required some hands-on responsibilities. But considering Sami Rizzo's reputation and her keen detective instincts, he couldn't merely park his sedan across the street from her home, monitor her actions, and observe the activities of the people who shared her home. No, Spencer had to take a different approach. And at this particular moment, he wasn't sure what that might be.

Maybe Spencer's longtime friend, Detective Chuck D'Angelo, a man who consistently walked a narrow line between ethical police work and self-indulgence, might offer some assistance as he'd done so many times in the past. D'Angelo was always looking for some action on the side. Short of homicide, he was game for almost anything—as long as the price was right. D'Angelo would retire soon and surely he could use a little mad money.

"You need help, Julian. Serious fucking help." Nicole massaged her shoulders right where his hands had left black and blue marks.

"I'm so sorry. I have no idea what came over me." He knew *exactly* what had come over him. He reached for her hand but she retracted as if a rattlesnake was trying to bite her.

"If my parents see these fucking bruises on my shoulders—"

"I've been under a lot of stress lately," he said. "I just lost control."

"You could have seriously hurt me. I'm not going to be able to sit down for a week. Is that the way you want sex? Are you into S and M?"

"Of course not."

"Well, something isn't right. And I can tell you firsthand that until you see a sex therapist about this fixation, don't even think about touching me. For now, consider our relationship platonic."

She was right. He *was* out of control. And he had to protect Nicole. After all, she had given birth to his beautiful daughters. Didn't he owe her something? "Would you feel more comfortable if we separated for a while?"

She fixed her eyes on him. "Seriously?"

"Maybe it's best."

She stood quietly for a minute, examining her fingernails. "Where would you stay?"

She knew nothing about his loft apartment. "There are lots of extended-stay hotels."

"What about the kids?"

"I'll pick them up a couple nights a week and take them on weekends. They don't have to know we're separated."

Nicole touched her shoulders again and let out a soft moan. "I think you should leave today."

Julian never dreamed that he'd have to take such drastic measures. But at this particular moment, he felt overwhelmed with both apprehension and anticipation. Being separated from Nicole was manageable. It gave him the freedom to aggressively pursue subjects for his research. But the thought of not seeing his daughters every day gnawed at him. Somehow, he had to focus.

The needs of the many outweigh the needs of the few.

✡ ✡ ✡

It had been over a week since Ricardo, his sister's lover, had summoned Al to Rio. Except for the few nights Al rented a hotel room out of sheer exhaustion, and the short breaks to get some fresh air or grab a quick bite of cafeteria food, he hadn't left Aleta's side. He spent hours talking to her, holding her hand, gently stroking her arm, but with each day that passed and she remained in a coma, he felt more and more hopeless.

He had even lost track of time. One day blended into another. He wasn't sure if today was Wednesday or Sunday. What difference did it make? He spoke to Sami every day, if for nothing else than to hear her voice. Thus far, he hadn't had anything new to report. He felt deep concern for Sami's welfare. He guessed that the captain, Chief Larson, and the mayor herself, would have little patience with the investigation. They didn't want to hear about dead-end streets, lack of evidence, or sketchy details. They wanted results. No excuses. No sob stories. In spite of his confidence in Sami's skills as a competent detective, Al couldn't help but feel that she might be in over her head. If she didn't apprehend the serial killer soon, her future as a homicide investigator would be in serious jeopardy. But as much as Al wanted to support Sami and be there for her, right now he had to focus his attention on Aleta.

He had always believed that South American coffee was the world's best. But the cafeteria convincingly disproved this theory. Never had he tasted such bitter rotgut. He only drank it to jump-start his brain.

Al walked into his sister's hospital room, sipping the last of the coffee, his face puckered as if he were drinking burnt molasses. He glanced at the heart monitor. Aleta's blood pressure was a little low, but her vitals were holding steady. He assumed his position on the uncomfortable steel chair next to her bed and as he had done every time he walked in the room, he kissed her on the cheek. Just then, Nurse Sofia walked in.

"Hello, Mr. Diaz."

He had told the head nurse repeatedly to call him Al, but she continued to address him formally. He guessed it was just part of the Brazilian culture.

"You're back again?" Al asked. Sofia had already been in to check on Aleta twice today, which alarmed Al. "Has anything changed?"

"Your sister is stable."

As the nurse checked Aleta's IV bag and performed other duties, Al noticed that she seemed a bit jittery. "Are you okay, Sofia?"

She continued with her tasks and looked at Al over her shoulder. "Everything is fine."

When Sofia finished with her duties she lingered as if she didn't want to leave. She approached Al and stood in front of him, obviously nervous. Tall and shapely, her eyes were as dark as espresso beans. When she smiled, her teeth looked like they could be in a Colgate commercial.

"Mr. Diaz, I hope I do not offend you, but I have watched you sitting here every day, hour after hour, by your sister's side. She is very lucky to have you as a brother."

"Thank you."

"I have heard that you are here alone without your family, and I feel sad that you are by yourself. Please excuse me for being forward, but I would like to invite you to my family's home for dinner. It would be very good for you to get away from the hospital for a short time. Our home is very close to the hospital, so if there was an emergency, you could return quickly."

Sofia had caught Al completely off guard. "That is so sweet of you, but—"

"My mother makes the best *feijoada* in all of Brazil. Please say yes."

"Let me think about it, okay?"

"As you wish." She smiled warmly and left the room.

It took Al a few minutes to gather his thoughts. He moved the chair closer to the bed, the sweet scent of Sofia lingering in the air.

"Good morning, Sunflower." He had given her this nickname when she was just a child. Their parents, impoverished as they were, had managed to save enough money to take a short weekend vacation. They went to a beautiful park with acres of six-foot-tall sunflowers. Aleta, barely four feet tall, was totally intrigued with these golden flowers towering over her. Since that day, he'd affectionately called her Sunflower.

Holding her hand and occasionally talking to her as if she were conscious, he felt his eyes growing heavy. He was about to stand up and stretch his legs when he felt Aleta squeeze his hand ever so slightly. He had held her hands for hours and hours, and never had she responded with even the slightest sign of life. Was it merely a reflex?

Al could barely find his voice he was so startled. "If you can hear me, Sunflower, squeeze my hand again."

Nothing.

"You can do it, Sweetheart. Please squeeze my hand."

Still nothing.

He sat quietly for a minute, guessing that he had dozed off and it was just his imagination. But then she squeezed his hand again. This time with a little more force.

"Sunflower, this is Alberto. I'm here, Sweetheart. Can you hear me?"

Again she squeezed his hand.

Al studied her face carefully, looking for any sign of consciousness. Her face looked frozen. No eye movement. No twitches. No nothing.

Not wanting to leave her for even a second, Al pushed the nurse's call button clipped to the side of the bed. In less than a minute, a nurse dashed in the room.

"Do you speak English?" Al asked.

"Little bit."

"Where is Dr. Souza?"

"He is making rounds."

"Find him and tell him to get here *immediately!*"

CHAPTER TWENTY-FIVE

Julian had just finished unpacking his three Vuitton suitcases, and neatly placed his clothes in closets and dresser drawers. Happy to be relaxing in his loft, the place he'd now be calling home for who knew how long, he poured himself a glass of Jordan Cabernet and sat on the sofa.

He wasn't yet sure how he would handle visits with his daughters. He certainly couldn't let them see his loft, particularly if he was conducting experiments. Perhaps when he picked them up he'd have to rent a hotel room. He'd take them out to dinner, of course, but wasn't quite sure what other activities would satisfy them. If it were up to him, just sitting next to his kids, sharing a bowl of popcorn, watching a movie would suit him just fine. He had promised Nicole that he'd pick them up two nights a week and on weekends. But depending on his activities, he might have to change the schedule. There was no way for him to predict when his research would conflict with his visits.

As content as he felt at this particular moment, flashbacks of what he had done to Nicole still troubled him. Was he losing control? Had his cousins warped him forever? For the last couple of years he had been struggling with his marriage. Hating any kind of altercation, he never confronted the difficult issues with Nicole. He just let them fester. But unlike Julian, Nicole loved a verbal showdown.

If he felt reasonably comfortable that his kids would be okay and not suffer from the deep emotional wounds so often inflicted by divorce, he might have had the nerve to hire a good attorney a long time ago. But he understood all too well what it felt like to be unloved. And he didn't ever want his kids to deal with the same psychological damage.

His unhappiness with their marriage still didn't address his motivation to hurt Nicole. Why would he force himself on her with no regard for her welfare? Had he been so caught up in the moment that for one brief period of time he got lost in his emotions? Was Nicole merely a vessel that allowed him to punish Marianne and Rebecca? One thing was certain: No matter what the circumstances, he could never let it happen again.

Julian gulped the last of the wine and flipped open his cell phone. He dialed the number he'd already memorized. "Have you made any progress?"

PI Spencer knew better than to discuss anything sensitive over the telephone. "Big Brother" was always listening. "The wheels are in motion."

"Do you have anything for me yet?" Julian asked.

"I've got a whole package of goodies."

"Are you familiar with Post Office Plus on Girard Street in La Jolla?"

"Next to the Italian bakery?"

"That's it. Would you mind dropping off the package this afternoon? I'll pick it up first thing in the morning. Do you still have my PO box info?"

"I do, Mr. Smith," Spencer said.

"Terrific. Anything else?"

"Call me tomorrow."

"How's your sister?" Sami asked, squeezing her eyes shut, preparing herself for his answer.

"Well, believe it or not, she's slightly improved." Al explained how his sister had squeezed his hand and that he requested the doctor perform another EEG.

"I am so glad to hear that."

"She's still in a coma, but her brain activity is almost normal."

"So what happens now?"

"It's still a waiting game," Al said.

"Is the doctor optimistic?"

"Cautiously."

"I can't imagine what you've been going through," Sami said.

"How you holding up? What's going on with the investigation?"

Al had enough on his mind, so Sami carefully filtered her answer. "I'm hanging tough. No major breakthroughs in the case, but I'm piecing things together."

"So, in other words, you've got nada, right?"

"Guess I can't bullshit a cop."

"Are the captain and chief turning the thumbscrews?"

"Not yet, but I expect to get bludgeoned at any moment," Sami said.

"Don't let 'em intimidate you."

"I can deal with them. I'm not so sure I can handle Mayor Sullivan."

"She's a tough cookie."

Silence.

"I have something I want to share with you, Sami."

How she hated when people started sentences like that. "Should I fasten my seatbelt?"

"You may need to."

Her mind flooded with a range of possibilities, all of which were unsavory. Did he meet some Brazilian hottie? Have a change of heart about their relationship? "Okay, now that my armpits are all sweaty, what's going on?"

"Since flying down here, I've had nothing but time on my hands. Time to think. Time to evaluate my life. Time to look at things from a different perspective."

She didn't like the way this was heading. But she held her breath and listened. She was hopelessly in love with Al, and if he was about to dump her from six thousand miles away...

"I've expressed how I feel about God and religion and evolution," Al continued.

"I know. God and religion are fairy tales and evolution is scientific."

"Well, maybe I've been wrong."

"In what regard?"

"You're not going to believe this, but I've been praying. And the strange thing is, I haven't any idea who I'm praying to. Watching my sister lying helplessly in that hospital bed, fighting for her life—"

"There's nothing wrong with praying. We all seek God when the chips are down. Haven't you ever heard the saying, 'There are no atheists in foxholes'?"

"Doesn't that make me a hypocrite?"

"No, it makes you human." Al didn't often expose his vulnerabilities. In fact, until this moment, Sami wasn't sure he had any. His willingness to share this intimate situation warmed her heart. "Don't feel you have to apologize for seeking God."

"But suppose she doesn't pull through? Suppose God doesn't answer my prayers?"

"I'm not exactly in good graces with God, so how can I give spiritual advice? Maybe you should talk to someone about this."

"Who?"

"Brazil is one of the most Catholic countries in the world. Surely the hospital has a priest or chaplain who visits sick patients regularly."

"That's not a bad idea," Al said.

"See. Once in a while I can actually say something meaningful."

"Thanks for listening to me whine."

"Not to worry. I fully intend to return the favor." She felt a bit choked up. "Send my love to Aleta."

Peter J. Spencer III was starting to think that his newest client didn't have the best intentions. Spencer had no problem operating outside the law. But when he drove to Post Office Plus and dropped off the package for his client, his gut instincts, which usually were reliable, led him to believe that "John Smith" might be involved in a sinister plan.

If, in fact, his mystery client and Detective Rizzo had been romantically involved, Spencer could understand why he might want to find out what she was doing and with whom. As a PI for over twenty-five years, he had seen it all—everything from jealous spouses to disgruntled employees to crooked politicians to Mafia vendettas to sexual perverts. Nothing could possibly surprise Spencer. But he felt certain there was more to the "John Smith" story. The logical side of his brain told him to let it go and just do what his client paid him to do. But his bloodhound nature wouldn't stop asking questions he could not answer.

Against his better judgment, Spencer decided to pay a little visit to Post Office Plus first thing in the morning. Surely "John Smith" would arrive in an automobile. One with a California license plate. A plate that could be traced by a number of Spencer's contacts.

CHAPTER TWENTY-SIX

"So, how's the investigation going?" Chuck D'Angelo asked, a smirk spread across his face.

Sami had just arrived at the precinct, hadn't even taken a sip of her Starbucks, and the last thing in the world she needed was D'Angelo busting her balls.

"No arrests yet, but I'm sniffing out a few leads."

"Any suspects?" D'Angelo asked.

"None worth talking about."

"You must be putting in lots of hours."

"A few more than normal, but I guess there really isn't a normal in this business, huh?"

"Any word from Al? How his sister is doing? When he's coming back?"

Just what she needed: a grand inquisition from her least favorite person, first thing in the morning. The Angels of Mercy must be angry with me, she thought.

"She's by no means out of the woods yet, but she's showing some improvement."

"Well that's good to hear." D'Angelo rested his butt against her desk. "How's your mom coming along after her surgery?"

In all the years she had worked with D'Angelo, they had never carried on a conversation for more than two minutes. Particularly one where he asked the questions and she provided the answers. Why the sudden interest?

"How did you hear about my mom?"

"Overheard a conversation between Al and the captain."

She wanted to say, "In other words you were sticking your nose where it doesn't belong. *Again!*" but thought it best to let it rest.

"My mom is coming along pretty well. Thanks for asking."

"Hey, we're all on the same team here."

She bit her tongue.

"Who's taking care of her while she recovers?"

"A good friend." No reason for her to be specific.

"Nice to have someone willing to help."

Wanting this conversation to end, she reached for the telephone, hoping he'd get the message.

He persisted. "Things working out with Osbourn?"

"Seems like a sharp kid."

"He's still a little green, but I think he's got the makings for a good cop."

"Well, when we arrest the serial killer, I'll be sure to give him credit for the collar. That ought to boost his career."

He gave her a sidelong glance. "Seriously?"

"You betcha. I have to make some calls, Chuck, nice talking to you."

With that, D'Angelo walked away.

Spencer arrived at Post Office Plus thirty minutes before it opened, hoping to find an ideal parking spot with an unobstructed view of the main entrance. Finding *any* parking spot in the Village of La Jolla was a formidable undertaking, let alone a select one. As luck would have it, Spencer pulled his car into the perfect spot.

He turned off the engine but left the key in the accessory position so he could pass the time by listening to his favorite cassette. Hank Williams belted out a twangy tune. Spencer felt a bit uneasy spying on his client. He had done some pretty underhanded things as a PI, all for the sake of a few bucks. But even criminals had a code of ethics. His first commandment as a PI was loyalty to his clients. Just how loyal was he, sitting in his car, trying to dig up some dirt on his client? For a fleeting moment, Spencer considered starting the engine and driving away, but when he saw a car park across the street and "John Smith," Chargers hat and all, get out of a new Ford Fusion, it was too late to abort his plan.

Spencer slid down in the seat, trying to hide the best he could, all the while fixing his eyes on "John Smith." Spencer's client got out of the car and almost jogged to the main entrance of Post Office Plus. He yanked on the door handle but it was still locked. Both Spencer and his client looked at their wrist watches at the same time. Seven forty-five. He watched his client pace back and forth, checking his watch every sixty seconds. Clearly, he was uneasy. At one point, his client even knocked on the door, perhaps hoping they might open a little early if they saw an anxious customer waiting outside. But the doors remained locked.

At precisely 8:00 a.m., a middle-aged blonde woman unlocked the front door and let Spencer's client, along with three other patrons, into the facility. Spencer couldn't observe the activities on the other side of the door, but guessed that his client would pick up the package Spencer had left, and quickly be on his way. Fortunately for Spencer, he could see the rear license plate on the Ford Fusion without having to get out of his car, so he made note of it.

Waiting for over fifteen minutes, Spencer wondered why his client hadn't come out yet. How long did it take to pick up a nine-by-twelve envelope? Maybe he was buying stamps? Mailing a letter? He dismissed his curiosity as inconsequential and tried not to give it another thought. But Spencer generally overreacted to most situations. And his suspicious nature had saved his hide many times. Better to be safe than sorry had always been his motto.

At eight twenty-five, carrying a manila envelope under his arm, his client walked out the front door of Post Office Plus and got into his car. Spencer started his engine, ready to follow his client. He waited and waited, but his client's car didn't move. Ah, Spencer thought, "John Smith" must be so anxious to read the information on Detective Rizzo that he couldn't wait until he got home. Finally, twenty minutes later, Spencer heard the hum of the engine and saw the backup lights. Careful to keep a safe distance, Spencer followed his client as inconspicuously as possible. If following someone in a car without being noticed was an art, then Spencer was Michelangelo.

While tailing "John Smith," following him through Bird Rock and Pacific Beach toward Freeway 5, Spencer contacted Detective D'Angelo, and without incriminating himself, almost talking in a secret code that few people would be able to decipher, he asked the detective to run the license plate number of his mysterious client. So anxious to find out who the mystery man was, Spencer felt like a kid on Christmas morning, waiting for the sun to rise so he could open the presents Santa left under the Christmas tree.

"John Smith" exited Freeway 5 at Del Mar Heights and headed toward the ocean. After traveling a mile or so, the mystery man parked his Ford Fusion in a small parking lot on 10th Avenue, next to a small, freestanding building. Spencer pulled to the curb across the street. When he saw his client walk in the front door, Spencer noticed the business name on the sign in front of the building, and had to look twice to be sure his eyes were not playing tricks.

Del Mar Fertility Center?

There were many things about detective work that Sami disliked, but at the top of the list, she despised interviewing relatives of a homicide victim. She'd never found an easy way to ask the questions she needed to ask. And no matter how diplomatic or tactful she was, the family members always misconstrued these questions as insensitive and inappropriate.

"I haven't had much experience interviewing family members," Osbourn admitted.

"Well I have," Sami responded. "It never gets any easier."

Osbourn drove and Sami gave directions from her worn-out *Thomas Guide*. The budget restraints were so tight in the San Diego Police Department that not even detectives could requisition a GPS system. The fact that higher-ranking officials like Captain Davidson and Chief Larson, superiors who did very little fieldwork, could enjoy this perk irritated Sami Rizzo to tears.

"Go straight past Orange Avenue," Sami said. "E Avenue is your second left. We're looking for number 2264."

Once over the bridge, Coronado Island looked and felt like a different world than San Diego, another dimension. Quaint and lacking a big-city feel, outdoor cafés and unique gift shops dotted the main streets. Kings, queens, movie stars, and presidents were frequent guests of the Hotel Del Coronado.

Osbourn pulled to the curb—first rule of etiquette was never to park in anyone's driveway—and let out a quivering sigh.

"You ready for this?" Sami asked.

"As ready as I'm going to be."

Approaching the front porch, she noticed a solid-wood swing hanging from brass chains. The wood looked as shiny as a gymnasium floor. Ceramic pots of geraniums, petunias, and coleus surrounded the entrance. The front door, accented with stained glass, looked like solid mahogany.

Before she could knock on the door, it squeaked open.

"Detective Rizzo?" the woman asked. Her dirty-blonde hair looked as if she'd just returned from the beauty salon. Her perfectly applied makeup could not conceal the dark circles under her puffy eyes.

Sami offered her hand. "Mrs. Stevens?"

"Please call me Elizabeth."

Sami gestured to her partner. "This is Detective Osbourn."

Elizabeth Stevens cocked her head to one side and studied Osbourn's face. "You're quite young to be a detective," she said. "You must be very bright."

"Thank you," Osbourn said.

Elizabeth Stevens invited the detectives into her home. She pointed to the Victorian sofa. "Please have a seat."

Surveying the pristine sofa, Sami felt like she was the first person ever to sit on it. She was surprised it wasn't covered with plastic.

"Can I get you some tea or a soft drink?" Elizabeth offered. "Ice water perhaps?"

Sami couldn't remember the last time a victim's relative extended so much hospitality. "Thank you, but we're fine."

Elizabeth Stevens sat on the matching chair adjacent to the detectives.

"Is Mr. Stevens joining us?" Sami asked.

"I'm afraid not." Elizabeth folded her hands on her lap in a proper manner, sitting upright with perfect posture. She looked like a tutor at an uppity charm school. "Connor's death has knocked the wind out of my husband. Joseph is currently under doctor's care, and he sleeps more than he's awake." She paused for a moment, noticeably choked up. "I've been able to function only through the grace of the Almighty."

Considering that her mom had expressed a desire to attend Sunday mass and Al had been recently praying to God to help Aleta, Sami wondered if God was indirectly sending her a message. He did work in strange ways, or so she'd been told.

"I'm deeply sorry for your loss," Sami said. "And I'm truly sorry that Mr. Stevens is having such a difficult time."

She gave Elizabeth a minute to regain her composure. "May we ask you a few questions?"

"Certainly."

Sami set the digital recorder on the cocktail table and removed a pen and notepad from her jacket pocket. "May we record this session?"

Elizabeth nodded.

"When did you last see Connor?" Sami asked.

"We had dinner with him the night he disappeared. He had just celebrated his twenty-seventh birthday, so we invited him over for his favorite dish. Turkey meatloaf, garlic mashed potatoes, and steamed broccoli. My son wasn't vegetarian, but he never ate beef or pork."

"Any idea where he went that evening or who might have been with him?"

"Connor had more friends than someone who'd just won the Lotto, so it could have been any number of them."

Sami felt a bit annoyed that Osbourn was sitting there like a stuffed animal, but she didn't have time to hold his hand. If he was as sharp as everyone claimed, he'd learn from this experience. "Is there any way you can provide us with a list of all his friends and possibly contact information?"

"All I can tell you is that my son spent hours on Facebook. Last he told me, he had over one thousand friends."

"I'm thinking more of personal friends who live locally. Friends he might hang around with."

"I don't have contact information, but I can give you some names."

"That would be great." Sami gave Osbourn a quick glance to be sure he wasn't sleeping. "Do you have any idea where your son went after having dinner with you?"

Elizabeth Stevens's amiable facial expression tightened. She looked angry. "I would guess he went to Henry's Hideaway."

Sami never heard of the place. "Have you been there?" she asked Osbourn.

He shook his head. "It's a gay bar in Hillcrest."

Sami didn't believe that the perpetrator was gay because unlike with his last female victim, he did not sexually assault Connor Stevens. "Elizabeth, was your son…gay?"

"Dreadfully gay. It was difficult for my husband and me to accept Connor's chosen lifestyle—and make no mistake about it—it *is* a choice. The Bible is very clear on this issue." She paused for a moment and reached for the box of tissues on the end table. "We begged our son to get help, but our efforts only made him more defiant. The more we tried, the more he'd rub it in our faces. You should see his wardrobe. He dressed like some flamboyant movie star."

"Did he have a steady partner, Elizabeth?" Sami asked.

She wiped the corner of her eyes and shook her head. "Sometimes I think every gay man in San Diego was his partner at one time or another. Connor lived a dangerously promiscuous life-style."

Obviously, Sami thought. That is likely why his bruised body lay on a cold slab. It sounded as if Connor Stevens hopped from bed to bed without discretion or fear. "Is there anything else you can tell us that might be useful?"

"I just want my son back. And that's never going to happen."

"Again, Mrs. Stevens," Sami said. "Our deepest condolences."

"Find this evil person, Detective, before another parent has to live this nightmare."

Peter J. Spencer III sat on a bench overlooking Sail Bay, enjoy-ing the cool breeze blowing off the water. The sky was perfectly blue, without even a trace of a cloud. He sipped his strong Ara-bian coffee and inhaled the smell of freshly cut grass. The mud hens had returned from their yearly migration. In large numbers and with carefree arrogance, they waddled across the boardwalk shoulder to shoulder in an organized fashion, stubbornly refus-ing to yield to joggers, cyclists, and rollerbladers.

From the corner of his eye, Spencer noticed Chuck D'Angelo approaching the bench. Without saying a word, D'Angelo sat beside Spencer.

"Lovely day," D'Angelo said.

"It's why we live here," Spencer responded. "What have you got?"

"A couple of interesting facts. First off, that license plate num-ber you gave me? The car's registered to Southwest Auto Rentals. Their office is on Grape Street in Banker's Hill."

"You're shitting me."

"'Fraid not. Here's the kicker. This guy claims he and Sami Rizzo were an item? Bullshit. The only one who's gotten into her knickers since she divorced that scumbag husband of hers is Al Diaz. And he works in homicide with me."

Spencer digested these surprising bits of information for a minute. "Wonder why this guy would lie."

"Not sure. But I can tell you this. He's up to no good and I think we ought to check him out. Next time you meet him, I'll tail him and find out where he lives, works, or plays."

"We're not going to meet face to face again."

"Ever?"

Spencer shook his head.

"Then give me his phone number. I can work with that."

Spencer lifted a shoulder. "Don't have one."

"I don't mind helping you out here, Spence, we go back a long way. But this whole thing reeks of foul play. I'm too close to retirement to fuck it all up. I think you're in over your head. I can't be part of it."

"I understand," Spencer said. "I hope this conversation is just between you and me. I mean, no one else needs to know, right?"

"If you're asking if I'm going to tell Detective Rizzo that someone's got her number, the answer is no."

"Think *I* should contact her?"

"That's your call," D'Angelo said. "The only thing I know for sure is that on August first, I'm going to clean out my office and put my personal things in a little cardboard box. And when I walk out that precinct door, I couldn't care less what happens. I'm going to spend the rest of my life sleeping in, smoking cigars, fishing, and occasionally fucking the old lady."

CHAPTER TWENTY-SEVEN

"Hi, Emily," Sami said. "Everything okay?" Sami had just left the precinct and was on her way to Henry's Hideaway. She hated working after the dinner hour, but when you were a homicide detective there was no such thing as a forty-hour workweek.

"Your mom nodded out on the couch watching an old Humphrey Bogart movie," Emily said. "And Angelina and I were playing Chutes and Ladders."

"Who's winning?"

"Angelina is kicking my butt."

"Does she laugh every time you slide down a chute?"

"Uncontrollably."

Oh, how Sami wished she were home, wearing her baggy sweats, sipping a cold Corona, and playing Chutes and Ladders with Emily and Angelina. "I'm not sure what time I'll be home."

"No need to explain. I've got it covered."

"What would I do without you, Cuz? You're at the top of my Christmas list."

"But how are you going to fit a Mini Cooper under the Christmas tree?"

"Wish I could afford to buy you one. Someday maybe."

"Drive safely, Cousin," Emily said.

"Don't let my mother sleep on the sofa too long. It's tough on her back."

"Actually, I planned to wake her just as soon as Angelina and I finished the game."

"Great. I'll see you when I see you."

Sami couldn't find a legal parking spot anywhere near Henry's Hideaway, so she cashed in on one of her official privileges and left her car next to a red-painted curb. She flipped down the visor to be sure the Official Police Business placard was visible through the windshield. One time, she had actually gotten a ticket from some rookie cop not quite understanding professional courtesy.

She had thought about calling her partner, but decided to let Osbourn enjoy a rare evening with his wife and kids. Sami remembered how often she'd eaten a cold dinner all by herself after an evening of surveillance or interviews. But she trusted Emily implicitly and felt great peace of mind knowing that both her mother and Angelina were in good hands.

As she approached the front door, she noticed a bouncer checking IDs. The guy must have been well over six feet tall, and Sami guessed he tipped the scales at three-fifty-plus. If this establishment wanted to discourage patrons from using fake IDs, then this guy would surely do the trick. But it wasn't just his imposing size that made him so intimidating. His ears were decorated with multiple earrings, and he had studs piercing both his nose and left eyebrow. She didn't even want to think about where else he might be pierced. Just to complete the ensemble, a collection of hideous tattoos covered both of his arms.

She had thought about cutting right to the front of the long line and flashing her gold shield, but she wanted to remain as inconspicuous as possible.

When Sami reached the entrance, she showed the big man her ID and badge with little fanfare. Up close, he seemed even bigger than she'd thought.

"I don't suppose you're here to party, are ya?" the big man said.

"Where can I find the owner or manager?"

"Well, the owner is never here in the evenings, but the manager should be floating around inside."

"Can I have his name?"

"Philippe something or other. He's a French dude." He stepped aside and opened the door for Sami. "Check with Patrick, the bartender. He'll be able to track him down."

"Thanks."

The first thing she noticed when she walked in the door was the size of the crowd. It exceeded legal occupancy by at least fifty people. The second thing she noticed was the blaring music, also louder than legal limits. But she wasn't here to issue citations for petty violations. She was elbows deep in a multiple-murder investigation.

She weaved her way through the mostly male crowd and squeezed between two young men at the bar. The bartender seemed like he needed two more hands to keep up with the drink orders, and he stood toward the end of the bar, twenty feet away from her. Rather than paw her way to the end of the bar, Sami leaned her back against it and waited for the bartender to wander down her way.

As her eyes observed the unreserved activity, the social commerce of the chase and the hunt, a soft kiss here, a pat on the butt there, it occurred to her that it wouldn't take more than two minutes for even the most out-of-touch person in the world to figure out that Henry's Hideaway was a haven for the gay community of San Diego.

Never considering herself to be homophobic, she did feel a bit uncomfortable in the thick of this crowd. Her discomfort had nothing to do with sexual orientation. The outrageousness of it all was what struck her. She had little doubt that she'd feel the same way in any bar where it was open season for alcohol, drugs, and casual sex. She'd never been a prude. In fact, living with Al and sleeping in the same bed with him contradicted her moral values. But, she thought, isn't it easy to modify your value system when it's convenient?

She caught a glimpse of the bartender heading her way. She motioned to him.

"What can I get you?" Patrick asked.

His flawless skin, soft cheekbones, full lips and subdued features might qualify him as the prettiest guy Sami had ever seen. "I'm looking for Philippe." She flashed her ID.

He pointed to the far corner of the bar, just past the dance floor. "See that office in the corner? You'll find him in there."

"Thanks for your help."

Sami negotiated her way through the thick of the crowd, inching her way to the corner, just past the dance floor. Suddenly, from out of nowhere, someone grabbed her hand.

"Let's dance, Cutie," the young woman with pink-streaked hair said. One of the few females in the bar, she seemed to blend in.

"Sorry. I can't." Sami tried to release her hand but the woman held on.

"C'mon. 'Right Round' is my favorite dance tune. Let's get wild."

"Please let go of me," Sami insisted.

The girl released her hand and walked away, mumbling something that the loud music drowned out. Sami guessed that whatever the pink-haired girl said was rife with four-letter words.

She reached the office door, unscathed from a second incident, and knocked with more authority than she normally would, hoping to overcome the deafening music. When Philippe opened the door, Sami had to do a double-take. If Michael Jordan had a twin brother, Philippe was his name. The man looked like he had dressed for the cover of *GQ* magazine. He wore an impeccably fitted charcoal suit, with a pale yellow necktie accented with tiny black diamonds. His shoes were spit-shined with military precision, and his perfectly shaped head was clean shaven.

Sami flashed her ID and badge. "Detective Rizzo, Metro Homicide. Can I ask you a few questions?"

"Please have a seat, Detective." From his thick French accent, Sami guessed he hadn't been in America very long.

Philippe sat behind his massive mahogany desk. Sami sat opposite him in a chair that looked like it weighed a hundred pounds. With the main door firmly shut, the quietness of the office surprised Sami. It looked more like it belonged to the CEO of a Fortune 500 company. The bar business must be lucrative.

"I'm conducting an investigation into the murder of Connor Stevens, a regular patron of your establishment. Does his name sound familiar?" She slid a recent photograph across the desk.

"Very tragic," Philippe said. "The world can be such a hostile place." He picked up the photograph and studied it. "I have seen this young man. But I do not mingle with our patrons. Perhaps you should talk to Tiny."

"And who might that be?"

"He's our security guard at the front door."

Sami couldn't suppress her laugh. "*Tiny?*"

"Considering the size of the man, it does seem a bit absurd," Philippe admitted. "But in spite of this obvious contradiction, he knows most of our regular patrons by name. The man doesn't miss a thing."

"May I speak with him?"

Philippe picked up a two-way radio and pushed several buttons. "Can you come to my office, Tiny?"

Sami drummed her fingers on the desk.

"Tell Raymond to screen IDs," Philippe said into the two-way.

In less than two minutes, Tiny entered the office, and sat adjacent to Sami, barely able to squeeze his wide hips between the armrests. Without asking permission, she set the digital recorder on the desk.

"Tiny, this is Detective Rizzo," Philippe said. "She would like to ask you a few—"

"This is about Connor, isn't it?" Tiny interrupted. "The guy that was murdered."

"How well did you know him?" Sami asked.

"Well enough that I'd like to spend ten minutes alone with the guy who snuffed him."

"So, you had a *personal* relationship with Mr. Stevens?" Sami asked.

Her question seemed to offend Tiny. "I wouldn't exactly call it personal. At least not *that* kind of personal. The guy was a regular—came into the place three, maybe four times a week. You get familiar with people when you see them so often."

"Did he typically come alone?" Sami asked.

"Most of the time. But he didn't usually leave alone. The guy was a mover and a shaker. If you can dig where I'm coming from."

"Tell me what you mean," Sami said.

"Hey, he lived life to the fullest. Sometimes I think he was trying to set a record."

"Can you recall anything specific about the last night he was here?" Sami asked.

"I remember the guy Connor left with, if that's what you mean."

"Can you give me a description?" Sami said.

"First off, the guy was about as gay as I am—and believe me, I'm as straight as they come. He tried like hell to look the part, but it just didn't work. Not that straight dudes don't pop in every so often. But they don't try to *look* gay."

"Anything specific you remember about his appearance?" Sami asked.

"When I asked for ID, he seemed offended. Told me he was forty-two."

"But he didn't look his age?"

Tiny shook his head. "Nope. The guy was a good-looking dude. I'll give him that much. If I swung from that side, I'd give him a jump."

Sami guessed that Tiny rarely filtered anything he said. Philippe looked noticeably uncomfortable with the big man's candor. "Could you point him out in front of a lineup?"

"Absolutely."

"Would you consider coming to the precinct and working with a sketch artist, so we can distribute a composite drawing of the suspect?"

"If it will help find this jerk-off—excuse my language—I'd be happy to."

"Thank you, Tiny. Did you happen to see his name on the driver's license or maybe an address?"

"No. But when he handed it to me, I caught a glimpse of another photo ID card in his wallet. I can't say for sure, but I think it had one of those medical symbols on it."

"What kind of medical symbol?" Sami asked.

"The one with the wings at the top and two snakes wrapped around a staff."

Sami had seen this image before. When Emily had showed Sami her nursing diploma, out of mere curiosity, she had asked her about the medical symbol stamped on the diploma, a symbol Sami had seen a hundred times. Fanatically detailed, Emily gave her a ten-minute lecture on the origin of the symbol. Sami even remembered its name: Caduceus.

"Anything else?"

"'Fraid not."

"You've been most helpful, Tiny," Sami said. She reached in her purse and handed business cards to both Tiny and Philippe. "Can you come down to the precinct tomorrow morning between nine and ten, Tiny?"

"I'll be there at nine."

"Call me if anything—even the most insignificant detail—pops into your head."

CHAPTER TWENTY-EIGHT

Julian couldn't quite figure out what Peter Spencer's angle was, but wondered why the PI was shadowing him. Spencer probably hadn't noticed, but Julian spotted him parked across the street from Post Office Plus. While Julian stood inside the office waiting to pick up the package Spencer had left there, Julian could clearly see outside, but the glare on the glass doors prevented Spencer from seeing inside. Julian could almost forgive Spencer's one indiscretion. Maybe the PI had a believable explanation. But when Julian again saw Spencer parked across the street from the Del Mar Fertility Clinic, the PI had lost all credibility. Spencer had claimed to be the "King of Discretion." Apparently, the PI's definition of discretion varied considerably from Julian's.

His thoughts shifted to his family. Other than a couple of perfunctory conversations when he'd picked up his two kids for an evening of burgers, fries, and a visit to the arcade at Belmont Park, Julian hadn't spoken much to Nicole. They hadn't discussed the issues they needed to discuss. But he felt content with that arrangement. The longer he could avoid any consequential dialogue, the better. He felt comfortable living alone in his loft, but he was still plagued with guilt for leaving his daughters. Troubling as his thoughts were, he could not afford to be distracted, and had to move forward with a search for another subject.

The temperature flirted with ninety today, so Julian grabbed a cold beer—not his usual thirst quencher. He had glanced at the information Spencer had given him when he'd left Post Office Plus, but his schedule at the hospital had been insane, so this was his first opportunity to examine the information in detail.

He studied page after page, detail after detail, but nothing in particular caught his attention. Nothing he could use. In his hands, he held enough biographical material on Samantha Marie Rizzo to write an exposé. The dates, names, events, and places revealed in this illuminating little package totally amazed him. With the right sources, it seemed to Julian, anybody could find out anything about anyone. Scary, he thought.

About to tuck away the package in a secure place, he noticed something. Sami's cousin Emily lived with her—her only cousin. Just turned twenty-two and just graduated from nursing school in San Francisco. Emily Rizzo regularly attended evening yoga classes at a downtown gym.

Yoga classes?

Julian had been overworking his brain trying to come up with an ideal place to meet subject number five. His next bit of research required that his subject be a female in excellent health. How could he go to a bar, randomly select someone and be sure she was healthy? The short answer was that he couldn't. But suppose he went to a place that promoted health? Suppose he went to a yoga class or a gym? Chances were if he selected a young, lean woman, she would likely be in good health.

Thank you, Emily.

Before her scheduled meeting with Police Chief Larson and Captain Davidson, Sami sat in one of the interrogation rooms with Detective Osbourn and gave him a brief summary of what she discovered at Henry's Hideaway. The young detective didn't seem particularly interested, nor did he ask many questions, which concerned her. Considering his participation in the investigation thus far, she now regretted not having him with her when she interviewed Philippe and Tiny. He obviously needed more frontline experience.

As a rookie detective, Sami remembered driving her colleagues crazy with question after question, like a first-grader wanting to learn everything about everything. Osbourn didn't seem to have that seed of curiosity so critical in a detective. She didn't want to overreact, but to this point, she was not impressed.

She looked at her watch. "We'd better get moving," she said to Osbourn. "Neither the chief nor the captain have much tolerance for tardiness."

"Is it important that I sit in on this briefing?" Osbourn asked.

"You're kidding, right?"

"You've already brought me up to speed, so why—"

"What the hell is going on, Richard? I chose you to partner with me on this case over four seasoned detectives. And it seems to me that you're somehow less than enthusiastic. Last night when I told you to stay home with your family and not to meet me at Henry's Hideaway, you didn't even flinch. Not one word of protest. Where's the ex-Marine that used to disarm IEDs in Iraq? Where's the guy who convinced me to partner with him? Did I make the wrong choice? Do you want out?"

"No, it's not that at all. It's just that…" His eyes filled with tears.

"What is it, Richard?"

"My wife had her second miscarriage two days ago."

Now, of course, she felt like an insensitive clod. But she wasn't a mind reader. "I'm so, so sorry." His announcement brought a lump to Sami's throat. "Why didn't you say something?"

"I wanted to leave my family business at home."

"But clearly you didn't. Under the circumstances, your lack of enthusiasm is perfectly understandable. But without that important piece of information, I could only assume that you had no fire in your belly and were sorry I chose you to partner with me. What would you think if the situation were reversed?"

"It wasn't my intention to let you down."

"Do you need a few days off?" She could see he was embroiled in an internal tug-of-war.

"I don't know if that would help. Some things just have to run their course. Besides, I think my wife needs some alone time."

"Let's do this. Come to the meeting with me—that will give you a little time to think—and we'll talk afterwards."

"Thanks for being so understanding."

The door to the captain's office was slightly ajar. Sami could hear Davidson and Larson whispering, but couldn't make out their words. Neither was known to be soft spoken; she could only guess they were probably making arrangements to tar and feather her if their meeting didn't prove fruitful.

As a courtesy, she knocked on the door before walking inside; Osbourn tailed behind. Sami and Osbourn sat in front of Captain Davidson's desk. Larson paced the floor.

"I hope you have something for us," Larson said. "I haven't bugged you but the mayor is driving me batty and I need to throw her a bone."

"We've come up with a couple of leads," Sami said.

"You mean *suspects?*" Larson said, his voice a few decibels higher.

She told Larson and Davidson about Tiny, that he was coming to the precinct this morning to work with a sketch artist, that he felt he could pick the alleged serial killer out of a lineup. She also told them about the symbol Tiny saw on the perp's medical ID.

"Does this witness seem reliable?" Davidson asked.

"He looks like he could play the lead role in a motorcycle movie," Sami said.

"What time is he coming?" Larson asked.

"Nine o'clock."

"Is our sketch guy onboard?" Davidson asked.

She understood that both the captain and chief were under tremendous pressure, but did they think she was still a rookie? "It's handled, Captain."

"So what's this about a medical symbol?" Larson said.

"Tiny is a bouncer at the bar where our perp met Connor Stevens. When our guy flashed his driver's license, Tiny noticed a photo ID with a caduceus symbol on it."

"A what?" Davidson said.

Sami had already anticipated this question and had the forethought to find a photo on Google and print a copy. She pulled a folded piece of paper out of her purse and handed it to Davidson. The captain studied it for a few moments and passed it to Larson.

"I've seen this symbol a gazillion times," Larson said.

Osbourn finally spoke. "The problem, of course, is that our man could be anything from a doctor to an orderly, or anything in between."

Sami didn't want to undermine Osbourn's attempt to participate, but based on the results of the autopsies and what Doctor Fox had told her, she had to correct him.

"Well, I doubt very much that our guy is an orderly. Based on the surgical procedures he performed on their hearts, more than likely we're dealing with a doctor gone awry. Perhaps even a cardiologist. But we can't rule out anyone working in health care."

"How do we narrow the field?" Davidson asked.

Sami had some answers but hesitated a moment to see if Osbourn would continue.

"Not all medical IDs have an imprint of the caduceus symbol," Osbourn said. "The process of elimination is going to be labor intensive. We are going to need every available body—detectives and support people as well—to find out who uses this symbol on their IDs and who doesn't. We're talking hospitals, clinics, outpatient surgical centers, anyone working for a health-care organization."

The young detective was starting to catch on, Sami thought. "And don't forget about private practices," she added. "We need to contact the AMA, the California Board of Nursing, and any other organization that maintains a database of health-care professionals."

"Well," Larson said, "seems like you and Detective Osbourn have made some headway. I had hoped for more, but if our eye witness helps the sketch artist come up with an accurate composite, we might be cookin' with oil."

"Can we make arrangements to have the composite sketch posted in all public places—trolley stations, bus stops, museums, post offices, beaches, parks—anywhere locals congregate?" Osbourn said.

"Sure thing," Larson said.

"And how about posting it on all the major billboards in the county?" Sami suggested.

"Those are all doable," Larson said. "I'm sure the mayor can make a few phone calls and help us cut through the red tape."

"It's not a secret that our budget is in the crapper," Sami said, "but is there any chance we can twist the thumbscrews and push the City Council to bump up the ten-thousand-dollar reward the Fosters are offering for the arrest and conviction of the perp?"

"Great idea," Davidson said. "That's how they nabbed the Parkside Strangler in LA. Cash is king."

"Hey, it never hurts to ask," Larson said. "Good job, Detectives. Let's plan on another powwow tomorrow morning at eight sharp. And Sami, if you run into any roadblocks or resistance from your colleagues, call me on my cell twenty-four-seven."

She thought the meeting was over, but when Osbourn and she stood and headed for the door, Chief Larson grabbed her arm.

"You can leave, Richard," Larson said. "But we need to speak with Sami privately."

She'd figured that this meeting wasn't going to be *that* easy. Rarely could she walk out of this office without leaving a piece of her hide.

Larson closed the door and gave Captain Davidson a look. Sami realized it was an ambush.

"Can we speak off the record?" Davidson asked. "Technically, we shouldn't be having this conversation with you, but—"

"If you two are comfortable, I'm comfortable."

"Have you heard from Al?" the captain asked.

"I speak to him every day. Sometimes twice."

"How's his sister?" Larson asked.

"She's holding her own. Still in a coma, but she's improved slightly."

"We hate to sound like ball breakers, but any idea when Al's coming back?" Davidson asked.

If she blurted the first thing that came to her mind, she might be unemployed. "It all depends on his sister."

"We don't want to be insensitive," Davidson said. "But we have a department to run here and Al is an integral part of the equation. We can't just give him an open-ended ticket to stay in Rio indefinitely."

"Under the Family Medical Leave Act," Larson added, "you can take up to six weeks to care for a spouse, parent, or child. But there's no provision for a sibling under this law. We want to support Al. Honestly, Sami. But there is no flexibility here. Our hands are tied. He needs to get back to work immediately."

"So if there was a way for him to qualify for the Family Medical Leave Act, both of you are onboard?"

"Absolutely," Larson said. "You have my word."

She didn't want to sound like a know-it-all, but if her superiors wanted to quote the law to her, they'd better damn well do their homework. "Neither of you have heard of Assembly Bill 849, which was passed in April of 2009? It's an amendment to the California Family Rights Act." She sensed that her tone was leaning toward sarcastic, so she had to be careful to tone it down. "This bill expands family leave to siblings, grandparents, grandchildren, and even a parent-in-law."

Larson and Davidson stared at each other, looking like she was speaking Russian. "I don't remember seeing that notice from HR," Larson said.

"Al has already filed the application with Judy in Human Resources and all she needs is your signature and approval, Chief Larson, and he's good to go for up to six weeks."

The color drained from Larson's face.

"Any chance you can sign it today?" Sami asked.

Clearly defeated, Larson coughed into his hand and folded his arms across his chest. "Well, um, I'll get over to HR later this morning."

"Thanks, Chief. Al appreciates your support. And so do I." She had to enlist every ounce of restraint to suppress her grin. "Will there be anything else?"

CHAPTER TWENTY-NINE

With help from Captain Davidson and Detective Osbourn, Sami organized a brainstorm meeting with four of her fellow detectives, six support people, and two administrative personnel. The group assembled in the conference room and congregated around the beat-up table that had been part of this room since the precinct was first opened. Osbourn and she stood in front of the group next to a whiteboard.

Never much of an artist, Sami drew an image of the caduceus symbol on the whiteboard as best she could. "This is the symbol we're looking for."

She wasn't surprised when her least favorite detective was first to speak.

D'Angelo stood with that smug look that made her want to smack him.

"So," D'Angelo said, "we're supposed to contact every doctor, lawyer, and Indian chief in San Diego just to find out if they have that weird symbol on their ID badge?"

"You can skip the lawyers and Indian chiefs," Osbourn said. He passed around a list of all the organizations they needed to contact, along with a photograph of the symbol.

"Each of you has been assigned specific health-care organizations to contact," Sami said. "We must verify whether or not this symbol appears on the ID cards of all their employees, associates, or members. If not, we don't need to go any further. But if they do use this symbol on their IDs, then we need a list of everyone involved in the organization that uses an ID card."

"Suppose they refuse to disclose any information because of confidentiality issues?" Debra Jones, Lab Tech, asked.

"They can either cooperate over the telephone, or we can show up at their doorsteps with search warrants and tear their offices apart. Whatever they prefer."

Sergeant McBride stood. "Not for nothing, but how the hell will you get a judge to sign a bunch of search warrants?"

"Judge Foster's daughter was the first victim. Needless to say, he'll do anything within the law to support our efforts to apprehend our guy."

"Okay," D'Angelo said. "We have a list of a gazillion health-care employees with badges that have that symbol on it. How does that help us nail this guy?"

She wanted so badly to call him a pinhead. "Whoever produced the ID cards also has a database of photographs. We have an eye witness who just this morning worked with a sketch artist to come up with a composite drawing of our perp. Once these photos are sent electronically, we'll compare them to the composite drawings."

"Sounds like a hefty undertaking to me," D'Angelo said.

"Between all departments, we have lots of help," Sami said.

"Still," D'Angelo said. "It could take forever."

"Not if we work around the clock. And that's exactly what we're fucking going to do." She fixed her eyes on D'Angelo. "Any more stupid questions or asinine comments should be directed to Police Chief Larson."

Just as he'd done repeatedly for the last two weeks, Al sat beside his comatose sister holding her hand, stroking her cheek, and softly talking to her. Eating very little and rarely three meals a day, he knew that he'd lost weight because he had to tighten his belt an extra notch to hold up his slacks. He had packed only a small suitcase, so every couple of days he had to use the motel Laundromat to wash and dry his clothes.

"Hello, Sunflower," Al whispered in Aleta's ear. "It was a beautiful day today. Warmer than normal for this time of year. The temperature hit eighty degrees. As soon as you're better, we'll grab a couple of cups of coffee and go for a long walk on Copacabana Beach. Would you like that, Sunflower?"

Exhausted and operating on reserve power, he sat back in the chair and closed his eyes. Almost immediately, the recurring nightmare that haunted him from the first day he landed in Rio de Janeiro played in his mind.

His sister lies in bed, unconscious. Plastic tubes snake out her mouth and nose. Her left arm is stuck with an IV. More than fifteen relatives, alive and dead, stand around the bed. Al sees his mother and father, cousins, aunts, and uncles. Their faces are chalk-white, walking corpses. As if they are given a cue from a movie director, each of them in harmony points to the electric cord plugged into the wall socket that powers the respirator keeping Aleta alive. In a chant-like manner, their declaration in unison, they say, "Pull the plug, Alberto!" Over and over they repeat this command. Each time they make this statement, their voices get a little louder. After only a minute or so, they point and scream, "Pull the plug, Alberto! Pull the plug!"

Al presses his palms to his ears but he cannot suppress the chant. He walks over to the electric receptacle, shuffling his feet as if he's wearing lead shoes, and grasps the power cord with his fingers. Hands shaking, he knows that the only way he can quiet the deafening declaration is to pull the plug. Louder and louder the chant continues. Just as he is about to yank the plug from the receptacle, ending his sister's life, he awakes out of a sound sleep.

Sweat covered his entire body and he could feel his heart thumping against his ribcage. Completely disoriented, as if awakening from a nightmare in a strange hotel room, he tried to gather his thoughts. He could not stop his hands from shaking. He tried to focus his eyes on Aleta, but the sweat blurred his vision. He swiped his sleeve across his eyes and looked around the room. No one was there. Just his sister and him. The chanting had stopped and his relatives had disappeared. Each time he had this dream, he awoke just before pulling the plug. He dreaded the day when it would not be a dream, when he might actually face a decision to end his sister's life.

Still out of breath and feeling unsettled, more than anything, Al needed some fresh air to clear his head. But not yet feeling that his legs would support his body, he thought it wise to remain seated for a few minutes.

"Sunflower," he whispered, "I'm here with you. Can you hear me?"

Fixing his stare on her face, he noticed the corners of her eyes twitching ever so slightly. He looked more closely and could see her eyes dancing around under her eyelids. In all the hours he had spent by her side, never once had he seen any facial or eye movement.

"It's Alberto, Sunflower. If you can hear my voice, please open your eyes."

He grasped her hand and held it firmly. He closed his eyes and prayed the prayer he had repeated over a hundred times, a prayer to a God with whom he had no relationship. Yet a God who Al believed could hear his plea.

He felt Aleta squeeze his hand.

His eyes sprang open and he focused on her face. When he saw her staring at him, her eyes partially opened, he thought that this was surely a dream. He squeezed her hand and she immediately squeezed his.

"Can you hear me, Sunflower?"

She nodded her head and pointed to her throat. Her face looked contorted as if she were in pain. Al figured out what she was trying to say. She wanted the damned respirator removed. He didn't want to leave her, but ran out the door to commandeer a nurse.

CHAPTER THIRTY

Julian looked at the giant headlines on the front page of the *San Diego Chronicle*:

HAVE YOU SEEN THIS MAN?

Below the headline, Julian glanced at the composite drawing, and at first, he panicked. But the more he looked at the sketch the less alarmed he felt. He could see a slight likeness, but the drawing was nowhere near spot-on. In fact, he guessed that a few thousand people could be more matched to the sketch than he could. It was an unremarkable representation.

Focusing carefully on his hair style in the sketch, it didn't take Julian long to figure out that whoever fingered him was at Henry's Hideaway the evening he had met Connor Stevens. That was the only time he had worn his hair in such a trendy, punked-out style.

He tried to recall whom he had encountered or spoken to long enough for them to remember what he looked like. Other than the bouncer checking IDs at the front door and a two-minute conversation with the bartender, nothing struck him. It was obvious, however, that the police had figured out he had met Connor Stevens at that particular bar.

He thought about his conversation with the bouncer, but could only recall that the big man had given him a hard time about his ID, even though he was twenty years beyond the legal drinking age. He studied the sketch again, more carefully this time, looking at the eyes, mouth, cheekbones, and lips.

"Nothing to worry about," he whispered. Still, maybe the police were getting too close.

Time for him to shift gears, to change his MO.

Time for him to join a yoga class.

Peter J. Spencer III paced the floor of his small office like a caged animal. He kept looking at the front page of the newspaper, shaking his head, unable to believe his eyes. Now it all made sense. The "John Smith" Spencer had met in the little coffee shop, the man who wanted to know everything there was to know about Detective Rizzo, the man who seemed so mysterious and so hell-bent on remaining anonymous, was likely the serial killer the *San Diego Chronicle* had named "The Resuscitator."

Thinking about his options, all of which seemed incriminating, Spencer wasn't sure how to proceed. If he contacted the police and told them exactly what had happened, he would be implicating himself as an accomplice—an accomplice to a serial killer. This wasn't some low-end criminal knocking off little ma-and-pa convenient stores. This was first degree, premeditated murder. And no matter how compelling his defense, trying to prove that he had no knowledge of the killings, Spencer had little doubt that the district attorney would want his head served up on a platter.

Another option was to contact Detective D'Angelo. But considering that the detective had given Spencer proprietary information about Detective Rizzo, D'Angelo would only be concerned about his own hide. And Spencer knew from past dealings with him that the seedy detective would not only play dirty, he'd do anything—including fingering Spencer—to save himself.

Even if Spencer contacted the police anonymously, what could he tell them that might lead them down the right path? He had no idea how to find "John Smith," nor did he know his real name, address, or where he worked. He wasn't even sure what kind of car he drove. He could pay a visit to the Del Mar Fertility Clinic, but without some official credentials or a search warrant, they would never betray a client's confidentiality.

Spencer had never been a squeaky-clean PI. Far from it. He had spent most of his career living in a grey world where nothing was ever black and white. He had done a lot of things he regretted, things that made him ashamed. But never had he been indirectly involved with a murderer. At least to his knowledge.

At this juncture, Spencer was unclear on how to handle the situation. But what he did know was that he couldn't just stand by and let this monster kill another innocent person.

"Good evening, Sami," Al said.

Sami hadn't heard his voice this animated since he'd arrived in Rio. "Please tell me you have good news."

"I have *extraordinary* news!"

She held her breath.

"Aleta has come out of the coma! And it's looking real good! Her vital signs are stable, and they've had her up and walking around. She still looks like shit, and she's really wobbly, but she's talking fine and the doctor doesn't think she has any permanent injuries."

"I am so happy to hear that. Thank God."

"Yes, we have to thank God." Al's voice sounded a little unsteady.

"Any idea when she'll be discharged from the hospital?"

"Once her appetite's improved and she can walk without assistance, the doctor will let her go home. But she will likely be here for a while. Ricardo has already made arrangements for in-home care until she is completely recovered."

"Terrific."

"How are you holding up?" Al asked.

"We've got a promising lead a bunch of us are working on right now. In fact, I just stopped home to check up on the gang, but I have to get back to the precinct in a little while."

"Graveyard duty, huh?"

"Pulling out all the stops."

"Chief Larson and Captain Davidson busting your stones?"

"Actually, they've been surprisingly supportive. They did try to strong-arm me on your medical leave, unaware that we're a step ahead of them. But I straightened them out."

"I'll bet you did." He let out a heavy breath. "I miss the shit out of you."

"You've always been such a smooth talker."

"That's what happens when you flunk out of charm school."

This was the first lighthearted conversation they'd had since he went to Rio. Sami almost forgot how much she loved the playful banter. "Don't worry. You may not be charming, but you're a good lay."

"You ain't so bad yourself."

Under the circumstances, she didn't even want to broach the subject, but she had to ask the obvious question. "Speaking of good lays—and I'm not trying to pressure you—do you have the slightest inkling when you're coming back to San Diego?"

"Once my sister is discharged I'd like to spend at least a few days with her. That okay?"

"Nothing is more important than your sister right now. You take whatever time you need. I'll be here when you get back."

"That's the only thing that keeps me going."

If only he realized just how much she needed to hear him say that. "I really have to get the show on the road, Honey."

"I'll speak with you tomorrow," Al said.

The moment the call disconnected, she felt utterly alone. She hadn't been feeling great lately. Queasy stomach. Indigestion. A little bloated. She'd felt this way before when stress had gotten the best of her. She needed to track down the Resuscitator. And she needed Al to warm her bed.

Driving another rental car from Southwest Auto Rentals, a hole-in-the-wall establishment run by three Iranian brothers who didn't require credit cards, only cash and a valid driver's license, Julian arrived at the Yoga for Life Center thirty minutes early and parked in a spot where he could watch the main entrance. He thought it wise to check out the ladies as they entered the building just in case someone in particular caught his eye. Julian assumed that the parking lot would likely be full, and when class let out there would be a mad scramble for cars. The situation left little opportunity for Julian to snatch anyone without someone noticing. He wasn't yet sure how he would proceed, or even if tonight would work, but without a clear plan, he figured he'd let his charm lead the way.

Five minutes before the scheduled starting time of the yoga class, Julian saw a faded red Sentra pull into the parking lot. The car looked like the owner had just come from a demolition derby competition. He could see that nearly every panel and door that *could* be dented *was* dented. Except for the roof. But how do you dent a roof?

He waited for the driver to get out of her car so he could get a good look at her. Wearing black capri pants and a tight-fitting sports bra, the young woman was about as muscular as a woman could be without looking masculine. As she briskly walked toward the entrance, he stepped out of his car and followed her toward the building. Using the name John Smith, he signed up for the class as a guest, paid the twenty-five-dollar registration fee, and grabbed a complimentary yoga mat. As discretely as possible, he watched the woman unroll her pink yoga mat on the hardwood floor, hoping that he could find a spot close to her. She wasn't much to look at, but her body was sculpted with distinct cuts between her triceps and deltoids. As she was small-breasted, her well-developed pectoral muscles showed clearly. If there was anyone in this place who had the strong, healthy heart he was searching for, she was the one.

Two participants had already taken the spots on either side of the woman, but as luck would have it, the spot directly behind her, the best position for Julian to observe her, had not been taken. He scurried over and positioned his mat on the floor. She gave him a quick glance, smiled, then sat on her mat and went through a series of stretching exercises. It didn't take long for him to figure out that she was no beginner. She twisted her body into positions that made it seem like her muscles were made of rubber. He, on the other hand, had never practiced yoga before, and had an eerie feeling his body wouldn't survive the hour-long class. He no longer spent three days a week at the gym, working with weight machines and doing a sixty-minute cardio workout. In fact, he felt a bit insecure seeing his reflection in the mirrors all around the room. Thank God for oversize T-shirts. Even if he hadn't abandoned his exercise routine, his workouts did nothing to make his body more flexible.

Trying to look like an expert at what he was doing, Julian sat on his mat, removed his sneakers and socks, and began a series of benign exercises, all the while watching the young woman. He guessed that she stood roughly five-foot-ten and tipped the scales at less than one-thirty. Tall and lean, her tiny waist complimented a perfectly shaped behind. As she stretched and bent and twisted her body into pretzel-like positions, he caught her checking him out several times. She didn't offer an obvious smile, but her eyes gave her away.

The yoga instructor, an attractive white man with exquisite muscle definition and long unruly hair pulled tight into a pony-tail, walked into the roomful of students and stood before the class. The instructor pressed his palms together in a prayer-like manner, and respectfully bowed forward. The students returned the gesture. Never having been to a yoga class, totally unfamiliar with yoga etiquette, Julian's actions were not in sync with the rest of the class. Already he felt uncomfortable and they hadn't even started with the first pose.

"Good evening class," the instructor said. "My name is Cour-age. Don't laugh. That is my legal name." He smiled. "Some of you look familiar, but I see a few new faces. Welcome, brothers and sisters. This is an intermediate class, so if you're new to yoga, please let your body speak to you and don't try any poses that seem too difficult. Please don't feel embarrassed to just sit in a resting position on your mat and watch the more experienced students. This is not a contest or survival of the fittest. It is an experience to join body, mind, and spirit." Courage pulled back his shoulders, widened his stance, and let his arms hang to the side. "Let's begin by stretching those back muscles."

Perspiring profusely fifteen minutes into the class, Julian real-ized that he was out of his element. Anyone who thought yoga was a woman's sport or an activity for wimps had never tried it. He had used muscles he didn't even realize he had. He sat on the mat, pulled his knees to his chest and watched the class, paying close attention to the woman in front of him. Julian might not be an expert or someone who could distinguish between good form and bad form, but he felt certain that this woman's fluid movement and graceful transitions from one pose to another seemed textbook-perfect.

During the next forty-five minutes, he tried several times to get into the rhythm. His attempts proved futile. Totally resigned, he surrendered and went from participant to spectator. Looking at his watch every couple of minutes, willing it to move faster, Julian thought the class would go on forever. Finally, the timer Courage had set at the beginning of class started playing an Indian song with the distinct sound of a sitar, and Julian felt like he'd been let out of prison. In retrospect, coming to this class had been foolish. Had he thought about it more clearly, he would have devised a more strategic plan. What was his next move? He sat there with thirty people around him, people who would soon be converging on the parking lot. How could he possibly think that this would be a fruitful evening?

He rolled up his mat and wrapped his towel around his neck, discouraged and highly irritated. Before returning the mat, he gave the woman one more look and smiled his best smile. Mat under her arm and towel over her shoulder, she approached him.

"First time?" she said.

"It's that obvious?"

"My first attempt only lasted five minutes, so you're way ahead of me."

"At least that gives me hope."

"Don't give up. Yoga is a great stress reliever. Besides, you never know when you'll meet someone interesting." Now she was grinning.

"Your form is exquisite," Julian said.

"And by *form* you mean my poses?"

He gave her a mischievous smirk. "That too."

She glanced at the wall clock. "I'd love to chat, but I really have to get going."

"How about I walk you to your car?"

"You didn't even tell me your name." She offered her hand. "McKenzie."

"John."

"My pleasure, John."

They walked side by side, heading for the door. With the entire class trying to exit the facility, it looked like a high school fire drill.

"Have you ever considered instructing, McKenzie?"

"I have. But in California you need a license and it's not easy getting one."

"Well, I for one would join your class in a heartbeat." Time to bait the hook. "Would you need a license to instruct one-on-one?"

"Good question."

"If you and your student kept things confidential, and you dealt in cash only, how would anyone find out?"

"I guess they wouldn't." She pointed to the beat-up Sentra. "That's my buggy. I call her the road warrior. I beat the crap out of her and she just won't die." She searched her purse for keys.

Julian looked around and there were at least ten people heading toward their vehicles. "This is going to sound totally off the wall, but would you consider giving me private yoga lessons?"

She stood frozen with her hand still in her purse. "Seriously?"

"Look, McKenzie, I would really like to learn yoga, but in a classroom environment I'm just too self-conscious. Besides, with one-on-one instruction, I can go at my own pace and work gradually toward more difficult poses."

"But every yoga center in San Diego offers private lessons. Why me?"

"Two reasons. First, I already looked into private lessons at three different studios and just didn't feel warm and cozy with the instructors. Second, I met someone interesting."

She fixed her eyes on his. "And where would I give these lessons?"

"Hey, we live in San Diego, where the sun always shines. We could meet at Mission Bay Park, Balboa Park—there are tons of outside options. And if you wanted an indoor facility, I have a huge loft apartment downtown that would be the perfect setting for yoga."

"As a currently unemployed college graduate, I'm really tempted."

"Let me sweeten the deal. We can meet at your convenience. Wherever you feel comfortable. And I'll pay you one hundred dollars per lesson—cash."

McKenzie pulled a piece of paper and pen out of her purse and scribbled her phone number. "I really have to fly, John. Give me a call tomorrow morning and maybe we can talk."

CHAPTER THIRTY-ONE

After an exhausting evening that didn't end until after midnight, Sami returned to the precinct at 6:00 a.m. to meet with Captain Davidson and Chief Larson. Last evening, Sami's associates, working from the leads the technicians, admins, and other detectives compiled, compared seven thousand photographs of male health-care professionals to the composite drawing Tiny and the sketch artist had jointly created. Fortunately, the organizations providing the databases and photographs were able to sort out the female photos, which accounted for the majority of health-care professionals with IDs displaying a caduceus. When the comparisons were completed, only seventeen health-care people resembled the composite sketch close enough for them to be considered possible suspects.

Sami and her colleagues now had to contact each of the seventeen suspects, and either interview them in their homes or ask them to come to the precinct. From her past experiences, most would cooperate, but a few would need to be detained as a suspect.

Although she felt completely exhausted when she'd gotten home at 1:15 a.m., for most of the night she could not unwind or sleep soundly. She just couldn't turn off the scenario in her head. Details of the investigation played over and over. For the last week she'd been running on reserve power and she figured that eventually she'd shut down and be totally ineffective. Thinking about her decision to quit school and return to homicide, she was not yet convinced she'd done the right thing. Was it ego? Was police work really in her blood, or was she merely living out her father's dying request? At this particular juncture, she faced several unanswered questions. The only two things she knew for sure were, one, that she had to find the killer, and find him soon; and two, she couldn't wait for Al to return. For now, she had to remove these troubling thoughts from her head and clear her mind for a meeting.

Walking down the long hallway to the captain's office, Sami felt like her shoes were made of concrete. Over the years, she'd heard the expression "dragging your ass" many times. Today it took on a whole new meaning.

She knocked on the captain's tightly closed door and waited for an invitation. When the door opened and she saw not only the captain and Chief Larson, but Mayor Sullivan as well, her already unsteady knees nearly buckled. That the three of them would meet her at 6:00 a.m. could qualify for an entry in the Guinness World Records. The fact that Davidson and Larson were dressed in suits and ties, and the mayor in a business suit at this early hour, surprised her even more.

Mayor Sullivan wasted no time with pleasantries or hand-shakes. Before Sami even had a chance to sit down, the mayor began the grilling.

"I have to be out of here in thirty minutes to catch a plane to Sacramento," Mayor Sullivan said, "so I don't have time for small talk." The mayor leaned against the file cabinet and brushed her hands across the front of her skirt. "What's the latest, Detective?"

Sami gave the three of them facts, figures, and a detailed account of what her colleagues and she discovered last evening.

"So, from nearly seven thousand photos," Mayor Sullivan said, "you narrowed it down to seventeen?"

"We'll contact the potential suspects beginning this morning," Sami said. "And interview them as quickly as possible."

"And by quickly, you mean *today*, right?" the mayor asked.

"Most of them. There may be a few—"

"I don't want to hear any excuses, Detective. I want all seventeen interviewed *today.*" Somehow. Someway.

"What I meant, Mayor, was that we may not be able to track down all of them. There may be a few out of town or some that we're unable to immediately contact."

"Pull out all the stops," Mayor Sullivan ordered. "I want everyone in the department working on this. In fact, I want every detective from homicide to narcotics tracking down these suspects. I don't care about job descriptions or roles. Chief Larson, contact the captains of each division and tell them this is a direct order from me. The only words I want to here at the end of the day are, 'We've made an arrest.' Is that clear?"

"Crystal clear, Mayor," Sami said.

When McKenzie O'Neill heard the telephone ring at nine thirty in the morning, she expected to hear her mom's voice. Every morning right around this time, her mother made her daily call to check up on her only daughter. McKenzie had left her hometown of Buffalo, New York, to attend college in San Diego with intentions of returning home. But four years of sunshine and sandy beaches had completely seduced McKenzie and she'd fallen in love with Southern California.

"May I speak to McKenzie?" the man's voice said.

"This is she. Who's calling?"

"This is the worst yoga dude in San Diego County. Remember me?"

"To be honest, I didn't expect to hear from you, John."

"You asked me to call this morning. Is it not a good time for you to talk?"

She didn't mind letting her toast get cold for an opportunity to make some money. "No, no, it's fine."

"Have you thought about my proposition?"

"How many times a week do you want yoga lessons?"

"Two, possibly three."

"And you're willing to pay me one hundred dollars per one-hour session and meet wherever it's convenient for me?"

"As long as you don't want to meet in Montana."

"I have an unpredictable schedule from day to day," she said, "and I doubt I'll be able to meet you during the day, so you're going to have to be a bit flexible."

"My schedule isn't exactly nine-to-five either, so we'll just have to play it by ear."

"So, how do I contact you?" McKenzie asked.

"Well, um, why don't I give you my cell phone number?"

"That would be great."

With the phone cradled against her shoulder, she wrote down the number, then said, "Looking forward to it, John."

"Likewise."

After Julian disconnected, he couldn't help but grin. He loved twenty-first-century technology. Especially the fact that he could buy an untraceable, throwaway cell phone without an ID or credit card.

Now that he'd made a connection with McKenzie, a woman he believed would be ideal as a subject, the next step was to get her to his loft. She seemed apprehensive when he made his proposition, which was perfectly understandable. What woman in her right mind would go to a strange man's apartment without learning more about him? Then again, Genevieve had defied this basic principle. But she was a careless, intoxicated woman. McKenzie seemed more responsible. And more cautious. He guessed that she would be more comfortable meeting him in a public place, so somehow he had to gain her confidence before he could ever expect her to consider going to his loft.

She was attracted to him. Catching her looking at him at yoga class made that obvious. This in itself was likely his most powerful weapon. Based on his prior experiences, women often thought too much with their hearts and not enough with their brains when it came to men. Many would go against the grain of common sense and risk everything for the possibility of love. To break through a woman's self-preservation fortress, nothing was more effective than the prospect of love. He did not have the luxury of time and had a significant amount of research to complete. But if he moved things along too quickly, he risked spooking McKenzie. He had to find a way for them to go from casual acquaintances to intimate lovers as quickly as possible.

CHAPTER THIRTY-TWO

Sami and her colleagues—fourteen of them from homicide, narcotics, vice, and arson—met in the conference room to organize an efficient plan to round up the seventeen possible suspects. Although the department's priority focused primarily on these leads, Sami's group was still tasked with the responsibility to follow every lead that came in through the hotline. Sami hadn't yet interviewed the relatives of Robert Winters or Rachael Manning, victims three and four, but it was high on her priority list and she had instructed Osbourn to set up appointments.

From her prior experiences, nearly all of the hotline tips proved to be a dead end. But, as a detective, she couldn't take anything for granted. Sometimes the most obscure phone call led to an arrest. Today would likely be another eighteen-hour marathon. And life for her would be a lot easier if lightning struck Detective D'Angelo. From her perspective, his retirement couldn't come soon enough.

Sami's cell phone, set to vibrate only, went off several times during the meeting, but she didn't dare answer it for fear the cranky group of detectives would hiss and moan. She did however take a quick call from Emily but cut her short. "Everything okay?" Sami had asked. When Emily put her mind at ease, she said, "In a meeting. Call you back ASAP."

"Let's split up into groups of two," Sami said. She pointed to the whiteboard. "To keep it simple, I've broken down the seventeen suspects by geography, so you're not driving from one end of the county to another." She passed out a stack of papers. "Here are names, phone numbers, addresses, and in some cases, employers. Most of you have only two suspects to track down." She looked directly at D'Angelo. "The homicide detectives will handle the remainder. Any questions?"

"I hope we're getting a little overtime pay in our next check," D'Angelo said. "President Lincoln freed the slaves a hundred and fifty years ago."

"Your concern has been noted. Next time I meet with Mayor Sullivan, I'll be sure to pass along your grievance. Unless, of course, you'd like to speak with her directly." Sami fished through her purse and pulled out a piece of paper. "I've got her personal cell phone number here if you need it, Chuck."

After the meeting, Sami walked over to Detective Osbourn. She could see a familiar concern in her partner's eyes. "Are you okay working all these hours?"

"Not crazy about it, but it goes with the territory."

"It's not a problem being away from your wife?"

"I'd rather be home, but—"

"If you feel you need to be with her, Richard, I can handle things myself. I've got plenty of help."

"Thanks, but that's not necessary. Physically she's okay. But it's going to take some time for her to get over the emotional stuff."

"If you need to cut your day short, don't be afraid to ask."

"I appreciate it."

She studied the list of the seventeen suspects whose likenesses resembled the composite drawing. There were three potential eye witnesses: Katie Mitchell, Genevieve Foster's best friend; Tiny, the bouncer; and Robin, the salesperson at Saks. Although anyone of them could possibly finger the perp, Sami felt strongly that she should run it by Robin first, and then contact Tiny and Katie afterwards. From what she'd learned thus far, Katie had seen the perp in a crowded, poorly lit bar, and Tiny only got a glimpse of him. So it made sense to interview a witness who spent time with the suspect under bright fluorescent lights and got a good look at his face.

"Before we try to track down these possibles, I think it would be a good idea if we touched base with the gal at Saks Fifth Avenue who sold our guy the outfit Genevieve Foster was wearing when we found her body."

"I thought Al already interviewed her."

"He did. And he's always thorough. But the game has changed now that we have a composite sketch and seventeen possible suspects. If she can finger one of these guys, we could both be home for dinner tonight."

"I'll drive," Osbourn said.

When Julian's cell phone rang, he knew it was McKenzie because she was the only one who had the number for his throwaway phone. "Jul…John speaking." He almost made a fatal mistake.

"Hi, John, this is McKenzie O'Neill. Remember me?"

"How could I possibly forget the yoga goddess?"

"That's a bit of a stretch, but thank you. And by the way, if you're trying to get a discount on the yoga classes by complimenting me, sorry, no deal."

"Not looking for a discount, but am hoping you've got good news."

"Well, I've tweaked my schedule a bit and if you're available, I can meet you tonight at around six thirty."

It was better news than he had expected. "Terrific. Where would you like to meet?"

"How about Balboa Park?"

The park was huge and generally crowded. He had hoped for a more secluded place. "That *could* work, but let me run this by you. What part of San Diego do you live in?"

"Clairemont."

"Have you ever been to Kate Sessions Park in Pacific Beach?"

"As a matter of fact, I was there last weekend for a concert in the park. The band Trigger was playing. They're awesome. Have you ever heard them?"

"Can't say that I have."

"If you'd rather meet at Kate Sessions Park, that's fine," McKenzie said. "It's pretty quiet there in the evening and the view of Mission Bay and the ocean is breathtaking."

That was exactly what he wanted her to say. "That works for me. Where do you want to meet?"

"How about we meet at the parking lot on top of the hill?"

"Perfect." Julian said.

"Let's meet on the east end of the lot."

"Looking forward to it, McKenzie."

"See you at six thirty sharp."

CHAPTER THIRTY-THREE

Sami and Osbourn searched for a parking spot in the filled-to-capacity ramp garage at Fashion Valley Mall. It seemed as though it were Christmas Eve and half the city scrambled to finish their last-minute shopping. Sami had always believed that San Diego was immune to the ebb and flow of the economy. No matter how grim the economic forecast, San Diego seemed to thrive. Crowds of people mobbed every restaurant in the county, especially on Friday and Saturday evenings. A crowded parking lot at a shopping mall in the middle of the week seemed like proof positive that her theory was valid. San Diegans had deep pockets and they loved their upscale cars, posh homes, designer clothes, and gourmet restaurants.

After circling for ten minutes up and down the ramp garage, hoping to find someone piling shopping bags in their trunks, Osbourn spotted someone leaving, and eased the Taurus into a tight spot designated Compacts Only. Sami could barely squeeze out her door, which reminded her that it was time to tighten the belt and get back to her daily runs around Balboa Park.

Osbourn, watching Sami struggle to wiggle her hips out the door, stood there with a big grin painted across his face.

"One smart-alecky remark," she warned, "and you'll be walking a beat in South San Diego with the pit bulls and drug dealers."

She slammed the door and brushed off her slacks. "I know low people in high places."

"I'll keep that in mind."

They weaved through the crowd and found the entrance to Saks Fifth Avenue. Osbourn had already contacted the store manager to set up a meeting with the salesperson.

"Who are we looking for?" Sami asked.

Osbourn referred to his notes. "The manager's name is Katherine Levy and the salesperson is Robin Westcott."

"Where are we meeting them?"

"Ms. Levy asked me to have her paged as soon as we arrived."

Once inside, the detectives headed for the first available salesperson. Sami had never been in this store. It was way out of her league. From the impeccably polished black marble floors to the outrageous chandeliers, the place was unmistakably a playground for the affluent.

While Sami craned her neck, perusing the decadence of the store, wondering if she'd ever have enough money to buy even a pair of pantyhose here, Osbourn approached a salesperson and explained the situation. The salesperson pointed to a door on the other side of the store, and they found their way, through racks of leather and linen, to Levy's office. Before they had a chance to knock, Katherine Levy opened the door and invited them inside the cramped and cluttered space. Already seated in the office was Robin Westcott, the salesperson who'd sold the perp the expensive cocktail dress.

"Thanks for meeting us on such short notice," Sami said. "We appreciate your cooperation."

"I hope we can help," Levy said.

Sami opened a brown folder and handed Robin Westcott a copy of the composite sketch along with seventeen photographs.

"I understand that Detective Diaz already spoke to you," Sami said. "But at that time we didn't have this drawing, or possible matches. Does the sketch or any of the seventeen photos look like the guy who bought the dress?"

Robin Westcott studied the sketch for at least a minute, cocking her head from left to right. Then she pointed to the sketch. "The features of his face are close, but not totally accurate. But what's completely wrong is the hair. He wore a Chargers baseball cap but took it off a few times. And believe me, this guy was as clean-cut as they come. Hair parted on the side like a kid making his communion. He certainly didn't have spiked hair."

Sami remembered that Tiny, the bouncer from Henry's Hideaway, had said that the perp was "trying to look gay," whatever that meant. She could only assume at this juncture that in an effort to blend in with the eclectic crowd, one of the things the perp had done was to change his hairstyle to something more contemporary.

"You said that the features of his face are close," Osbourn said. "How do they differ from the guy you saw?"

Robin looked at the sketch again. "First off, the guy's chin was chiseled. In this sketch it's not nearly as pronounced. Now I'm not talking about a chin like Jay Leno. More like an Armani model."

Before Sami could ask for clarification, Katherine Levy handed Robin the Saks Fifth Avenue summer catalog and pointed to a particular model. "Is this what his chin was like, Robin?"

Robin vigorously nodded and handed the catalog to Sami. Now she could see exactly what Robin meant.

"Another thing that doesn't seem quite right is the shape of his face," Robin said. "It was more triangular than oval." Robin nervously scratched her head. "I can't say for sure, but I think his nose was a little more prominent, too. Not big, but…" She paused for a moment and stared at the wall. "Do you remember the actor, John Barrymore, the guy who played Sherlock Holmes?"

"Of course," Sami said.

"That kind of nose."

"Do any of the photographs look familiar?" Osbourn asked.

One by one, Robin flipped through the photos, all the while shaking her head.

"I can't absolutely swear to it, but I don't think that any of these guys is the one who bought the designer dress."

Sami sat back in the chair and began reviewing the last forty-eight hours. She and her colleagues had examined thousands of photos and narrowed them down to seventeen possible suspects. But the likeness was based on the sketch that Tiny and the artist had come up with. It was perfectly understandable that Tiny got the hair wrong. How could he know that the perp parted it on the side? But he had gotten other, more important features wrong. Right now, a bunch of detectives were likely interviewing the wrong suspects.

"Robin, would you consider coming to the precinct and meeting with our sketch artist, so we can get a more accurate composite drawing?"

Robin glanced at Katherine Levy as if silently asking for her approval. Levy nodded.

"When would you like me to do this?"

"ASAP."

"How about first thing in the morning? Around nine?"

"Perfect." About to leave, Sami had to ask a question to ease her mind. "One more thing, Robin. Is there a reason why you didn't agree to help us with a sketch when Detective Diaz met with you?"

Robin stared at the floor. "I was scared. When he asked me if I could, my brain went blank. I remembered certain things about the guy, but his face just wouldn't come into focus. Now that I see this sketch, my memory is starting to come back."

"But now you can remember what he looks like?"

"Yes."

Sami gave Robin Westcott directions to the main precinct. "Thanks for all your help. We appreciate you talking to us." She handed both of the women a business card and glanced at Osbourn. He got the hint and handed each of them his business card as well.

"So what do you think?" Osbourn asked.

The two detectives headed for Saks's front door.

"Basically, if I can be blunt, I think we're temporarily screwed."

"My thought exactly," Osbourn agreed.

"I thought Tiny was a reliable source, but you can never be sure."

Like a gentleman, Osbourn opened the door for Sami and they headed for their car.

"All things considered," Sami said, "it seems that Robin has a more credible snapshot of what our guy looks like. As a bouncer at the front door of a busy bar, Tiny must look at a couple hundred faces and IDs every night. And how long does he see each of them as he screens them at the front door? Maybe ten seconds. Not to mention the limited lighting. But Robin spent some time with our guy. Talking. Listening. And looking at his face under bright lights. Stands to reason that she would have a more reliable memory."

"Right now," Osbourn said. "There are a whole lot of detectives on a wild goose chase."

"Don't say anything to the captain or anyone else for that matter until we get this sorted out."

"I won't breathe a word of it."

"If the mayor finds out, she's going to have a shit-fit. And you and I will be eating army-surplus peanut butter."

"What now?" Osbourn asked.

"Back to the drawing board."

CHAPTER THIRTY-FOUR

"Hey there," Al said. "How's my one and only?"

"Oh, I've been better and I've been worse, but right now I'm feeling really shitty."

"Are you sick?"

"Not that kind of shitty. Although my stomach's been on the rampage lately."

"Is it work?"

"Forget about me and my continuing saga," Sami said. "How is Aleta?"

"She's doing real well. Not quite ready to run a marathon. She tires easily and still has a few battle scars, but she seems on her way to a complete recovery. Only thing that concerns me is her short-term memory. She forgets what she had for breakfast and seems really absentminded. But the doctor feels it's temporary."

Sami so desperately wanted to ask him when he might be home, but didn't want to put him under anymore pressure. "That's wonderful news."

"So tell me what the hell's going on."

She explained the inaccurate sketch, the wasted hours chasing a ghost, and her fear that the mayor was going to go postal on her. "It's not your fault. You had what you believed to be a reliable source and moved forward. What else could you possibly do? Twiddle your thumbs until another victim showed up on the front steps of City Hall? You win some, you lose some. You have to take every lead seriously."

"I should have asked more questions. Dug deeper. I guess that my two-year hiatus away from the department dulled my cop instincts."

"I don't believe that for a minute."

"Well, I'm happy I've got at least one fan."

"How's the clan doing?"

"Everyone is fine."

"Oh, I almost forgot." The tone in his voice changed. "Think you can put up with my snoring again?"

She didn't want to get too excited but…"Is that your subtle way of telling me you're coming home soon?"

"If you'll have me."

"Well, D'Angelo *has* been hitting on me lately and I'm really tempted."

"Tell him I'm going to cut his balls off when I get back."

"I don't think he has any."

Al laughed. "I catch a flight in two days, and I'm thrilled. I just love to fly!"

The last thing she wanted was for him to second-guess his decision, but she had to ask. "Are you sure, Al? I mean, are you really okay with leaving your sister?"

"We made a pact. No more huge gaps between visits. She promises to come to San Diego at least four times a year. I invited her and Ricardo to join us for a July fourth barbeque. That okay?"

"You have to ask?"

"Just trying to be courteous."

"Your sister and her boyfriend are welcome anytime," Sami said. She looked at her watch. "I'd love to talk more but—"

"Yah, yah, I remember the routine. Don't let the mayor rough you up."

"I won't."

"I'll e-mail you my flight info. Think you can pick me up at the airport?

"Nothing would make me happier."

Just as she had promised, Robin Westcott showed up at the main precinct at 9:00 a.m. sharp. Sami whisked her off to a private room where Robin and the sketch artist, Israel Martinez, could hopefully come up with an accurate composite of the serial killer. When Sami introduced Robin to Israel, he scratched the back of his head.

"Didn't we already do this?"

"That was just for practice," she had said. "This one's for real."

By the way Israel looked at her, it was obvious he wasn't amused.

She faced the daunting task of meeting her colleagues with her tail between her legs, and having to explain why they'd been chasing a ghost for the last twenty-four hours. She wasn't yet sure how she'd make this announcement without coming under attack—especially from her favorite detective: Mr. Big Mouth D'Angelo. Surely, he would thoroughly enjoy taking her to the mats. If she'd learned anything as a detective, she'd learned that when you deliver bad news to your colleagues, be sure you follow it up with good news. As soon as she had the new sketch in hand, she would convene with her colleagues and break the news. Then, they would have to run another comparison of the new sketch against the database of photos they had collected.

Not all was lost. In spite of the faulty composite drawing, the basic premise was still valid: the perp was likely in health care, he had an advanced medical degree, and his medical ID had a caduceus imprinted on it. Also, both Tiny and Robin Westcott believed they could pick the perp out of a lineup. *So*, she thought, *maybe I'm not nearly as screwed as I thought.* Her phone rang and Police Chief Larson, his voice a familiar growl, summoned her to his office. Immediately.

When Sami saw Mayor Sullivan sitting in the captain's office yet again, she suspected that she was about to be horsewhipped.

Davidson gestured for her to sit adjacent to the mayor. Her irritable stomach announced its displeasure.

"Where's Osbourn?" the chief asked.

She couldn't tell Larson that she let him make a quick trip home to check on his wife. "He's knee-deep in paperwork."

The chief wasn't buying it. "He needs to be here."

"No worries," Sami said. "I can get him in here. But if I do, we'll never have our reports completed by the end of the day." Larson was a stickler for paperwork, so Sami rolled the dice.

"Forget it," the chief said. "You can fill him in."

Mayor Sullivan leaned toward Sami as if she was going to whisper in her ear. The volume of her voice was anything but a whisper. "I understand that your team has done a fine job tracking down and interviewing the seventeen suspects. Is that correct, Detective?"

"It is." She could tell that the mayor was weaving a web.

"And is it also true that none of the seventeen suspects resulted in an arrest, or were even worthy of a more in-depth interrogation?"

"I'm afraid so, Mayor."

"So we spent hundreds of man hours on a wild goose chase?"

"Not at all, Mayor. Through our efforts, we found another witness who can pick our guy out of a lineup. In fact, she's with Israel Martinez as we speak."

"That's terrific, Detective," the mayor said. "There's only one minor problem. We have no suspects—not even one—so we have no lineup."

"What's the witness doing with Martinez?" Larson asked.

"She got a much better look at our guy so we're adding a little more detail to the original composite sketch."

"Who's the witness?" Larson asked.

"The salesperson at Saks."

"Wait a minute," Larson said. "Didn't Al already interview her?"

Sami nodded.

"And he never asked her if she could identify our guy?"

"He did. But at that time the witness claimed she couldn't help with a composite drawing. You know how it goes, Chief. Sometimes witnesses suffer from temporary amnesia."

"I have to be honest with you, Detective," the mayor said. "In spite of your efforts, I'm not only disappointed at the lack of progress in this investigation. I have to tell you, I'm seriously losing my patience."

"Let me ask you a question, Mayor, if I may. What should I be doing that I'm not already doing? Because if you have any suggestions at all, if I need to move in a different direction, or completely change my course of action, I'll act on your suggestions immediately."

"I'm not the lead detective on this investigation, you are. I don't tell you how to do your job and you don't tell me how to do mine. My only concern is results. And I don't care how you get there, as long as your methods are within the guidelines set by the department."

"With all due respect, Mayor, considering the short time I've been lead on this investigation, I think we've made great progress.

We have two eye witnesses, and soon we'll have a revised sketch that will narrow the field. Our guy is more than likely in health care, and his medical ID card has the caduceus symbol on it. I know that I don't have to tell you this, but police work is a process of elimination. You get a lead. You chase it. If it takes you to a dead end, you move in a different direction. Wouldn't you agree that we're heading in the right direction?"

The mayor stood, leaned her backside against Larson's desk, and folded her arms. "So what's your game plan, Detective?"

At times like this, Sami regretted being half Sicilian. Oh, what she wanted to say to the mayor. "As soon as the revised composite sketch is done, I'll be meeting with the entire crew and coordinating distribution to all city, state, and federal locations. We'll also compare the sketch to the database we've compiled of health-care professionals that meet our criteria. Once completed, we'll hit the bricks again and interview potential suspects based on their resemblance to the composite sketch."

"Okay," the mayor said. "I'm going to give you lots of rope here. Hopefully, you won't hang yourself."

CHAPTER THIRTY-FIVE

Julian arrived at Kate Sessions Park a few minutes early, feeling excited and nervous at the same time. Except for three teenagers tossing around a Frisbee, a family of four enjoying a picnic, and a young woman walking her Golden Retriever, the park was quiet. And that was exactly the way he wanted it. Not that he had any intentions of snagging McKenzie here—that would be way too risky. But the fewer people who saw them together, the less chance anyone would make the connection when she went missing.

Although he had made some interesting, and he felt important, discoveries, his research was not progressing nearly as well as he had hoped. At the hospital, he had unlimited resources—medications, surgical tools, and cutting-edge equipment, not to mention an entire research staff available at his beck and call. And he had access to the most sophisticated medical equipment in the world. From a surgical standpoint, his loft, at best, was little more than an underfunded clinic. Grabbing a handful of scalpels, or a rib spreader, or anesthesia, was easy. They fit neatly into his briefcase. But the only piece of diagnostic equipment he had at his disposal was a dated heart monitor he had purchased second-hand from a medical supplier. He couldn't just walk out the hospital door with a ten-thousand-dollar piece of equipment under his arm.

A woman appeared out of nowhere, walking across the lawn holding hands with two young girls about the same age as Julian's daughters. His thoughts drifted to Lorena and Isabel. He had faced fierce guilt and a profound sense of loss when he had packed three suitcases and moved out of his home. He had believed that the separation from his daughters would prove devastating. Sure, when he dropped them off after spending time with them, he'd felt horrible. But he didn't feel the intense emptiness he had anticipated. Was he a rotten father? Would he ever be able to repair whatever damage he'd caused? Children didn't always reveal their emotions. Fears and insecurities were often buried deep inside. How well he knew this. When he was young, unloved, and desperately seeking his parents' recognition, no one was aware of his private hell. No one could ever understand what he felt in his broken heart.

Thoughts of Nicole took hold of him. Separated from her, he now realized that he had been silently unhappy with his marriage for years. Sometimes denial conveniently masks the obvious. Had it not been for his daughters, he might have found the courage to walk away from his marriage years ago. Now more than ever, he needed to secure the research grant from GAFF. Once approved, he would be in an ideal position to ask Nicole for a divorce and fight for custody of his daughters. For now, he'd have to endure. There was no way he could handle the pressure from the research and emotional strain of a divorce at the same time. Everything came into focus. His objectives crystal clear.

He looked to his right and saw McKenzie O'Neill parking the "road warrior" right next to him. He watched her get out of the car, and in that moment, he wanted her the same way he had wanted Eva and Rachael.

"Sorry I'm a little late," McKenzie apologized. "The traffic coming into Pacific Beach was horrendous."

"No big deal. I was just sitting in my car admiring the view of Mission Bay." Julian grabbed the yoga mat he had purchased just that afternoon, tucked it under his arm, and draped a towel around his neck. "Pick a spot."

McKenzie pointed to a level area under a palm tree. "How about over there?"

"Hey, you're the instructor, so it's your call." He reached in his pocket and peeled five crisp twenty-dollar bills from a sizable wad of money. He handed the money to McKenzie. "Here you go. I thought it best to give you the money in advance just in case you have to drive me to emergency."

She laughed. "Not to worry. I'll take it easy on you for the first couple of lessons. Then you're in big trouble."

She walked slightly ahead of him, leading the way. He liked what he saw. Perfectly proportioned with highly defined muscle tone, McKenzie's body didn't have an ounce of fat. But oh, what an ass.

She rolled out her mat and set her towel and gallon bottle of water on the grass. "You didn't bring any water?" she asked.

"Afraid not."

"Well as long as you're not scared of getting cooties, you're welcome to share mine."

"Thanks. The last thing I'm worried about is getting cooties from you." He stared at her long and penetrating. Julian could feel strong chemistry between them.

His stamina and flexibility surprised him. Of course, McKenzie was really taking it easy.

She glanced at her watch. "We're twenty minutes into it. How you holding up?"

"I'm fine now. But wait until I try to get out of bed tomorrow morning. I'm going to need a crane."

"You'll be fine. Sore muscles are a good thing. It's your body trying to tell you something."

"Yes. Telling me to take up basket weaving."

"Okay, watch closely. We're going to go into downward facing dog."

Julian studied her form carefully and tried his best to hold the position.

"Don't overdo it. If you feel too much strain in your lower back or shoulders, move to a cat-cow stretch on all fours. Remember how to do that?"

"I do."

Thirty-five minutes later, Julian was completely spent and about as drenched as he could be without stepping into a shower. "Can we call it a night?" he asked.

"Had enough?"

"Don't worry. I won't ask for a refund."

"That's a good thing. Because my fee is nonrefundable."

They gathered their things and walked slowly toward the parking lot. Julian turned and looked west. "Looks like a beautiful sunset."

"Yes, it does."

"Are you in a hurry?" Julian asked.

"That depends. What did you have in mind?"

"We could drive to the ocean, get a couple of iced drinks from Starbucks, and watch the sun set."

She looked at her watch. "I'm tempted but I've got an early-morning appointment and really should get going."

"But wait a minute. You're still on my dime, right? The least you could do is give me my money's worth. Besides, it's my treat."

She didn't say anything but he could tell she was seriously considering his proposal.

"C'mon. It'll be fun. Maybe we'll see the green flash."

"I've never seen one," she said. "Have you?"

"Only once."

She chewed on her lower lip. "Okay. But just as soon as the sun sets, I have to leave."

Parking at the beach was always difficult, but it was too early for the bar-hopping crowd and too late for the sun worshipers, so at this particular time, both McKenzie and Julian found parking spots only two blocks from Crystal Pier, a landmark in Pacific Beach. Conveniently, Starbucks was on the way to the ocean.

"I'll run in and get the drinks," Julian offered. "You can sit out here and look at the beautiful sky. What's your pleasure?"

"I'd like a Very Berry Hibiscus."

"That's a joke, right? You're trying to set me up so the Starbucks folks think I'm looney."

"Nope. It's one of their limited-time promotional drinks. I had one yesterday."

"Okay, but if I'm not out in ten minutes, come rescue me."

"Sure thing."

He was glad she hadn't ordered a frothy drink with lots of whipped cream. That would make it nearly impossible to spike her drink. He ordered a Very Berry Hibiscus for her and a green tea Frappuccino for himself. While he waited, he kept an eye on her. With her back to him, he could see that she was facing west and watching the colorful sky. *Perfect.*

When the order was ready, he grabbed the drinks and headed for the condiment bar. As he reached in his pocket and removed a small packet of the Rohypnol he had prepared earlier today, he looked left and then right to see if anyone was watching. As quickly as he could, he poured the drug into McKenzie's drink, grabbed a stir-stick, and thoroughly blended the drug with the drink.

"Enjoy," he said as he handed McKenzie the drink.

They headed for the ocean.

They weren't fortunate enough to see the green flash, but the orange and red and yellow sky dancing on the calm ocean was begging to be on a postcard.

"I gotta get moving," McKenzie said. "I'm suddenly really tired."

"It's probably the ocean air. Just about every time I come down here, I fall asleep on the beach."

They left the beach and headed for their cars. Julian noticed that McKenzie walked like someone with concrete shoes.

"Are you okay?" he asked, trying to sound legitimately concerned.

"Wow. My head is spinning. I feel like I'm drunk."

"Is it that hibiscus drink?"

She shook her head. "I seriously doubt it."

"Has this happened before?"

"Never."

Only a half block away from her car, he didn't think she was going to make it.

"I have to sit down," McKenzie said. "I feel like I'm going to pass out."

"We're almost there. Take my arm."

"I don't think...I can drive. What am I going to do?"

"There's an urgent care a few blocks away. I think you should get checked out. Why don't I drive you there?" From his past experience with Rohypnol and the dose he'd given her, he guessed that it would take hold in about five minutes and she'd be passed out cold.

"I don't want to trouble you," she said, her voice almost garbled.

"It's no trouble. Honestly."

CHAPTER THIRTY-SIX

The effect of the drug didn't wear off for more than three hours. When McKenzie awoke, she found herself lying on a strange bed in a pitch-black room, and not only did she feel as if she were still dreaming, her brain was a collection of incoherent thoughts. She tried desperately to piece together the puzzle but the only thing she knew for certain was that John—if that was even his real name—had drugged her. But why? She didn't even want to think about the obvious, but couldn't stop herself from taking a quick inventory. She didn't feel any discomfort "down there," but in her current state how could she be certain that her sensory signals told the whole story?

For most of her adult life, McKenzie had been careful—obsessively careful. Why had she let down her guard with John? Was it the money he had offered her? Was it his innocent charm? Back in college, three of her closest friends had been drugged with "roofies." One got pregnant, one was a victim of a gang rape, and one ended up in therapy. Whatever he had planned for her, she feared the worst.

She tried to sit up but felt something tug on her wrists. It took a minute for her to realize that she was bound to the bed with something unidentifiable. She further discovered when she tried to bend her knees that her ankles were also tied to the bed. Her temples were throbbing unmercifully. She lay perfectly still and listened. But all she could hear was the tick-tock of a clock.

Her mouth felt as dry as sawdust, so she tried to produce enough saliva to speak, but the best she could do was generate a barely audible sound.

"John, are you here? Can you hear me?"

She could hardly hear her own words. How did she expect anyone else to hear them? All she could do was lie quietly and wait.

On her way to the airport, Sami felt first-date nervous. She and Al had been together for nearly two years, yet she still got goose bumps in anticipation of seeing him again. If "absence makes the heart grow fonder," then she was living proof. She hoped that her nervousness was a good sign. After all, what was left when the sweaty palms and anxious stomach were replaced with ho-hum yawns?

She tried to time her arrival a few minutes after his plane landed, allowing some time for him to retrieve his luggage. Just ahead, she could see the lighted JetBlue sign where they had agreed to meet. Standing just below it, holding one suitcase in each hand, she spotted a familiar silhouette. Al dropped one of the suitcases and waved his arm like the president about to board Air Force One.

Unable to find a curbside spot, she double-parked next to a black Lincoln. Al left the luggage by the trunk and before she could even say hello, he wrapped his arms around her. It seemed as though it had been years since she felt the security of his firm hug. She didn't want him to let go.

"How are you, stranger?" he said.

"I'm much better now."

Al let go of Sami and lifted the suitcases into the trunk. She tried to help him but he grabbed her arm. "Not with that back of yours."

They hopped in the car and headed for the exit toward Freeway 5.

They both started talking at the same time. "I guess we both have lots of questions," Sami said. "You go first."

"How's your mom?"

"Coming along, stubborn as a mule. Fortunately, Emily seems to have more persuasive powers than I do."

"Everything okay with Emily living there?"

"I hope she never leaves. She's my savior."

Al coughed into his hand. It seemed as though he were choosing his words carefully. "Any progress with the investigation?"

"Lots of cold trails. But we do have what I hope is an accurate composite sketch."

"From an eye witness?"

"From the salesperson at Saks who sold the perp the cocktail dress we found Genevieve Foster wearing."

"Robin Wescott, the gal I interviewed?"

"That's the one."

"But she told me she couldn't help us with a sketch."

"Apparently, the fog lifted."

"I guess I should have pushed a little harder."

"Maybe you were a little distracted."

Al felt strongly that this was not the time or place for this conversation to take place. But Sami opened the door, so he had no choice but to tell her what he'd been struggling with. Waiting would only make it more agonizing. He reached over and laid his hand on top of her thigh. "You know that I love you, right, Sami?"

"I already don't like the direction of this conversation."

"Answer my question, please."

"Up until this minute, yes, Al, I believed you loved me. But I have this eerie feeling you're about to drop a bomb."

"No, Sami, love has never been the problem. I was in love with you before you even knew I existed. Remember your first day with homicide, when Captain Davidson introduced us? I took one look at you and I knew you were the one. I've never felt anything like that in my life. It's corny and sounds so Hollywood, but for me it was love at first sight.

"Then the more I got to know you, the more I learned about what made you tick, the greater my love. I guess I fell in 'like' with you too."

"Are you trying to tell me that you don't feel that way any longer?"

"Not at all, Sami. I love you with all my heart. But…"

"You're walking on eggshells, Al. Just tell me what's on your mind. Please."

"I feel as though the fire is gone. It's as if we're two people who love each other but live separate lives under the same roof. There's no time for romance. No time for intimacy. And no time for sex. I need more."

"You don't think *I* need more?" She put on the turn signal and merged onto the freeway. "Sometimes life gets in the way. I don't mean for that to be an excuse, but maybe this is a good thing. Maybe this conversation can get us back on track. Maybe we should talk to a relationship counselor."

He stared at the floor mats. "It's not that simple."

"I never said it would—"

"I slept with another woman."

Sami wanted to pull off the highway, park on the shoulder, and puke. His confession completely blindsided her. She knew from the start that there would be rough spots along the way. They both brought baggage to this relationship. But she always felt that no matter what, they could work things out because love could leap over even the biggest hurdles. Never in her wildest dreams did she think he would...

Feeling that Brazilian women were among the most beautiful in the world, she tried to imagine what the other woman looked like. She guessed that she was a tall, thin, black-haired beauty with generous lips, ample breasts, and a cute little ass, unlike Sami's, which at this particular moment felt the size of the Goodyear blimp. The images flashing through her mind replaced her speechless shock with intense anger. She felt so used. So betrayed. If she weren't driving the car at seventy miles an hour, she could envision herself slapping him silly.

"Are you in love with her?"

His head snapped toward Sami. "Of course not. It was just sex."

"*Just* sex? You say that so casually, as if all you did was hold her hand."

"I was lonely and depressed," Al said. "I would never do something like this under normal circumstances. It just happened."

Oh, how his matter-of-fact attitude opened old wounds. Her deceased ex-husband, Tommy DiSalvo, always tried to make light of his sexual escapades by excusing them as "just sex." When she had suggested she should have the same privilege, Tommy became enraged. Why was it okay for a guy to cheat, but if a woman did the same thing, she'd be a tramp?

"How many times did you fuck her? Was she a regular piece of ass?"

He didn't answer right away, which spoke volumes.

"It happened only once," Al said, his voice barely audible. "I swear."

"Are you sure about that? Your word doesn't mean much right now."

She could see that his eyes were glazed over, and this made her even more enraged. Did he think for one minute that an emotional display would make it easier for her? "Where did you meet her?"

"She's a nurse."

"What's her name?"

Al hesitated again.

"What's her fucking name!"

"Sofia."

"So while you were sitting by Aleta's bed, so concerned about her welfare, you found the time to get it on with one of the nurses, right?"

"Sami, I'm sorry. What do you want me to say?"

"I want you to tell me why. What have I done to make you cheat on me?"

"I was vulnerable and weak. She was there and you weren't. That's all there is to it."

For the rest of the ride home neither of them uttered a sound. Sami pulled in the driveway and the two of them sat quietly in the car. After several awkward minutes, she grabbed her purse from the back seat and opened the door.

"I can't sleep in the same bed with you. And with Emily and my mother here—"

"I'll stay at a hotel tonight. Can we talk tomorrow?"

"We're going to have to deal with this thing one day at a time." She pulled the trunk release and, without saying another word, headed for the front door.

Al ran to her and grabbed her shoulder.

"What?"

"I love you, Sami."

"Love is not enough."

Fortunately for Sami, everyone was sound asleep when she walked in the front door. She didn't have it in her at the moment to explain why Al wasn't with her. She guessed that no matter what she said, her mom would push the issue until she coughed up the truth. Her mom could extract top-secret information from the director of the CIA.

Sami doubted that she'd ever be able to fall asleep with so many disconcerting thoughts coming at her from all angles, so instead of going to bed and tossing and turning, she curled up on the sofa and turned on the TV. As she clicked through the channels, hoping to find a mindless movie to watch that didn't require an ounce of brain power, she came upon a movie called *The Ugly Truth*. She'd seen this movie before. It was a romantic comedy with a basic premise that women are naïve when it comes to men, falsely believing that sensitive, caring men actually exist, when in reality, all men are pigs and the only thing they care about is getting laid. There are no White Knights in shining armor, only self-centered clods that let the little head think for the big head. At this point in time, this movie seemed like the perfect companion for a woman who felt that every man on the planet should have his balls cut off.

She stared at the screen and heard the words spoken by the actors, but nothing really registered. She loved Al more than she loved any man she'd ever met. But how could she ever forgive him?

CHAPTER THIRTY-SEVEN

For most of the night, Sami slipped in and out of consciousness until her cell phone awakened her. She looked at her watch. At six thirty in the morning, she guessed it was either police business or the wrong number. She wanted it to be Al, begging for her forgiveness, crawling on his belly like the snake he was, but as much as this fantasy tugged at her feelings right now, she didn't think it was him.

"Sami Rizzo."

"Sorry to call so early," Captain Davidson apologized. "Late last night a missing person's report came in on a McKenzie O'Neill, and I'm afraid she might have been abducted by the serial killer."

The captain's timing couldn't have been worse. Sami felt like a zombie. "What's the connection?"

"No one has seen her for a couple of days. Her parents said when they couldn't reach her, they started calling her friends. One gal—her closest friend—said that the last time she saw McKenzie was at a yoga class. She said McKenzie seemed smitten by a man her friend had never seen before. Her description of him pretty much matches our guy."

"I just need to take a quick shower, Captain. I'll be there in an hour."

"Did Al come back from Rio last night as planned?"

She could hear herself saying, "Yes, the lyin', cheatin' sack of shit did come home last night." "Made it home safe and sound."

"Chief Larson and I have been talking, and with your nod, we'd like Al to partner with you on the investigation."

She was speechless.

"There are lots of implications here, and I'm sure that the rumor mill will kick into high gear. But we don't have time to pussyfoot around. You and Al are the best we've got, so if some-body's nose gets bent out of shape because of your personal rela-tionship with Al, too fucking bad. I've never been a big fan of political correctness. Besides, we got the okay from Mayor Sul-livan. Let the naysayers deal with *her.*"

Trapped like a rat. Under the circumstances, the thought of working side by side with Al, morning, noon, and night, was as unsavory as anything she could imagine at this particular point in time. Her wounds were still raw. But what could she do? As much as it pained her, she had no choice but to do what was best for the department. Whatever became of their romantic relationship, they had to find a way to separate business from personal.

"No problem, Captain. I'm sure Al and I can set our relation-ship aside and stay on task."

"I was hoping you'd say that. Do you want me to call him or would you like to break the news?"

"Oh, I think it should come from you, Captain."

"See you in an hour."

She set down the phone and headed for the bathroom. On the way, she saw her mother standing in her robe, just outside Sami's bedroom.

"Are you okay, Mom?"

"Where's Alberto?"

Sami didn't have time to explain, so she lied. "He had an early-morning appointment."

"Why didn't he sleep here last night?"

How could she possibly know this? "Can we talk later? I really have to get moving."

Josephine gave Sami a look she had seen many times, and Sami was certain that their next conversation would not be pleasant.

McKenzie had no idea how long she'd been lying on the bed in that dark room. Although her head was far from being clear, the effects of whatever drug John had given her had lost its grip. She had no concept of time. At this particular moment, the only thing she knew for sure was that she had to use the bathroom.

"Is anybody there? Can you hear me? I have to go to the bathroom."

Nothing.

Wetting herself was the least of her worries. Obviously, John had other plans for her. She tried not to think about the possibilities. But no matter how hard she tried, she couldn't help but believe that she had been duped by the serial killer she'd read about in the newspaper and seen on TV. Who hadn't heard the grisly details of what that maniac did to his victims?

McKenzie was fearful of what he might do to her, of course. But for some reason, she wasn't out-of-her-mind terrified. Shouldn't she be? Had the drugs diluted her senses?

Before she could muster another thought, she heard something in the distance, a door opening with squeaky hinges that needed lubrication. Then she heard the door click shut.

Footsteps. A man's heel-pounding footsteps. The cadence of someone walking slowly toward her. She strained her eyes to make out his image, but the room was too dark. Then, bright lights flooded the room and she squeezed her eyes shut until they adjusted.

"Hello, McKenzie."

The voice was familiar. She opened her eyes slightly to confirm what she already feared. "What's your real name?"

"Julian."

"You're the one, aren't you?"

"The *one*?"

"The Resuscitator."

"That's such an impersonal name, don't you think?"

"Would you please cut me loose and let me go to the bathroom?" She hoped that the thought of her soiling herself might motivate him to let her use the toilet.

Next to the bed, McKenzie now noticed a small cart holding odd-looking tools and instruments. She couldn't make out what they were. Julian reached for what looked like a scalpel and cut the two nylon straps binding her ankles. He held the scalpel inches from her face. "You're not going to try anything silly if I cut you loose, right?"

His face looked much different than the face of the charming man she had met at her yoga class, the man who had broken through her self-preservation mechanism, the man who would surely be her executioner. She saw an intensity in his eyes that sent chills through her body.

He cut the straps binding her wrists and led her to the bathroom, following only half a step behind. "You've got five minutes."

She went into the bathroom, her mind aswarm with terrifying thoughts of her fate. She now knew, beyond a shadow of a doubt, that her captor was the man the *San Diego Chronicle* referred to as the Resuscitator, the serial killer who performed barbaric experiments on his victims. Now, wide-awake and free of the side effects of the drugs, McKenzie O'Neill was indeed out-of-her-mind terrified.

As she sat in the bathroom, shivering uncontrollably, she realized that the only possible way for her to survive this ordeal was if somehow she overpowered Julian before he bound her to the bed again. But how could a hundred-twenty-five-pound woman ever expect to get the best of a two-hundred-pound man? Frantic, she gently opened the vanity drawer, looking for a makeshift weapon.

"Three more minutes, McKenzie," his voice echoed from the other side of the bathroom door.

She found nothing in the vanity drawer. Now she checked the medicine cabinet. Aspirins. Antacids. Cotton swabs. Toothpaste.

Panic set in.

Her last hope was the area under the vanity that concealed the bottom of the sink and the plumbing. She opened the doors, squatted down, and pushed a variety of items out of her way.

Mouthwash. Cough syrup. Bandages. Sunblock. Softsoap.

About ready to give up, McKenzie spotted a pair of scissors. They looked like the kind hair stylists used for trimming, the blades pointy and about four inches long. What could she do with these scissors? Could she inflict enough damage to incapacitate Julian just long enough for her to flee out the door? Maybe she'd get lucky and even kill the asshole? Quite to her surprise, McKenzie O'Neill, pacifist, vegetarian, animal activist, found the concept of killing Julian quite appealing. The woman who stepped over ants while walking down the street was embracing the thought of killing another human being. Was she really capable of such a deed?

"If you're not out of there in one minute," Julian warned, "I'm coming in."

Yes, she thought, I could end his life.

Her mind was scrambling, trying to think of how she could distract him long enough to strike a blow. Where on his body would an assault be most effective? Suppose she missed her mark? What would he do to her in retaliation? Harsh reality replaced her conflicting thoughts.

He's going to kill me anyway, so if I piss him off what difference does it make?

McKenzie carefully slid the scissors, point first, down the back of her capri pants, but realized that if Julian walked behind her and followed her back to the bed, he'd see the outline of the scissors through the form-fitting material. But where else could she hide them, in her bra?

No time to second-guess.

She walked out of the bathroom and stood by the door, facing Julian. If she could get him to lead the way back to the bed, maybe, just maybe she could plunge the scissors deep into the side of his neck and puncture his carotid artery. This, she felt certain, would incapacitate even the Incredible Hulk. Maybe even kill him.

Julian pointed. "That way."

McKenzie didn't move.

"What's the problem? Do you want me to drag you over there?"

She had to engage him in dialogue. Something to divert his attention. "Can I just sit down for a while and talk to you, without my hands and feet bound to that bed?"

"There's nothing to talk about."

"There isn't? I think there's a lot to talk about."

"I'm not playing this game." Julian grabbed her arm.

While he escorted her toward the bed, almost dragging her, McKenzie was careful not to give him a rear view of her body. As he tugged on her arm, leading the way, she reached behind her back, slid her hand down her capri pants and grasped the handle of the scissors. Walking slowly, he looked straight ahead, but every so often gave her glances as they moved closer to the bed. She had to wait for the perfect moment. She would get one shot and one shot only.

She tightened her grip on the scissors.

He stopped in his tracks, his grip on her forearm tightening. "What are you hiding behind your back, McKenzie?"

Shit! "Nothing. My back muscles are a little sore. That's all."

This was the moment of truth. In an instant, he would spin her around before she had a chance to stab him and her plan would self-destruct.

Just as he tugged on her arm, pulling firmly to turn her around, with one quick motion, McKenzie cocked her arm like a trip hammer, and aimed for the side of his neck, thrusting forward as forcefully as she could. His quick reflexes stunned McKenzie. He moved swiftly, but not quite quickly enough. Just as the tip of the scissors pierced the skin on the side of his neck, he grasped her wrist and stopped her forward motion. Only the tip of the scissors penetrated his neck. What she didn't realize was that she missed her mark and the scissors struck him several inches away from the carotid artery. Nonetheless, he went down on one knee and released his grip on McKenzie's wrist, but still held her forearm.

She used a maneuver she'd learned in her self-defense class, and with a rapid circular motion, she twisted her arm counterclockwise, and freed her forearm from his grip. Now it was a foot-race. She bolted toward the front door, her legs and feet scrambling like a cartoon character's.

She peeked over her shoulder and saw him still on one knee, gripping his neck.

Almost there.

She reached the door, grasped the doorknob, and twisted it with all her might. It didn't move. Utterly frantic, she realized it was locked, so she clicked the lock a quarter turn and the doorknob now moved freely. But the door still would not open.

She looked over her shoulder to see if he had regained his composure and was moving toward her, but strangely, he was sitting on the floor cross-legged, his hand pressed against the wound, looking as if he didn't have a care in the world. In fact, she could see a smirk on his face.

McKenzie tried again to open the door, twisting the doorknob in both directions and tugging on it with all her might. She looked up and saw a deadbolt.

Of course, she thought.

When she reached toward the deadbolt to unlock it, instead of seeing a thumbturn like on her door at home, what she saw was a keyhole. Without a key, she could not open the deadbolt. McKenzie now understood why he had not run after her. Where could she go? She figured that whatever he originally had in store for her, he would now make her pay a higher price for her foolish stunt.

She sat on the floor with her back against the door, trying hard not to be emotional, but unless a miracle happened, her fate was sealed. Choked up and feeling as hopeless as she'd ever felt, she watched him disappear into the bathroom, obviously confident that she had no way out of the loft without the key to the deadbolt. She could run to a window and yell for help, but the loft might be located in a remote area, far from civilization. Soon he'd come out of the bathroom and she would no doubt end up bound to the bed again completely at his mercy. Could she somehow reason with him? Maybe bargain with him?

Foolish girl.

How do you bargain with a madman? Besides, she had only one thing to bargain with—the mere thought of it repulsed her— but he could take it if he wanted. And she suspected he would.

CHAPTER THIRTY-EIGHT

When Sami heard Al's voice, she wanted to smash her cell phone against the concrete wall. She had just parked her car in the precinct parking structure and was walking toward the main entrance.

"The captain just called me." Long pause. "He said you're okay partnering with me?"

"Do I have a choice?" she asked.

"It wouldn't be a popular choice with the department, but yes, you do have a choice."

"And what do you suggest I say to the captain, that my boyfriend fucked another woman and—"

"I can say I'm sorry for the rest of my life, Sami, but if you can't let it go—"

"Let it *go*? How about letting me catch my breath? Twelve hours ago you told me that you slept with another woman and you expect me to just dismiss it as if you kissed her on the cheek?"

"People make mistakes."

"Yes, they do. But I don't consider you screwing another woman a mistake."

"If you want me to call the captain and tell him I have to go back to Rio, I still have some time under the Family Leave Act."

"Back to Rio? Why? So you can fuck Sofia again?"

Al didn't say a word.

Sami had to get back on task because this conversation was going nowhere. "We need to nail this guy before he murders another person."

"We may be too late," Al said. "I assume the captain told you about the missing person's report."

"He did. Are you capable of separating personal from professional?"

"Hey, I'm the one on the hot seat here. The question is whether or not *you* can work side by side with *me* without letting your personal feelings get in the way."

"I guess we'll just have to find out."

Al breathed heavily into the phone. "There is one more thing, Sami."

She held her breath, hoping he wouldn't drop another bomb.

"Should I look for an apartment? Room with a friend? I'm not quite sure how to proceed."

Nor was she. On top of everything else, the last thing Sami wanted was to explain to her mother why Al no longer shared her bed. Even if she let him sleep on the sofa bed, her mom would still play twenty questions.

I hope I don't regret this.

"How would you feel about sleeping on the sofa bed?"

"You're okay with that?"

She wanted to say, "*No, I'm not okay with it,*" but didn't think brutal honesty would help the situation. "If I wasn't, I wouldn't offer."

"Thanks, Sami. I'll give you as much space as you need."

Space is not what she needed. What she needed was a way for her to trust him. "Are you coming to the precinct?"

"Be there in thirty minutes."

Great. She wasn't so sure she'd made the right decision.

✡ ✡ ✡

After Al flipped his cell phone closed, he stood silently staring at the Winslow Homer reproduction hanging above the bed. He was intrigued that the Holiday Inn Express had chosen the perfect watercolor to exemplify his emotions. Homer had poignantly captured his utter feeling of solitude and despair. In the painting, a man sat in a small rowboat, hunched forward, grasping the oars. The sky was dark and dismal, but the water calm. He couldn't see the man's face in the painting; the man's back faced him. But he could tell that the artist's intention had been to convey loneliness. He was no art critic, but from what he could see, Winslow Homer had captured the essence of loneliness. The painting now seemed as if it were an omen.

He sat on the bed, his mind a hornet's nest of troubling thoughts. For so many years, he had quietly been in love with Sami Rizzo, never believing that anything would come of it, that his love for her was hopeless. When she had revealed her true feelings, telling Al how much she loved him, he felt as if he'd just won the lottery. Now, the thought of losing Sami was more than Al could bear. He knew her well enough to know, or at least hope, that eventually she'd find it in her heart to forgive him. He also feared that his indiscretion would forever tarnish their love. No matter what he did to beg her forgiveness, her heart was fragile, and this wound might never heal.

How many times had he cursed Tommy DiSalvo, her ex-husband, when he had cheated on her and she had called Al in the middle of the night looking for a firm shoulder to cry on? How many tears had he watched spill out of her puffy eyes? Now *he* was the villain, the unfaithful fool who jeopardized their relationship.

He remembered what Captain Davidson had told him when he'd asked about Al's relationship with Sami: "*What you've got is the brass ring, Al. Don't fuck it up.*"

Alberto Diaz could only hope that he hadn't completely destroyed the most precious part of his life.

After retying McKenzie's wrists to the bed with nylon straps, leaving her legs unbound and her body lying prone, Julian went into the bathroom to dress the wound on his neck. Fortunately for him, the scissors had not punctured a major artery or vein, so he felt confident the wound did not require stitches.

He understood her motivation to escape. If he were facing a similar fate, wouldn't he do the same thing? He actually admired her courage and resourcefulness. He'd learned through years of experience with sickly patients that the will to survive is the strongest instinct.

He checked his neck in the mirror to be sure that blood was not oozing through the gauze, then he headed for the bed and sat beside McKenzie. Obviously startled, she jumped but didn't say a word. He studied her form. Admiringly. Lustfully. His mind flooded with delightful possibilities. Thoughts of Eva. Thoughts of Rachael. He no longer fought the good fight like he'd done with Genevieve. No more troubled conscience or moral dilemmas. He surrendered to his deepest desires without the slightest concern for McKenzie's welfare. His hunger to fulfill his fantasies far outweighed morality or reason. He wanted her the way he wanted her, and that was that.

He laid his hand on the small of her back and gently slid it over her butt. My, how firm she was. No doubt the results of her rigorous yoga workouts. She turned her head and stared at him, a look of total disgust on her face.

"Take your fucking hands off me."

He admired the grit and determination in her voice. She was like a wild filly, fighting not to be saddled. Oh, how he'd break her will. He ignored her order and again slid his hand over her butt; this time his fingers lingered.

She struggled with the nylon straps binding her wrists to the headboard. She kicked her feet violently and twisted from side to side, but the straps restricted her mobility.

Julian eased off the bed and stood over the cart with the surgical instruments, carefully taking inventory. He picked up a pair of dressing scissors and sat down again on the bed. Without uttering a sound, he slipped the scissors under McKenzie's sports bra and ran it up the middle of her back, cutting it from bottom to top.

"You fucking pig!" More pointless struggling.

Now, he grasped the top of her capri pants with both hands and yanked them over her butt and down her legs. He tried to pull them over her ankles and feet, but her violent thrashing made it impossible.

With his mouth only inches from her ear, scissors pressed firmly against her neck, he spoke softly. "If you don't lie still, I promise you, you'll regret it."

She must have concluded that his was not an idle threat. She stopped resisting and lay as motionless as a corpse as she let him remove the capri pants.

Julian removed his clothes and knelt on the bed, his knees straddling McKenzie's thighs. Now the tears began. She cried uncontrollably.

"Please don't do this," she begged, her voice no longer spirited.

So focused on his own needs, Julian could not evoke an ounce of empathy or compassion for her. Her plea fell on deaf ears. He closed his eyes and drifted back to his childhood. As he lost control and savagely took her, he spoke through gritted teeth.

"This is for you, Marianne.

"This is for you, Rebecca."

By the time Al arrived at the main precinct, Sami and the captain had already gone over details of the investigation and discussed the likelihood that the missing girl, McKenzie O'Neill, had, in fact, been abducted by the Resuscitator.

Al knocked on the captain's door, pushed it open, and peeked inside.

"Don't be bashful, Detective," Captain Davidson said. "Get in here and join the party." The captain stood and extended his hand. "Welcome back to the shit-storm. Glad to hear your sister is doing well."

"Thank you, Captain." Al glanced at Sami, who was studying her fingernails. "Hi, Sami."

Sami nodded, gave Al a quick look, and he could feel the icicles.

This isn't going to be easy.

The captain brought Al up to speed on the investigation and gave him some details about the missing girl. Through it all, Sami sat silently.

Captain Davidson lit a cigarette and filled his lungs with the soothing smoke. "Do either of you want to tell me what the hell is going on?"

Al and Sami briefly made eye contact, then they looked at the captain.

"I'm not following you, Captain," Al said.

"Well, follow this," the captain answered. "First off, Sami hasn't uttered a sound since you walked in the door. And considering that she's rarely at a loss for words, I'd call that curious, wouldn't you? Second, I'm getting a really weird vibe from both of you. You can cut the tension in here with a knife."

"There's nothing going on, Captain," Sami said. "I just didn't sleep well last night." Now Al could feel her cold stare.

"You two better not bullshit me," the captain warned. "You need to be totally focused on one thing only. Your personal lives take a back seat until we catch this guy. If there's even the slightest friction between you two, and it's going to interfere with the investigation, I need you to tell me right now." The captain took another hit on his cigarette. "Are we on the same page?"

"We're on it, Captain," Sami said.

"Well, then, go catch that douche bag."

CHAPTER THIRTY-NINE

Quite to McKenzie's surprise, she was able to suppress her pain and hadn't so much as let out a moan while Julian tore into her. She'd been with only a few men in her life—she had preserved her virginity until she turned nineteen—some quite aggressive in bed. But never in her life had she imagined that a man could be so vicious. In spite of his violent thrusts, she refused to give the son of a bitch the satisfaction, so she squeezed her eyes shut, and tried to focus on her breathing exercises to relax her muscles. Now finished with her, Julian sat on a chair adjacent to the bed, looking so satisfied and content she wanted to claw his eyes out. It felt as if her lower torso was on fire. He had taken her every way a man can take a woman. Through it all, she endured.

Now, McKenzie faced the bitter reality of what he'd do next. Would he rape her again, perhaps even more violently? How many more times could she handle it? What other vile acts was he capable of?

Lost in her thoughts, she didn't even notice that he approached the bed and sat next to her. Without saying a word, he cut the nylon straps binding her wrists to the headboard. She let out a heavy sigh and massaged her bruised wrists.

"If you promise to behave yourself," Julian said, "I'll leave the straps off. For now."

She had no delusions about his gesture. She guessed that he'd cut her loose for his own perverse reasons, not to make her feel more comfortable.

"Lie on your back," he ordered.

So that's it, she thought. He must be bored with screwing me from behind. For just a moment, she thought about rolling over and kicking him in the side of his neck, right where she'd wounded him. But he still held what looked like a scalpel in his right hand.

"Are you in pain?" Julian asked.

"What do you think?"

"Would you like to take a nice warm bath?"

"You rape me and now you're concerned about my *comfort*?"

"I'm sorry. It wasn't my intention to..." He paused for a minute, as if he couldn't think of the right word.

"Fuck me like a dog?"

"*No*! It's hard to explain."

"Who are Marianne and Rebecca? A couple girls who rejected you?"

"*What*?"

"You called their names when—"

"You're full of *shit*!"

"Then how would I know their names?"

He thought about that.

"Is this going to happen again?"

Silence.

"Answer me."

"I...don't know."

She wondered if his offer to let her soak in a warm tub was a sincere gesture, or if he had a sick agenda. The thought of soaking in a tub seemed quite inviting. But she suddenly realized that she lay there completely naked, and she could almost *feel* his eyes touching her. She shuddered to her core. As insane as it seemed, maybe a bath might be a good idea. Would he give her some privacy, or gawk at her as if she were someone in a freak show?

"You're going to let me take a bath *alone*?"

He nodded. "If you prefer."

Is this guy fucking kidding? "That *is* what I prefer." She eased off the bed, her lower torso throbbing, uncomfortably aware of her nakedness. As she headed for the bathroom, he grabbed her arm. "When you come out of the bathroom, you come out naked with your hands up in the air."

"Can I wrap a towel around me?"

"Naked, I said."

While McKenzie prepared her bath, Julian took advantage of the situation and telephoned Nicole.

"Hi, Honey," he said, acting as if everything was rosy between them. "Sorry about last night."

"Why didn't you pick up the girls?"

"I had emergency surgery at the hospital."

"And you couldn't call?"

"I got rushed into surgery and—"

"You are *so* full of shit!" Nicole was almost screaming. "When I didn't fucking hear from you and couldn't reach you by cell phone, I left the kids with Julie next door and drove to the hospital."

He had to think fast but hadn't a clue what to say. She had bushwhacked him good.

"And guess what? No one had seen you all day. Why are you lying to me? What the hell is going on? How could you do this to your daughters? They sat out on the front steps for over an hour waiting for you. Isabel cried her eyes out. You promised to take them to Belmont Park, remember?"

No, he didn't remember. One day blurred into the next. "I'm really sorry, Nicole."

"You can take your 'sorries' and stick them where the sun don't shine!"

"It's the research grant. It's consumed me."

"Well, then maybe it's time for you to make a choice: your family or your precious A-Fib study."

"Why can't I have both?"

"Obviously, you can't handle both."

"I am so close, Nicole. In another two weeks I'll have the data I need."

"So the girls and I should just sit around waiting for you to be a husband and father again?"

"It's a ten-million-dollar grant. I'm ninety-eight percent there."

"Well, you're one-hundred percent losing your family."

The next thing Julian heard was a dial tone.

As McKenzie O'Neill soaked in the bathtub, the hot water soothing her muscles and her aching behind, it was as if a giant fog lifted from her conscious thoughts. How absurd that she would be taking a bath in the home of a madman, a madman who would likely end her life. Shouldn't she be concentrating on a survival plan? She had already failed at her first attempt to overpower him, and now that he was on to her, how could she possibly devise a plan that might work? How could she surprise him?

She had no weapon, no way to get the advantage. Besides, even if she were to temporarily put him out of commission, without a key, there was no way she could get past the dead-bolted door. How then could she survive this ordeal?

She eased her way out of the tub, still feeling as if her internal organs were ablaze. As someone who loved TV programs like *CSI*, or any crime show where the police tried to outsmart the villain, McKenzie was fascinated with the idea of a serial killer, and had followed the Resuscitator and the four homicides closely. Not only had she read everything written about the crimes in the *San Diego Chronicle*, she also viewed national coverage on CNN and other major networks. Familiar with every detail of how he had murdered his victims, she felt chilled to the bone.

Terrified he would likely kill her in a most gruesome way, she felt overwhelmed with panic. She sat in the warm water, unable to quiet her sobs.

She heard a gentle knock on the door.

"Everything okay in there?"

"I'll be out…in a few minutes."

"Remember. Naked."

If only she had a gun.

CHAPTER FORTY

"How do you want to work this, Al?" Sami asked. After their meeting with the captain, she had the dubious task of telling Detective Osbourn that he was no longer her partner on the serial murders investigation. It took a great deal of diplomacy for her to convince him that the department's decision had no reflection on him or his qualifications. It was merely an experience issue. To ease Osbourn's understandable disappointment, and to make him feel more involved with the investigation, Sami asked him to follow up with the families of Robert Winters and Rachael Manning, victims three and four. They had learned that both their families lived out of state, so Osbourn was going to set up phone interviews. And if the victims' families had video capabilities like Skype or some other Web cam system, they would conduct a video interview.

"For the sake of time," Al suggested, "I think it might make more sense if I interviewed McKenzie O'Neill's parents and you spoke with her girlfriend. Or the other way around. Whatever you prefer."

She didn't have to think about his proposal for more than a nanosecond. In fact, she imagined that she'd take advantage of every opportunity to work independent of him during the investigation. Seeing him every day at work, living under the same roof, playing a game of deception so no one would suspect they were at odds, seemed like more than she could bear. Sami wasn't sure who would give her more grief if they uncovered their little masquerade, the captain or Sami's mother. Of most issues whirling around in her mind right now, few were clearly defined. But on one particular issue, Sami was crystal clear: Every time she looked at Al, she wanted desperately to kick him in the balls. Not exactly the most productive attitude for a detective trying to track down a serial killer.

"I'll take on O'Neill's parents, and you can interview her friend," Sami said.

Before Al could even respond, she turned her back on him and walked toward the parking ramp.

Ignoring Julian's mandate to exit the bathroom naked, McKenzie, hoping to restore just a morsel of dignity, walked out the door with a towel wrapped around her, intentionally defying his instructions. Although the last thing she wanted was to provoke him, she just couldn't bear the thought of exposing herself to a man who molested her with his eyes.

Sitting on the bed with his back to her, he seemed uninterested as she walked toward the bed. As she approached his back, she wished she had a baseball bat in her hands. She noticed a few additions to the area around the bed. First, she saw what appeared to be a video camera resting on a tripod. The perfect accoutrement for a pervert, she thought. What really caught her eye was a small monitor mounted on a silver stand with about a dozen long wires hanging from it. She'd worked as a candy striper, volunteering at a local hospital when she was a teenager considering a career in health care, and she'd seen monitors like this one all the time. It wasn't merely a monitor. It was a heart monitor.

Julian looked over his shoulder and McKenzie could see his eyes locked on her.

"You don't follow directions very well, do you?" he said.

"This loft is freezing. I'm just trying to warm up."

"Sit on the bed," he ordered.

Still holding the bath towel in place, hoping he wouldn't force her to remove it, she sat on the bed as far away from him as possible.

"Are you going to rape me again?"

He stood and walked toward the cart holding all the surgical instruments. Julian opened the drawer and removed a syringe. "I want you to remove the towel, lie on your back, and close your eyes."

McKenzie's body shivered. Looking at the syringe, imagining what awful drug he would inject in her veins, she now understood that rape was the least of her worries. She felt an odd pressure in the center of her chest, as if a heavy weight lay on it, a sensation she had never felt before. She could hardly breathe. Panic set in. Was she having a heart attack? Now she could feel a rapid heartbeat. "Something is wrong."

"What is it?"

"It feels...like an elephant is sitting...on my chest. I can't... breathe."

He pawed through the drawer in the cart, grabbed a stethoscope, and pressed it to her chest.

"It's just a stress-induced rapid heartbeat." He took a syringe off the cart.

"What are you...going to do?"

"Give you something to calm you down."

"You're going to...kill me, aren't you?"

"The needs of the many outweigh the needs of the few."

✳ ✳ ✳

"How are you feeling, Mom?" Sami asked. They had just finished dinner and Emily was cleaning up in the kitchen. Sami and Josephine sat on the sofa.

"So-so. My back still aches and I get out of breath easily. But I don't have any chest pain."

"That's great."

Sami was still struggling with how to tell her mom that Al would be sleeping on the sofa bed, trying to come up with a logical explanation. No doubt, no matter what the reason, this change in living arrangements would evoke much speculation. Emily, Sami could deal with. Her mother would be a handful.

"Oh, by the way," Sami said matter-of-factly, "I just wanted to tell you that Al will be sleeping on the sofa bed for a while. I didn't want you to wander into the living room in the middle of the night and be startled."

It took Josephine less than a second for her red flag to go up. "Trouble in paradise?"

"Nothing like that. It's just that I haven't been sleeping very well—lots of things on my mind. And Al snores at night, which makes falling asleep even more difficult for me."

"I see. And how long is this going to go on?"

"Just for a few weeks."

"And in a few weeks Alberto will be miraculously cured of his snoring?"

The old woman was sharp as ever, Sami thought. She felt dangerously close to checkmate. The door opened and Al walked in. He stood in the foyer and looked confused, as if he'd walked into the wrong home.

"Did I miss dinner?" he asked.

"There are plenty of leftovers," Josephine said. "Emily made linguine with clam sauce."

Al hung his jacket on the coat tree. "Sounds great." He walked past the two of them as if they were barely acquainted with him, and headed for the kitchen.

"He must really be hungry," Josephine said. "Not even a peck on the cheek for the love of his life."

Checkmate.

Julian was amazed at McKenzie's resilience. During his two procedures, both complicated and performed with her ribcage spread wide open, her heart maintained a normal sinus rhythm and wouldn't go into atrial fibrillation even when he introduced powerful drugs. He found this quite puzzling—and medically remarkable. Obviously, her heart was strong and resistant to electrical disturbances caused by medications. This fact in itself compelled Julian to follow a completely different path. McKenzie O'Neill just might be the subject he'd been searching for. For the next experiment, he carefully stapled her ribcage closed.

When finished, he stood over her, admiring the textbook precision of his work. Feeling parched and ready for a short break, he went into the kitchen and grabbed a sparkling water from the refrigerator. Just about to take a sip, he heard the heart monitor going berserk. He dropped the water bottle on the floor and it exploded on impact, the carbonated water gushing out of the plastic bottle like a mini-geyser.

Julian rushed to the bed, looked at the heart monitor, and nearly gasped when he saw that the young woman was in cardiac arrest. With medical skill and a meticulous technique, he began CPR, hoping to restore normal rhythm. As he performed compressions, blood squirted from the fresh incision, and some of the staples broke free. After several minutes, he stopped to catch his breath. He then resumed CPR, his eyes locked on the monitor.

He continued with the compressions but could not restore a heartbeat. He guessed that for whatever reason, McKenzie suffered from a delayed and adverse reaction to the drugs he'd given her. Now her heart felt the full impact of the potent medications. He had made an irreversible error in judgment and his hopes to uncover critical new data through never-before-performed experiments were lost.

McKenzie O'Neill was dead.

His disgust escalated to rage. He dashed to the monitor, grasped the power cord, and yanked it out of the electrical socket. He never wanted to hear that annoying sound again. He had risked everything to secure the research grant: his wife, children, career, and reputation. Not to mention the very real possibility of spending the rest of his life in prison. Or worse. He really believed that his experiments on McKenzie would have produced the data he required to satisfy the Global Atrial Fibrillation Foundation and ultimately fulfill their requirements to approve the research grant.

So close. So *painfully* close.

Suddenly, Julian realized he didn't want to spend another minute in the same room with McKenzie's corpse. She symbolized failure. No self-recrimination—there'd be plenty of time for that later. No shopping for designer clothes. No critical thinking about where to dump her body. For the sake of his prior subjects' families, he'd been careful to leave the bodies where they could be easily found. But he didn't have the time or the patience to pay McKenzie the same courtesy. He wanted her out of his life immediately. He wrapped a sheet around her, lifted her off the bed, and headed for his car.

After lying awake for nearly two hours, checking the time on her clock radio every few minutes, Sami decided to raid the fridge for a light snack, in spite of the fact that once again she felt nauseous. Although her body needed additional calories about as much as a centipede needed another leg, she'd always found comfort in food, particularly fattening food. She'd always believed that if God was truly all-knowing and all-merciful, He would have made broccoli taste as good as chocolate cake, and never would have invented the word *calorie*.

It had been a fruitless day. Sami's interview with McKenzie O'Neill's parents yielded nothing she could run with. And according to Al, McKenzie's friend could only offer a description of the mysterious man at the yoga class, which pretty much matched the composite sketch.

She'd spoken to Osbourn about his interviews with the families of Robert Winters and Rachael Manning, but they offered very little information that would help the investigation. Not living in San Diego, neither family knew much about the victims' daily activities, whom they hung around with, or where they went for entertainment. Robert Winters's parents didn't even know that Rachael and he were engaged. Not exactly a close-knit family.

What puzzled her most was the scarcity of leads coming in since they'd distributed the new sketch. Typically, when the police department circulated a sketch of a suspect in a murder investigation, the toll-free hotline lit up like the Fourth of July at Disneyland. And what made this even more baffling was the fact that Judge Foster, the father of the first victim, Genevieve Foster, was offering a ten-thousand-dollar reward for information leading to the arrest and conviction of the serial killer. Where was this guy hiding?

With the refrigerator door open and her head poking inside, Sami shuffled the contents around looking for something appealing. She spotted a small slice of carrot cake tucked away in the corner, the remains of a get-well gift a neighbor had baked for her mother.

About to rearrange the contents of the fridge so she could reach the carrot cake, Sami heard someone's feet padding along the floor. She let go of the cake and looked over her shoulder.

"Got the munchies?" Al asked.

"I've always had a passionate relationship with midnight snacks."

"Don't let me stop you." He pulled out a chair and sat at the kitchen table.

Sami had no idea why he wasn't sound asleep. "Is the sofa bed uncomfortable?"

She closed the refrigerator and leaned against the counter, suddenly aware that all she wore was a long T-shirt and panties. He had seen a lot more. Many times. But things were different now.

"The sofa bed is fine. I heard someone in the kitchen and hoped it was you."

Looking like a mad professor, Al combed his fingers through his hair. "Can we talk?"

She could deal with talking business at one in the morning, but if he wanted to discuss their relationship, she just couldn't handle it right now.

He didn't wait for her to answer. "I really screwed up. You're the best thing that ever happened to me, and the thought of losing you—"

Her cell phone rang.

Saved by the bell, she thought.

"This is Captain Davidson."

She looked at Al and silently mouthed the captain's name. "I don't suppose that this is a social call at one a.m.," Sami said.

"When *my* phone rings in the middle of the night, *your* phone rings. That's the deal. Where's Diaz?"

"Sitting right next to me."

"You two have insomnia?" the captain asked.

"Something like that," Sami said.

"Put me on speaker," the captain said. "I need to talk to both of you and don't want to repeat myself."

Sami didn't think that the captain would call in the wee hours of the night to chew their asses. He much preferred doing that face to face. She guessed that something significant was brewing with the investigation.

"Remember McKenzie O'Neill, the missing young woman?" the captain said.

Sami feared what was coming next. "We do, Captain."

"She's not missing anymore. Our guy dumped her at Torrey Pines Park, right near the public parking lot."

"Same condition as the other victims?" Al asked.

"Except for one minor detail."

They could hear the captain sucking on a cigarette.

"What's that, Captain?" Al asked.

"She's alive."

Sami and Al gave each other a long, penetrating stare.

"Is she conscious?" Sami asked.

"She's barely breathing. Real faint heartbeat. Fortunately, the guy who found her—a late-night jogger—was an EMT and had the presence of mind to check her pulse and call nine-one-one. From what I understand, by looking at her, you'd think she was dead."

"Where is she right now?" Sami asked.

"Fighting for her life in the ICU at Saint Michael's. Not looking good."

"Where are you, Captain?" Al said.

"Drinking rotgut hospital coffee in the waiting room."

"What do you want us to do, Captain?" Sami said.

"Get your little asses to the hospital ASAP, so I can go home and get some sleep. If she regains consciousness even for a minute, I want you two here."

CHAPTER FORTY-ONE

Barely awake, occasionally dozing off for brief periods, Sami and Al sat in the hospital ICU waiting room with two vacant chairs between them. Silent as two heavyweight fighters mentally preparing themselves for a title fight, they seemed totally disconnected. Sami knew why she wasn't talking, but she wasn't sure if Al's tight lips were voluntary or a matter of exhaustion. Whatever the reason, she was glad he hadn't continued his speech about how sorry he was. With her wounds still raw, she didn't want to hear it. She looked at her watch just as the hour hand hit four.

She did not understand why Captain Davidson insisted that both of them remain at the hospital, like sentries guarding a palace. What was the point? Wouldn't it make more sense for them to alternate shifts, so both could get some rest? If McKenzie did regain consciousness, what could two detectives do that one couldn't?

To make the wait even worse for Sami, this particular waiting room evoked bitter memories. She had sat in this exact chair only a short time ago after her mother had a heart attack. She didn't even want to think about the days she'd waited in this prison, biting her fingernails while her father fought a losing battle with cancer.

Now sitting in this quiet, dimly lit room with Al, her lover gone astray, she felt uncomfortable. Although they'd been intimate in so many ways—physically and emotionally—he now seemed like a stranger, a man about whom she knew nothing. After her troubled marriage with Tommy DiSalvo, a dirtbag who could have authored a textbook on infidelity, she never thought a man would earn her trust again. Then Al came along and she thought he was different. Sami anticipated that his battle with alcoholism might strain their relationship. Never in her wildest dreams did she think Al would sleep with another woman. Here she sat, broken-hearted and revolted by the mere thought of him ever touching her again. How could she hope to survive this? How could she ever trust him again?

No one from the hospital—nurses or doctors—had come to the waiting room to update them on McKenzie O'Neill's condition. Sami and Al had impressed upon the medical staff the critical importance for them to be informed if McKenzie showed even the slightest sign of consciousness. The physician she initially spoke to—Sami couldn't remember his name—didn't look old enough to vote, let alone like a man qualified to treat critical patients in the ICU. Oh, how she wished Doctor Templeton were here. But considering his high rank in the hospital, she didn't expect that he worked many graveyard shifts unless it was an extreme circumstance.

At five fifteen in the morning, Sami awoke when someone walked into the waiting room and gently shook her shoulder. Disoriented and suffering from a severe case of the shakes, Sami tried to clear her head and focus her eyes on the young man wearing a white lab coat.

"Detective Rizzo, I am Doctor Chung, one of the physicians treating Ms. O'Neill." He glanced at Al, who appeared to be sound asleep. "Perhaps you wish to wake your partner?"

Sami leaned toward Al, stretched her arm past the two chairs separating them, and not so gently grasped his arm and squeezed. He jumped and his eyes sprang open. "What the hell is going on?" Al twisted his knuckles into his squinty eyes and blinked like a man who had just walked out of a dark movie theatre into bright sunlight.

"This is Doctor Chung," Sami said, pointing to the man who barely stood five feet tall.

Doctor Chung bowed to both of them in a respectful manner. "May I speak to both of you?"

Al stood and stretched. Sami didn't move.

Doctor Chung clasped his hands and shook his head ever so slightly. "Doctor Hastings and I have been examining Ms. O'Neill for several hours, and we have performed a number of diagnostic tests."

"Has she regained consciousness?" Sami asked.

"I'm afraid that is highly unlikely," Doctor Chung said. "Both Doctor Hastings and I are amazed she's alive."

"Is she going to make it?" Al asked.

"Not without extremely complicated heart surgery."

"What's the prognosis?" Sami asked.

"That is a very difficult question to answer until we actually perform the surgery. We believe she suffers from a condition called stress-induced cardiomyopathy or broken heart syndrome. It is a rare condition—usually temporary—brought on by severe stress, and it mirrors the characteristics of heart failure." The doctor's lips tightened to a thin line. "Under normal circumstances, we would treat this condition with medication and in a week or two the patient usually recovers. With Ms. O'Neill, we have multiple issues—all serious. The echocardiogram and angiogram show a malfunction of both the mitral valve and aortic valve. Repair or even replacement may be necessary. But this is a temporary fix. Frankly, she may need a heart transplant. As I said, we cannot answer these questions until we perform the surgery. Until we find a suitable donor, we may have to temporarily install a heart pump called a left ventricular assist device, or LVAD. This procedure makes the surgery even more difficult."

Not having a clue what the doctor just said, and not wanting a long complicated medical explanation, Sami opted for the obvious question. "How quickly can you operate?"

"As soon as we get a team together. This is not your everyday open heart surgery," Doctor Chung said. "We've already consulted the chief of cardiothoracic surgery, and he will be part of the team."

"Doctor Templeton?" Sami asked.

The doctor nodded. "Have you heard of him?"

"He performed bypass surgery on my mother," Sami said.

"That is most fortunate," Doctor Chung said. "He is one of the best bypass surgeons in the country."

Al stepped closer to the doctor. "How many times has Saint Michael's Hospital performed this kind of surgery?"

"If we replace both valves *and* install a heart pump, to the best of my knowledge, it will be the first time. We have already put in a call to Doctor Jonathon Fisher in San Francisco, the foremost heart surgeon for this type of procedure."

"And if he's not immediately available?"

"We can keep the patient stabilized for at least a week if we have to wait a few days for Doctor Fisher."

"Isn't that a little risky?" Sami asked.

"Not as risky as trying to perform this specialized surgery without the benefit of Doctor Fisher's vast experience."

"Have you spoken to Ms. O'Neill's family?" Sami asked.

Dr. Chung nodded. "They requested a private waiting room near ICU. In situations like this, many family members want total privacy."

"I ask that you suppress any information about Ms. O'Neill from the media," Sami said.

"I'm afraid it's too late. I understand that several local news stations were present when Ms. O'Neill was found."

Bad news, Sami thought. It would be an advantage if the killer thought O'Neill was dead. Then again, if he learned that the victim survived her ordeal, the perp might panic and make another attempt on her life. Not that Sami would want the victim to be used as bait, but it could help them grab this guy.

"I want to be clear on one point, Doctor," Sami said. "You're saying that the damage to this woman's heart resulted from severe stress?"

"The cardiomyopathy, yes. But the valve problems, no. Someone seems to have performed some unexplainable procedures on this young lady and I can only guess that he's some sort of mentally unbalanced person."

Sami didn't need to hear the doctor's confirmation to understand the type of monster she was dealing with.

After he had dropped McKenzie's body at Torrey Pines Park, Julian turned off his cell phone, something he rarely did. Doctors, particularly cardiologists, needed to be available for emergencies day or night. But after his outrageously disappointing situation with McKenzie, he didn't want to speak to anyone no matter how critical the issue.

As he usually did in the early morning, he turned on the local news, half paying attention, half dozing off. After a restless night, an evening that yielded little sleep, he could barely keep his eyes open. But when he saw the Breaking News banner crawling across the bottom of the television screen, and next to it a photo of McKenzie O'Neill, it grabbed his attention. He turned up the volume.

"McKenzie O'Neill, a young woman apparently left for dead at Torrey Pines Park, a woman who may have been the Resuscitator's intended fifth victim, miraculously survived her brush with death. Doctors are working feverishly to save her life. However, based on a statement from an undisclosed source at Saint Michael's Hospital, the prognosis is grim. Stay tuned to KTAK Action News for the latest on this breaking story."

Julian felt like someone had jammed the butt end of a two-by-four into his stomach.

She was *alive*?

How was it possible? Her heart had flat-lined for more than ten minutes while he'd worked frantically to resuscitate her. Julian's mind searched for answers. It just didn't make sense. He carefully reconstructed everything he'd done to McKenzie. Coming up empty, he walked over to the heart monitor and attached the ten electrodes to his body. Wrists. Ankles. Chest. He turned on the monitor and EKG device and lay on the bed. It took a few seconds before the mechanism interpreted the signals from Julian's heart and deciphered them.

At first, everything seemed normal: heart rate 81, EKG normal. Suddenly, the warning alarm blared in his ear, and when he looked at the monitor, he watched in shock as a flat line crawled across the screen. According to the monitor and EKG, he was in full cardiac arrest.

In his panic to resuscitate McKenzie, Julian now realized that he never took a moment to check her pulse or listen to her heart—an action that should have been as fundamental as taking a patient's blood pressure. In his disoriented state, Julian had ignored prudent medical practices and relied solely on the heart monitor, never even thinking that it would malfunction. These were the actions of a fool, not of an experienced cardiologist. He had no idea whether or not she was conscious, and if she was, what she might have told the police. He had plenty of contacts at the hospital and could discretely inquire about her condition. After all, would it seem strange for a heart doctor to be interested in the welfare of a heart patient?

Julian disconnected the ten electrodes and turned off the heart monitor. He felt a rush of rage coursing through his body, an uncontrollable urge to scream. Instead, he kicked the monitor like an awkward martial arts student and could feel the muscles in his groin area pulling. His kick knocked the monitor off the stainless steel stand and he watched it bounce against the wall and crash to the floor. The EKG device, still wired to the monitor, bounced on the floor as well. His hands were trembling and he felt enraged by his carelessness.

Calm down. Keep your cool. Think clearly.

He turned on his cell phone and decided to check in with the hospital to see if he could get any information on McKenzie's condition. But before he could speed dial the number, his voice mail music, a tune by Kenny G, alerted him that several messages waited for him. He punched in his password and waited to hear the first message.

Julian, this is Ted Hastings. We have a situation at the hospital and need you as soon as possible. It's too lengthy to give you a complete explanation, so give me a call on my cell and I'll explain. Thanks.

Situation? Ted Hastings, a fellow cardiologist, could only be calling for one reason. And that reason had something to do with McKenzie O'Neill.

The next three messages were also from Doctor Hastings, each one a little more panicky than the prior one. In Doctor Hastings's last message, he gave Julian the details about McKenzie and the surgical plan, but he didn't say whether or not she was conscious.

He had little choice but to go to the hospital and see for himself.

CHAPTER FORTY-TWO

When Peter J. Spencer III watched the morning news and connected the dots, he no longer wondered if the mysterious John
Smith and the Resuscitator were one in the same. He'd been kidding himself into believing that the whole thing was merely a
bizarre coincidence, when all along he'd been denying the truth.
Through his own self-preservation instincts and selfishness, he'd
chosen to ignore the obvious and not call the police hotline. He
now felt directly responsible for McKenzie O'Neill's circumstances. His blatant negligence and cowardice placed the young
woman in a life-threatening situation, one Spencer could have
prevented.

Having lost his appetite, he set down his bowl of oatmeal,
grabbed the remote control, and turned off the TV. He could
no longer ignore what he needed to do, regardless of the consequence. But he wasn't sure if he should call the hotline or try
to reach Detective Rizzo directly. After careful consideration,
he feared that even with modern-day technology, messages still
occasionally get lost in cyber-space, and he realized that each
moment he wasted put another innocent person at risk. He had
to take action.

After Doctor Chung assured Sami and Al that the prob-
ability of McKenzie regaining consciousness before her surgery

was highly unlikely, Captain Davidson agreed to let the detectives leave the hospital—at least for the time being. The captain arranged for a uniformed policeman to be stationed outside McKenzie's hospital room twenty-four hours a day. By now, the Resuscitator had most certainly heard that the young woman had survived, and Sami was relieved that the department offered her protection.

Sami and Al drove separately from the precinct to her home, but they pulled into the driveway at nearly the same time. To avert another emotional conversation with Al, Sami had hoped to beat him home, retire to her bedroom for a few hours sleep, and then head back to the precinct. Considering her aversion for Al, she hadn't a clue why she'd invited him to sleep on the sofa. Obviously, she had not thought things through carefully enough before making the offer, and had no idea of how uncomfortable she'd feel. At this juncture, she didn't want to ask him to leave, but she would do everything in her power to keep away from him—except, of course, during the course of police business.

Wanting to avoid lengthy dialogue with any household member, Sami kissed her mom on the cheek, gave Emily a quick hug, and bent over and kissed Angelina on the forehead.

"Sorry to abandon you guys," Sami said, "but I've had a long night and need to get some rest." Sami looked at her watch. "If I'm not up by ten thirty, please wake me."

Sami walked in her bedroom and sat on the bed for a moment, trying to gather her thoughts. Just about to rest her head on the down pillow, her cell phone rang.

"This is Detective Rizzo."

"Hi, Sami, it's Richard Osbourn. Sorry to bother you—I know Al and you pulled an all-nighter at the hospital, but this is really important."

Sami's first thought was that something happened to McKenzie O'Neill. "Don't ruin my morning, Richard. It's already on its way to sucking."

"Actually, I think this might *make* your morning."

"I'm listening."

"We got a call from some guy who claims he has information that will reveal the identity of our guy, but he won't talk to anyone but you. He insists that he remain anonymous."

Sami wanted to get excited, but over the years, how many times had she heard this story only to discover that the call was a hoax? "Did the call come in on the hotline?"

"It came in on *your* work line."

"*My* line? So this hot lead came in from a guy who wants to remain anonymous and forfeit the ten-thousand-dollar reward?"

"That seems to be the case."

"Was he on the phone long enough for us to trace the call?"

"Negative."

"How do I contact him?"

"He said he'd call back at twelve noon sharp."

"Thanks, Richard. I'll see you around eleven."

Julian arrived at the hospital at eleven thirty, an hour before his scheduled meeting with Doctor Hastings to review McKenzie O'Neill's chart, to discuss the proposed surgery, and to coordinate the help of Doctor Fisher in San Francisco. He put on his lab coat, clipped his photo ID to the front pocket, draped a stethoscope around his neck, and headed for the ICU. Feeling nervous and a little jittery, he hoped he didn't run into any other cardiologists on his way to McKenzie's room. He felt certain that a look of guilt covered his face.

Twenty paces from her room, he spotted a policeman sitting next to the entrance.

Shit.

He nodded at the policeman and smiled as if they were old friends, and walked past him toward the entrance to the room, acting as if he had every right to be there. He was about to push open the door, when the officer sprang up and blocked the doorway. Julian stood over six feet tall, but still he had to look up at the towering cop.

"Can I help you, Doctor?" the officer said, his tone soft and polite.

Julian pointed to his badge. "I'm one of the physicians treating Ms. O'Neill. I need to examine her."

Squinting to focus his eyes, the policeman studied Julian's ID badge, then fixed his stare on his face. He looked at his clipboard, and stepped to the side. "Your name is on the list, Doctor. You're cleared to go in."

"Thank you."

"But I have to accompany you."

That's not what Julian wanted to hear. Suppose McKenzie was awake? One look at him and surely she'd remember. He'd given her various drugs during his experiments, but hadn't found it necessary to give her one that induced amnesia. He had hoped to be alone with her. Now he felt trapped. His only hope was that she still remained unconscious.

CHAPTER FORTY-THREE

Sami programmed her office telephone so that all calls would automatically ring in Captain Davidson's office. Two communications technicians had already set up the wiretap, hoping that Sami could keep the anonymous caller on the phone long enough to trace the number. For all she knew, the guy could, in fact, be the serial killer.

Four of Sami's colleagues sat in the office with her, anxiously waiting for the phone to ring, none of them having much to say. If legitimate, this phone call could break the investigation wide open. The captain sat at his desk, rocking back and forth, sucking on a cigarette. Al sat slouched in the corner of the office, looking like a schoolboy punished for unruly behavior. They had decided that Al would monitor the call and try to trace the location. Sami wasn't shocked to see D'Angelo joining the party. In fact, she would have bet on it. Based on her prior experiences with the asshole, she expected him to break her balls with that patronizing grin and snarky remarks. But she had a little surprise for him. Richard Osbourn, sitting next to her, was there to learn.

"This could be your big day, Detective Rizzo," D'Angelo said. "Your name might be written across the sky as Homicide Detective of the Year."

"Thanks for the vote of confidence," she answered, "but my ego doesn't require fanfare."

"C'mon, Sami," D'Angelo said. "We all enjoy a little pat on the back."

She could no longer hold her tongue. "And tell me again why you're here, Detective, when you explicitly declined to be any part of this investigation?"

Davidson sat forward, seemingly anxious to hear D'Angelo's answer.

"I didn't want to steal your thunder. I've had my share of glory days. I've come to the end of my career and want to go quietly."

Quietly?

"You know what I find rather curious, Chuck?" Sami said. "You understand how our new telephone system works, right?"

D'Angelo looked confused. "To be honest, I do the basics and don't give a rat's ass about all the newfangled gizmos. Are you going to give me a demonstration?"

"Actually, I'd like to tell you about a very interesting feature." she gestured to the captain and pointed to his phone. "May I, Captain?"

"Be my guest."

She turned the telephone 180 degrees and started pushing buttons. She directed her attention to D'Angelo. "These new phones have a memory. They can track the last twenty calls and identify whether a call came in directly, was transferred, or was forwarded." She pushed a few buttons and pointed to the display. "Curiously, when the call came in from the anonymous guy, it didn't come directly to my line, nor was it transferred from the main operator." Sami locked her eyes on D'Angelo.

"What does this have to do with anything, Sami?" D'Angelo said. "Are you accusing me of something?"

"Well, Chuck, perhaps you would be kind enough to explain how the call I received from the anonymous guy was forwarded from *your* telephone."

D'Angelo's face flushed with blood.

"How did this anonymous caller get your number, Chuck?"

"What the hell do I know? The fucking call came in on my line, the guy asked for Sami Rizzo, and I forwarded the call. What's the big deal?"

"Why didn't you say something about this, Detective?" Davidson asked.

"Because it's bullshit. Should I keep a log of every fucking call I transfer?"

"Chuck," Sami said softly, "you do realize that every call that comes in or goes out is recorded, right?"

D'Angelo looked like his bones had just turned to Jell-O. Before he could utter another sound, the captain's telephone rang. Sami looked at her watch and it was exactly twelve noon.

"This is far from being over, Chuck," Davidson warned. "Get your sorry ass out of here and wait for me in the conference room."

The conversation with the anonymous caller ended much quicker than Sami had hoped. Obviously, the caller purposely cut the conversation short. The moment she hung up, she looked at Al, hoping he'd traced the call, but he shook his head.

"Not long enough to get the location."

"Replay the call," Captain Davidson said.

Al pushed a few buttons, turned on the speaker, and they all listened.

"This is Detective Rizzo."

"If you want the identity of the Resuscitator, match his DNA sample with the database at the Del Mar Fertility Center."

"Why?"

"'Cause I believe he's a donor."

"I'm not sure we have his DNA. Why can't you give us his name?"

"'Cause I don't know his name."

"Do you have any idea where he lives, or where he works?"

"Look, all I've got for you is the fertility center. Check it out and you'll track down the killer."

"Can you give us—"

Click.

Fortunately for Julian, McKenzie remained unconscious. He put on a little show for the policeman and examined her from head to toe.

Looking at McKenzie, studying her chalky complexion, Julian felt no remorse or sadness for her. Only anger. She had placed him in a very incriminating position. She had unwittingly sabotaged his research and now forced him to search for one more ideal subject. He looked at her chart and felt a bit relieved. Her prognosis was grim to say the least. Stress-induced cardiomyopathy. Valve repair or replacement. Possible heart pump. Possible transplant. From what he'd read and from what he remembered about the experiments he had conducted, her only hope was a transplant. He didn't know how, but he wasn't going to let that happen.

Immediately after a little powwow in Davidson's office to devise a plan of attack, Sami and Al nearly jogged to the crime lab on the fifth floor to see Betsy, Forensic Crime Scene Investigator.

When they walked into the lab, Betsy was sitting in the corner of the room, alone, sipping a Starbucks coffee.

"Nice life," Sami said. "They actually let you guys take a break up here?"

"Been here since six a.m.," Betsy answered. "Without a little caffeine boost, I'd be out cold." She finished the last of the coffee and tossed the cup in the trash. "I assume this isn't a social call."

"Can we talk?" Al said.

Betsy led them to a tiny room that served both as a supply room and mini conference room. It was barely big enough to be a closet.

Betsy closed the door. "Hope neither of you is claustrophobic."

Noticing only two chairs and a beat-up table, Sami folded her arms and leaned against a metal file drawer. "You two can sit. I need to stretch my legs."

"What can I do for you?" Betsy asked.

"We want you to help us catch the Resuscitator," Al said.

"Nothing would please me more."

"Is there an easy way for us to get our hands on a fertility center's database so we can see if our guy's DNA sample matches one of their donors?" Sami asked.

"Are you talking about a private center?" Betsy asked.

"It's the Del Mar Fertility Center," Al said.

Betsy thought for a moment. "Have you approached them?"

"We wanted to talk to you first," Al said. "You always have a bag of tricks up your sleeve."

"I'm afraid my bag is empty. If they don't voluntarily agree to share this information with you—and it is highly unlikely they will—the only alternative is a court order. I'm sure you were already aware of that."

Yes, Sami suspected that this is exactly what Betsy would say, but she was hoping for a miracle. No matter how compelling the argument, no fertility center would voluntarily share proprietary donor information with anyone. Not even cops.

"Sorry," Betsy said. "I wish I could tell you what you want to hear."

"No worries," Sami said. "I still have one trump card left."

CHAPTER FORTY-FOUR

Believing that it would be a waste of time to contact the Del Mar Fertility Center and ask them to disclose confidential client information, Sami, with Al trailing behind, rushed straight to her desk.

"Any chance you'd like to share with me why you're in a foot-race?" Al asked.

"You'll see."

When they reached her desk, Sami, one of the few people in the Western world to still use a Rolodex, flipped through the alphabet until she reached the *F*s.

Her fingers couldn't dial the number fast enough.

"Keep your fingers crossed," Sami said to Al.

"Foster residence."

Sami couldn't make out the woman's accent, but she definitely sounded European. "Good afternoon. This is Detective Sami Rizzo calling from Metro Homicide. May I speak to Judge Foster, please?"

"I am sorry but he is on vacation and will not be back for two weeks."

That seemed odd, Sami thought. Just a short time ago the Resuscitator brutally murdered his daughter, and he felt cheery enough to take a *vacation*?

"May I ask who I'm speaking to?"

"My name is Helga. I am the Fosters' housekeeper."

"Helga, this is a high-priority police emergency and I really need to contact him. Can you please give me his cell phone number?"

Long silence. "I am terribly sorry but I cannot do that. Judge Foster would fire me if I gave his personal number to anyone. Even the police."

"Okay, I can appreciate that. How about calling him and asking him to contact me? Could you do that?"

"I am sorry. I cannot."

"Listen to me, Helga, and listen carefully. We are moments away from apprehending the serial killer who murdered Genevieve Foster. But without Judge Foster's help, the killer is going to slip through our fingers. How do you think the judge would feel if we passed up an opportunity to catch this guy?"

"It broke my heart when Genevieve was murdered. Poor Judge Foster still cries when anyone mentions her name. I just don't know what to do."

"Do the right thing and call the judge immediately."

Again, a long silence. "May I have your telephone number, please, Detective."

"We just got a call from Doctor Fisher," Doctor Hastings said. "He can be here in less than forty-eight hours."

Julian sat in Hastings's office feeling somewhat relieved that he had a forty-eight-hour window to take care of business. How he would ultimately solve the problem, he wasn't yet sure. To make things even more trying, dealing with the policeman posted by her door would most certainly limit his options. What he had to do was address the situation before McKenzie went into surgery. No matter how skilled a surgeon, there was no way he could make a purposeful blunder in surgery without his esteemed colleagues recognizing his actions.

"Based on the medical information we shared with Fisher, what's his opinion?" Julian asked.

"Well, as experienced as he is with stress-induced cardiomyopathy, he didn't offer a lot of hope."

"That's not good news," Julian said.

"According to Fisher, no matter what we do, she will ultimately need a transplant. Her troponin levels are off the charts: 425 nanograms per milliliter. As you know, at 500, her heart muscle is virtually dead. There are too many critical issues to deal with. The surgical procedures we're facing are merely to keep her alive until we can find a suitable donor."

Well, I'm going to do everything in my power to ensure that she never makes it to the operating table.

"This better be good," Judge Foster warned. "What's so important that you have to pester me halfway around the world, Detective?"

"Helga didn't brief you?" Sami said.

"I didn't give her a chance to."

"I'm truly sorry to trouble you on your vacation, but—"

"*Vacation*? Do you actually think I'd take a vacation right after my daughter was murdered?"

"Sorry, Judge, that's what Helga told me."

"Helga cooks and cleans. That's it. I don't share my personal life with her."

Sami was curious what the judge was doing "halfway around the world," as he coined it, if he *wasn't* on vacation, but she didn't dare ask. "Well, whatever you're doing Judge Foster, I hope—"

"Considering that so many people seem to have a sudden interest in my personal activities, let me tell you, Detective Rizzo, what I'm doing. Were you aware that over a billion people worldwide drink filthy, polluted, bacteria-infested water?"

"I never heard that, Judge."

"It's a pitiful fact. And one of the worst places on the planet per capita is the Fiji Islands. That's where I'm calling from right now. I'm on the board of directors for an organization called Clean Water International. We organize mission trips to areas where people desperately need clean water. The volunteers install a simple, ingenious filtration system that converts swamp water into ninety-nine-percent-clean drinking water. Do you have any idea how many children die from dysentery every day? The number is staggering." His voice suddenly softened. "I can understand why it seems strange that I would leave San Diego while my daughter's killer is still at large. To be honest with you, I just couldn't stand being in that city any longer. My entire family thinks I've lost it, and maybe I have. Working here in Fiji, helping these poor people gives me a reason to get up in the morning." Now his voice was unsteady.

Sami could hear him breathing heavily into the cell phone. She guessed that it was hard for him to show his human side. From her experiences with judges, most were steel-fisted. His story touched her heart. But at this particular moment, Sami had to stay focused on her agenda.

"I guess you didn't contact me to hear a lecture about water pollution, right, Detective? Please, tell me that you apprehended my daughter's killer."

"Well, Judge, with your help we can do exactly that." She told him about the fertility center, the fact that the perp was likely a donor, and the court order she so desperately needed to access their database.

"A court order like this, Detective Rizzo, is a slippery slope. I turned my head the other way when you asked me for a stack of search warrants, and you can't even begin to imagine how badly I want that monster to rot in jail. But…" The phone went silent. "How quickly do you need it?"

"Not to sound disrespectful, Judge, we need it yesterday."

"A court order is not like a warrant. It's a very delicate matter. Don't forget that I'm thousands of miles away. How do you propose I sign a court order?"

"Does it require a wet signature to be valid?"

"There has to be an original document on file with a wet signature, but you can serve a copy to the fertility center."

"So your intern can draft a court order based on your instructions and e-mail it to you as an attachment. You can print it, sign it, scan it, and e-mail it back to your office. You'll have the original on your person, and I can use a copy to serve the center."

By the long pause, Sami hoped he was weighing the issue carefully.

"I'm really uncomfortable with the legal and ethical implications, Detective Rizzo. What you're asking me to do really pushes the legal envelope."

"I appreciate that, Judge Foster. But you must also understand that there is another young woman lying in a hospital bed right now, fighting for her life. What this maniac did to her is unspeakable. Somehow, she survived. Please don't let him hurt another woman."

"Well, Detective, I'm less than two years away from retirement. And if the timeline gets shortened, it might not be the worst thing in the world. I only hope I don't end up in front of a judicial committee on ethics charges."

"If your court order results in an arrest, and we get this guy off the streets, I don't think anybody would question your ethics."

A long silence.

"Okay, Detective, you've got your court order. I'll have it completed and signed within the hour. Now find this scumbag and put his ass behind bars."

The moment Sami disconnected the call, she clenched her fist like Tiger Woods after sinking a twenty-foot putt, and yelled, "Yes!"

Al, standing next to Sami, listening to her half of the conversation with Helga and Judge Foster, clapped his hands. "Well done, Sami. Well done."

Detective Chuck D'Angelo sat opposite Captain Davidson in the small conference room and nervously drummed his fingers on the metal table.

"Mind telling me what the fuck is going on, Chuck?" Davidson barked.

"I think everyone is blowing this way out of proportion. Especially Rizzo. She's got it in for me and I have no idea why."

"This has nothing to do with Detective Rizzo and you know it."

"She's trying to hang me out to dry."

"Then how about we call the IT people and listen to the conversation you had with the anonymous caller before you transferred the call to her? That should clear things up, no?"

D'Angelo thought for a moment. "That's not necessary, Captain."

"We've known each other for a long time. Talk to me, Chuck."

He weighed the captain's request. "There's a PI I've been acquainted with for a few years. Every once in a while we cross paths. He's helped me out a few times, and I've returned the favor."

"And every time you've scratched each other's back it's been on the up-and-up?" Captain Davidson asked.

"Not everything has been squeaky-clean, but we never broke the law. You've been out there, Captain. You know what it's like. Nothing would ever get done if we played by all the rules."

"Why did this guy call *you*?"

"Because he thinks one of his clients might be the Resuscitator. He didn't want to just call in on the hotline, so he contacted me and asked who he should speak to. When I got the call, and he explained to me what was going on, I transferred the call to Rizzo."

"Let me get this straight. You get a call from a guy, he tells you that he thinks he can finger our perp, and you just transfer the call to Sami?"

Chuck nodded. "That's right."

"Are you fucking shitting me? You get a lead like this and you just transfer the call as if it was a telemarketer selling time-shares in Timbuktu? Why didn't you say something to me so we could nab the guy and bring him in for questioning?"

"He wanted to remain anonymous."

"Why?"

"I never asked."

"You didn't find it strange that this guy would pass on a ten-thousand-dollar reward?"

"I guess it never occurred to me?"

"C'mon, Chuck. Who the fuck do you think you're talking to? You're way too experienced a detective to overlook something so obvious. The guy wanted to remain anonymous cause his fingernails are dirty." The captain fixed his stare on D'Angelo. "And you know what I think, Chuckie Boy? I think some of that dirt has rubbed off on you. You're less than two months away from retirement. Do you really want to jeopardize your pension and face possible criminal charges?"

"Please don't do this, Captain."

"You did it to yourself. Now give me the guy's name."

CHAPTER FORTY-FIVE

"How about we ride to the courthouse together?" Al suggested. He guessed that Sami was avoiding alone time with him. He really wanted to speak to her one-on-one, but he could still see pain in her eyes.

I'm a piece of shit.

"It really isn't necessary that you accompany me," she said. "I'm just going to pick up the court order and go directly to the Del Mar Fertility Center."

Just as he suspected. She'd do anything to avoid him. "Even with the court order, you still might run into a snag. Besides, I'd like to talk."

She grabbed her purse, rummaged through it, and found her keys. "I think your dick said everything there is to say."

"Please, Sami. I just want a chance to explain."

"You're wasting your time. But if flapping your lips makes you feel any better or helps you deal with the guilt, at least it takes care of one of us."

They walked out of the precinct and headed for the parking structure, Sami leading the way like a woman competing in a walking marathon. Al had rehearsed his speech many times, but suspected that once they sat in the confines of her car, his brain would go blank and he'd have to improvise. The courthouse was less than five minutes away, not nearly enough time for him to plead his case. Not wanting any gaps in his plea for forgiveness, he decided to wait until they drove to the fertility center, which was a twenty-minute ride.

Sami pulled her car to the yellow-painted curb designated for commercial vehicles only, flipped down the visor with the placard marked "Official Police Business," and turned off the ignition.

"For a guy who has a lot to say, you're awfully quiet."

"I thought we'd talk while driving to the—"

"Let's get this over with right now. You talk. I'll listen."

Not expecting to be blindsided, he tried to organize his thoughts, but they were all jumbled together. "I'm not going to bore you with a long speech. So I'll cut to the chase. You may not believe this, and you have every reason not to, but I love you with all my heart. It sounds so cliché, but it's true. I have never felt this way about anyone. My actions, unfortunately, don't support my claim. I can't explain why I did what I did. All I can say for sure is that I was in a strange place. I thought my sister was going to die. I needed comfort. I felt completely alone. I'm sure this is going to piss you off, but it wasn't about sex. It was about having someone comfort me at a time of need. The sex just happened.

"I'll do anything not to lose you. Just ask. All I want is another chance to prove to you how much I care for you and how deeply sorry I am. If you tell me to hit the road, I totally understand. I'll move out today. I'll even get transferred to another precinct. I'll do whatever it takes to ease your pain."

He could see her eyes welling with tears. During his entire speech, she hadn't once looked at him. She blankly stared out the windshield.

"Sami, I beg you to forgive me."

She turned her head and faced him. He searched her eyes but had no idea what she was thinking or what she might say.

"This isn't about forgiveness. And it isn't about love. I know you love me. This is an issue of trust. You, more than anyone, know my history with Tommy. You know how difficult it is for me to trust a man—any man." Now tears were running down her cheeks. "I need some alone time. Time away from you. I can't work with you every day, live under the same roof, and think this through clearly. We have to work together, but we can divide our tasks. If I need help, I'll ask Osbourn. The captain doesn't need to know this. I'll keep you posted and you do the same. All it takes is an e-mail or phone call. My Blackberry is on twenty-four-seven."

"Fair enough. I'll move my stuff out today."

"Just take your essentials. For now anyway."

That she wasn't booting him out completely gave him a glimmer of hope.

"Where will you go?"

"I'm not sure right now. I'll manage." He touched her hand but she recoiled. "What are you going to tell your mother?"

"The truth."

When Peter J. Spencer III heard a gentle knock on his office door, he grabbed his wallet and rushed to open it. He hadn't had time for breakfast this morning and felt ravenous. He wasn't crazy about Domino's Pizza, but at least it would stop his stomach from growling. Besides, they delivered.

When he opened the door, he expected to see a young kid holding a pizza box. Instead, two men dressed in dark suits stood shoulder to shoulder. With a couple of pairs of sunglasses, Spencer thought, they could easily audition for the next *Men in Black* movie. He'd been around long enough to recognize who they were.

That fucking *D'Angelo.*

"What can I do for you?" Spencer asked, well aware why they were there.

"Are you Peter Spencer?" the younger cop asked.

"The one and only. In the flesh."

"I'm Detective Osbourn and this is Lieutenant Ramirez. May we speak to you for a minute?"

Spencer stepped to the side and invited them in. He pointed to a beat-up leather sofa in the far corner. "Have a seat, gentlemen."

Spencer wheeled his high-back executive chair across from the detectives. "Can I get you something to drink?"

"This is not a social call, Mr. Spencer," Ramirez said.

"How did you guys find out?"

Osbourn and Ramirez looked puzzled. "Find out what?" Osbourn said.

"That I was the anonymous caller."

"We got a tip," Osbourn said.

"And that tip's name wouldn't happen to be Chuck D'Angelo, would it?"

"Why do you ask?" Ramirez said.

"A couple of suits show up at my door a few hours after I speak with Detective Rizzo. I don't need to be Einstein to figure it out."

"What's the guy's name?" Osbourn asked.

Giving them carefully edited information, Spencer told them about his mysterious client and his long-time association with Chuck D'Angelo.

"So this 'John Smith' hired you to get personal information on Detective Rizzo?" Ramirez asked.

Spencer nodded. "That is correct."

"And you didn't have any ethical issues with his request, or suspect he was up to no good?"

"First of all, I didn't break any laws. Much of the information I shared is public knowledge—if you know where to look for it. Second, I *did* suspect the guy was shady. Hence the call to Detective Rizzo."

"Do you have any idea what John Smith's real name is?" Ramirez asked.

"If I did, I wouldn't be calling him John Smith."

"When you spoke to Detective Rizzo," Osbourn said, "you told her she could get the Resuscitator's true identity through the Del Mar Fertility Center. Where did you get this information?"

"When I suspected something wasn't kosher, I tailed the guy one day and saw him walk into the place. I figured he was a sperm donor, and that the center would likely have his real name—not to mention DNA."

"What's D'Angelo's part in all this?" Osbourn asked.

"Only that I had a prior relationship with him, so instead of calling in the tip on the hotline, I called Chuck and he put me through to Detective Rizzo. No mysteries. No huge conspiracy."

"Are you wealthy, Mr. Spencer?" Osbourn asked.

The question came from nowhere and caught Spencer off guard. "Well, if I were, would I work out of a shit-hole office like this?"

"I find it rather curious," Osbourn said, "that a man who surrounds himself with such an austere environment wouldn't be the least bit interested in the ten-thousand-dollar reward for information leading to the arrest and conviction of the Resuscitator. Why is that, Mr. Spencer?"

Spencer fixed his eyes on Osbourn and folded his arms across his chest. "I'm not answering any more questions, fellows. If you want to arrest me, go ahead. Otherwise, this conversation is over."

"It may be over, Mr. Spencer. But as soon as we listen to the recording of your conversation with D'Angelo, you just might be unemployed."

The room went silent. For the first time since the detectives walked in the door, Spencer felt rattled. Having no skills worthy of any other career, if he lost his PI license, he'd be lucky to find a position at a 7-Eleven. He knew all too well how the police department worked. A simple philosophy governed the world of law enforcement and it was called the barter system. Even if there were no grounds to pull his license, if the detectives talked to the right people, Spencer's PI license wouldn't be worth the paper it was written on.

He could not remember verbatim what D'Angelo and he had discussed on the telephone prior to speaking with Detective Rizzo, but he feared that the conversation would ultimately incriminate him in some way. Time to play Let's Make a Deal.

"If I come clean on D'Angelo, and give you a little history lesson of his extracurricular activities, can I walk?"

Osbourn gave Ramirez a quick glance as if he were asking for approval, and the lieutenant nodded. Obviously, Spencer thought, he was still a wet-behind-the-ears detective, and couldn't wipe his ass without permission.

"As long as you haven't committed a felony," Osbourn said, "I think we can work out something."

"But that's not a guarantee," Ramirez added.

CHAPTER FORTY-SIX

Sami and Al walked into the Del Mar Fertility Center and approached the reception desk. Sami flashed her badge, but the young woman behind the desk paid little attention to it and continued talking on her cell phone.

Sami waved the badge in front of her face. "Please hang up."

The receptionist finished her sentence and disconnected the call. "I'm sorry, but that was a very important call."

"Well, I think our business here might be slightly more important," Sami said. "We need to talk to the manager, supervisor, owner, whoever runs this place."

"May I ask what it's regarding?" the young woman said.

"No, you may not," Sami answered. "It's confidential police business."

The receptionist stood and parked her hands on her hips. "Let me see if Ms. Cardoza is available."

Sami removed the court order from her purse and held it up so the receptionist could see it. "This is a court order. She needs to *make* herself available."

While waiting for the receptionist to return, Sami checked out the waiting area. By the way the place was exquisitely furnished and decorated, she guessed that the semen collecting business was booming. Other than a young man sitting in the corner, reading a copy of *GQ*, likely waiting for his date with a paper cup, the room was vacant. Just as Sami and Al were about to sit down on a cushy leather sofa, the receptionist returned with a tall, stunning Latino woman who looked like she could win the Miss Universe contest. Oh, how Sami wished her hips were as slender as this young woman's were. But what really struck her was an image of Al in bed with a woman who looked like this. Did his Brazilian hottie look this good?

"I'm Detective Rizzo and this is Detective Diaz."

The woman extended her hand. "I am Maria Cardoza. I manage this facility. How can I help you?"

"May we talk privately?" Sami asked.

Cardoza pointed. "Certainly."

Al followed Sami through the door and Cardoza led them to her office. Like the waiting area, the office was lavishly appointed. Sami was not surprised.

"Our receptionist tells me you have a court order," Cardoza said.

Sami laid it on her desk. "We are searching for a man who we believe is one of your clients." Sami handed her the DNA analysis, noticing that Cardoza was looking at Al even though Sami was doing the talking. "We've already scanned the FBI's National DNA Index System and did not find a match. We need to find out if anyone in your database matches this DNA."

"That might take some time," Cardoza said.

"We don't have time," Al said.

"Our central office is in San Francisco," Cardoza said. "All of our confidential client information is kept there. Court order or not, I'll need approval from a higher power to release this information. I'm sure you can appreciate the sensitivity of the situation."

"And I'm sure you can understand that this information could be a matter of life and death," Al said. "We're not just detectives, Ms. Cardoza, we're *homicide* investigators."

"Let me make a couple phone calls," Cardoza suggested. "Would you mind waiting in our lounge area. I'd appreciate some privacy."

Julian was running out of time. What made things even worse was the call they'd received from Doctor Fisher. Apparently, he'd had a critical surgery scheduled, but the patient died, so instead of having to wait forty-eight hours, Dr. Fisher would be in San Diego mid-morning tomorrow and McKenzie's surgery was scheduled for early the next day.

Julian's original thought was to find a way into her room without the policeman shadowing him. He could do what he needed to do and be out of there in five minutes. If he could overcome the cop problem, though, he still faced another obstacle. All ICU patients hooked up to life support and heart monitors were carefully observed at the nurses' station. If he injected McKenzie with a lethal drug, the moment she arrested, the nurses' control panel would light up, and the warning buzzers would go off. Even if he found a way in and out of McKenzie's room unnoticed, the police, no doubt, would perform a thorough autopsy, and they would discover that she'd been murdered. This would initiate a massive investigation that could easily lead the police to his doorstep. No, he hadn't thought his plan through carefully. This was no longer viable.

Although it would pose great difficulty, the only logical solution to his quandary would be to sabotage the surgical procedures. Granted, it was a tricky undertaking requiring planning and precision that would not attract the attention of his fellow surgeons. This would be next to impossible. Fortunately, the complexity and unusual nature of McKenzie's surgery did offer him a couple possibilities for covert subversive actions. When dealing with delicate heart surgery, one millimeter can be the difference between life and death. He had lost patients before, and no one ever questioned his competency. Every day, patients died on the operating table, so to lose McKenzie O'Neill, a young woman with only a small chance of survival anyway, would not likely raise any questions. He just had to be careful and not do anything too obvious.

Having explored several options, painstakingly considering the risk and feasibility of each, Julian still hadn't determined what might work. At this point, he had no idea what little slip of the scalpel would end McKenzie's life. He wasn't yet sure if he would cause a total bleed-out and watch her die on the operating table, secretly weaken one of the valve replacements, or do something to affect the heart pump's ability to function properly. He could only hope that the difficult surgery and multiple procedures involved would offer an opportunity for him to solve this problem once and for all.

When Chuck D'Angelo walked into Captain Davidson's office and saw David Costello, assistant district attorney, and Oscar Jones, special agent from Internal Affairs, he sensed he was about to be ambushed. He braced himself for what would undoubtedly be a bloodbath.

"I think you've met David and Oscar, Chuck," the captain pointed to the two men. "Have a seat."

D'Angelo shook their hands ever so briefly and sat in the only available chair.

"Something has bubbled to the surface, Chuck, and we need to have a little chit-chat," the captain said.

"Well," D'Angelo said, "let's get this over with. I've got a full afternoon ahead of me."

"Tell me," Agent Jones said. "What is your relationship with Peter Spencer?"

I'm gonna cut off that motherfucker's balls!

"The PI?"

Agent Jones nodded.

"I wouldn't call it a *relationship*. More like an acquaintance."

"That's not exactly what he's telling us," Agent Jones said.

"So you're going to believe some two-bit PI over me?"

"Detective D'Angelo," Costello said, "We listened to a tape recording of your conversation with Spencer the day he called and you transferred the call to Detective Rizzo. Do you want to change your story about your relationship status with Spencer or would you prefer that we listen to the recording together?"

"Okay, okay, so I knew the guy and worked with him on a few cases. What's the big deal?"

"The big deal, Detective," Agent Jones said, "is that if only half of what he told us is true, you've got some serious explaining to do."

"Hey guys, I've been with the department for over thirty-five years, and I've got twice as many collars as any other detective. I fucking put the bad guys behind bars. If once in a while I have to work around the system, I do. If we detectives didn't push the envelope every now and then, we'd be sitting at our desks with our thumbs up our asses while cold-blooded killers walked the streets of San Diego. Instead of jerking off, reading police policies and procedures, I get the fucking job done."

"We're not talking about violating police protocol, Detective," Costello said. "We're talking about actions that may result in criminal prosecution. I hate to say this, but pending a thorough investigation, you risk losing your pension."

Feeling helplessly pigeonholed, D'Angelo had to retreat. "I think before this party goes any further, I'd like to have an attorney present."

While Sami and Al waited quietly for Maria Cardoza to contact the San Francisco office of the Del Mar Fertility Center, they sat in the lounge. Al read a three-month-old copy of *Sports Illustrated* and Sami browsed through the *San Diego Chronicle*.

Feeling nauseous again, which lately seemed to be mainstream for Sami, she went outside for some fresh air.

"Be right back," Sami said.

She wasn't sure if her desire to go outside was driven more by her queasy stomach or having reached her limit on the awkwardness between Al and her. Something had to give. Either she had to bury her pain and give him another shot, or she had to break it off completely, which created new problems. It was one thing for him to move out of her house, and quite another telling Captain Davidson that they could no longer work together.

If she truly were a good cop deserving of the confidence Mayor Sullivan had placed in her, her personal life would temporarily remain in the background and she'd be totally focused on apprehending the Resuscitator. In spite of what she believed was the right thing to do, thoughts of Al's affair and the status of their relationship had dominated her thoughts. At the heart of the issue was one immutable fact: Samantha Marie Rizzo was deeply in love with Alberto Diaz. And if Hollywood films and Gothic novels were even partially true, love could conquer any obstacle.

Right now, all she wanted was a two-pound box of Godiva chocolates.

Al popped his head out the door. "She's ready for us."

They went to Cardoza's office and sat down. Cardoza closed the door.

"Well, I spoke to the regional manager and I think we can give you the information you're looking for."

"Fabulous," Al said.

"How soon can we get a DNA match, personal information, and a photo?" Sami asked.

"First thing in the morning."

Sami looked at her watch. Three o'clock. "With all due respect, tomorrow morning might as well be Christmas. At the department, we can match DNA samples in minutes. Why is it going to take eighteen hours?"

"Because you have access to the FBI's National DNA Index System. Our system, although efficient, is no match for the FBI's. It's like comparing a black-and-white TV to a high-definition plasma. I can't make the system respond more quickly than it's capable of responding. It's a technical issue. Barring any unforeseen obstacles, I can have the information tomorrow morning at nine."

Sami wanted to argue, but to what end? They'd already discovered that the perp's DNA was not registered with the FBI's database. Not to mention the fact that the database for the Del Mar Fertility Center was private information. Even with a court order, not Judge Foster or the mayor herself could force them to comply immediately. In fact, the court order itself stated that the Del Mar Fertility Center must provide DNA information matching the sample supplied by the San Diego Police Department "as soon as logistically possible."

"We'll be back tomorrow morning at nine sharp," Sami said. "If for any reason you should get the results sooner, please call me on my cell phone." She handed Marie Cardoza a business card.

CHAPTER FORTY-SEVEN

Sami dropped off Al at the precinct parking garage. Although things were really heating up with the investigation, Sami needed a little time to decompress. Besides, it felt as if she hadn't seen her family in decades. "I'm heading home. Going to take my mother, Angelina, and Emily out for a quick dinner. Can you move your stuff out while we're gone?"

Al opened the door and stepped out of the car. He leaned inside and looked at her. "If that's what you want, you got it."

"No, it's not what I want. It's what has to be."

"Call me just before you go to dinner and I'll be out of there in thirty minutes."

"Remember what I said. For now, just take your essentials."

"You mean a toothbrush and deodorant?"

"I think you might want to grab some underwear."

This exchange was the closest they came to lightheartedness since he'd confessed to having an affair. She missed their banter and camaraderie.

"I'll meet you at the fertility center tomorrow morning," Al said.

"You don't have to meet me. I can do this on my own."

"I *want* to be there."

"Suit yourself."

Sami wanted to drive off but Al still stood there with the door opened.

"Tell the clan I said hi."

"Will do," Sami said softly.

Sami and her family sat in a booth sipping sodas, waiting for the waitress to take their orders. Sami wasn't really in the mood for Italian food tonight, which was a rare occasion, but her mom insisted that they go to DeMarco's, Josephine's favorite restaurant. As usual, her mother always got her way. At least Angelina would be happy. She loved their mac and cheese.

"Thanks for the nice surprise, Sami," Emily said. "I didn't really feel like cooking tonight."

"My pleasure, Emily," Sami said. "You deserve a hell of a lot more than dinner."

"Mommy, can I have some 'ronis and cheese?" Angelina asked.

"Of course, Sweetheart," Grandma Rizzo said.

Sami hated when her mother answered a question directed to her. It was just one of many things that got under her skin.

Wanting to make the announcement as matter-of-factly as possible, Sami just blurted without forethought. "Al is moving out."

"Where's he going, Mommy?"

How could she answer this question? "He's getting his own place, Honey."

As Sami expected, her mom gave her a sidelong glance with a suspicious look in her eyes. Emily stared blankly at Sami as if she'd seen a ghost.

"Is this permanent?" Josephine asked.

"Is anything permanent?"

"Apparently not."

Sami held her tongue. Originally, she had thought about coming clean and telling her mother and Emily that Al had an affair, but she now realized the idea bordered on insanity.

"I knew when Alberto moved to the living room sofa bed, that his next move would be out the door," Josephine said.

"Are you okay?" Emily asked.

Sami swallowed hard. "I'm…fine."

"What made Alberto move?" Josephine asked. "What did you do?"

"*I* didn't do anything. *We* just decided that we both needed some time and space to think."

"Time to *think*?" Josephine repeated, the tone of her voice laced with sarcasm. "Once two people split up, it's never the same again. Remember Aunt Florence and Uncle Rocco?"

How could she forget? When Sami's aunt and uncle split up—Sami had just turned ten—Aunt Florence moved in "for a while," which turned out to be over a year. Florence never uttered a civil word to Rocco when they talked on the telephone, and Sami got a daily dose of their verbal confrontations. Eventually, when Florence filed for divorce it became the center of family gossip. If ever there were a mismatched couple, those two won the prize. Was this her destiny with Al?

"Gee, Mom," Sami said. "Thanks for comparing Al and me to Aunt Florence and Uncle Rocco. That's such a compliment."

"All I'm saying is that once two people go their separate ways, there's no going backwards. If Alberto moves out, you can kiss him goodbye."

Sami hated to admit it, but in part, her mother's viewpoint made sense. Over the years, she had seen more divorce than reconciliation—not only in her own family, but through friendships and friends of friends. Maybe her mother was right. Maybe Al moving out was the beginning of the end.

"Hi, Julian. It's Ted Hastings. Can you do me a huge favor?"

Julian slipped on his Bluetooth. "What's up?"

"I was scheduled to perform the pre-op tests on the O'Neill girl first thing in the morning, but I've got a conflict in my schedule. Any chance you could stand in for me?"

A key component to the prescreening process prior to surgery included a comprehensive evaluation by one key member of the surgical team. Julian didn't really want to substitute for Doctor Hastings—it could prove risky—but he had little choice.

"No problem. I can handle it."

"Terrific. I'm really looking forward to meeting Doctor Fisher and assisting."

"It should be quite an experience," Julian said. "Maybe we'll even make the front cover of the *American Journal of Cardiology*."

"What we're doing isn't exactly groundbreaking, but if we save this girl, it's going to grab some attention from the entire medical community."

Save *her? Not a chance.*

"Thanks again, Julian. Contact me if you run into any problems."

Shortly after dinner, Josephine went to bed and Sami helped Angelina slip into her Sponge Bob Square Pants pajamas, while Emily sat in the living room sipping a glass of Ferrari-Carano Rosato di Sangiovese. Sami tucked in her daughter and sat on the edge of the bed. She bent forward and kissed Angelina on the forehead.

"Good night, Sweetheart."

"Mommy, is Al going to be with Daddy up in heaven?"

Heaven was the last place Tommy DiSalvo would spend eternity. "No, Honey."

"Then how come we can't see him anymore?"

"You *will* see him, Honey. He's just not going to sleep here."

Angelina thought about Sami's answer. "Will he still take us out for ice cream?"

Wouldn't that *be awkward?* "Well, if Al can't take you, I still can."

"But he's funny, Mommy. He makes me laugh. And he tickles better than you do."

Sami could hardly hold back the tears. Her daughter had already suffered one loss. And now she might be facing another. When she and Al first decided to live together, Sami had thought long and hard. The last thing she wanted was to bring another man into Angelina's life, only to watch him disappear. Angelina had just validated her biggest fear.

"Well, Sweetheart, maybe Mommy can learn how to tickle you like Al did."

Sami kissed her again, turned on her nightlight, and walked in the living room. Emily had already poured Sami a generous glass of wine.

Emily patted the sofa cushion next to her. "Have a seat, Cuz."

Before sitting down, Sami gulped two mouthfuls of wine.

"We're not slamming tequila," Emily said. "It's a sipping wine."

"Then maybe we should bring out the Patrón."

"Want to talk about it?" Emily offered.

Sami *didn't* want to talk about it, but if she didn't vent to someone she trusted really soon, her head would surely explode. Whom in her life could she trust more than Emily?

"Things have gotten rather complicated," Sami said. "When Al was in Rio tending to his sister, he…"

Emily reached over and grabbed her hand.

"He had an affair with a nurse."

Emily went silent for a moment. "Wow. That knocks my socks off."

"Why? That's what men do, isn't it? They wine and dine you, make you fall in love with them, and then they rip out your heart and stomp on it."

"I can't back you up on that one, Cuz. I haven't had time to date since high school."

"Trust me. You're better off."

"Is it over?" Emily asked. "I mean *really* over?"

"I can't answer that question right now. I'm still waiting for my anger to settle down. How can you think clearly when you're seething?"

"Does that mean you're considering giving him another chance?"

"Not sure. Just not sure."

Emily slipped her arm around Sami's shoulders and gave her a hug.

"Want some advice from a snot-nosed kid?" Emily asked.

"Sure. You're wiser than most people twice your age."

"I don't understand much about relationships, so this is coming from my gut. But I think what Al and you have is something special. Something rare. Maybe you can't see it, but when he looks at you, I can tell that he just loves you to death. He's a good guy. Sometimes good people screw up. I would guess that when he was in Rio, thinking that his sister would die, he was weak and vulnerable. This nurse came along and gave him comfort. I don't think it was about sex or a negative reflection on his feelings for you.

It most certainly wasn't about his feelings for the nurse. It could have been anyone close enough to offer him emotional support. If I can be so bold as to offer my opinion, don't let him get away. Give him another chance to prove his love. He's worth it, Cuz."

Sami squeezed back the tears. "I love you, Emily."

CHAPTER FORTY-EIGHT

Julian stopped by the nurses' station and commandeered a nurse to assist him with McKenzie's pre-op tests. Again, a policeman stationed just outside McKenzie's hospital room stopped him at the door.

"Hello, Doc. Back again, hey?"

"Ms. O'Neill is scheduled for surgery early tomorrow so I have to run some pre-op tests." He pointed to the nurse. "Ms. Oliver is here to assist me."

"Okay if I join you?"

"Do I have a choice?"

The cop shook his head. "'Fraid not. It's standard procedure."

Julian didn't care that the cop tagged along because he had no intentions of harming McKenzie in any way. He'd already decided that her moment of truth would come during surgery. But in spite of Julian's indifferent attitude, he couldn't deny that the cop annoyed the hell out of him. "So, doctor-patient confidentiality means nothing?"

"Not in this situation."

Julian walked in the room with the cop and nurse following behind. Nurse Oliver knew exactly how to proceed without direction. While she drew blood from McKenzie's left arm, Julian went through a series of diagnostic tests, one of which was to check her pupils to see if they reacted to light. Just as he backed away,

McKenzie's fingers twitched and her eyes opened slightly. Julian didn't think that either Nurse Oliver or the cop noticed this, but he stood directly over her and her eyes locked on his face.

"It's you," McKenzie said softly.

Julian backed away as if she'd hit him in the gut with a battering ram.

"It's you," she said again, a little louder this time.

If she regained total consciousness, there would be no place for him to hide.

"Did you hear that?" Nurse Oliver said.

"Hear what?" the cop said.

"The patient said something. Did you hear it, Doctor?"

"I heard her mumble something, but I don't think she's conscious. It's not uncommon for a comatose patient to experience brief moments of responsiveness."

"It's you," McKenzie said. This time much more pronounced.

"I must resemble someone she knows," Julian explained, hoping they would buy into his reasoning. "Considering the critical condition of her heart, we can't let her get riled." He turned towards Nurse Oliver. "I need 10 milligrams of diazepam, *stat*. I'll update her chart and make the appropriate notations."

"Right away, Doctor." Nurse Oliver left the room immediately.

"Forgive me, Doctor," the cop said, "but the detectives assigned to handle this investigation asked me to alert them the moment the patient regained consciousness. A five-minute conversation could help us apprehend her assailant. I don't quite understand why you're going to sedate her."

Julian wasn't sure if he could hold himself together, but he did his best to stay calm. If the cop prevented Nurse Oliver from administering the sedative long enough for Detective Rizzo to get here, everything in his life would come crashing down.

"She may appear to be lucid," Julian insisted. "But I assure you, the only thing that's going to come out of her mouth is incoherent mumbling. Her heart is barely functioning. If we don't keep her completely at rest, she may never make it to surgery tomorrow morning."

"Okay, Doctor. Point well taken. I still have to follow my orders and contact the detectives at once. Whatever they decide to do is between you and them."

"Fair enough."

Just then, Nurse Oliver returned with the syringe. While the cop was facing the other way, talking on his cell phone, she injected the sedative into McKenzie's IV.

Unless Sami Rizzo was driving a rocket ship, Julian thought, McKenzie O'Neill would be out cold long before the detective got here.

For the first time today, Julian felt a slight sense of relief.

After a long dose of soul searching, Sami prepared herself to meet Al at the Del Mar Fertility Center. Just seeing him was painful. During the night of restless sleep, Emily's words played in Sami's mind like an endless CD. Over and over again, Sami kept hearing the same words: "Give him another chance to prove his love. He's worth it, Cuz."

Sami didn't doubt that Al was worth it. His worth was not the issue. What she doubted was her ability to ever trust him again. Without trust, a relationship is doomed. If he came home a little late, would she give him the third degree? If he went out with the guys for a beer, would she chew on her fingernails wondering if he was on the prowl? If she picked up a strange scent when she hugged him, would she accuse him of being with another woman?

All these troubling questions and few answers.

Just as she was about to pull in the driveway of the fertility center, her cell phone rang.

"Detective Rizzo."

"It's Officer Dolinski. I just wanted to tell you that for a brief period, Ms. O'Neill opened her eyes and mumbled a few words."

"What did she say?"

"Her words were barely audible. I couldn't quite make them out."

"Is she still conscious?"

"The nurse—I believe her name was Ms. Oliver—gave her a sedative to help keep her calm. The doctor said that her heart is very weak and if they didn't sedate her, she could go into cardiac arrest."

"What's the doctor's name?"

"So many doctors fly in and out of her room, his name escapes me. My shift just ended and I'm walking to my patrol car. The clipboard with the list of doctors and nurses authorized to see Ms. O'Neill is with Joe Martinelli, the officer who relieved me. I've had some difficulty getting a cell phone signal in the hospital, but I'd be happy to go back upstairs, check the clipboard, and call you right back."

"That's not necessary, Officer. You go home and get some sleep. I'll contact Doctor Templeton directly and find out what's going on. Thanks for calling."

She parked her car in the lot next to the fertility center and flipped open her cell phone. She didn't think she'd find Doctor Templeton in his office this early in the morning, but remembered that he had called her from his cell phone a few days ago. She pushed a few buttons and went into the "Received Calls" menu. Sure enough, she found his cell phone number.

After three rings, she expected to hear a voice mail prompt. Instead, she heard the doctor's voice.

"This is Doctor Templeton." His voice sounded labored.

"Hi, Doctor, sorry to bother you so early in the morning, but—"

"No need to apologize, Detective Rizzo. I've been awake since the wee hours. Just started my morning cardio workout, so I might sound a bit out of breath. What can I do for you?"

"I understand that McKenzie O'Neill regained consciousness for a brief period, but some doctor ordered a sedative to put her out. Was that you, Doctor?"

"No, that would likely be Doctor Hastings, a fellow cardiologist. He was scheduled to complete some pre-op tests on the patient early this morning. We haven't spoken yet."

"Why would he sedate her? We left explicit instructions to contact us if she even twitched. We may have missed an important opportunity to speak with her that might lead us to her assailant."

"Well, Detective, it's hard for me to comment without first speaking to Doctor Hastings. However, to me, it sounds like he made the right call. This young woman is clinging to life by the skin of her teeth. Any excitement at all could place her in a life-threatening situation. Under normal circumstances—if there even is such a thing in medicine—we would have already operated on this young woman. Unfortunately, without some guidance from Doctor Fisher, a cardiothoracic surgeon up in San Francisco, the risk to operate would be greater than the risk of a short postponement. Doctor Fisher is flying in later this morning. He and I, along with two other heart surgeons, will evaluate Ms. O'Neill's condition and determine exactly how we will proceed. We've scheduled surgery for first thing in the morning, and if we're successful, she should regain consciousness within twenty-four hours. When she does, you can speak to her for as long as you like without it endangering her life."

How could she, a layperson, dispute his professional opinion? "Thanks for the explanation, Doctor. Any idea at this point how long you expect her to be in surgery?"

"It's hard to say. The surgical procedures we're dealing with will likely take ten to twelve hours. Ultimately, Ms. O'Neill will need a heart transplant, which, believe it or not, might be less risky than what we're facing. Unfortunately, thus far, we do not have a donor, so our goal is to keep her alive until we find one. Without the surgery she faces tomorrow, I doubt she'd live another seventy-two hours."

"I can't thank you enough, Doctor. Hope you have a great workout."

"These old bones ain't what they used to be. Have a nice day, Detective Rizzo."

Almost like clockwork, Sami disconnected Doctor Templeton, and Al pulled up next to her. He got out of his car and waited for her to grab her purse, check her face in the vanity mirror, and step out of the car.

"Mornin', Sami."

Sami barely acknowledged him with a quick wave.

The center would not open for another ten minutes, so Sami hoped their conversation would remain professional and not personal.

"Have you spoken to this Doctor Hastings?" Al asked.

"The only one I've met on the surgical team is Doctor Templeton, but I'll contact Hastings when we're finished."

"I hope it amounts to something," Al said.

"Officer Dolinski couldn't make out what she mumbled. But maybe Doctor Hastings did. I would think that if she'd said anything significant, uttered a name, or something even remotely tangible, Doctor Hastings would have contacted us."

"One would hope so." When they walked into the center, the receptionist immediately acknowledged them with a smile, which was a dramatic change from the tepid greeting they'd received the day before.

"Good morning, Detectives. Can I get either of you a cup of coffee or some water?" Her tone was saccharine sweet.

Sami shook her head. "No thanks."

"I'd love a cup with cream and two teaspoons of sugar," Al said.

"Please have a seat. Ms. Cardoza will be with you in a minute." They barely had time to sit down when Ms. Cardoza appeared from the back room.

"Nice to see you again, Detectives. Please come into my office."

As Al passed the receptionist, she handed him the coffee and Sami noticed that the young woman winked at him.

"Thank you," he said.

This was *exactly* the situation Sami dreaded. Was it an innocent wink, or was she outwardly flirting? Was he attracted to her? Did he wink back? If they reconciled, wouldn't she be sentenced to a life of paranoia and suspicion? She now realized that she needed to speak with Doctor J again. Maybe she could clear Sami's head and help her sort out her conflicting emotions.

When they all sat down in Cardoza's office, Sami tried to read the woman's eyes, but they gave her no clue of what was coming next.

Maria Cardoza set a manila folder on her desk and pushed it toward Sami. "We found a DNA match. However, this particular client is one who requested to remain anonymous, so he goes by a pseudonym."

"You allow that?" Sami asked.

"It's not the norm, but if a client insists on remaining anonymous, who are we to challenge that request?"

"And what name does this guy go by?" Al asked.

Cardoza opened the folder. "John Smith."

"How utterly original," Sami said.

"It would surprise you," Cardoza said, "if I told you how many men use John Smith as their name."

"Do you have his photo?"

"As part of his anonymity, he did not want a photo taken."

"So," Sami said, "when a client comes in looking for a sperm donor, what would make them choose an anonymous donor when they have no information on him? For all they know, he could be Charles Manson's brother and have the IQ of a housefly."

"Detective Rizzo, I didn't say that we knew nothing about our anonymous donors. Only that they use a pseudonym and do not have a photo taken."

"Tell me about this guy," Sami said.

Cardoza slipped on her reading glasses and studied the file. "First off, he's of English descent. He's slightly over six feet tall. He's forty-two years old and has dark hair and blue eyes."

"That describes about twenty million men, just in California alone," Al said. "Can you give us any distinguishing features or something more specific?"

"Well, all potential donors are required to take an IQ test and a Global 3 Personality Test. His IQ is 147 and his character pattern of behavior, thoughts, and feelings lean toward assertiveness, competitiveness, perfectionism, dedication, and altruism. What seems a bit out of the ordinary is the fact that rarely does a personality trait of altruism combine with these other traits."

Sami and Al's eyes met.

"I appreciate your efforts, Ms. Cardoza," Sami said, "but this information doesn't really help us. We've got nothing except a broad description." Sami paused for a moment. "When is this donor scheduled to come in again?"

"Most clients just pop in without an appointment. I guess it has something to do with their mood on any particular day. I'm sure you understand."

"Here's my card," Sami said. "Next time he wanders in, call me immediately. And find a way to detain him until we get here."

Sami and Al stood. Sami offered her hand. "Thank you for your help."

Just as Sami and Al reached the reception area, Maria Cardoza called Sami's name.

"Something just occurred to me," Cardoza said. "I'm not sure if this helps, but when I originally interviewed this guy, I couldn't help but notice that he had a dimple on his left cheek—a very pronounced dimple."

"Only on his left cheek?" Sami asked.

Cardoza nodded. "That's correct."

Sami and Al stood in the parking lot, both leaning against their cars.

"Any brilliant ideas?" Al asked.

"Well, you were right, Al. Bad judgment on my part. We have to speak with Doctor Hastings ASAP. It would also be a good idea to speak to the nurse who injected McKenzie with the sedative."

"We could put out an APB for anyone with a left dimple on their cheek," Al said.

"Good luck with that."

"I'll follow you to the hospital," Al said. "If you lose me, call me on my cell and I'll meet you in the main lobby."

"The way you drive, I doubt that Mario Andretti could lose you."

Odd, Sami thought. Their playful interactions almost seemed normal. Then a disturbing image of Al making love to the Brazilian tramp flashed through her mind and everything turned sour again.

CHAPTER FORTY-NINE

As Sami had predicted, Al pulled into the hospital parking lot right behind her. In fact, he parked his car right next to hers. Under normal conditions, Al would grab her hand or drape his arm around her shoulders whenever they walked side by side. Now they walked together separately.

Neither of them spoke as they approached the main entrance. Al held the door for her, so at least one factor in their relationship hadn't changed. Aside from his often vulgar mouth, he had always been a gentleman.

She pushed the up button for the elevator and the silence between them continued. A good number of people were scattered about the hallway. Some appeared healthy, others were in wheelchairs or pushing walkers. It seemed like a mix of visitors and patients. One woman in particular caught Sami's eye. Obviously in pain, the woman's face was a picture of misery. Hunched over in the wheelchair, her backbone looked severely deformed.

Is this what I have to look forward to in my golden years?

They waited for the less-healthy people to board the elevator, then they barely squeezed in. Sami pushed the button for the sixth floor. Of course, everyone else behind them wanted to get off the elevator before the two of them, so it was like a game of musical chairs.

Finally, the sixth floor.

"Where we headed?" Al asked.

"Before we find Doctor Hastings, let's talk to the officer stationed at McKenzie's room."

"Do you remember where her room is?" Al asked.

Sami pointed. "Intensive care is down the hall and through the double doors on the right. I think it's room six twenty-five."

Double-timing their pace, they sailed down the hallway, passing nurses and doctors and an assortment of other people. When they turned right, Al pushed the saloon doors open and held one for Sami. She stopped dead in her tracks when she saw an empty chair in front of McKenzie's room.

Where the hell is Officer Martinelli?

Sami and Al gawked at each other.

"Something ain't right," Al said. "Let's check with the nurses' station."

"Excuse me," Sami said to the tall blonde nurse. "Have you moved McKenzie O'Neill to another room?"

"Are you a relative?" the nurse asked.

While Sami dug through her purse, Al whipped out his badge from his back pocket. "We're homicide detectives, miss. Can you tell us where Ms. O'Neill is?"

Sami had an eerie feeling that the answer to Al's question would not be good news.

While the blonde nurse banged on her computer, Sami noticed that the nurses' station looked like the control room for NASA. Modern medicine had truly evolved.

The blonde nurse stood and cocked her head to one side. "I'm afraid that Ms. O'Neill took a turn for the worse and was rushed into emergency surgery."

"Can you tell me who's operating?" Sami asked.

The nurse checked the computer again. "Doctor Hastings is leading the surgery, and Doctor Templeton will assist, but I'm not sure who else is on the surgical team. She deteriorated rather quickly, so they had to assemble a team stat."

Sami tried to remember the name of the nurse who gave McKenzie the sedative. Olivia was the only name that rang a bell. "Is there a nurse here by the name of Olivia?"

"No Olivia here," the blonde nurse said. "There is a Nurse Oliver."

"That's it!" Sami almost yelled. "Can I speak to her, please?"

"She just went on break, but she's probably in the employee lounge just down the hall."

When Julian had gotten the call from Doctor Hastings, he could hardly contain himself. Maybe he wouldn't even have to take action. Doctor Fisher still wasn't due in for a couple of hours so Julian and his colleagues were on their own. If she didn't die on the table, which now seemed quite possible, it would be much easier for him to sabotage the heart pump surgery without Doctor Fisher standing next to him. Furthermore, this particular procedure required three cardiothoracic surgeons, each busy with their own responsibilities, so his actions would go unnoticed.

After a brief discussion, which had included feedback from Doctor Fisher by telephone, Julian and the other surgeons determined that the safest course of action was to install the heart pump *before* the valve replacement surgery. Julian hadn't had a great deal of experience installing a left ventricular assist device, and he had no experience whatsoever with the unit they chose to install, the HealthMate II, the smallest, least cumbersome of all LVAD devices. Consequently, if he did make a fatal error, no one would ever suspect that it was anything more than an honest mistake.

The team of doctors, nurses, and surgical technicians stood at various stations in the operating room, each of them with a defined role. Doctor Hastings, who had more experience with the HealthMate II than the other surgeons, stood over McKenzie's spread-open ribcage.

"Before we begin," Doctor Hastings said. "This is how it's going down. As usual, Doctor Mickelson will monitor the patient and adjust the anesthesia as necessary. He will also administer Heparin to prevent clotting. We need to make three incisions: one at the base of the left ventricle, one in the aorta, and one in the right side of the abdominal wall. Before we install the LVAD, we will reroute the blood to the heart-lung machine and it will pump and oxygenate the patient's blood. We then must form a pocket for the LVAD in the abdominal wall as well. After that, we'll insert a tube to channel blood from the ventricle to the LVAD. Another tube will be connected from the pump to the aorta. When the pump is adequately supporting the patient's heart, and her vital signs are stable, we can move forward with the mitral and aortic valve replacement. Any questions?"

No one uttered a sound.

"Let's proceed."

Sami and Al found their way to the employee lounge, so crowded that Sami wondered who was running the hospital.

"Is there a Nurse Oliver in here?" Sami yelled over the buzz of the crowd.

A nurse standing at the counter, buttering a bagel, turned her head and waved the hand holding the knife. "That would be me."

Sami and Al flashed their badges simultaneously, as if it were a coordinated plan.

"I'm Detective Rizzo and this is Detective Diaz. Can we talk privately?"

"Sure thing. Just let me check out with the charge nurse."

When Nurse Oliver returned, she led the detectives to a small room used for patient consultation.

"This is about the O'Neill girl, isn't it?" Nurse Oliver asked.

"What would make you ask that?" Sami said.

"First off, everybody in the free world has heard what happened to this poor girl, the news media revealed her name. Second, a police officer is posted at her door twenty-four hours a day."

"The police officer posted at Ms. O'Neill's door told us that you were in her room when she regained consciousness," Sami said. "Is that right?"

She nodded vigorously. "I wouldn't exactly call it consciousness. She mumbled a few words and seemed a little agitated, so the doctor asked me to give her an injection of diazepam, which is generic Valium."

"Could you make out what she mumbled?" Al asked.

"Not really."

"We understand that Doctor Hastings was the one who examined Ms. O'Neill and asked you to give her the sedative, correct?"

She shook her head. "It wasn't Doctor Hastings."

"Are you sure?" Sami asked.

"Absolutely positive. I *know* Doctor Hastings."

"Then who was it?" Al asked.

"To be honest, I'm not sure what the doctor's name is."

Sami looked at the nurse in disbelief. "You work here and you don't know the doctors' names? Please understand that it's absolutely crucial we speak to the doctor who examined her. He might have understood what she mumbled and that could be a significant piece of evidence."

"I'm sorry, Detective. I've been a nurse for almost twenty-five years, but I've only worked at Saint Michael's for about a month. And I was just transferred to the ICU a week ago. Do you have any idea how many doctors buzz in and out of this place day in and day out? I suspect it's going to take me several months before I know everyone by name."

"How can we find out who examined Ms. O'Neill?" Sami asked.

"Whoever it was must have signed her chart."

"And how do we get our hands on that?" Sami asked.

"I'm still feeling my way through procedures. Give me a minute and I'll ask one of the other nurses."

Sami and Al waited in silence, and once again, everything seemed out of sync between them.

With guidance from Doctor Hastings, Julian made the first incision at the base of McKenzie's left ventricle. Once cut, he proceeded to carefully insert a small plastic tube in the incision and secured it with a special clamp.

"Nice work," Doctor Hastings said. "Make sure the clamp is tight enough to prevent leakage and loose enough to allow blood flow."

Julian did his best not to grin. He knew *exactly* what had to be done. He checked the heart monitor and noticed that McKenzie's heart rhythm was erratic.

Time to play good doctor.

"Can you stabilizer her?" Julian asked Doctor Mickelson, the anesthesiologist.

"Doing my best, but I can't give her narcotics. I don't want to risk her heart rate elevating. She's tracking at forty-eight beats per minute, and that's right where she should be."

Again Julian made an incision, this time in the aorta, approximately five centimeters above the heart. This was the clamp he had to compromise. But not quite yet. Once all of the procedures were completed—installation of the LVAD and valve replacements—they would remove her from the heart and lung machine, and turn on the heart pump to be sure it worked properly. Then, as was normal procedure, Julian would check the clamps one more time and make minor adjustments just before they closed her. And at that time, if he made the aortic clamp just loose enough, it would fail as soon as her blood pressure elevated slightly, and that would happen the moment she regained consciousness, or better yet, if she had a nightmare. Either way, she wouldn't last through the day.

Julian couldn't have written a more perfect script.

Nurse Oliver walked into the consultation room, let out a heavy sigh, grabbed the clipboard from under her arm, and dropped it on the table. "Well, Detectives, this is really embarrassing."

Sami reached for the clipboard and flipped through the pages. "I don't understand. Didn't the doctor we're trying to track down sign Ms. O'Neill's chart?"

"Nope. He didn't follow procedures, which is not uncommon for doctors. Some are a real pain in the butt. I asked a bunch of nurses if they knew who performed the pre-op, but busy as they are, no one remembered. That's why we keep patient charts, but they're worthless if we don't play by the rules."

"Then how do you propose we track down this phantom doctor?" Al said.

"Doctor Hastings would know, but he's knee-deep in surgery. And I can tell you firsthand, the surgery he and his team are performing on that young girl requires his undivided attention."

"Do you have any idea how long Ms. O'Neill will be in surgery?" Al asked.

"I've seen valve replacements and heart pumps installed, but never at the same time. My guess would be that they won't be out of there for another seven or eight hours. I'm really sorry, Detectives, I feel like an incompetent boob."

"It's not your fault," Al said.

"Now what?" Sami asked.

"I guess we wait until O'Neill is out of surgery," Al said.

"Something just occurred to me," Nurse Oliver said. "I can't believe I didn't think of this earlier. There is an observation tower that overlooks the operating room. When a team of surgeons, nurses, and surgical techs work together on such a complicated procedure, each of them will take a short break now and then, even the head surgeon. No one can remain alert and on top of things for ten hours straight without a break. They all share responsibilities, so no one member of the team does it all. I'm sure there are three, maybe four surgeons working on the patient. There are windows of time when all they're doing is observing. I can get you into the observation room and find out if Doctor Hastings can break free just long enough to tell you which doctor performed the pre-op tests. What do you think?"

"Excellent idea," Sami said. "Show us the way."

For the moment, Julian was finished with his part of the procedure. Doctor Hastings was now exhibiting his surgical talent. As Julian watched closely, he admired Doctor Hastings's ability and meticulousness. Over the years, he had seen his share of sloppy surgeons, those that seemed like they were racing the clock with little regard for the comfort and well-being of the patient. He appreciated a real craftsman, and that is exactly what Doctor Hastings was.

Julian guessed that Doctor Hastings would complete the valve replacements—a tedious, labor-intensive procedure—in another three hours. At that time, Julian would have the opportunity to make his final adjustments, alterations that he felt certain would once and for all free him to continue with his research.

He'd had quite enough of McKenzie O'Neill, and couldn't wait until she was out of his life.

CHAPTER FIFTY

Nurse Oliver, walking swiftly and swinging her arms as if she were engaged in cardio exercise, led the way to Surgical Room One. Of the six operating rooms, Number One was the biggest and most technologically advanced. They walked up a stairway to the second level and entered the observation area overlooking the operating room. To Sami, it looked like a sky booth you might find at a football stadium.

Nurse Oliver pointed. "The surgeon in the middle is Doctor Hastings. I have no idea who the other two are. I'm going to get into some surgical scrubs, pop my head in the operating room, and speak to one of the nurses. Wish me luck."

Sami counted heads, finding it hard to believe that the surgical room was crowded with over fifteen medical professionals. All were wearing surgical masks and caps, so it was hard for her to see their faces. One of the surgeons turned his head toward the observation room and she recognized that he was Doctor Templeton. Thus far, they recognized two of the surgeons, but hadn't yet identified the third one. Sami did notice that Doctors Hastings and Templeton seemed to be working together on a procedure, while the third, unidentified surgeon observed.

"So that's what goes on in an operating room, huh?" Al said.

"Sure doesn't look anything like *Grey's Anatomy*."

"Is it any wonder health-care costs are through the roof?" Al said. "Don't get me wrong. I'm happy that they're pulling out all the stops to save Ms. O'Neill, but can you even imagine what the tab is going to be?"

"No, I can't," Sami said. "I just hope the poor girl makes it."

Sami noticed the door to the operating room open and Nurse Oliver walk in. She tapped another nurse on the shoulder, and the two of them disappeared through the door.

From this distance Sami couldn't quite make out what was going on inside McKenzie's chest. She saw plenty of blood-stained scrubs and sheets. She imagined that witnessing open heart surgery was a lot more difficult than witnessing an autopsy.

Sami saw the door to the operating room open and a nurse, presumably the one Nurse Oliver had spoken to, made her way through the group and approached the unidentified surgeon. He looked up at the observation room for what seemed like a long time. He nodded a couple of times and followed Nurse Oliver out the door. A few minutes later, the door to the observation room opened and in walked the surgeon.

He loosened his surgical mask and removed the nitrile gloves.

"Nurse Oliver had to return to the ICU. You wanted to see me?"

Sami thought it odd that he didn't introduce himself. Then again, he'd been in surgery for the last few hours trying to save a young girl's life. She guessed that etiquette was the last thing on his mind.

"Thanks for taking the time, Doctor. I'm Detective Rizzo and this is my partner, Detective Diaz." The moment the word "partner" slipped off her tongue she cringed.

"I'm Doctor Youngblood. How can I help you?"

"I realize you have more pressing issues to deal with, so we'll try to make this as brief as possible," Sami said. "We're trying to determine who performed the pre-op tests on Ms. O'Neill."

"Look no further, I performed the tests."

"You ordered the sedative when she regained consciousness?" Sami asked.

"She wasn't really conscious—at least not in the traditional sense. She was, however, clearly in distress and needed to be calmed down quickly."

"Were you aware that we left explicit instructions to contact us the moment she showed any signs of consciousness?" Sami said.

"With all due respect, Detectives, my primary concern was for the welfare of the patient, not following police protocol. If she had been stable and I wasn't concerned that her heart might arrest, of course I would have kept her conscious. But the situation called for an immediate medical decision."

Sami couldn't quite figure out why he was so defensive. In spite of his lecture, his voice remained calm.

"Before you sedated her," Al said, "we understand that she mumbled a few words. Can you tell us what she said?"

"Unfortunately, they were incomprehensible."

"Was there anyone else in the room that might have heard what she said?" Sami asked.

"Only Nurse Oliver and the officer, and they were farther away from her than I was."

"Is there anything else you can tell us?" Sami asked.

"Only that I have to get back into surgery." He extended his hand first to Sami, then to Al. "I'm sorry I can't help. And equally sorry if I came on a little strong. But this is a very difficult surgery and I'm running on reserve power."

He smiled.

At first, Sami didn't notice, but then she focused on his left dimple.

His *only* dimple.

She could feel her face getting hot. Was it merely a bizarre coincidence? The more she studied his face, the more he resembled the composite drawing. Was she standing inches away from the Resuscitator?

If he *was* the killer they'd been searching for, he remained remarkably composed. Too composed actually. His surgical cap was soaked through with perspiration, but he showed no signs of nervousness or fear. Could a serial killer occupy the same space as the detectives trying to track him down without showing even the slightest sign of anxiety? Could anyone's blood run that cold?

Sami's brain kicked into overdrive. She tried to fit together all the pieces of a very complicated puzzle. Sure, he resembled the composite drawing and fit the description two eye witnesses had shared with her, but that was still circumstantial evidence. He was extremely handsome and his build appeared to be average. He was also the right height. What else did she have? As a cardiologist, he was perfectly capable of performing the same experiments the killer had performed on each of the five victims.

Sami focused her eyes on the ID badge clipped to his scrubs, and there it was: the caduceus symbol.

"Before you leave, Doctor," Sami said. "I'd like to know if you're acquainted with a private investigator by the name of Peter Spencer?"

She studied him closely and could see tension in his eyes. The cool and composed doctor showed signs of nervousness.

"Well…Um…The name doesn't ring a bell."

Al grabbed Sami's arm. She could see that he was confused with her line of questioning. Obviously, he had missed it. She eyeballed Al and ever so slightly shook her head, signaling, hopefully, for him to let her continue without interrupting. Her lips tightened to a thin line.

"What would you say if I told you Mr. Spencer was on his way to the hospital?"

"I fail to see what relevance that has to anything," Doctor Youngblood said. "Now if you would *please* excuse me—"

"Are you sure you never met him?"

"I don't have time to play these foolish games, Detective."

"Okay, Doctor Youngblood. That is your name, isn't it?"

"I don't appreciate this harassment—especially when I have a critical patient lying on a surgical table."

"My apologies," Sami said. "I just have one more question. Would you prefer to be called Doctor Youngblood or John Smith?"

Sami looked into Doctor Youngblood's eyes and saw the same eerie darkness she had seen in Simon's eyes. She had little doubt that he was the killer. About to arrest him, she reached for her Glock, but before she could draw her firearm or even form a word on her lips, Doctor Youngblood did a hundred-eighty-degree turn and was out the door before either Sami or Al could react. Sami didn't have to explain. Al finally figured out exactly what was going on. They bolted out the door after him, lagging behind the doctor by a long distance. He must be a gazelle, Sami thought.

Doctor Julian Youngblood dashed down the hall like an Olympic sprinter, past the nurses' station and past the doctor's lounge. Out of shape, running as fast as he could, he was out of breath. What now? Where could he run? Where could he hide?

As he dashed down the corridor, grazing people as he kept up a blazing pace, he suddenly felt as if everything moved in slow motion. It was like a dream, when you're trying to get away, but your body just can't move.

He pushed on.

Sami and Al ran down the corridor shoulder to shoulder. They'd lost sight of the doctor and were pursuing him blindly.

"Better call for backup," Sami yelled.

Al flipped open his cell phone and dialed 911.

"Nine-one-one, what is your emergency?"

"This is Detective Diaz. I'm at Saint Michael's Hospital on Hillside Avenue and am in pursuit of a suspect in a murder investigation. I need backup to secure all exits as soon as possible. Last seen, the suspect was wearing green surgical scrubs. Subject is a Caucasian male, approximately six feet tall, with an average build. He has dark hair and his name is Doctor Youngblood."

"Got it, Detective," the operator said. "Help is on the way."

Julian two-stepped it up the stairway where an alarmed door offered access to the hospital roof. He realized that if he triggered the alarm, the detectives would be on him in a few minutes. But he knew there was no exit if he ran down the stairs. He felt trapped and didn't know what to do. Out of sheer panic, he opened the alarmed door and stepped onto the roof. Frantically, he jogged around air conditioning compressors, vents, and equipment he did not recognize, searching for another exit, hoping that maybe he could find a way out of the building.

On the other side of the roof, he spotted another access door and ran toward it. He grasped the doorknob and yanked hard, but the door wouldn't open. Of course, he thought. He needed a four-digit security code to unlock the door.

He stood motionless for a moment, his mind racing out of control. It felt as if his entire life was flashing in front of his eyes. He walked toward the edge of the roof, and stopped just short of the two-foot ledge, facing Fourth Avenue. In the distance, he could hear sirens getting louder by the second. He also heard the "whop-whop" sound of a helicopter rapidly approaching. Soon the detectives would track him down. He had to find another way off the roof.

Sami and Al jogged to the nurses' station, both panting and trying to catch their breath. Sami could hear a fire alarm blaring. They stopped and spoke to the first nurse they saw.

"Did you see Doctor Youngblood run by here?" Sami asked.

The young nurse pointed. "He flew by like a marathon runner and went to that stairway, but that's not an exit. It's only for access to the roof. What the hell is going on?"

They had no time to answer.

Sami and Al jogged to the stairway, Al leading the way. Handguns drawn, poised in front of them, they slowly eased their way up the stairs.

"Careful," Sami whispered, as they approached the wide-open access door. "He could have a weapon."

"I don't think he was packing while in surgery."

"Smartass."

Al watchfully stood on the threshold of the roof and motioned for Sami to proceed. Cautiously, they inched their way onto the roof and quickly scanned the area, looking for the doctor. He was nowhere in sight.

"You go left and I'll go right," Al said.

Sami nodded. She turned, but before she could take a step, Al grabbed her forearm. "Please be careful," he said.

Utterly panic stricken, Julian squatted behind an air conditioning compressor to gather his thoughts and catch his breath. How foolish he had been. Of all the exits in the hospital, he chose a one-way path to nowhere. Except for the main stairway, there was no other way off this roof, and at any minute, it would be flooded with cops. How had he gone from esteemed surgeon to fugitive? What might have happened if he had completed his research? No time to play "what if."

As inconspicuously as possible, he peeked over the compressor and saw Detective Diaz making his way toward the locked access door to the second stairway. Julian turned around and rested his back against the compressor. Could it be that the detective knew the security code?

Julian needed a plan and he needed it now. He looked down and noticed a three-foot-long piece of electrical conduit lying on the floor. He picked up the conduit and snuck up behind the detective, the makeshift weapon ready to strike.

Al approached the door, mindful of his surroundings, taking nothing for granted. He had no idea where the door would take him. It could be another stairway, or might just be a storage area. For all he knew, the doctor could be hiding behind the door, waiting to pounce. Al grasped the doorknob, trying to be as quiet as possible.

He tugged on the doorknob, twisting it clockwise, then counter-clockwise, but the door would not open. About to turn around, Al felt something strike him in the back of his head. He could hear ringing in his ears, but only for a few seconds. His eyes went blurry and he fell to the floor.

Julian stood over the detective, having no idea what to do next. He noticed a pistol lying near the detective's right hand. He picked it up and stared at it as if it was a foreign object he'd never seen before. He had never held a handgun, let alone fired one. He could hear the helicopter, now within eyeshot. He surveyed the surroundings. The situation was getting out of control. His options were few.

Having walked the entire perimeter of the roof, searching for Doctor Youngblood, Sami peeked around the corner and saw Al lying face down on the floor. The doctor stood over him, looking like a statue. Seeing Al's motionless body, Sami felt a surge of adrenalin rushing through her veins. A wave of terror crashed over her. Logic quickly took control. If the doctor had shot Al, she would have heard the blast. So even though she had no idea the extent of Al's injuries, she could at least feel relieved that a hot piece of lead wasn't lodged somewhere in his body.

Sami realized that the doctor, standing frozen, hadn't yet noticed her. He seemed so preoccupied with Al that he paid little attention to anything else. Al, thank God, was beginning to stir. He grasped the back of his head, turned over, and sat upright, resting his back against the door.

Sami noticed a piece of silver pipe lying on the floor next to the doctor's foot, and quickly figured out what had happened. Holding her Glock with both hands, arms extended, elbows locked, she pointed the gun at Doctor Youngblood. "Drop your weapon, Doctor, and get on your knees with your hands behind your head."

Before the last word slipped off Sami's tongue, the doctor immediately reacted and aimed the handgun at the center of Al's chest. "Don't come any closer," he warned.

"Are you okay, Al?" Sami yelled.

"I will be when we cuff this asshole."

Al's comment eased her frazzled nerves. After all, if Al was seriously injured, would he make such a flippant statement?

"I'm going to say this one more time, Doctor," Sami said. "Drop your weapon and get on your knees!"

Julian tried to steady the gun but his whole body was shaking. Suddenly, he heard a commotion behind him. Appearing through the main access door to the roof, Julian watched a literal parade of policeman converging on the roof, slowly walking towards him, each with their weapons pointed directly at him. They all wore riot gear and carried shields. They looked like modern-day gladiators.

Sami feared that even if a sharpshooter put a bullet clean through the doctor's head, a nerve reflex still might twitch his trigger finger. If this happened, Al would likely take a bullet square in the chest. "Don't shoot!" Sami yelled, waving her arm at the backup.

"Wise decision, Detective," Dr. Youngblood said, directing his statement to Sami. He waived his gun at Al. "I want you to stand up and turn around with your back facing me. If you so much as flinch, I'll put a bullet between your shoulder blades."

Al eased up, supporting his back against the door. The cobwebs hadn't yet cleared and the back of his head was throbbing. He felt a little woozy, but managed to find his legs. Having no other option, Al complied with the doctor's order and turned with his back facing him.

Slowly, Julian moved toward Al. With his peripheral vision, he could see Sami inching toward him and the gladiators moving in his direction. "Don't make another move," Julian yelled. "Unless, of course, you want Detective Diaz to meet his maker."

Julian grabbed Al by the back of his shirt collar and pressed the barrel of the gun against the back of Al's head. "Let's walk," Julian said.

Gripping Al's shirt tightly, the handgun still resting against the back of Al's head, Julian stepped away from Sami and her gladiators and moved toward the edge of the roof. Once there, Julian noticed a two-foot ledge around the perimeter. He tightened his grip on Al's shirt.

"Step up, Detective."

Sami watched in horror as Al stepped up on the ledge, his body teetering slightly. Was this how it was going to end? So many thoughts flooded her mind. If Al plunged to his death without her ever forgiving him, how would she ever forgive *herself*?

"Now listen to me carefully," Doctor Youngblood yelled. "I want you, Detective Rizzo, and your pack of wolves to get the fuck off this roof. If you're not out of here in less than a minute, Detective Diaz is going to perform an Olympic-style high dive into a pool of concrete. And while you're at it, call the boys in the copter, and tell them if they land, Diaz flies."

What frightened Sami most was Doctor Youngblood's sudden composure. In spite of his hopeless situation—there was no way he'd ever leave this hospital alive—he appeared to be in complete control of his emotions. In a matter of seconds, he had gone from panicky to rock-steady. Sami knew from her prior experiences with cold-blooded killers that those most composed were generally the most dangerous. She thought, for a moment, about trying to negotiate with him, but feared what he might do.

"I don't see anyone moving," Julian said. "If you're not—"

Julian made the fatal mistake of taking his eyes off Al for just a moment, long enough for Al to react. Still shaky and lightheaded, Al maintained enough wits about him to take advantage of the situation. He swung his right elbow and caught Julian square in the nose. Reacting without thought or reason, Julian dropped the gun and covered his face with both hands. Blood poured out of his nose. Al tried to step down off the ledge, but Julian grabbed his shoulders and tried to push him off the roof. Al had no idea how he maintained his balance, but he stood firm.

Sami watched them struggle for only a second. She rushed toward them as quickly as she could, the backup right behind her. By the time she got there, Al had managed to overpower the doctor and step off the ledge. Both men were still locked in battle, swinging and tugging and pushing. She saw the handgun the doctor had been holding lying on the roof. She raised her weapon.

"Dr. Youngblood, get on your knees and put your hands behind your head! *Do it now!*"

As if rehearsed, both Al and the doctor loosened their grip on each other. Dr. Youngblood put his hands behind his neck, but instead of getting on his knees, he jumped up on the ledge with the grace of a gymnast mounting a balance beam.

He stood on the ledge with perfect balance, as if he didn't have a care in the world, as if it were a lazy Sunday afternoon and he was enjoying a panoramic view of the city.

"Doctor Youngblood," Sami yelled. "Please step off the ledge."

He turned toward her, but held his ground. The blood from his nose was painted on the front of his scrubs.

"Please, Doctor, put your hands behind your head and step down."

He didn't move.

"Last chance, Doctor," Sami said. "Off the ledge and on your fucking knees."

"What are you going to do, Detective, shoot me?"

"If we have to," Sami warned.

"Then go ahead and shoot."

"Do you really want it to end this way?"

Dr. Youngblood turned around, his back facing her, his toes near the edge of the roof.

"Why, Doctor?" Sami yelled. "Why did you kill those people?"

"The needs of the many outweigh the needs of the few."

Julian thought about Nicole, how he'd betrayed her. He thought about his daughters, how much he loved and missed them, how much he'd hurt them. He thought about his career and the research grant, his legacy now one of notoriety. Most of all he thought about all the subjects he had put in an early grave, of the dreadful things he had done to his female subjects. In one moment of clarity, Julian understood why he had ravished Eva and Rachael and McKenzie and Nicole. It had nothing to do with them; they were merely substitutes for Rebecca and Marianne, victims by default. He'd given up all hope that he could ever repay his cousins for the emotional damage they had inflicted on him, for alienating his entire family by accusing him of attempted rape. The only means by which he could temper his rage was to redirect his hunger for revenge. There was no other way for Julian to find even an ounce of consolation.

He couldn't imagine spending the rest of his life in prison. Then again, any responsible jury would surely sentence him to death. Death would be a gift, much easier to deal with than rotting in a cage. But how would he deal with the guilt while he waited to die? No, he would not subject his family to a long, protracted trial or allow the news media to dismantle the lives of his wife and daughters. He had no choice but to do the righteous thing.

Doctor Julian Youngblood, husband, father, gifted cardiologist, inched forward, his toes now hanging slightly over the side. He leaned into the wind until the weight of his upper torso pushed him forward like an Olympian diving off a platform. Once airborne, it felt like his stomach was heaving into his throat. Soaring toward the ground, the air rushed past his scrubs, making the sound of a flag flapping in the wind. His arms and legs were helplessly flailing, and his last thoughts were of Isabel and Lorena.

Sami rushed to the edge of the roof, stopped a few feet short, carefully leaned forward, and looked over the ledge. Horns were blowing and tires squealing. She could see Doctor Youngblood lying motionless on the concrete sidewalk, face down. Behind her, a police helicopter landed on the helipad. She tried to feel pity for him, but all she could feel was an unusual sense of relief.

"When you get to hell," she whispered, "tell Simon I said hi."

Al moved toward Sami and they stood toe to toe for what seemed like an eternity. Eyes speaking, tongues still, Al put his arms around her and pulled her toward him. They embraced.

"Thanks for saving my life," Al said.

"All in a day's work."

"How can I repay you?"

"No need. I owed you one. Remember?"

CHAPTER FIFTY-ONE

When Sami and Al walked into the precinct, they were greeted like celebrities. Their fellow detectives and the support staff applauded as if they had just won an Academy Award. Even though she felt energized beyond anything she could imagine at this point in time, she didn't feel like a movie star or a heroine. Four innocent people had died at the hands of the killer and a fifth was fighting for her life. What had she done that was so extraordinary during the investigation? Anything worthy of such fanfare? Wouldn't any other detective have taken the same steps and followed the same leads?

She had been distracted during this investigation, overly concerned about her personal life. Had she made mistakes, or overlooked some obvious facts that might have helped her close the investigation sooner? Once again, she doubted her competency and wondered if the homicide department was where she belonged.

Al was shaking hands with everyone, celebrating as if he'd just won the California Lottery. The blow to the back of his head caused a minor concussion and the doctor warned that he might suffer from lingering headaches. But overall, he gave Al a clean bill of health. Sami stood in his shadow as they weaved toward Captain Davidson's office. She hoped to remain as low-key as possible. Detective Osbourn approached her with a chimp-like grin on his face.

Osbourn offered his hand, but then withdrew it. "Screw the handshake. You deserve a hug."

He put his arms around Sami and held her tight. "Congratulations."

She really liked this young man.

"Have you heard about D'Angelo?" Osbourn asked.

Sami shook her head.

"His goose is cooked."

"What happened?"

"Seems that he hasn't been satisfied with his detective wages for quite a few years. You name it, and he's done it. Extortion. Drug trafficking. Stolen property. Assault. The DA wants his ass. Looks like the poor slob is going to do time *and* lose his pension."

Sami found it difficult to feel any sympathy for him. "You know what they say. 'Mess with the bull and you get the horns.'"

Davidson poked his head out of his office. "Hey, Rizzo. Grab Diaz and get your asses in here."

Al was still busy celebrating. The precinct looked like the locker room of the Super Bowl champions, minus the champagne. Sami grabbed Al's arm and dragged him to the captain's office.

"Mayor Sullivan is delighted. She wants to take both of you to lunch next week."

"All the credit goes to Sami," Al said. "All I did was a high-wire act."

"Whatever the case," Davidson said. "That asshole got what he deserved. I just feel sorry for his family. Turns out, he had a wife and two daughters. It's a damned shame."

The captain pulled a cigar out of his desk, carefully unwrapped it as if it was a sacred ceremony, and lit it. "I've been waiting for a long time to find a reason to smoke this cigar. It's a Montecristo. Best cigar in the world."

"You do know that Cuban cigars are illegal, right, Captain?" Sami said.

He took a long hit and filled the room with blue smoke. "So arrest me." The captain smiled a rare smile. "Let's get serious. How's the O'Neill girl?"

"She's out of surgery," Sami said. "Doctor Templeton is pleased with how everything went. But no matter what, he says she needs a transplant as soon as possible. Unfortunately, heart donors are hard to come by."

"Well," the captain said. "Let's hope for the best." He handed Sami an envelope. "Open it."

"It's a bit early for a Christmas card, Captain," Sami said.

"But not too early for a raise."

Sami tore open the envelope and pulled out an official-looking letter signed by Police Chief Larson.

"Congratulations, *Sergeant* Rizzo," the captain said. He handed her a new gold shield.

Sami couldn't form a syllable.

Sitting right next to her, Al leaned over and gave her a quick hug. "You deserve it, Sami."

"How did this come down so quickly?" Sami said. "I mean, we just solved the case a few hours ago."

"This has been in the works since we reinstated you," the captain said. "It's just a coincidence that it became official today. I'm not sure about you, but I think the timing couldn't be better."

Sami glanced at Al and noticed a strange look on his face. She'd known him long enough to be sure that his sentiments were sincere. Still, he had to feel slighted.

"I want you and Al to take a week off—with pay, of course. Compliments of Mayor Sullivan. Go have some fun. Plant a tree. Go on a cruise. Or just watch soap operas all day. Now get the hell out of here while you can. But remember one thing, Sergeant: Along with your shiny new badge and title come more responsibilities and more politics. Be ready for a shit-storm when you return."

Sami sat across from Doctor J and wasn't sure how to start the conversation. When Sami had contacted her, she hadn't expected to get an immediate appointment. She guessed that the good doctor was making a concession on her behalf.

For the first two days of Sami's vacation, she wore her favorite lounging pajamas day and night and didn't once leave the house. It was now time to integrate back into the world.

"You must feel an incredible sense of relief," Doctor J said.

"If another serial killer shows his ugly head," Sami said, "I'm packing my bags and moving to Montana."

Doctor J laughed. "Tell me, you haven't been in this office for quite a while. What brings you back?"

"Brain damage."

"That's rather vague. Please elaborate."

She explained to the doctor about Al's trip to Rio and about his affair with the Brazilian nurse. "He's begged me to give him another chance, but I'm not sure I can ever trust him again."

"Are you in love with Al?"

"He calls me three or four times a day, wanting to meet for coffee or join him for lunch. I keep telling him that I need some time. He never argues with me or tries to convince me to meet him, but I sense he's getting impatient."

"You're not answering the question. *Are you in love with him?*"

"I was."

"And you feel that his affair has extinguished your love?"

"I'm sitting here with you because I don't know what I feel."

"And you expect me to figure it out?"

"I'm just looking for some guidance."

"That can only come from your heart. I can tell you what to do, but this is a decision only you can make. If you don't feel you can ever trust him again, then I can assure you that at best your relationship with Al will always be on shaky ground."

"How can I trust someone who's betrayed me?"

"Under the right circumstances, good people do bad things, Sami. From what you told me, Al was in a terrible place sitting by his sister's side, uncertain whether she'd live or die. He had no one to comfort him. It's my guess that your voice on the telephone and support was not enough. This wasn't about sex, Sami. Al didn't cheat on *you*. He simply needed a safe harbor."

"I'm really growing weary of everyone telling me that it wasn't about sex."

"Well, Sami, it may not be what you want to hear, but in most cases of infidelity, it's *not* about sex."

"Suppose he does it again?"

"Then you'll be faced with another decision. Life is a series of crossroads, some significant, others less important. Each and every day of our lives, we reach these crossroads and have to decide which way to go. If you're looking for perfect love, or searching for a flawless man, you'd better prepare yourself for a rough ride."

Sami thought about her words, but as poignant as they were, she still didn't know what to do. There was one fact, one monumental fact, she neglected to share with Doctor J. Maybe she just needed to sit down with Al and bare her soul.

* * *

After Sami left Doctor J, she headed home, but impulsively made a U-turn on Genesee Avenue. Doctor Templeton had called Sami yesterday and said that McKenzie O'Neill had regained consciousness and was responding to the surgery much better than anyone had anticipated. Never having met her, she decided to visit her at the hospital and introduce herself. She wanted to meet this courageous young woman face-to-face.

When she pulled into the parking garage, she was overcome with an eerie feeling. This is where it all happened. Saint Michael's hospital would never be the same.

She found her way to the entrance, and hopped on an elevator to the sixth floor. She'd heard from Doctor Templeton that McKenzie would remain in the ICU for at least another two weeks. She wasn't sure if McKenzie was still in the same hospital room, so she went to the nurses' station.

As luck would have it, Nurse Oliver was on duty. The nurse looked up from the chart she'd been studying, stood, and smiled.

"Detective Rizzo, so nice to see you."

She wanted to correct the nurse. After all, she *was* a sergeant. But did her title really have any impact on anyone other than her?

"Hello, there. How you holding up?"

"Still a little shaky, Detective. It isn't every day you're part of a CSI series. I've spoken to a number of people and everyone is in shock that Doctor Youngblood was the Resuscitator. It certainly is disconcerting that such a well-respected doctor could be a cold-blooded killer. I guess one never knows where evil lurks."

"Sometimes the least likely people have the darkest souls."

Nurse Oliver nodded. "What brings you here, Detective?"

"I'd like to visit McKenzie O'Neill. Can you tell me what room she's in?"

"Sure thing." Nurse Oliver checked her computer. "She's in a private room—six forty-five." She pointed. "Go down the hall and turn right."

"Thank you," Sami said.

"Have a nice visit, Detective."

When Sami walked into the hospital room, McKenzie appeared to be sound asleep. She tiptoed to the side of the bed and sat on the metal chair. The young woman's body looked like something out of a horror movie. She couldn't find a visible place on her body that didn't have a hose or wire attached to it. She saw a heart monitor, an oxygen sensor, and other equipment she didn't recognize. Sami could hear hissing and sucking and pumping sounds. She guessed that McKenzie was heavily sedated because no one could sleep through such a racket.

One nurse after the other zoomed in and out of the room, checking her vital signs, adjusting IVs, making notes on McKenzie's chart. That she slept through it all, amazed Sami. The nurses were cordial, but said little more than hello.

After waiting for more than an hour, Sami decided that McKenzie wouldn't soon awaken. Just as she was about to leave, a nurse walked in.

"Hi there," the nurse said. She gave Sami a once-over. "You're the detective that figured out Doctor Youngblood was the killer, right?"

Sami nodded.

"We haven't had that much drama around here since the bomb threat back in the mid-nineties. Did he really jump off the roof?"

"That he did."

"God rest his soul." The nurse walked toward her. "I'm Sister Mary."

"Detective Rizzo." As soon as the words came out of her mouth she realized that it would take some time for her to get used to her new title.

"Have you been here long?" Sister Mary asked.

"For more than an hour."

"I guess you're tired of waiting, huh?"

"I was hoping to talk to her, but it looks like she's going to be sleeping for a while."

"Actually, I'm here to wake her and prep her for surgery."

Sami felt goose bumps all over her body. "Is there a problem?"

"Quite to the contrary. It seems we found a donor. She's scheduled for a heart transplant in less than an hour. Her new heart is on ice right now."

Sami couldn't believe her ears.

"When I wake her I can give you a few minutes alone with her if you like."

"I appreciate the offer but I'll come back in a few days. She's got more important things on her agenda than chatting with me." Sami fished through her purse for a business card. "Would you be kind enough to call me after her surgery and let me know how she's doing?"

"I'd be happy to, Detective."

"I'm curious though. When I spoke to Nurse Oliver, she didn't say a thing about the transplant."

"That's because the call came in a short time ago. We don't waste any time with heart transplants. Everything happens pretty quickly."

"Who's the donor?"

"A young man in his mid-twenties was in a motor vehicle accident as a passenger in his friend's car."

Sister Mary walked to the bedside and checked the flow of the IV bag.

"Tell me, Detective, do you believe in miracles?"

"I never really thought about it much."

"I think you're Ms. O'Neill's guardian angel."

"Why do you say that?"

"We had little hope that we'd find an ideal donor for Ms. O'Neill. Her blood type is O negative—the rarest type of blood. She can only receive an organ from an O negative donor. But because it's so rare, she was number one on the waiting list. That some young guy in Northern California with O negative blood would suffer fatal injuries seems statistically unbelievable. Especially when you consider that the driver of the car walked away with only a broken nose from the impact of the air bag. To make it even more mind-boggling, not only does the blood type match, but the tissue samples are compatible, and the chest cavity of the recipient is perfectly proportioned to accommodate the size of the donor's heart."

"I still don't think I'm anybody's guardian angel."

"It gets better. It just so happens that the young man's driver's license identifies him as a registered organ donor. Just to add even more food for thought, he didn't die until he arrived at the hospital, which ensured that his organs could be harvested while they were still viable. All this happened while you were quietly sitting here in her room."

"I guess you could call it a miracle, but one person had to die for another to live. Where's the miracle in that?"

"According to the victim's father, his son suffered from chronic cystic fibrosis, an insidious disease. The young man was always in pain. In a way, his death might have been more merciful than what he was facing alive. In fact, his father said his son's death gave his family a sense of relief. They didn't know how much longer they could endure watching him suffer. His father was happy that the young man's heart would live on."

Sami left the hospital in a daze. She tried to process what Sister Mary had told her, but she just couldn't get her head around it. Considering all the factors, what *were* the odds that a donor would come along at such a crucial point in time? Was it really a miracle?

The other issue that troubled Sami was Dr. Youngblood's motivation. What would possess a respected cardiologist to perform such gruesome experiments on innocent people? Why would he brutally rape the women? Until these questions were answered, Sami didn't consider the investigation closed.

CHAPTER FIFTY-TWO

Al sat on the bench at Crystal Pier in Pacific Beach, overlooking the unusually calm ocean, waiting for Sami to arrive. He was pleasantly surprised when she called and asked him if they could meet. What pleased him even more was the fact that she had suggested they meet where he first revealed his love for her. Was this a good sign? He sat nervously, his eyes focused on the boardwalk.

The marine layer was thick this morning. The sun hadn't yet burned through the stubborn clouds. But the air was still warm. Al believed that what happened today would reshape his life in a profound way. Whether he walked away holding her hand or shuffled along by himself, rejected and beaten, today would redefine who he was.

Lost in his thoughts, he didn't notice Sami approaching until she stood five feet away.

He bolted up like a boot-camp corporal, ready to salute his drill sergeant, and moved toward her, hoping she would welcome his hug. She didn't back away, but the hug was more perfunctory than intimate.

"Thanks for meeting me, Al."

"I should be thanking you."

They sat together on the bench, but she kept her distance.

"Would you like a cup of coffee or something to drink?" Al asked. "I can run over to Starbucks."

"Thank you, but no. My stomach's on another rampage." Sami paused for a minute and looked out at the ocean. She shared with him the details of McKenzie O'Neill's transplant and her favorable prognosis. "Sometimes I think God speaks to us through miracles but we don't hear Him."

"I think we've witnessed a lot of miracles over the last thirty days," Al said.

"How so?"

"First off, my sister survived a car crash and your mother survived a heart attack and bypass surgery. Then, Emily came along as a gift from heaven to care for your mother and Angelina."

"I guess I took those things for granted," Sami said. "Closing the investigation on the Resuscitator ranks up there as well." Sami briefed Al on Dr. Youngblood's research grant and his presumed motivation for the surgical experiments. No one could answer questions about the sexual assaults. Sami guessed that the reasons were put to rest along with Youngblood and would forever remain a mystery.

"And let's not minimize your promotion, Sergeant Rizzo."

She laughed. "Now *that's* a miracle."

They sat quietly for a few minutes, enjoying the peacefulness of the ocean air.

"I have something to tell you, Al."

He had a feeling that she hadn't met him to talk about McKenzie O'Neill. "Before you say anything, can I get something off *my* chest?"

"If you must."

"I'm not going to beat a dead horse because there's nothing I can say that I haven't said already. You know that I love you and also that I deeply regret what I did. The thought of losing you has opened my mind and made me realize that I never really proved to you how deeply I love you."

Al stood up, pulled a small box out of his pocket, and dropped to one knee. He opened the velvet box and showed Sami the princess-cut engagement ring. A small crowd of curious onlookers stopped in their tracks and watched.

"Make me the happiest man in the world, Samantha Marie, and agree to be my wife. I promise to spend the rest of my life proving my love for you."

Sami desperately wanted to say yes, but not until she revealed *her* secret. If this didn't scare him away, then she'd know for certain that it was meant to be.

"There's no easy way for me to say this, so I'll cut to the chase. You know that my stomach has been out of sorts for a long time, and that when I'm stressed, I occasionally miss a period and my whole body goes on a rampage. Well, when I missed two periods in a row and puked nearly every morning, I finally went to the doctor."

She could see his face tighten and his eyes narrow suspiciously.

"I'm pregnant, Al."

His face lit up like a Christmas tree. "I'm going to be a *father*?"

Sami nodded. "I guess that's just another miracle."

Lost in his thoughts, Al stood speechless.

"I've got a great idea," Sami said. "Why don't we head home, pick up the clan, and go to Sunday services at Saint John's Church?"

Al thought about that for a minute. "Okay. But I must warn you: the foundation of the church might shake when I walk in the door."

"I'll take my chances."

Al leaned toward Sami and they kissed. There was little doubt in Sami's mind that Alberto Diaz and Samantha Marie Rizzo would soon walk down the aisle as husband and wife. Sami had no unrealistic expectations. All might not be rosy. But in a fairy-tale kind of way, she felt in her heart that love could conquer almost any obstacle. And those difficulties beyond love's healing power, she would pass on to God.

ACKNOWLEDGMENTS

I would like to thank the following people for their invaluable contributions to the creation of *Resuscitation*. Without their marketing brilliance, technical expertise, editorial feedback, medical knowledge, and words of encouragement, writing this novel would have been nearly impossible. If I've forgotten anyone, please accept my deepest apologies.

Larry Kirshbaum, Terry Goodman, Sarah Tomashek, Jacque Ben-Zekry, Jenny Williams, Charlotte Herscher, Jennifer Chasser, Anthony Annechino, Kristin Peters, Richard Shade Gardner, Paula Brandes, Cayla Kluver, Kimberly Phifer, and Elena Stokes.

ABOUT THE AUTHOR

Daniel Annechino wrote his first book, *How to Buy the Most Car for the Least Money*, in 1992, while working as a general manager in the automotive business. But his true passion has always been fiction, particularly thrillers. He indulged his taste for suspense during his former career as a book editor specializing in full-length fiction. He spent two years researching serial killers before finally penning his gripping and memorable debut novel, *They Never Die Quietly*. A native of New York, he lives today in San Diego with his wife, Jennifer. When not writing, he enjoys cooking, drinking vintage wines, and spending time on the warm beaches of Southern California.